FROM A WATERY GRAVE . . .

Harumi carefully removed the contents of the yellow rubber pouch. For a moment, she reexamined the brilliant gold seal she had just broken.

"My God, Benny," she said, touching the pouch with a shiver. "Where did this come from?"

"I told you, the *Arizona*. From a compartment in the aft section of the ship. What's the big deal?"

"Do you know what this is? It's gold. The gold chrysanthemum. The imperial seal of the Japanese emperor!" She fingered the stack of envelopes in front of her, each sealed with its own gold chrysanthemum. "What a find!"

"It has to go back," he said. "I stole something from a monument. A cemetery."

"But this could be a find of major historical significance!"

Ben Spain smiled broadly. "Aren't you being a little melodramatic? A few sealed envelopes in a waterproof pouch aren't exactly the Rosetta Stone."

Harumi pounded her fist.

"How the hell do you know?"

PINNACLE BOOKS HAS
SOMETHING FOR EVERYONE —

MAGICIANS, EXPLORERS, WITCHES AND CATS

THE HANDYMAN (377-3, $3.95/$4.95)
He is a magician who likes hands. He likes their comfortable shape and weight and size. He likes the portability of the hands once they are severed from the rest of the ponderous body. Detective Lanark must discover who The Handyman is before more handless bodies appear.

PASSAGE TO EDEN (538-5, $4.95/$5.95)
Set in a world of prehistoric beauty, here is the epic story of a courageous seafarer whose wanderings lead him to the ends of the old world — and to the discovery of a new world in the rugged, untamed wilderness of northwestern America.

BLACK BODY (505-9, $5.95/$6.95)
An extraordinary chronicle, this is the diary of a witch, a journal of the secrets of her race kept in return for not being burned for her "sin." It is the story of Aiba, that rarest of creatures, a white witch: beautiful and able to walk in the human world undetected.

THE WHITE PUMA (532-6, $4.95/NCR)
The white puma has recognized the men who deprived him of his family. Now, like other predators before him, he has become a man-hater. This story is a fitting tribute to this magnificent animal that stands for all living creatures that have become, through man's carelessness, close to disappearing forever from the face of the earth.

DEADPOINT

STEPHEN CASSELL

PINNACLE BOOKS
WINDSOR PUBLISHING CORP.

PINNACLE BOOKS

are published by

Windsor Publishing Corp.
475 Park Avenue South
New York, NY 10016

First Printing: February, 1993

Printed in the United States of America

*For my gramp, David Bennett Cassell,
who raised me as his son and taught me
to set and stay my course. I will always
carry that debt with honor.*

"For in much wisdom is much grief and increase of knowledge is increase in sorrow."

— Ecclesiastes

"It has been decided that the battleship *Arizona* will always lie in state in the mud of Pearl Harbor as a living shrine and tribute to those sailors who so bravely gave their lives for the fight against world tyranny."

— President Franklin Delano Roosevelt
December 2, 1942

Tokyo
November 12, 1941

One

The 1930 canvas-topped Rolls Royce slid silently from the curb at Shimbashi train station into the wet blackness that smothered downtown Tokyo. The tempo of the rain beating against the cotton roof increased sharply as the driver picked up speed turning into Tenth Avenue. Even inside the Rolls, the stinking damp was bone piercing. It was a night when people huddled close for protection, occasionally glancing over their shoulders. Sr. Lt. Toshiyuki Mizutari pushed his exhausted body deeper into the false warmth of the red leather seats. Damn rotten November weather.

The Rolls turned sharply into the gaudy neon brightness of Ginza Street, still alive despite the fact it was two A.M. on a Thursday morning. Picking up speed, the chunky eleven-year-old limousine moved north on the wide sweeping Ginza, the right rear fender shimmering in the wet neon glow, revealing five simple white stripes that offered the hope of Imperial protection.

"How was your journey, Lieutenant?" asked the escort sitting next to him. Toshiyuki glanced at the man for the first time, and suddenly realized he wasn't an escort at all, but a guard.

Quickly, he lowered his eyes, mostly out of respect but partly out of dread for a full colonel of the Japanese Secret Police, the Kempei Tai. Despite the dismal light filtering into the rear compartment of the bulletproof car, he could make out the perfectly groomed head bobbing slowly inside a stiff red and khaki uniform collar. The effort to achieve perfection was ruined by misshapen yellow teeth that crossed one another like maverick-growing ears of miniature corn.

"The train ride was long. A normal hour and a half from Yokosuka, took four hours, with a long stop in Yokohama. But my journey did not begin from the naval base at Yokosuka."

"Oh?" The ruined face moved closer.

"My journey began from the south China coast. I have not slept for the past forty hours."

"I don't understand?" The secret police face wrinkled, having missed some small shred of information.

"As senior gunnery officer aboard the *Ushio*," Tushiyuki explained, "I was responsible for the cleaning and repair of all gun mounts, after a solid week of intensive shore bombardment. DesRon Six, my destroyer squadron, or what's left of it, pulled into Yokosuka and there was an imperial rescript waiting for me."

"I see." The colonel smoothed his sleeve with a gloved hand. "Well, this China business has certainly changed everything for us."

"What have I done, Colonel?" Toshiyuki blurted out. "What act of dishonor have I committed against my shipmates, my country, to be ordered by the emperor and the imperial staff to the Imperial Palace in the dead of night?"

The colonel shook his head thoughtfully. "God only

knows in these times. But my orders were explicit."

"Could there be a mistake?"

"There is no mistake. I was ordered by the imperial staff to pick you up. It is truly the strangest command I have ever carried out, but these are strange times." He glanced sideways in the dimness at the young naval officer and bowed his head in false, but polite sympathy.

Toshiyuki worked to focus his energy, to rebuild his inner strength for whatever horror or dishonor awaited him. The Rolls momentarily slowed and off to his right, Toshiyuki could see the towering and brightly lighted Imperial Hotel.

Often when he was little, no more than seven or eight, his mother and entourage would journey from their home to Hibiya Park, across from the Imperial. All day they would romp in the grass and feed the swans and smell the fragrance of spring and summer. Tokyo was still in ruins from the great earthquake of 1923, but it didn't matter. That was a fine feeling to hold onto. He had written his first Haiku after one such trip:

A Spring Bloom
In Fragrance
Blue Sky Memories

Toshiyuki's thoughts drifted back even further to the one time his father Baron Mizutari, long since dead, brought a little Toshiyuki and his older sister into Tokyo, from the family estate in Kyoto. It was a grand time and they had traveled with great excitement across the Sumida River on the old wooden Kachidoki Bridge for an entire day's outing in the waterfront gardens of Hama Rikyu. It was the only time his father had ever engaged in play, and the only time he had ever embraced his son Toshiyuki. Late in the afternoon his father had taken them on the water bus along the Sumida and for the first time he had seen the city's squalor and poverty near Azuma-bashi, the drooping, rotting match box cottages along the riverbanks outlined against the tattered wash, hanging next to each shack. What stood out for Toshiyuki in that warm fragment of memory, were the bobbing pink paper lanterns glowing in the weeds at sunset.

". . . There is a great deal of strain all around us, Lieutenant. These are strange times."

Toshiyuki glanced over and realized the colonel had been talking incessantly. More than half of his destroyer squadron had departed two weeks before for a destination somewhere in the north of Japan. Some obscure anchorage, probably that frozen and always miserable Tankan Bay in the Kuriles. The worst duty in the fleet. Scuttlebutt was rampant that ships were pouring into Tankan from all over the empire. He had even heard from his gunnery chief that the great carrier *Akagi* was on her way north, as part of the awesome Kido Butai Japanese strike force.

The threat of war had been in the air for many months now. If war was truly imminent, Toshiyuki prayed to be part of it, even if it was war with the United States. He had deep feelings for his many American friends, but serving the empire was a cherished honor that his father would have been proud to share. He had trained all his life for war and to serve his dead father's tradition. Samurai blood from the Shimzau Clan ran deep in his veins, back to the times of the great Emperor Jimmu. Now, he wondered, in the softness of his gut, if

12

he would survive the night to fulfill that warrior promise.

The ugly colonel started again. "Lieutenant, you are a fine, brave officer, with a spotless war record in the China campaign. The *Ushio* is a fine destroyer and you have served well. Even as a Black Dragon at Etajima you were left untarnished." The colonel's voice forced Toshiyuki to look up and it was then he noticed that the Kempei Tai man's eyes reflected a cold fierce light that made them translucent.

"I am sure your record and the honor of your family will work in your favor."

I'm dead, Toshiyuki thought. I won't live through the night. He bowed his head formally, attempting to end the one-sided conversation. He knew the man was playing with his fear, but what he needed now, was more time to steel himself for the coming imperial ordeal. But the colonel would not have it.

"Lieutenant, I've been instructed to inform you of the necessary protocol, once you've arrived at the palace. You will be ushered into the presence of the Lord Keeper of the Privy Seal, Marquis Kido. He will instruct you in the correct way to behave in the presence of the emperor. Is that clear?"

"*Hai!*"

"You are true Samurai and you will conduct yourself with dignity and honor even in death. There will be no honor if you fail."

"I understand, Colonel." He looked up. "I understand only too well."

Through the side window of the Rolls Royce, Toshiyuki recognized Nijubashi Bridge, the formal entrance to the Imperial Palace grounds. Only with the greatest discipline did he keep himself from shaking apart inside as the limousine rolled to a stop at the massive palace doors.

Two

The imperial grounds were blanketed with darkness and hostility. Alien forms and pungent odors pushed at Toshiyuki as he was marched by three metropolitan policemen along a narrow path that wound, it seemed, through the black shadows of the entire two hundred forty-seven acres of woods, gardens, and pavilions. Mercifully, the path finally gave way to a lighted terrace that sloped down into Fukiage Gardens, a remote corner of the imperial compound.

"Move along, you're expected immediately!" prodded a police captain with a sour voice and a thick hand against Toshiyuki's shoulder. Briskly, the group made its way into a thick belt of trees that guarded large steel doors carved into a naked toe of a hill in bunker fashion.

As they marched through the doors, Toshiyuki remembered his brief encounter with Marquis Koochi Kido, Lord Keeper of the Seal, the emperor's most trusted aide and window to the outside world. Kido had promised that if even the slightest taint of dis-

15

honor was committed against His Majesty, retribution would be swift and sure.

They were ushered through another set of vault-thick blast doors and Toshiyuki suddenly found himself in a brightly lighted conference room decorated with brilliant red and gold silks adorned with cherry-wood paneling. He stood for a moment letting his eyes adjust to the dazzle of lights and colors, before spotting three large *tatami* mats of finely woven fiber in the corner of the chamber.

He lowered himself cautiously to the mat nearest the doors and waited in silence, his back at rigid attention and his head bowed to his chest. He must show *Kodo!* The emperor's code for warrior conduct. What he had been taught since his youth and his naval academy days at Etajima. He must not dishonor his father's memory. Dying was easy. Living honorably in the presence of the emperor was not. He must have the courage to speak intelligently when called upon and die with dignity.

Just as Marquis Kido had instructed, Toshiyuki focused his eyes to a spot on the *tatami* and promised himself that if he could be allowed to survive the night he would visit the sacred Yasukuni Shrine and pray for all Japanese war dead and their families. It would be the only way he knew of giving thanks.

The sound of delicately shuffling cloth broke his concentration. With his head bowed to his chest it was difficult to see, but he was able to make out a brilliant orange color moving toward him with astonishing quickness. He held his breath and waited, fighting every instinct to raise his head.

For a long time the figure in the orange court robe was quiet. Then, without preamble, the emperor began. "I will speak and you will listen to my comments and instructions." The voice was shrill and effeminate. Toshiyuki was embarrassed by his own assessment.

"I am about to charge you with a royal mission that I hope will save us from certain destruction. This will be the most important sortie of your life!"

Toshiyuki couldn't believe what he was hearing! His emotions flooded with relief. Mission? What mission? This was the emperor speaking to him! This night had to be a mistake!

"Raise your head and face me, Lieutenant!"

Mizutari had never seen his emperor's face except in photos. It was forbidden without royal permission. In the streets people were forced to bow their heads until the royal procession passed from view. The emperor's deeply set brown eyes windowed a smooth oval face. Thick round wire-rimmed glasses sat efficiently on His Majesty's small even nose. There was a grace and durability to his emperor's face that Toshiyuki liked. But something about the royal face nagged at him. It was the emperor's chin. It was weak and out of character for the son of heaven. The face was human!

"I am instructed that you are well suited for the task at hand," Showa Emperor Hirohito said. "But we shall see. The empire, under the direction of a government run by Premier Tojo, is heading for an armed clash with Britain and the United States. I am very distressed by that fact."

Hirohito began pacing, moving lightly on his feet. "There is great treachery against me, Toshiyuki. That

17

is fact, not paranoia. I do not want war with the Allies, but I walk a delicate tightrope between the army and navy. They all strut like peacocks eager to blood themselves in my name." Anger seeped into his voice, fueled by a deep turbulence. "This is a conflict that can only end in disaster, but my ministers have outfoxed me through protocol. There is little wisdom in Tokyo these days."

Hirohito looked down at the young officer who was staring up at his emperor with iron obedience masking his bewilderment and confusion. "Your father carried out important court missions for my father, Emperor Taisho. When he died, I inherited the throne when I was not much older than you." He smiled for the first time.

"From the moment I was six years of age, I was trained for my role to come. Admiral Togo, who defeated the Russians in the great sea battle of Tsushima Straits, taught me the virtues and duties of *Bushido*. He was a man of principle and honor. A man of his word who accepted the surrender of Admiral Rojestvensky with humble honor. Not like that bastard Tojo. Does my candor disturb you, Lieutenant?" It was a veiled question.

"I am not certain what to say. Lord Keeper Kido ordered my silence."

"Forget Kido," Hirohito grunted sulkily. "He watches over me like I was a child, still in training at Peers School. I am forty years old with the responsibilities of a nation. I am not a god, despite what you hear from the Ministry of Propaganda. We must find a way around the fanatical thinking that has been engendered by the likes of Tojo and his compatriot Baron Oshima in Berlin. They have poisoned the thinking of our Officer Corps."

Hirohito leaned closer to Toshiyuki. "Speak and counsel with me as a *Samurai*. I understand you have studied in the United States."

"Yes Your Majesty, at Whittier College in California."

"Your English is sound and you are familiar with American customs?"

"I believe so. I lived with a family of American Quakers near the campus for three years. I made many friends."

Hirohito nodded his approval. "Good. Then what I am about to order you to do, may help save you from having to go to war with those friends."

"My friends are Quakers who do not believe in war, Your Highness. They are pacifists. Over the years we had many discussions. Their convictions are as deeply rooted as the *Samurai* upbringing that molded me as a warrior."

"I know of your family's integrity, Toshiyuki. That is why you were summoned in the middle of the night. You are an act of faith for me." The emperor paused. "I must have your word as a *Samurai*. You can never reveal these truths that are revealed here tonight until I personally release you from your pledge."

"I pledge my word, Highness! As a *Samurai* and as the son of Baron Mizutari!"

"Very well." Hirohito cupped a hand to his mouth and instinctively his voice dropped. "This court has unsanctioned ears. This past August, I began secretly communicating, by a series of letters, directly with American President Franklin Roosevelt and his Secretary of State Cordell Hull. No more than ten men outside of this room are aware of these secret cables. The current Tojo military clique is certainly not privy to this written dialogue."

Toshiyuki shivered, not understanding the full impact of the words.

"We discussed peace in our letters, Lieutenant," Hirohito explained. "A lasting peace for all Pacific partners. There can never be a repeat of the horror of Nanking three years ago. The thought sickens and shames me. We discussed Japan's withdrawal from China and the lifting of the American trade restrictions and the ending of the oil embargo."

The emperor paused, searching for the right words. "We discussed face and trust. The need to begin to rebuild Japanese-American trust, that has decayed for the past forty years into a vulgar hatred. I promised Roosevelt in writing, that I would work toward those ends, that Japan can live as a peaceful neighbor."

"They have tried to strangle us, Your Highness!" Toshiyuki blurted out. "Only when we are sitting in their hip pocket do they consider it peace. They believe us to be inferior. Little yellow men!"

Hirohito frowned, and Toshiyuki bowed his head. "I have dishonored you. I am not worthy of your—"

"Nonsense. With luck this might ripen into a healthy discussion between two men who care about Japan's future. It is true that American acts have been designed to strangle us. By the same token, we have tried to purify China to our standards. China is

America's great ally. We are just as racist as the United States."

Hirohito turned and pointed to the east. "Our destiny lies in that direction. I know of plans." His voice dropped to a whisper. "I know of irrevocable plans to make war. My approval even adorns those plans through trickery within the general staff and the cabinet. Please stand, Lieutenant, and face me as a trusted aide, whom I will count upon in the weeks to come."

Toshiyuki rose and prayed that the emperor could not see the trembling of his legs.

"I must convince Roosevelt of my intentions to stop this insidious impulse to commit national *seppuku!* With that in mind you will proceed immediately to the Marianas by flying boat."

"I am confused, Your Highness."

"Confusion is the beginning of understanding. The sea plane is under command of the Imperial Household. The plane will land in Tanapag Harbor on the Island of Saipan. You will be escorted directly to Garapan Prison, run by the *Kempei Tai*. My direct orders will release two prisoners to your custody. Senior officers loyal to me will be waiting to assist you. You will then fly without escort to American-held Johnston Island, in the Central Pacific, where you will be expected."

Toshiyuki's eyes grew wide with unanswered questions.

"It will take at least a week to set up the flight. Then you will have one week to take care of your business and your mission on Saipan. The exact time of your rendezvous on Johnston Island, within an eight-hour limit, has been set for December first, Tokyo time. That will be your only chance to make contact with United States representatives and it will give me time to deal with Admiral Yamamoto. Nothing can be guaranteed beyond that point, including your mission or your life. Once past that date, things will happen automatically."

Hirohito stared at Toshiyuki in disciplined silence. Then, "You will be met by an American battleship, where the transfer of prisoners and certain documents will take place. I will hold you responsible for that success. Is that clear?"

"Perfectly, Your Highness," Toshiyuki said and bowed his head.

The emperor went to a small table across the room where he retrieved a bright yellow rubber pouch. Toshiyuki had seen that type before aboard the *Ushio*. It was waterproof and used to store secret fleet codes and orders in ship's safes.

"Within this double jacket," the emperor said, "I have compiled certain documents and plans for the eyes of President Roosevelt only. As a sign of my integrity, each paper carries my imperial seal so they cannot be tampered with. I have also enclosed a flag presented to me by Admiral Togo, when I ascended the throne in Nineteen twenty-six. There are only two in existence. It is the Z signal flag that Togo raised going into battle against the Russians in Nineteen hundred and five. The other flag will adorn the battle mast of carrier *Akagi,* in the days to come, if I cannot stop all this. This flag is symbolic of Japan's final

22

emergence as a modern nation state and my personal link with the honor of Japan's past.

"I am charged with the lives of eighty million of my countrymen. I will now live up to that responsibility. I am staking the life of my country on the strength of these documents and your prisoners to convince Roosevelt of my intentions."

Hirohito moved to another table and brought forward a brown envelope. "Your orders under the Imperial Seal and my signature. From this point on, I must sever all direct contact with you and the mission. Will you succeed for me and for the future of Japan?"

Toshiyuki bowed. "I am honor bound to give my life for you and this mission."

"I don't want your life, but your success!" Impulsively, Hirohito clasped Toshiyuki's shoulders. "I am not a demonstrative man, but the fate of our country, for a hundred years to come, is in your hands. No one must ever know of this mission — this night or of this conversation."

"I never left my ship in Yokosuka, Your Highness."

Hirohito nodded solemnly. "When I ascended the throne, I called for 'Enlightened Peace' during my reign. Thus far, it has been Japan's bloodiest. If you succeed, where I have failed, we will at last have some measure of peace. Kendo will no longer be the way of war but the way of the ceremonial sword. I now award you the Order of the Golden Kite, Japan's highest decoration for bravery."

Toshiyuki suddenly found himself moved to the point of tears, yet he was washed in a great serenity. His fate had been sealed. Haltingly, he began to silently sing "Kimigayo," the national song, allowing his feelings to become one with his emperor. After all was said, how many mortals could actually say they had been given the opportunity to personally serve their emperor.

Three

The old spoon bows barely pulled the dark, un-
gainly bulk of the ancient battleship through the
mountainous morning swell of the Central Pacific,
seven hundred miles south southwest of Honolulu.
Without warning, the little Kingfisher scout plane,
rigged precariously aft, atop main gun battery C,
began to shake fiercely in protest to the Force Eight
seas.

The thin, deeply tanned face of Capt. Franklin
Van Valkenburgh peered down at the scene from the
bridge. "Fucking deck division people! Just a bunch
of goddamn liberty hounds! Have someone lash
down that Sikorsky before she breaks free! Jesus, the
Guam Boys could do better!"

A sharp buzz punctured the tension in the large
compartment overlooking the foam-swept bows,
struggling once again to throw off tons of melon-
green seawater.

"Look alive, damn it!" the captain said, his voice

eroding into a snarl. "This sure as hell isn't a suite at the Royal Hawaiian."

An ensign in starched khakis, looking as green as the heavy seas, reached for the bulkhead phone.

"Captain—Sky Lookout reports Johnston Island in sight."

"Where for Chrissakes? I'm not Houdini!"

"Sorry, sir. Sky reports Johnston bears three points off the starboard bow. No other targets in sight." The ensign took a deep breath, trying desperately to make peace with the mass rising in his throat.

Van Valkenburgh rubbed his jaw, thinking it through, not liking his predicament one bit. He raised his glasses, trying to separate Johnston Island from the dirty ocean and blurred horizon. Then he turned and grabbed the phone from the bewildered ensign. "Any sign of that Japanese seaplane? It will be coming at us from the southwest, from somewhere out of the Mandates."

"No, sir," snapped the telephone voice. "We're all set up here, looking for that large four-engined Jap flying boat."

"Watch out for any funny business, sailor! It's not just a sea plane that bothers me! We could run into a whole damn Japanese task force trolling out there in this shit for weather! We don't have any damn escorts and if they jump us out here, our asses will be deep sixed in a flash."

"Aye, aye, Captain. We've got five pair of trained eyes up here searching for smoke on the horizon as well as for that *Kawanishi* flying boat."

"Very well, Maintop, stay damn sharp! If a whale farts out there I want to know pronto!"

Valkenburgh drew a deep troubled breath, knowing how impossible it would be if his ship was ambushed. Slowly, he cradled the phone and then picked up another. "Conn, this is the captain. Reduce speed, all ahead one-third, all shafts. Steady on the course, two four six degrees, relative. Let's go to condition ZED now, close and dog all X and Y doors. Take the crew to battle stations and for Chrissakes, look alive! This is still real Indian country."

He replaced the phone to discover Rear Adm. Isaac Kidd hovering nearby. "Well, Admiral, we've got Johnston off the bow, about eighteen miles out, just barely popping out of a nasty line squall. I'm about to call Johnston radio. I just hope to hell this isn't some kind of a trap; I'm too damned close to Johnston Island to run a zigzag to counter submarines in the area!"

Admiral Kidd searched the captain's ruddy face with steady brown eyes. "I know," he said quietly. "I feel naked as hell, too. It's my ass, if something goes wrong. Remember, it's my battleship division."

"Then I don't understand why—"

Kidd held up a hand and motioned Van Valkenburgh to a corner of the bridge. "Look, Frank, this sortie is purely political, all the way from Washington. That job we just did in the Philippines is also on the QT. For god's sakes, Kimmel didn't even ap-

27

prove this. It came directly from the White House, if you want to know. I don't really enjoy parading around out here, without air cover, looking for a damn sandbar, with the Japanese ready to jump us! But, Harry Hopkins was very persuasive."

"What about approved channels, Admiral? Are things that haywire these days? Who the hell is that mystery guy we picked up at Pearl? He raised holy hell at ten ten dock before coming aboard, like a fucking sultan. He's bitched his head off ever since we left Manila! I don't even know his name. No name, no orders, nothing. Just verbal commands!" Van Valkenburgh shook his head in disgust. "He eats alone and last night spent more than two hours on a secure channel, on the twenty-seven sixteen circuit, with some black chamber CINPAC type at Pearl. He's moved all types of equipment, including an emergency radio transmitter, into a compartment near the fantail fuel bunkers. Then he has the fucking crust to declare the spaces off limits!"

"Sand Island Radio reports contact with the Japanese flying boat," a Bridge voice called out. "The Catalina confirms the plane is our target and is now about sixty miles out. ETA is about twenty minutes."

"Admiral, I'll be damned if I'll endanger my ship or my crew without knowing what the hell is going on." Van Valkenburgh rubbed his closely cropped salt and pepper hair with a thick, callused hand. "What right does that guy have, sequestered in my ship, changing my orders and taking us to Johnston?"

"He has every right." Kidd grabbed Van Valkenburgh's shoulder and smiled. "Frank, here's the straight shit. He's Roosevelt's man. He could sleep on the deck of your bridge and all you could do would be to ask him where he'd like to have his rations served. Stop being a seaweed politician. It isn't smart. Let's take care of this business, and beat it back to Pearl, no worse the wear for it."

Valkenburgh nodded stiffly and took a deep breath. He didn't like, nor was he used to, not having complete control over his ship. "You're right, Admiral," he said. "At least I hope to hell you are, or this old girl is in real trouble."

"Approaching Rene Reef," called out the stricken ensign.

Slowly Valkenburgh made his way to the bulkhead telephone system. "Conn, this is the captain. Ready your whaleboat crew on the starboard quarterdeck. Prepare to launch at my command and rendezvous with that Japanese flying boat."

Minutes later: "PBY *Cactus One* Patrol reports that Jap flying boat is approaching on a heading of zero eight zero, on the deck," the ensign reported. "Speed is one six four knots."

Valkenburgh trained his field glasses on the tiny black dot that was quickly growing into a large sea plane. A moment later, the Japanese plane, dressed in dark olive drab paint, offset against large blood red rising suns, flew over the *Arizona* with engines roaring, at two hundred feet. Slowly the plane

29

banked and dropped her nose looking for a clean stretch of Lagoon water. For some reason Valkenburgh shivered inside and couldn't let go of a deep, empty feeling — like nothing he'd ever experienced.

Pearl Harbor, Hawaii
March 26, 1991

Four

Benjamin Spain watched the purple designs floating lazily in the green oil-slicked water and shivered at their beckoning.

"Remember your lifeline, Ben," cautioned Park Supervisor Jack Scruggs as he centered the twin SCUBA tanks on Spain's back. "Visibility is a lousy ten feet this morning, so take it real slow."

"Slow is all I can do down in that tangled mess," Spain said. "Better let me see that blueprint again. Help me over to the chart table." Awkwardly, Spain waddled over to a highly detailed construction blueprint of the U.S.S. *Arizona,* in the Marble Shrine Room of the *Arizona* Memorial, floating on piers over the rusted carcass of the sunken battleship.

"The word is that she's a real bitch inside. A diver's nightmare!" Scruggs removed his flat-brimmed Jack Pershing Ranger hat and rubbed his long thin nose. "We're goin' on gut here, Benny. We think and it's only a guess, that the oil leak is originating somewhere near the tiller room." He drew a long fin-

33

ger over frame eighty-five of the diagram, near the port wing tanks and torpedo voids. "You'll have to go in through the main access hatch, between three and four main after turrets. Your arc light should give you plenty of illumination."

"You're sure this is necessary, Jack? The damn hulk's been leaking oil forever! Who the hell cares?"

Scruggs nodded. "Until last week it was only a few drops, every few minutes. Don't know what the hell gave way, but now it's a steady stream. In a few months, the whole East Loch will be fouled. The *Zona* carried close to six thousand tons of bunker oil, when she went down."

"It's your nickel." Spain's face relaxed for a moment.

"That's right, it is my nickel, so listen up, wolfman! Don't play any games this time! This dive is purely exploratory. A pathfinder exercise. You've got to descend through five decks of death. I think our target is somewhere around here." He tapped a finger on the diagram, at a compartment marked D-105 EFO. "Emergency fuel oil compartment, frame ninety-five. Flat against the double bottom and next to the tiller room. Damn tricky stuff. God only knows what type of debris is down there. It will be confusing! Just don't disturb anything. You know the rule. *Arizona* is a sanctuary."

Ben Spain's mind was slipping away from the chatter. "Don't worry. I just hope a wing tank hasn't let go. I'll drown in the damn oil!"

"At the first sign of trouble, just get out. The keel

34

is buried in twenty feet of mud, so it will be cold as a witch's tit down there."

"Okay, Jacko, let's get this pony show on the road." Spain sucked in a mouthful of sweet Hawaiian air, surveying the morning. The lush Waianae Mountains thrust themselves up into a deep blue sky, punctuated with white masses of fast-moving clouds that were pushing hard against the green cleavage of Kolekole Pass. It was spring in Hawaii, the best time of the year, and Spain felt good. Low humidity, soft lovely days, with cleansing rains, fueled his life.

"Stop daydreaming!"

Spain glanced at Scruggs who was impatiently waving him down to a temporary floating platform, just behind the memorial. A special orange marker buoy set off the invisible stern of the dead ship.

Spain had memorized his route. He knew the *Arizona* in death as well as anyone. Two years before, he had worked with United States Park Service divers surveying the *Arizona,* in an effort to finally find what ultimately killed her. After a year of methodically charting her rusted and crusted exterior hulk, she had almost become a friend. At least, something familiar, but with the potential of sudden death always waiting. *Arizona*'s entire fore deck, some hundred feet of ship, between the bridge and bow, had evaporated, under the power of more than a million pounds of smokeless explosives ignited by a Japanese bomb that had scored a direct hit on the ship's magazines.

Ben Spain couldn't complain. This was considered

hazardous work, and the National Park Service was paying five hundred a day. Ironically, in death, the *Arizona* and the more than a thousand souls she still possessed, had given him a real measure of freedom, even a strange peace, and certainly time for Harumi.

Cautiously, Spain nosed over and descended through a rusted trunk hatch using the thick white beam of light as his guide and only link with sanity. The sound of rasping from his demand regulator was his frail lifeline of compressed air. Slowly he moved through four decks of debris, visualizing in his mind the final moments for the men trapped below decks, when the *Arizona* went down. Nine minutes, he kept saying to himself. It took only nine minutes to destroy all those lives as the ship settled in the mud. He shivered at the images of trapped men breathing their last, struggling in tiny pockets of lost air, waiting for a rescue that never came. The ghosts kept pushing at him:

> *All right you swabbies*
> *Reveille!*
> *Let go'a your cocks*
> *And grab your socks!*

He froze before the sight of a full skeleton draped at a crazy angle across a narrow passageway. A clean silver dog tag and thin chain were still wrapped delicately atop the man's rib cage. Spain began breathing heavily as he aimed the beam of light over the

36

few tatters of T-shirt that lay next to the remains, undulating in the soft black current as white ribbons of surrender. Carefully, he rubbed a gloved hand over the compartment door sign, as the first tremors rocked his body:

D-418 AFT GYRO COMPASS ROOM

Spain suddenly feared he was losing control. His heart was pounding in his ears. He had another full deck to descend before he could even get close to the emergency fuel compartment. The only life was the rise and fall of his chest!

Don't panic. Don't think about it. Jesus! Don't let yourself want a drink. For long moments he gripped a hatch handle fighting to regain control of his fear, forty feet below the surface of Pearl Harbor, inside a six-hundred-foot rusted tomb.

Breathe, damn it! Inhale. Exhale. One human skeleton. What the hell's the matter with you? The man knew death a half a century ago. What's it matter now? But the myths were right. Divers stayed away from *Arizona* like the plague. Ten men had died in various salvage operations on the ship during World War II. Swallowed alive by this cursed rust bucket.

Swim, damn it! Swim or die! Forcing himself to concentrate, Spain held the underwater light with both hands to keep it steady, as his powerful legs pushed him down the narrow hatch ladder to the fifth and lowest deck. He desperately needed to vomit, but somehow forced the mass to settle in his stomach, as his senses slowly regained control.

Ten minutes after making his way through the Steering Motor Room, Spain's hand made little circles on the ooze and rust covering the hatch door number plate:

D-104 FLAG STORES

The rubber cord around Spain's neck holding the light took the slack as he used both hands to push down on the hatch handle. Surprisingly, the hatch handle gave way with hardly any pressure. The force of his pushing had propelled him inside the compartment, slamming his body hard against an interior steel bulkhead wall. He knew the suspect emergency fuel bunker was just beneath his feet.

Automatically he checked his air supply. In his panic he'd used up more than half of his entire store. The gauge registered less than five hundred pounds. Enough to take him topside, but not much else, except to mark the cabin and check the decks and bulkheads for signs of oil leakage. Cautiously, he played the beam of light around the small compartment, suddenly blanching in fear as it caught a brownish skull resting casually on a steel table. He jerked the beam away and spotted another skull without its skeleton. Taking a deep breath, he tricked his senses away from panic and death.

The compartment, filled with debris, bones, and an old-fashioned vacuum tube shortwave radio transmitter, didn't show a trace of oil. Slowly, Spain turned himself around, breathing in short rasping spurts, careful to keep his air tanks from tangling in the clutter. Life in the compartment was slow motion against a backdrop of blackness. Time to go, my two friends, he muttered silently, as he swam gingerly through the debris. His right hand came up feeling for the hatch as a yellow rubber pouch glided past.

Spain reached out and pulled it in. For a moment he played the light on the bag, studying its surface. Impulsively, he pulled the case closer to his faceplate for examination. Then he let it slide away. As he reached for the hatch he turned back to find the pouch riding in his wake. He shrugged to his long dead audience and swam from the compartment with the pouch tucked inside his tool sack.

Five

Spain rubbed his damp, curly gray-blond hair, staring out into the small but well-manicured garden behind the shingled cottage on Kealaolu Drive in Kahala. At that moment, the garden was being carefully patrolled by Mollie, a two-year-old black lab, with large soulful eyes. A gentle gust of the afternoon trades rustled the pink hibiscus and red poinsettias, pushing the afternoon light off the flowers in dances of color.

"I lost it today, Harumi," he said quietly as Mollie positioned herself for a late afternoon sunbath. "I wanted a goddamn drink forty beats down inside the stink of the *Arizona*."

He watched the sunlight ripple the dog's thick black coat with streaks of red and brown. For a moment he thought that the *Arizona* wasn't real. How could it be, in the peace of that moment?

Harumi van Horn snapped her head up from the soft green electronic fuzz of the computer screen and fixed her eyes on the back of Spain's head and thickly rounded shoulders.

"What did you say?"

"I'll always be a flophouse drunk. I just can't climb out of the damn darkness." Spain turned slowly, fear and anger rimming the dark pockets beneath his deep-set eyes. "I hit the wall again this morning and all I wanted was a damn drink!" He searched her exotic Eurasian face for answers. "I've struggled all day and I still want one. I'm tired of struggling! Right now, alcohol and urine would do just fine."

"Did you have a drink?" Harumi rose from her chair. "Did you take one?" she demanded.

"I might as well have. I'm still a damn street alky. I'll never get past it. At the first sign of trouble, I'm ready to sabotage myself by jumping back into a bottle of shaving lotion!" He held a full bottle of amber unblended Scotch up to the light. "For the last two hours I've stared at this bottle as if it contained all the fucking secrets of the universe." He looked back to the garden. "This place is the end of the rainbow. There's no place left to run."

"*Shaving lotion?*"

Spain made a bitter sound. "The last time I hit bottom. Not even the good stuff, just rotgut supermarket shit. Partial dreams for ninety-seven cents plus tax and a need to believe in God."

"How long has it been, Benny? How long?"

"Who the hell cares!" Spain snapped, then shook his head.

"How long has it been since you stopped drinking?" Harumi repeated evenly.

"Three years, give or take." He nodded solemnly. "Three tough years, but at least I remember them!" He frowned, wrinkling his weathered face, as he continued to purge himself. "It's been three years since I left the mainland, stopped practicing law, developed a real belief in God and learned to live with my sobriety. I don't miss L.A. or the law one damn bit." His burden began to lift and he smiled at Harumi, his confidence still alive.

Harumi turned off the computer, pushing her shoulder-length raven hair away from her slender face. "How did it happen, Benny?"

Spain shook his head, and then carefully placed the Scotch bottle on an antique French sideboard, happy for the small victory. "I can't pinpoint it exactly. In counseling, I was told it was the way I internalize stress; the tensions of life." He drew in a deep breath, reaching into himself. "I know all the clinical terms, all the psychobabble crap, that in the beginning helped me live with the gut-pounding emotions, one day at a time!"

He tracked the softness and intelligence in Harumi's eyes and knew it was all right to go on. "Each person has a trigger. Some damn thing that puts them over the edge. For me —"

"What?" she urged quietly.

"Ah, it was the end of my tour in Nam. Until then, it was really nothing special. I suppose you have every right to know all this."

"No," she said thoughtfully. "My rights are only if you want me to know."

42

"Is that your Japanese or Dutch speaking?"

"Neither. It's my womanhood."

"I fell out of a banyan tree a couple of years ago and landed here, with a failed life behind me and you accepted me."

"I accepted your reality a long time ago. We live on many different levels and offer each other various gifts." She bowed her head, letting the words soothe him. "Besides," she said, laughing, "you like fish heads and tofu burgers. There is real harmony in us." She cocked her head, knowing Spain had to say more.

"What was the trigger, Benny?"

Spain jerked his head as an expression of agony filled his face. "The trigger was a horrible two months in Haiphong, after our war ended. Before that, Nam was tolerable. Real nutsville, but I knew inside I could make it, if I could manage to stay alive." He shook his head, remembering. "Then the fucking wheels came off."

"Haiphong!" She turned over the word with surprise.

"It was just after the 'peace with honor' crap that came out of Kissinger's asshole. Some damn patriot in the Pentagon fingered my dive team, which was stationed at Da Nang. They offered us up as sacrificial lambs. We were sent off to that great never never land of North Vietnam, to defuse a shitload of mines we had dropped to blockade their major port facilities."

His face took on a dark, faraway cast. "We had

43

almost made stateside rotation," he said softly, still living the ancient nightmare. "It was just lousy luck. We lost thirty-six guys out of a hundred. Sent home in fucking body bags. I still can't get that smell out of my nose. Those kids never got any older, but I did. I was the fuse puller, so I survived."

Harumi moved close to touch Spain and take away his hurt. Slowly she reached up and wiped his tears. "I've heard enough. You don't have to say anymore, Benny."

He smiled, still lost somewhere in his past. "The hell I don't. If you're too chickenshit to listen, don't, but I've got to say it or it'll choke me to death. It's the nightmare or the Scotch, so take your pick. De-activating those bastard mines, fused with active homing devices, was impossible. When the navy dropped them they were designed to be tamper proof, and by God they were. Monster mines called *Quick Strike*. Cute, huh? Five-hundred and one-thousand-pound explosive loads. They didn't kill slopes, just us. When one went bang, it would turn my kids into instant Jell-O at a hundred yards. But we kept trying and we kept dying."

Spain slumped into a white cane rocker, wringing wet with sweat. "Then some planning-desk bastard decided it would be a brilliant idea to send a few of us upstream, in the Red River, to a sleepy little hamlet called Hai Duong to defuse errant mines that had missed their targets in the harbor by thirty kilometers. Some miss, huh?"

Harumi laid her head against his heaving chest

44

and wrapped her arms around him, to ease the hurt.

"One terrific morning, my chief, with a quick, easy smile, a twenty-two-year-old kid named Michael Collins, was surveying a mine and was shot through the face and both eyes by a sapper, right in the middle of the damn river!" Spain rocked his head in cadence to his body in the chair. "He kept screaming my name, 'Benny, Benny, oh God, don't let me die here? Please Benny!' When I got to him his face was gone above his mouth. Just shot away into something inhuman. But the kid was still human, damn it! He kept talking to me with that mouth. He finally bled to death in the red mud and weeds along the riverbank, an hour later. I didn't have the guts to end his suffering. I was helpless and weak. Villagers washing their clothes in the water ignored our screams for help, as if we were all dead."

Spain cupped his thick, worn hands gently around Harumi's face. "That did it. I was all washed up. I was educated sewer water. I couldn't even take a piss without shaking to pieces. I felt the constant touch of dead men on me. I hated myself for what I'd seen and what I knew. How do you change that? Making it through each day became tougher and tougher. When I finally went home, I was already alcoholic. Other guys smoked dope, collected necklaces made from fresh VC ears and then shot up with H." Spain laughed darkly. "I was civilized. I was a lawyer, cut above the common combat grunt. A clubby court-house professional, who just drank booze."

Harumi kissed him gently.

"My old man told me it was a mistake to leave the high sheep meadows of the Western Sierra. 'Basques don't belong in the cities,' he said. 'Too many people and ideas poison the mind.' Funny thing, the old guy was right, with his sixth-grade education. He was a wise old bag of bones and sheep shit. So I had to overcome my past, with a law degree and a navy commission. I should have known."

Finally, Harumi broke the spell. "How did you come to Honolulu?"

"Jack Scruggs was my old division commander in Nam. I was married to his sister for three years."

Harumi raised her eyes for a moment, then the thought and surprise were gone.

Spain smiled. "Even Jack hates his sister. We lost contact after Nam, then by some stroke of luck he was in downtown Los Angeles on business and found me begging in front of the Bonaventure Hotel for quarters. I told you I was a street fleabag."

"I didn't realize you were reduced to that."

"And more. Jack nursed me back to health and shoved me kicking and screaming into a tough-assed AA program. Finally, I made it sober to a halfway house with two squares and a warm, lice-free bed, for the promise of coming to Hawaii to work with him on the *Arizona* survey project. I owe Jack my life."

Harumi took Spain's face into her hands. "What the hell do I know. I teach current American history to a bunch of spoiled *Haoles* from the mainland."

46

Craving his tenderness, she laid her head on his knee. "I didn't really understand the depth of it before. I was always cautious to ask. I knew you'd talk about yourself when it was right for you." She shook her head. "I live in books, in my classes and my research. I can only feel your experience through your pain. Not a very exciting existence."

"What you do is most important of all. I know how damn good you are. Why the kids are here doesn't matter." His face grew lighter as he pulled her into his lap. "All I want is what's inside your head, and that's the difference age makes."

"Bullshit, Spain! How can you have done all those things and be so insecure about yourself? Besides, you're as much a letch as I am."

His hand brushed her firmness. "Very easily, Harumi. I'm thirteen years older than you. A tough thirteen years. You've got your whole career ahead of you in teaching and research. I'm fine for right now, but that's probably all. I'm filled with scar tissue, you're filled with dreams. You're a veggie-burger Buddhist and I'm a nonpracticing human, without credentials." He pursed his lips. "I've hidden too long in my own fear. I'm an exile from life. In truth, I'm over the high side and you haven't even seen it yet." Suddenly the conversation had gone further than Spain wanted.

Harumi smiled. "Let me make my own decisions!" She felt her voice rising. "I have a thing for bagmen, so stop being an ass!"

"Spoken like a true chair merchant." Idly, Spain

fingered the rubber pouch he'd retrieved from the *Arizona*.

"Benny, my dad went through hell as part of the Dutch Resistance, during World War Two. He survived that trauma, the drinking, and nightmares and the death of his first wife. He built a new life for himself here in the Islands. He didn't marry my mother until he was in his late forties. He and my mother were eighteen years apart and very happy until she died. That was even after my mom spent the war on Sand Island, as a Japanese undesirable." Suddenly she noticed the pouch in his hands. "What on earth is that?"

Spain shrugged. "I pulled it out of the *Arizona* this morning. Some kind of a sealed pouch. It'll have to go back. House rules."

"Let me see it." Harumi took it from him and moved across the small open den to the computer console, her dark hair and well-shaped body flowing musically, despite the blue work shirt and loose fitting safari pants.

Spain sucked in a deep breath of fresh air. Harumi had talked him away from his dark abyss and he was grateful for the reprieve.

"My God, Benny!" She bent around the console and eyed him. "Where'd this come from?"

"I told you, the *Arizona*." He held up his hands. "From a compartment in the aft section of the ship. What's the big deal?"

Harumi didn't answer.

"What's the mystery?"

48

But Harumi was now totally absorbed. Suddenly she forced out an animal noise. "My God, Ben! Do you know what's inside this thing?" Her voice was trembling. "I can't believe it! This package is personally addressed to President Roosevelt from Emperor Hirohito."

"What's the big deal?"

"Who else knows about this, Benny?" Her voice was ice cold.

"No one."

"Thank God for small favors." She touched the pouch, shivering inside.

Six

"Look at this, Benny." Carefully she removed the contents of the pouch. For a moment, she reexamined the brilliant gold seal she had just broken.

"What is it?"

"Gold, Benny! It's the Imperial Seal of the Japanese emperor! The gold chrysanthemum. And it's never been broken! It looks so new and untouched, after all these years." She looked up at Spain. "Is that possible?"

Spain picked up the empty rubber pouch, carefully running his fingers through the inside seams and outside seals. Finally he nodded. "Everything's intact. It seems airtight. There's no reason why it wouldn't keep out the water and the humidity."

Spain thought of the skeleton blocking the passageway — a dead guard on a dead ship. "There is no way of telling how long this has been submerged. I mean it might have taken years for the water to have completely flooded the compartment, if there was enough air pressure."

"What a find!" Harumi whispered as she fingered

the stack of materials, each envelope sealed with its own gold chrysanthemum.

"It all has to go back," Spain said sharply. "I took something from a monument. A cemetery."

"Come on, Ben! This could be an historical find of major significance. I'm a historian, remember? Don't you know what this find could mean for me?" She paused. "For us?"

Spain smiled broadly. "Aren't you being a little melodramatic? A few sealed envelopes in a pouch are not exactly the Rosetta Stone."

"How the hell do you know?" She pounded a fist against the side of the computer. "God, Benny—" She stopped before losing her composure. "Look, I'm sure you were one fine litigator, a trial lawyer who understood detail, control, and manipulation. But this is my turf, so let go." She reached over and took his hand. "I'm not the enemy here. Work with me?" she asked, her voice evening out. "Just let me evaluate what's here, then make copies of the documents. This could mean so much to so many people."

"If Jack Scruggs found out, I'd be finished."

"He doesn't have to know, Benny."

"I know, damn it! Besides, I owe that man my life and ultimately finding you. I won't lie to him or let him down."

Harumi steepled her hands. "Okay, listen to me. We'll do the right thing. Sit with me and help me see what we've got here. Working together, we can go through these materials in a few hours. I read Japanese and at the least, it will allow me to know

51

what kind of a judgment to make. When we're done, we'll have dinner and then hit the all-night fast copy place in Waikiki. Then tomorrow you can return this pouch and the documents to the *Arizona*. Fair enough?" She touched his face and felt the texture of his rough skin. "What do you say?"

Spain nodded. "Sure, why not. There's not a damn thing here worth fighting about, anyway."

Carefully, Harumi laid out the rules. More than an hour later, each envelope had been opened and marked for repacking. Spain set up a 35mm Nikon with a strobe light to photograph each envelope and its contents.

As the stubborn light settled to the west over Olomana Peak, Spain built a warming fire from local driftwood, then ordered a pizza to be delivered. He knew they would never leave the house that night. Harumi was too heavily involved with painstaking examination, cross-checking, and precise note-taking. When called upon, Spain would photograph certain documents and charts.

Finally, sometime after ten that night, Harumi called to Spain in a strange and distant voice. "Benny, I have a rough overview of these materials, but I can't figure out a couple of the pieces." While munching cold pizza, she handed Spain a stainless-steel wrist bracelet marked with Japanese characters and a date on the backside:

Spain shrugged after turning it over. "A simple ID tag of some sort. What's it say?"

Harumi referred back to her notes to be certain. "The literal translation is F.N. GARAPAN KTP.NR16020."

Ben repeated the initials. "Doesn't mean a thing. The numbers don't register." He gave her a blank stare. "It's tough to be brilliant when you don't know."

"The numbers came up in another document, referring to some type of a book. It's within the context of a personal note from Emperor Hirohito to Roosevelt." She paused, letting the words push at Spain.

He let out a slow whistle. "Personal note?"

Harumi nodded solemnly, then burst into a wide grin. "Bingo! This is the real damn stuff. It has to be!" She pulled his hand to her breast. "My heart's beating like a machine gun. God, this is exciting!" She shook her head. "I just can't believe what's here. This all confirms so much that we thought and speculated about, but could never prove. It—"

"Hold it, Harumi! The documents go back to the *Arizona.* That's a given."

"Christ, Ben!"

Spain shook his head. "If this gets out, I'm done with Scruggs and the Park Service."

"I can't let the information die here, Ben. It's too

large an issue. There's too much truth here, to let it die," she said firmly.

"I said I would help you copy all this—"

"All right. I guess I don't have a choice, do I?"

"No! Now tell me what's so damned important?"

Harumi bent down to rub Mollie's ears as she began, her face glowing in the den's firelight. "The material in that pouch confirms that Roosevelt knew about the attack on Pearl Harbor in advance!"

"Old news, kiddo. Every schoolchild has heard about it. I don't care what's been confirmed."

Harumi smiled vaguely. "What your little school kids don't know and this pouch confirms beyond legal doubt, is that Roosevelt and Hirohito exchanged secret letters by diplomatic courier weeks before the attack. It seems that Hirohito provided Roosevelt with precise military information on the Pearl Harbor raid long before it took place!" Harumi closed her eyes for a moment, swallowing into her dry throat. Then her face clouded over. "What I don't have a clue to, is how and why the emperor's pouch ended up inside the *Arizona!*"

"Why the hell would the emperor inform Roosevelt about their surprise attack on Pearl Harbor? That's utter nonsense! I can't buy it!"

"Not utter nonsense, just historical intrigue. Could anyone have planted those documents on the *Arizona,* after the war?"

Spain shook his head. "I don't think so, and why would anyone want to?"

She nodded. "I guess you're right. Is there any

way I can steal a look at the log of the *Arizona*? It might clear up how the pouch ended up aboard."

"I really don't know. I'll call Jack. Maybe he knows."

"Ben, if you ask, it might arouse suspicions and then we've blown it."

"Harumi, nobody cares! Suspicions about what? Let me handle it. But I don't want Jack hurt or betrayed."

"Promise, Benny, more than you know!" She reached up and held him tightly. "I love you too much for that. I wish you would hear that."

Spain grunted and reached for the phone.

"Darlene, hi, it's Ben. Hope it's not too late. Good. Yes, I'm treating Harumi all right. I just have a sec. Is Jack around?"

"Ben, don't blow it, please!"

"Damn it! Be quiet."

"Jack, sorry to bother you, but Harumi wanted me to ask you a couple of questions. She was too shy." He winked at Harumi.

"She's doing this academic monograph on the Pearl Harbor attack and has been bugging me for weeks. Maybe you can help. She's written to the Navy Department, but of course they haven't answered yet. Has the *Arizona* been disturbed since she was sunk?"

"Answer is no, Ben. Today, you made the first check dive below second deck. I thought I told you that. Three months after the attack, divers went

55

down to crack open the paymaster's safe and retrieve the ship's payroll. Attempts were made to go deeper, but a number of divers became entangled in debris or were overcome by noxious gases and that was that. Does that help?"

"Sure does. Oh, one last thing. Harumi wants to glance at the deck log of the *Arizona,* to help with her paper. Where can she do that?"

For a long time the other end of the phone was silent. "I thought you knew, Ben." Scruggs's voice had changed, but Spain wasn't certain how. "The log was never found after the attack."

"Harumi will be sorry to hear that. She's talked about seeing it for months." Ben could feel something growing on the other end of the line. "Thanks, Jack."

"See you in the morning. I think we'll dive together tomorrow, Benny."

Spain hung up the phone and shrugged off a mildly unpleasant feeling of an old cold ghost clawing at him.

"What'd he say?"

Spain told her about the conversation and then moved close to Harumi. "I want to know exactly what we're getting into with your historical intrigue. Walk me through it as best you can with as much detail as you possibly can. I won't be able to guard my rear or yours, unless I know what the hell those documents are all about. If you are right about the Roosevelt-Hirohito relationship, there must be a hell'va lot more!" He walked to the fire and stoked a

56

red hot log, the amber light deepening his tired features.

Slowly he turned to her. "It's really crazy. That ship went down a half century ago, but she won't die. I just have this feeling." Then he smiled. "All right, Doctor van Horn, tell me a bedtime story."

"First let me show you something. A small map dated November twelve, Nineteen forty-one, is included. It's titled 'Naval Task Force Route Final Approved Naval Ministry.' It's in Japanese, but you'll get the idea of what Hirohito was giving to Roosevelt."

For a long time Spain stared at the map, orienting himself to the Pacific and the significance of the plan. Then he turned to stare at Harumi. "My God, this is part of Yamamoto's battle plan!"

Seven

The zodiac idled slowly in the blackness. Off in the distance, the *Arizona* Memorial squatted protectively over her rotting tomb in the shadow of a dense bamboo grove along the shore of Ford Island. The entire scene was eerily backlighted by the glow of Pearl City.

"We have to be back at the Visitor Reception Center by midnight, or—"

"Or what? You turn into a pumpkin. God, Benny, come on!"

"That's when the navy S boat makes its rounds of the *Arizona* complex," Spain offered patiently. He found himself whispering for no reason. If someone wanted to find them, all they would have to do was follow the harsh whine of the outboard engine or their phosphorescent wake churning up the East Loch of Pearl Harbor.

"I'm sorry, Benny. I'm nervous." Harumi finished

zipping up her wet suit to fight the chill coming off the black water. Suddenly she took his hand. "Look, Ben, thanks for this. I know the risks you're taking. If this wasn't so important—" Her voice faded into the drone of the outboard motor as she traced the faint outline of his face in the dark.

"I must be nuts!" A deep rumbling cut him off. Instantly, Spain killed the engine. "Quiet!" he hushed. "Don't move!" Out of the blackness a primordial shape became an omnipotent form, moving toward their small rubber boat.

"It looks huge, Ben!" She was startled.

"It is. Looks like a missile destroyer standing out to sea on the tide."

"What can we do?"

"Not a damn thing. We stay put and drift, if we don't want to be seen. Hopefully, his bow wave will push us out of the way. He's only doing five knots."

Hardly breathing, they both watched in a trance, as the six-thousand-ton warship loomed larger and darker in their eyes.

"It just turned, Ben. It's heading directly for us!"

"It just seems that way." Spain watched the knife-shaped bows and knew she was right. "Easy. Take it easy," he soothed, uncertainly.

"Don't they see us?"

"Let's hope to hell not! We're too small and a black rubber raft on a black night won't even register," he shouted above the freight-train roar of the destroyer. Quickly, Spain assessed their complete vulnerability. Too late to put on their tanks or just swim for it. Maybe it didn't matter, after all, trading his life and Harumi's for a goddamn rubber *maru* and a wild-goose chase aboard the *Arizona*. The roar of the ship bearing down on them was deafening and now they could hear deckhand voices above the engine and propeller noises. The sounds of a small city about to eat them.

Instinctively, they held each other, watching the growing monster. "Let's go over the side, Ben! At least we can try to swim to shore." Harumi was terribly frightened.

"Can't. We're too fucking close! That bastard's screws would suck us in and chop us into shark food. The engines are too damn powerful. He's running gas turbines. Same as seven forty-seven's," he shouted. He stroked her hair and knew she didn't know what the hell he was talking about.

Spain stared up at the enormous animal about twenty yards from them. "Hold on!" he screamed, as they were captured by the vortex of frothing sea and a massive wall of cold, shadowless steel.

"I love you, Spain!" Harumi was saying goodbye. She touched his cold cheek just as the bottom dropped out. The next few moments slipped away into nothing, as alien slow-motion shapes ripped at her. Self-anger welled up in her, for pressuring Spain. All for what? she thought angrily. An overactive imagination. I've always been too damn full of myself. Then she was engulfed.

60

For a long time they lay silent, holding each other, as the raft bobbed and rocked in the destroyer's foaming wake. Finally, Harumi spoke. "I got us into this mess and I almost got us killed. I'm so sorry."

Spain ignored her, rising carefully to check the integrity of the small boat and the outboard engine. "Seems, okay. I don't know how we dodged that bullet. I think someone's trying to tell us something."

"Let's go back, Benny."

"After all this? For Chrissakes!" He felt his voice carry across the Loch. "We go, Harumi!" he said angrily. Then he hit the start button, forcing the engine into life. Quickly, he steered across the remainder of the channel and swept in behind the darkened memorial, around the stern of the *Arizona*. He drifted for a moment, then decided to tie up to the ancient white mooring pier that once held the dead ship's lines. In silence they glided to their target next to Ford Island.

They helped each other with their tanks and slipped into the dark water tied together with a six-foot lifeline. "Harumi, this is my turf. Do *exactly* as we planned. This tomb has killed before and I know her as well as anyone. She's a black hole. No changes from what we talked about. Agreed?"

"Agreed," she answered, testing her regulator-mouthpiece. "Ready, Benny?"

He nodded and led the way as they descended

into the black oily water, guided by Spain's powerful arc light. Ever so slowly they swam down through the first four decks. To survive, Spain forced his breathing into a steady cadence, this time refusing to acknowledge the death surrounding them. Inhale, exhale. Spain allowed the music of the bubbles and the rasping of the demand regulator to steady his focus, as they finally pushed down into the fifth deck. Yet he knew the blackness was always close to engulfing them.

Slowly, Spain moved the light down the narrow companionway, searching the grim rusting decks and bulkheads, littered with debris and skeletons. Harumi followed Spain through the blackness as he found the hatch door marked FLAG STORES. Cautiously, this time, Spain swung the hatch outward and then they were inside. He stopped and checked his air gauge. Better this time, he thought. He then checked Harumi's. She was more relaxed, having used up less air. All told, they had about thirty minutes remaining.

He took his slate and wrote 15 MINUTES, tapping Harumi with the light, then illuminating his board. Certain she understood, he checked his watch and then set about exploring the compartment, allowing Harumi to take the lead. His beam touched a skull on the deck and suddenly his throat constricted with fear. Harumi didn't notice, excitedly pointing with her light to something.

At first Harumi moved carefully, then as her confidence built, she allowed herself to feel the history and the moment. It was an incredible emotion, totally devoid of fear, as she explored the cluttered darkness. Something caught her beam of light, then she lost it in the blackness. It was yellow! She was sure of it. Damn, where is it?

Wildly, she crisscrossed the beam, but the yellow patch was gone, swallowed by the murk. Startled, she felt something on her shoulder. It was Ben signaling five minutes. Only five minutes! She panicked, not having accomplished anything she had intended. Her own slate was empty. She had planned to sketch the entire layout of the compartment and mark the places where the skulls were located. She knew Ben would never do this again. What a waste! He had risked so much to allow her this chance. Her beam found a bank of old-fashioned shortwave radios and what looked to be the teleprinter for some sort of primitive code machine.

A moment later, she felt the dreaded final tap on the shoulder and without turning knew it was time to begin the ascent to the surface.

"Damn, I blew it, Ben! My one shot." Disgusted, she threw her mask in the bottom of the boat. "I had it in my sights, then I lost it!"

"What's that?" Spain was distracted, moving quickly, letting go of the lines to the *Arizona* mooring stand. He climbed over her, started the engine and opened the throttle to its maximum setting. Harumi tried to stand and instantly fell back as the zodiac leaped forward.

"You all right?" he called. "We've only got half an hour. I cut it too close. The damn navy will have my ass, to say nothing of Scruggs and the Park Service!"

"I blew it, too, Ben!"

"What the hell are you talking about?"

"Another yellow pouch—"

She turned to meet Spain's steady gaze. "Are you sure?"

She nodded silently as Spain guided the boat behind the Visitor Reception Center. As he tied up, Harumi told him about it. "I didn't survey the room."

"I've got something that might help you." He pointed to his dive bag. "Take a look, but be careful."

Slowly she opened the nylon bag. "A skull. You brought up a skull!"

"I thought we could have some private forensic tests run. Who knows."

Gingerly, she replaced the skull in a towel." Thanks, Benny. I know how hard all this is for you. The skull is a real start. At least I hope it is."

"You hear something?" Instinctively, he fell flat into the bottom of the boat, pulling Harumi with him.

They were quiet for what seemed forever, listening

to the gentle lapping of the water against the concrete pilings of the visitor center. "God, I swore I heard someone close by," he finally whispered to her. "Maybe I felt it." He looked into her eyes in the dim light and felt his groin stir, suddenly wanting her.

Harumi felt his firmness through the wet suit and laughed. "You pick the damndest times. Not here, Ben. Not with all your paranoia."

"A little paranoia might go a long way, from this point on!"

Eight

The fire suddenly flared, throwing a muted glow across the den. It was a diffused yellowish cast, transmitted from another time. Harumi shivered, despite the fire's warmth, and ran her long graceful fingers over the fissures and frighteningly smooth surface of the skull.

"Who are you?" she whispered aloud. "Did you belong to that pouch?" Harumi bit her lip as the old light danced off the skull's jutting mandible and the square brownish teeth that mocked her presence with a hollow smile. In fact, it was more of a sneer than a naked death smile — an expression of the skull holding onto some ultimate secret.

For some unexplained reason, it was the dark hollows between the teeth that struck the sharpest terror within Harumi, giving the skull a grisly Halloween power. Harumi continued to fondle the skull, mostly out of a need to push through her own fear and uncertainty. Those staying qualities had won Harumi a hard-fought victory in her academic life, with her appointment as the only tenured woman in the history department at the University of Hawaii.

66

Harumi leaned back and allowed the fire's warmth to wash her fatigue, as Mollie stretched with a long moan on the bare oak floors. She reached up with a porcelain arm and swept a glass of red wine from the table sloshing it on the floor. "I can't feel sad until I know something about you. How did you lose those teeth? It looks like someone—"

"He looks like some poor mother's son from Topeka, Kansas, who happened not to be on liberty at the right time, a million Sunday mornings ago and became the space between the cracks."

"So you say." She reached up and rubbed the back of Spain's neck. Carefully, she searched his face as they embraced. "How was it today?" Even her whisper could be an inviting smile.

"Tiring. We dove three tanks on the *Arizona*."

"And?" Harumi stiffened.

"And nothing. I steered Jack away from your little mystery palace and we hit pay dirt. I think we found the source of at least one oil leak. That prospect lightened Jack's load considerably. The navy is all over his back to plug up the old girl, before all of Pearl is fouled with that bunker oil. But there is something. Something I can't touch about Jack." He sat next to Harumi, thinking it through.

"What is it?" She could feel the tension behind his eyes.

"Maybe nothing. Maybe my old arthritic paranoia acting up, but I think Jack knows we took the zodiac last night. I felt it all day. I couldn't shake the feeling that he was watching me.

He smiled, brushing off the instinct. "How was your day? Did you share our find with anyone on campus?"

She laughed, tossing her head in a funny way. "Are you serious. Those bastards! I'd blow hot air up their asses from the fires down below, before I'd share any of this." Her voice trailed away with a deep, bitter resentment. "Those small-minded male idiots made me feel like a fire hydrant that was peed on for seven long years, before I earned tenure!"

"Nice talk." Spain held her close. "Sorry, I just thought some immediate input would help."

"You couldn't have known, Benny. I haven't said much about it before. It must be my Japanese stoicism. See the things we're learning about each other. If we have anything here with the historical impact I think it has, those six old men would be the last one's I'd involve. They'd steal us blind."

"Okay, okay," Spain soothed. "We take no prisoners. But we have to start trusting someone, sometime, lady."

"So, make a suggestion."

"Your skull playmate, here." He pointed with a soft drink can in his hand. "Let's find out who the hell he is."

"Brilliant." Harumi rolled her eyes. "And maybe he's a she." Then she laughed darkly. "That would be a pleasant surprise wouldn't it."

Spain nodded. "More than you know. I don't think a woman, legally, ever set foot below decks in *Arizona*." He rose to let the dog out.

"Anyway, Doctor van Horn, I suggest we find a friendly dentist who has some understanding of forensic identification using teeth. At least it's a start." Slowly, Spain reached to the table and picked up the skull, searching its hollows for something more. "Speaking of teeth, it looks like our friend had an accident with all those missing pearls."

"I have looked for the past hour." She tapped the skull with a pencil. "I've been trying to convince myself that this thing is just a pumpkin, not the remains of a human being." Harumi snuggled close to Spain for warmth, if not comfort.

"Jesus!" Suddenly she sat up. "We can take our friend to see Kimmie." Harumi brushed hair from her eyes and kissed Spain lightly. "Solutions are all around us. If anyone can help, it has to be Kim!"

"Who is she?"

"We grew up together, from the time we were in junior high, in Kona. Her family owned a great deal of land on Maui's Kaanapali Coast, before it all became hotels. She's big bucks with no pretense."

Spain rubbed his tired face. "So?"

"She's also a dentist. Kim Dubin, DDS. She has her office, or what passes for one, at Kahuka. We lived together at Berkeley. She graduated from Cal Dental School a few years ago, then bummed around with a few friends surfing heavy-duty spots on the African and Australian coasts. Then she came home and passed her Boards."

"Is that why she lives on the North Shore?"

"It's really the Windward Coast," she corrected. "But yeah, when the big stuff rolls in from the Gulf of Alaska, she closes her practice, from November to early March. Money never has been a problem."

"I gather—" Spain fell silent, stood and moved toward the kitchen. Harumi watched his mood change with that awful street pallor and tightness rising to choke his features.

"Benny, what is it?" she called. The overhead lights in the kitchen clicked off. "Ben?"

"Quiet," he called.

"For God's sakes, what's going on?"

"Shut up!"

"Sometimes you're such a shmuck, Spain!" Harumi started for the kitchen just as the dog let out a death-curdling yelp from the yard. "Mollie!" she screamed. "Stop messing around, Ben!" Suddenly the house went dark.

"Down on the floor!" Spain hissed.

Harumi sagged to the hardwood floor in confusion. "Ben, what the hell is it?"

The silence of the gentle trades and the crackle of the soft fire, were now her only companions. "Ben?" she called again, her heart pounding in her throat. Carefully, she looked about as her eyes adjusted to the blackness and undulating shadows of the fire. After a few moments, Harumi rose to her feet and started for the sliding door. As her hand reached for the latch, an earth-shattering explosion of noise, light, and glass tore at her face, just as a hard force slapped her to the floor.

The frightening waves rose up the hard sloping curve of the unforgiving black lava rock beach, crashing in great falls of water. With each crashing torrent, the waves grew larger, reaching for her paralyzed body, laying helpless and naked. Then it came. An angry wall of yellow water topped with an enormous crest rolled in a deep curl toward her. Powerless, Harumi screamed as the mountain of water crashed over her prostrate form. Just before consciousness left her, Harumi began to shake with fear.

"Harumi—" A bright, painful shaft of light forced her eyes to open.

"You all right?" Spain cradled her head in his thick hands.

"Wh—what happened? There was a crash and this giant wave and I was shaking. It was weird." Her mouth was filled with dry cotton. "God, it was so real."

"We had a visitor. He must have slipped over the back fence and then he mixed it up with Mollie. There's a trail of blood."

"Is Mollie all right?" Harumi forced herself into a sitting position, her head spinning.

"She's fine. The yelp was probably after Mollie grabbed his arm or leg, then she was thrown. But she's fine. The girl's a trooper. Our visitor will no doubt need stitches. He lost a fair amount of blood, if what's all over the back grass is any indication.

"What about the lights?"

"That was me. I felt someone was out there and I went for the fuse box in the kitchen. How's your head?"

"My head?" She felt it, suddenly remembering the explosion and the concussion. "It's spinning. What happened?"

Spain pointed to the snowfall of shattered safety glass strewn all about Harumi. "Whoever it was got off a shot, despite Mollie's teeth. He was damn good. If only you would have stayed down, like I told you!"

"A shot! What the hell are you talking about? Who'd want to shoot at me?" Her body quivered, just like in the dream.

Spain picked her up to keep her bare feet from the glass litter. "I don't understand any of this, Benny." She felt a sob rising in her throat. "We don't have anything worth shooting at."

Spain carried her to the couch and laid her down.

71

"Maybe we do." He motioned to the skull still resting on the coffee table. "Maybe we have a great deal more than even you think."

Spain disappeared and returned a moment later holding a small pistol.

"What the hell is that, Ben?"

He frowned. "One of the few things I kept from the past." He held up the small weapon trying to interest her. "It's an M-52, nine millimeter. A Czech-made automatic that I picked up in Nam. "For a moment he stared at the weapon, a talisman of his past. "It's dependable and easy to use. I want you to learn to use it."

Angrily, Harumi rubbed her hands through her hair. "Damn you! I don't use guns! This is really stupid. I'm not into that barbaric crap. Besides, this is a police matter."

Carefully, she threaded her way through the broken glass, finally retrieving the phone. She glared at Spain, with tears streaking her cheeks.

"That's right, go ahead and call them." Spain shook his head, his movements and voice hard and bitter. "When the cops get out to the house, they'll ask about motive and you can show them the pouch and its contents, stolen from the *Arizona,* as well as the skull! Nothing like a little national monument grave robbing. You might as well have stolen the remains of the unknown soldiers from Arlington, based upon the hard time we'll both serve, to say nothing of the publicity."

"That asshole wasn't after the skull or documents at all." Her voice was a defensive shrill.

"Nice try, van Horn." Spain held up the used automatic, its dull metallic surface scratched and scarred. He pointed it toward the opening where the sliding door had been shot away, his tone dropping to a whisper. "He was definitely a pro. That was a warning shot. He probably had a nightscope. He could have dropped you anytime he wanted. He wanted to miss, to scare us away from our little find and this amateur black-bag operation of ours!"

"No one knew, Benny." She dropped her face into her hands. "Nobody knew, damn it!"

Spain shook his head. "Someone's been smelling our stink, whether we like it or not. Somebody who is damn good."

"Bullshit!" she screamed. "It doesn't make any sense! Besides, they missed me."

Spain whirled and pulled her toward him. "Listen, Harumi, my tough-assed academic. That gunman left a calling card, so we would do just what we're doing right now, eating our own tails. Do you want to follow through with this thing? It's all your historical garbage, anyway. I don't need this or your damn historical intrigue! I can dump it all behind the house in the alley, or drop it back in the *Arizona* and our problems will be over! Because our friend will try again! What do you say?"

"Shove it, Spain!" She wrestled free of his grasp. "This is our ticket. I know what's best for us, even if you don't. No son of a bitch is going to scare me off!"

Spain paused, then suddenly smiled. "Good, I'm glad it was straightened out." He pulled the eight-shot clip from the butt of the gun. "Tomorrow, you start carrying this automatic in your purse. Tonight, I'll teach you how to use it and what to look for if someone is following you. Clear?"

Harumi nodded sullenly. "First help me clean up this

73

mess." She bent down into a squat and started picking up the glass, then looked up. "Thanks, Benny. As long as I know the rules I'll be all right."

Spain touched her shoulder gently. "That's the point, Harumi. There are no rules, just results and a belief in your own skill. That's all that is going to count from now on."

Nine

Harumi kicked the twenty-year-old Toyota Land Rover into overdrive as she accelerated north across Oahu through the tunnels on Pali Highway, while Spain did his best to avoid conversation as they moved through sparse Saturday morning traffic. Off to his right and far below, the rounded, soft green velvet shapes of the weathered Waimanalo Forest mountains took shape against the thick layers of gray clouds, lingering in the morning air. A moment later, the long, shimmering ribbon of Manoa Falls came into view as it plunged into the shadows below. Somehow the beauty of the landscape was a rebuttal to the purpose of their business.

"You're too quiet. What are you thinking, Ben?"

Spain glanced sideways with a distant look. "You really want to know?"

"Of course, you dumb *Haole*."

"You won't like it."

Harumi raised her eyes as she turned northwest onto Kamehameha Highway, heading for Kahuka on the Windward Coast. "That never stopped you before."

"I never should have taken the damn pouch. Then by taking you down into the *Arizona,* I only compounded the felony. I need this kind of trouble like I need a bottle of Scotch to cure myself. It's my fault it all developed. I put my life back in order and this happens."

"How could you have known what was in that pouch, Benny?" She touched his hand.

"It's not right," Spain blurted out. "That's from my gut. Those poor bastards should be left alone in the *Arizona!*" He was disgusted. "And I don't care how you feel, historical significance aside. Those kids gave up their lives so we could drive Toyotas! Jesus!"

"I do know what you mean, believe it or not. I've thought about it a great deal, since that bastard shot at me the other night. It's *kapu."* She shook her head. "Disturbing a grave."

"Kapu?"

"It's Hawaiian for forbidden." She bit her lip. "You may not believe it, but I understand." She turned her head, tears rimming her eyes. "But I can't stop now."

"You mean you *won't* stop!"

"All right, I won't stop! I know what's inside that pouch!" She was pleading for his understanding. "It's a hunger in my stomach. An ache I can't soothe. I have to know what happened in that compartment before the attack. I can't let it rest, least of all for all those men who died in that ship. We owe them the truth!"

Harumi turned her eyes back to the highway. "I'm even paranoid now. I've had this feeling for the past two days that someone has been watching me. I have the feeling now that we're being followed." She shook her head, the fear and tension crawling up the back of her neck. Out of the corner of her eye, she saw Spain pull the automatic pistol out of his jacket that she had refused to carry, and place it on his lap.

Spain appraised the dental office on the floor above Lindy's Food and Dry Goods Store, just off Highway 83, in Kahuka. Despite the small quarters, the single-chair office and tiny dental lab were immaculate.

"Well, do I pass inspection?"

Spain turned to find a woman with a deep bronze tan burned into her skin. Her faded blue eyes were windows to an open, austere face, offset against strawberry blond hair that swept in long curls over her white dental coat.

"Did I have that look?" he asked feebly.

"Yes. But so does everyone the first time they come to the office. Just because I'm a surf bum, doesn't mean I don't know how to practice dentistry." She smiled. "Hi, I'm Kim Dubin and you must be Ben Spain. Your name sounds like a restaurant!" She laughed at her own joke.

"I'm Spain all right."

"People hear surf bum, they think quacko or rich kid playing around." Suddenly, she appraised him. "So you're Harumi's squeeze? She sure has kept you under wraps long enough."

Playfully, she moved a hand over his arms and shoulders, lightly patting his hard stomach. "Well, a little long in the tooth, but he still looks like good healthy stock."

"He's okay for now." Harumi laughed.

Dubin squared her shoulders and hard frame in front of Spain. "Ben, I take my dentistry as seriously as van Horn takes her teaching."

Spain grunted. "I guess we're all in trouble."

Dubin shot Harumi a puzzled look, then went on. "I'm a rural dentist here on the Windward Coast and the

77

north shore. People depend on me and that makes me feel good." Dubin glanced from Harumi to Spain in one sweep. "So? Your phone call was very bizarre. What's all the mystery? Where's that skull you wanted me to examine?"

A few minutes later Spain returned to the office with the roll bag containing the skull. Carefully, Dubin ran a dental pick and small lighted mirror into the jaw area, taking a small sampling of a metal filling for analysis. She then reached into a drawer of her lab workbench and pulled out a micro tape recorder and began to speak.

"Fillings seem to be composed of silver, not zinc oxide, although that fact has to be confirmed by analysis."

Dubin then ran her fingers over the remaining jaw teeth. "The only teeth remaining in the lower jaw are the bicuspids and anteriors."

An hour later, Dubin had shot and developed a series of X-ray films. "Look at this, Harumi." Dubin snapped the films into place on the white viewing screen. "Look at those soft tissue markings. It appears that considerable decalcification is present and the dentine is worn moderately, but not significantly."

"What's that mean?" Harumi asked.

"Well, the minimal wear on the teeth suggests an American diet, but there is some evidence of coarser foods. Interesting."

Spain traced a hand over one of the films of the skull. "How old is our friend?"

"Moderate. I'd guess between the age of thirty-five and fifty."

Harumi sat heavily in the cramped office. "This doesn't help one damn bit."

Dubin laughed. "Still no patience. Always in a hurry. Some Buddha head you are. Well, at least you haven't changed."

"What's next?"

"Ben, I'll make impressions of the remaining teeth, do more X-rays from all angles, and then I'll start tracking with the Naval Bureau of Medical Records in Saint Louis. I'm basing that start on his navy background, circa Nineteen forty-one. Sorry I can't do more right now."

At the door, Kim Dubin cautioned them. "Without complete dental records, this identification could be long and expensive, if not impossible. There just aren't any guarantees we can find out who this person was. It was a half century ago." She took Harumi's hand. "I know what this means to you and I promise I'll do what I can." She smiled and kissed her friend goodbye.

Spain moved slowly in the dawn light. His hand fumbled out from under the warmth of the electric blanket, reaching for the ringing telephone.

"Yeah? Oh, Doreen, everything okay?" He sat up in bed. "What is it?"

"Jack's dead?" he repeated the words without emotion. "The navy found him an hour ago during their rounds at the memorial. My God, Doreen, what are you saying!" Spain's body jerked.

Then the voice on the other end broke down. Slowly, Spain hung up the phone.

"What is it, Benny?" Harumi sat up in bed, her breasts spilling over the blanket in the pink light.

"Somebody cut off Jack's head and dumped his body

in the water at the memorial." His voice was numb as he began to dress. "I've got to go to Doreen. I have to help her!"

"My, God! Let me go, Benny. I want to do something."

"Damn you! You've done enough with your fucking *Arizona* project!" he screamed. "If you would have left it alone, like I wanted, this never would have happened." Spain grabbed the keys to the Toyota and bolted from the house.

Ten

It was dark by the time Spain let himself in. He found Harumi sitting cross-legged in a straight-backed chair. From the one small light burning in the living room, he could tell her face was swollen and tear streaked.

"I'm sorry, Harumi. What I said to you was horrible. It's just that Jack was—" His voice broke. "Jack was the one person who checked me back into the human race. He gave me a chance and—"

"And you couldn't help him," Harumi said quietly.

"They cut off his head, Harumi! Jesus, why? He never hurt a soul." He wrapped his arms around his chest. "They did an autopsy late this afternoon. The pathologist said his neck had been severed with a sword of some kind. A sword!"

"What can we do for Doreen, Benny?" Her voice shared his ache.

Spain shrugged. "Nothing. Her parents are flying in from Boston in the morning." He turned to her, his face vulnerable and tired in the meager light. "Doreen's in shock. I guess I am, too." He looked up. "I'm sorry about this morning."

"I know that you're hurting terribly, but you must know that I've never been so deeply hurt that way before." She looked at Spain, wanting to touch and comfort him.

"I don't know what to say about your pain. I'm just very frightened right now. Everything is turned upside down. What should have been the greatest day of my life went down the toilet."

Spain followed her across the living room with his eyes, as she paced. "I don't know if this is the time to tell you."

"Tell me what?"

"I heard from Kim Dubin this morning."

"What's the news?" he asked wearily.

"She found out who our pumpkin friend was." Spain followed her into the den and looked out into the darkness of the backyard and suddenly everything seemed cold and dead.

"St. Louis's computer center for naval personnel didn't turn up anything, so Kim checked with the military branch of the National Archives in Suitland, Maryland."

Spain turned. "So?"

"So, Maryland came up with something. The man's name was Noonan. Ring a bell? He was a civilian at one time, employed by the old Civil Aeronautics Authority in Washington."

Spain turned away, losing interest.

"It took Kim a week to do all the computer cross-checking, but it finally turned up that another former employer was Pan American. Kimmie's tough. At Pan

Am she squeezed out dental records for comparison."

Cautiously, Harumi moved closer to Spain. "Mean anything, yet?"

"No, not really. Sounds like a civilian technician of some sort. It's still common practice in the navy to have specialists aboard for installing and checking equipment. So much for your historical intrigue," he said bitterly. "The guy was just at the wrong place at the wrong time."

"No," she said evenly, "that's not what it was at all. The man was identified as Fredrick J. Noonan. That name also corresponds to the initials FN on the steel bracelet I found in the pouch. Remember?"

Spain opened his hands in an empty gesture.

"Do you recognize the name?"

"No, damn it!"

"Then try Fredrick J. Noonan, navigator for the around-the-world flyer, Amelia Earhart. Both were lost at sea or picked up by the Japanese, sometime after July one, Nineteen thirty-seven, when their plane was reported missing. They were never found!"

Spain shook his head. "What the hell are you saying! I find a skull in the *Arizona* and now you're trying to tell me it's Earhart's navigator? It's impossible. Jesus, this is all crazy!"

Harumi shook her head and touched him for the first time. "No mistake, Benny," she whispered.

"That comfortable mythology of 'lost fliers' obviously has nothing to do with the truth." She rubbed her eyes "I just don't know. I couldn't even begin to—"

The sound of the doorbell interrupted them. Spain leaped flush against the wall, next to the door. In one motion he pulled the Czech pistol from his belt and chambered a round with a dull click. Then he gestured with the gun, for Harumi to open the door.

"Who is it?"

"Telegram."

Spain tensed. Before he could catch Harumi's eye, she opened the door.

The Young Hawaiian messenger handed Harumi a yellow envelope and then she signed his clipboard. Slowly, she closed the door, glancing at Spain holding the pistol.

"I signed for you. Mrs. Ben Spain." She tried to smile, but couldn't.

Spain tore open the envelope and read the message. For a frozen moment, his features grew thick and stooped as he took on the appearance of a man approaching the last summer of his life.

"What is it, Ben? You look awful. Another ghost?"

Spain was silent for a long time. Finally he drew a breath. "I have seen a ghost! Harumi, we can't stay here anymore! We just can't. Everyone that has had anything to do with that pouch is in danger. You better call Kim."

"Ben, what is it? What danger are you talking about? That's what the man said on the phone this afternoon."

"What man?"

She grimaced. "I don't know. At first I thought it was just one of those phone calls, but I guess not."

"What did he say?"

"Ah, something about us being in danger."

"Was that all?"

"Well, he said something. He said 'tell Oboe he's in danger.' The man said you would understand. What's Oboe mean, Benny?"

"I can't explain now, but we've been warned. We have

to get off this island right now! I can smell the death all around me."

Harumi looked at Spain and began to feel the fear crawling over her again, just like in the dream.

Eleven

The pilot of the twelve-passenger Cessna 402 red-lined the throttles on both engines and released his toe brakes on runway twenty-six left, at Honolulu International. Moments later, the Royal Hawaiian commuter plane jumped up into a mild tropical rainstorm sweeping the southern edge of Oahu, shrouding Diamond Head in cloud. Routinely, the pilot banked sharply, pulled in his landing gear, leaned his fuel mix and began to claw for altitude in the rough air.

Spain stared at the rain beading on the small fuselage window as Pearl Harbor came into view, the lochs splashed aquamarine against the leadened sky. Harumi leaned over from her seat and searched the waterscape below.

"It looks so tiny and benign up here." She pointed to the *Arizona* Memorial, a meager nondescript white block shape far below. Tentatively, she took Spain's hand as the Cessna cleared Barber's Point, then swept out to sea, setting a course one hundred eighty miles to the southeast.

"As benign as a rattlesnake, Harumi." Spain squeezed his temples.

She turned away and tried to laugh, but the hurt was too close. "I'll probably lose tenure now. Feeble excuses in the middle of a semester don't really work. As my learned colleagues would say 'it isn't good form.' "

"You have sick days."

"There are sick days and then there are sick days." Harumi stared at Spain. "This fall's under fright days, doesn't it? I wonder what the professors' union would say about it?" She shuddered. "Who do you think it is?"

"Who?"

"Trying to kill us," she whispered.

Spain shook his head. "I don't know. I don't even know why for Chrissakes. None of it fits. Trying to take us out for a few lousy documents and the skull of a flyer who died so long ago. It's all I've been thinking about." He moved very close to her seat. "There has to be something more. A great deal more."

A man across the narrow aisle looked at them with a puzzled expression. Spain shrugged and rolled his eyes indicating the intrusion. Harumi leaned back in her seat and drew a long breath; as the engines pulled the aircraft out into the vastness of the morning Pacific and away from the Oahu storm, into wisps of snow white cloud floating in a deep blue sky. Half an hour later the plane found and then followed the Ka-lohi Channel to the emerald green softness of the island of Molokai.

She looked down and thought about her fear, her

uncertainty and her own ego. As the Cessna swept past Molokai's desolate Kalaupapa coast, her thoughts turned to the few lepers still living on the island in near isolation. Now she was a leper, carrying something awful and deadly. As Harumi lost herself, the Cessna banked slowly toward the pineapple island of Lanai and the tiny deserted isle of Kahoolawe. Forty minutes later, the Cessna bumped smoothly down on the rural mountain airstrip of Kamuela in the shadow of the thirteen-thousand-foot volcano of Mauna Kea on the Big Island of Hawaii.

The small airport was deserted except for a man Spain observed, standing and watching, in the corner of the small terminal. "Your father?" Spain nodded in the man's direction.

Harumi nodded and smiled. "That's my dad. He's being standoffish because of you." Without another word she marched off to her father and wrapped her arms around him. A moment later she led him back to Spain.

Erik van Horn was a large thick man somewhere in his early seventies, Spain guessed, still carrying a barrel chest and a shock of snow-white hair atop a rather odd, tense face. Spain knew this wasn't going to be easy by the look in the elder van Horn's steel-gray eyes.

"Daddy, this is Benjamin Spain." Harumi beamed.

Erik van Horn moved forward reluctantly, never taking his eyes from Spain. "So you're Spain?" The voice sounded like a murder indictment.

"I'm Spain," he offered, all at once, feeling like a beaten-down drunk Gypsy.

Erik van Horn extended an enormous hand, measuring Spain's strength, despite his advancing years. Finally, Spain pulled away when the viselike grip became too much.

"I always wondered how I'd feel when I met the man who finally took my Harumi away from me." The elder van Horn removed his broad-rimmed straw planter's hat and wiped the humidity from his face.

Spain and Harumi exchanged glances. Quick, fast, clever verbiage was something Spain wasn't good at. "I'm not sure what to say, except that I treasure my time with Harumi."

The steely eyes widened. "You'd better, or I'll kick your ass from one end of this island to the other!" There was only a slight trace of a Dutch accent left in his voice.

"Jesus, Dad! That was totally inappropriate."

"Maybe, Harumi, but if your mother knew you were shacked up, she'd turn over in her grave. I still honor her traditions in our home."

"I know that Father, but I love Ben. Your anger can't make this something trite. I thought you trusted my judgment? You always did before. What changed?"

Spain watched something finally give way in Erik van Horn's eyes.

"I do honor Mother's Japanese traditions," Harumi said softly. "Her blood runs in my veins and so does yours. Ben Spain has nothing to do with that fact. He never will. He also has nothing to do with losing Mom." There were tears in her eyes.

"Ben Spain is decent and honorable. Please don't spoil this for me. I've worked so hard for a life."

Van Horn grabbed her shoulders and hugged his daughter. "Damn, you're right, Harumi!" He shook his head a bit bewildered. "The house has gotten very lonely."

"I know, Dad. It's been difficult for both of us, but she'll always be with us."

The elder van Horn smiled sheepishly. "God, Spain, let's try this hello business, again. I promise to be civil. I'm not a bad sort once you get to know me." He extended his hand and smiled warmly. "Harumi does have a way about her. I've been overly protective, when it's way past my time to do so."

"I understand Mister van Horn."

"Erik, please. Welcome to the land of the Parker Ranch, the world's largest, and the land of the *paniolos*." Instantly, the hostility was gone, replaced with energy and curiosity. Spain had never seen anyone shift emotional gears so quickly.

The distraction of the luggage cart banging through the swinging doors in the desolate little terminal diverted their attention.

"You brought her!" van Horn was genuinely pleased. Atop the cart was a large cage with a very unhappy dog's face mashed against the screen. "Well, let's get Mollie out of there!" The dog heard van Horn's voice and began whimpering.

Suddenly he stopped. "Where's the rest of your luggage?"

Spain held up a small tote bag. "That's all."

"Harumi?" He looked at his daughter.

"Same."

"You sure as hell travel light. A fast getaway, huh. Who the hell is chasing you?" He laughed.

Harumi and Spain exchanged glances. "Whoever it is," Spain said evenly, "is trying to kill us. They've already tried once."

Van Horn cocked his head and felt his face flush cold in the air. He watched Harumi bite her lip and knew there wasn't the slightest humor in their faces, only fear.

Twelve

"What the hell's going on?" Erik van Horn fishtailed the mud-splattered Ford wagon through the light rain, west along the rich Mauna Kea plateau of rolling green hills, dotted as far as the eye could see, with grazing beef cattle.

"I'm not without experience." The gruff voice was laced with uncertainty and concern. The old man glanced over at his daughter and grunted.

Harumi barely nodded, her eyes filled with sadness. "I know you have that kind of experience."

"I hate to be blunt, but killing is still killing," he added, taking a sharp hairpin curve on three wheels. "That hasn't changed in a thousand years. It's just wholesale now and a helluva lot more indiscriminate."

Carefully, Harumi took her father through the series of events and finally the phone warning for Spain. At the end she tried to stifle a yawn and at last gave in, dozing off against the dog laying next to her. She finally felt secure enough to sleep.

The old man mashed his jaw and was deep in thought for a long time, as the wiper blades thumped endlessly back and forth across the windshield. At last, he looked at Spain through the rearview mirror, watching him carefully.

"Good Christ, Ben," he suddenly blurted out. "It's just damn hard to believe. I lived that war. I still do, every little stinking detail in the dark corners of my mind. It's only pleasant to people who weren't there." Van Horn shook his head. "Imagination always does fall short of the truth. But these events tied together? It's staggering! You have any theories? After all, you found the goodies."

Spain rubbed his stubbled chin. "Not a clue."

"What the hell was Fred Noonan doing aboard the *Arizona?*" van Horn mumbled almost to himself.

Spain read his eyes in the mirror and knew what was coming.

"I hope you've tucked away that little pouch and Mister Noonan for safekeeping. Whether you like it or not, the two of you have become the custodians of these secrets."

"The package is in a very safe place." Then he laughed darkly.

"Something funny?"

"If I've learned anything, Erik, it's that there are no secrets. Obviously someone somewhere knows about the *Arizona* find and is just waiting for the right moment to jump on my frame. The dirt under my fingernails isn't even safe anymore. I just don't know why it would matter enough to kill for."

The eyes stared uncertainly at Ben, again. "You have to let me help." Van Horn looked over at his sleeping daughter. "What's your next move?"

Spain laughed again with a hollow groan. "Our next

move is to stay alive and then find out what we've really got here."

"How much more is there?"

"God only knows what is still inside that compartment on the *Arizona*." Spain looked out at the deepening forest of monkey pod and eucalyptus, rubbing his tired eyes.

"It sure doesn't look like Hawaii. It feels like the Sierra, where I grew up."

"Parker Ranch country," van Horn grunted. "They say there's more than fifty thousand head of beef cattle spread over a quarter million acres. That's alot of cow shit. The land has a special smell when the wind blows just right." He looked up in the mirror but wasn't laughing.

"Ben, there's a real smell right here, at least I think there is. Something's missing. I'm just not sure what. I don't even know all the questions yet, let alone the answers. If you really want my help, you'll have to tell me everything."

Spain felt himself shiver inside.

"I wish to hell we'd met under different circumstances. Don't get me wrong, Ben. I don't want a war with you. That would be stupid and besides, I'd lose. I know Harumi. She's much younger than me, with twice the savvy. I'm really trying to like you. My daughter sure as hell does. Living is precarious enough without this type of thing rearing its ugly head. I know what it's like to be on the run. There's a special hollow feeling in the gut." His voice was a low guttural whisper.

"I know this is very personal, but with Harumi involved, this is high-stakes poker for me. Tell you what. I'm ready to talk when you are."

Spain held the old man's gaze in the mirror for what seemed forever, measuring him. "Fair enough."

Spain withdrew in silence, concentrating on the slippery two-lane road that wound through thick forest lands now including sugar pine, and ironwoods edged with brilliant patches of island orchids. As the road worked its way to the northeast, they passed numerous abandoned sugar cane mills, their tin roofs rusting silently in tones of red and brown in the dampness and the tall grasses, always bending to the trades.

At last the rich tablelands gave way to deeply eroded tropical rain forest valleys cut by delicate ribbons of arcing waterfalls, as the road dropped steeply to meet the jagged and hostile Hamakua Coast molded volcanically to the northeast corner of the island.

Spain dropped his head to the top of the seat, exhausted. His instincts were dulled and uncertain, shot through with self-doubt and guilt. Jack Scrugg's death had been devastating. He had lost a parent. Someone who cared far beyond words. He was alive because Scruggs had picked him out of the gutter, cleaned him up and given him another chance at life. He felt his frail insulation, built up so painfully these past three years, eroding away, just like the deep valleys they were passing through. He was damaged again, his fabric torn, but just how extensively he didn't know.

"Ready to talk yet, Ben?" This time van Horn's voice was quieter. Maybe he had sensed Spain's pain and resignation.

"Sure, why not."

Van Horn removed his planter's hat and rubbed a hand through his white hair. "We might be family one of these days, so the sooner we get it all on the table, the better. I've been there myself. We all have baggage in our lives. So what's this *Oboe* business?"

Spain forced himself to smile out of respect. He was beginning to grow fond of the old man. He was direct and open, with a mind like a steel vise. He was using his age as a cover and Ben also liked that part of van Horn. The old man focused down on just one fact that Harumi had presented to him in passing.

"My name was Oboe." Spain looked out the window. "I suppose I'll always be Oboe. They'll etch it into my gravestone." Then carefully and slowly, Spain laid out his past. Finally after twenty minutes, he shrugged. "That's it, Erik. I didn't tell Harumi about that part of my life, because she didn't need to know. I thought she wouldn't ever have to know. It wasn't to deceive her, it was to protect her."

Silently, van Horn swung the old wagon into a long narrow gravel driveway that wound down through a dense tropical forest to a house of rough redwood and glass, cut out of the black lava, with a remarkable view of the pounding surf far below. The landscape was filled everywhere with sad trees and liquid shadows of stream water pouring down the black lava cliffs, with multicolored impatiens growing from the rocks.

After he turned off the ignition and gently stroked Mollie's ears, van Horn turned slowly to face Spain. Real fear was etched into his eyes.

"Thanks, Ben." He nodded his head. "I think I like you. I just hope to God you didn't bring that string of death to this house. Jesus," he muttered softly, "this is my last sanctuary!"

Thirteen

Despite the leaden overcast buttressed by line squalls swirling upward in piles of soft black gauze, the sky swept on forever out into the whitecapped Pacific. Erik van Horn's home, built into a carved knuckle of an ancient lava field a thousand feet above the black sand beach, stood square in the face of a mystical view of the desolate northeast coast of Hamakau and the Waipo Valley. The real Hawaii that had escaped the travel guides.

"Beautiful view, isn't it, Ben?" Van Horn smiled patiently at Spain. "That's Earth's spawning ground out there in the Pacific. We've never gotten tired of it. It's always renewed me and been a source of comfort."

Spain shivered as a line squall slammed at the shoreline far below. The closing weather seemed to fit his dark mood. Suddenly, large droplets of rain, pushed by a driving northeaster, pounded viciously at the expansive tempered-glass windows. Nervously, he swirled a half-filled mug of steaming black coffee, looking for some small measure of warmth wherever he could find it.

The old man placed a strong hand on Ben's shoulder, then pointed down to their right into the shadows of the awesome Waipo Valley, a deep green tear in the steep cliffs, anchored by a peaceful meandering stream that fed into the sea.

"See that angry scar halfway up the valley's wall?"

Spain shrugged, half listening.

"In Nineteen forty-six an Alaskan quake triggered a series of sixty-foot tidal waves that swept up the entire three-mile valley, without warning, killing every damn living soul including a herd of wild horses. People stood up here on the cliffs and just watched those massive waves roll in and they couldn't do a damn thing."

"That's great." Ben looked sideways at Harumi's arched eyebrows, then out to sea to the faint gray shadow of Maui, bleeding into the distant horizon, as he felt her eyes bore into his back.

"I wanted to fill in some missing pieces, Harumi, and get a piano off my back," he whispered.

Erik van Horn pulled from his Jack Daniel's, adding another layer of blush to the eroding features of his thick face. "Damn good idea, Ben." He walked to the window and stared out at the deepening twilight descending over the lumpy, pink ocean. "Harumi needs to know."

"Know what? What the hell is this?" Harumi cocked her head in a funny way, restlessly moving her eyes from her father to Spain, her smile vanishing in the heavy air. Finally, her large brown eyes settled again on Spain. "What missing pieces, Benny?" Her voice rose defiantly to meet the scent of betrayal. "What's going on here?"

Spain rubbed his tired face, raising his eyes to meet Harumi's cold glare. After her nap and a hot shower, with her long raven hair pulled back in a ponytail, Harumi looked so unsoiled. For a moment Spain forced himself to remember her razor-sharp mind and the mental toughness behind her sculpted Eurasian face.

Suddenly he shivered, inwardly. "Harumi, your father asked me some hard questions on the drive from the airport, while you were sleeping." Spain's mouth trembled as he sat heavily on the edge of the thick, textured sofa.

"What I'm going to say may be a key to saving our lives. That's the only reason we're having this talk." Spain drew a stale breath to fuel himself, glancing sideways at the elder van Horn.

"Ah, there was a period of time, from Vietnam until Jack Scruggs found my moth-eaten hide in Los Angeles, that you don't know about. Very few know about." He made an empty, pathetic gesture with his hands.

That little movement broke Harumi's heart, as her anger faded, watching him struggle, the old pain growing as a cancer on his face.

"When my alcoholic law practice and marriage fell apart, I made a desperate attempt to help myself. I found an old navy buddy from my Nam days, housed in a cushy civilian job with the Department of Defense, in Washington. He was a field wheel in deep black programs. I needed to live; I had developed skills he wanted, and all at once I found myself involved. The work was easy and I could function almost without being sober and the pay was steady and all in cash. I was strictly shadow material."

"Shadow material? I don't understand—"

"Harumi, if you didn't interrupt me, I'd be lost." Spain paused and sipped from the mug. "I became a spook, a covert operative for the Naval Investigative Service, an offshoot of the Office of Naval Intelligence. It was my job to spread good cheer wherever Top Floor wanted, in a black program called Bandit."

"I don't understand any of this, Ben!"

"What's Top Floor?" the elder van Horn probed.

"The White House."

"Jesus!" Van Horn's old gray eyes grew wide.

"Well, that might begin to explain the gun." Harumi looked at Spain sharply.

"I wish that's all it was," Ben said gently. "In Nineteen eighty-three, I became an adviser to an early Contra group on the northeast Nicaragua, Honduras, frontier, called the Salvador Perez Regional Command. It was drawn from seven hundred down-and-out kids, dirt-poor tenant coffee farmers, and cow punchers, all struggling to survive in the damn rain forest."

"Ben, I don't —"

"Shut up, Harumi! Just once shut up while I have the guts to do this!

"I worked directly with a rebel commander, all of twenty-six years old. He was a tough-assed kid I ended up naming Sheriff. Then there was his staff and runners, all kids with names I gave them like Harmonica Pete, American Gothic, Smiley, Happy, Schmedley, and Little Orphan Annie."

Harumi and her father stared at each other, then burst out laughing. I guess the names sounded comical to outsiders, Spain thought, but it was dark humor, as dark as the blackest night that could be imagined. They were just poor kids and old people who cared enough about something, at least in the beginning, to die for it.

"Most were dead within a year. Sandanista-Cuban ambushes, mountain leprosy, malnutrition, and a lethal type of arthritis, of all things." Spain raised his strained and bloodless face to Harumi. "In Nam when I lost my people, it ripped me apart. By eighty-three, I thought I couldn't feel anything. You know the old saying, I was living in my past, peeing all over the present. There just wasn't a whole lot of myself left, or so I thought." He paused, listening to the rain pound against the windows, giving into the comfort of its steady rhythm.

"Go on, Benny," Harumi urged softly.

"Ah, five months after I dropped into Jinotega Province in northeast Nicaragua, the Sandanista's and Cubans came after our unit in force. Commandante Ruben, aka Sheriff, decided to be brilliant and counterattack by raiding a Sandanista outpost near the hamlet of Pantasma.

Spain's eyes took on a far away cast. "It was in a thick forest of cherrywood and mahogany, with a creek that ran red. Their camp was damn well protected, but we needed the food, boots, and the ammunition and our limited intelligence told us they had three cows we could slaughter for meat. At least that was Sheriff's justification for the attack. For four nights we moved undetected through the dampness and slime of the rain forest, more than forty kilometers, finally crossing the Gusanera River with damn latrite clay soil in my nose and every pore of my body."

Spain gulped a swallow of coffee, now lukewarm and tasteless. "On the fourth night we surrounded their encampment, kinda like Custer surrounding the Indians at Little Big Horn. I manned the radio to give a blow by blow to our base across the frontier. Besides, it wasn't smart for an American adviser to be found in the middle of a fire fight, so I stayed behind at the River and their radio was supposed to relay information to me on the quarter hour. As often happens in these things, it was chaotic and confused once the small arms and mortar fire started zeroing in. After an hour of dead silence, except for the occasional report of a pistol, I moved in to see what the hell had happened. My controls across the frontier in Honduras were screaming for information."

Spain pulled his weight from the sofa arm and shuffled like an old man into the kitchen to refill his coffee mug, the gray in his hair now prominent. Once, he looked out of the kitchen and could clearly see the van Horn family examining him with morbid curiosity.

"I made my way into the compound and found that Sheriff had secured the area," he said, putting down the coffeepot.

"Meaning?" Harumi smiled dully at Ben as he moved slowly back into the glass-filled room.

"Meaning, Sheriff had taken some thirty-odd prisoners, including a number of Cubans and one Soviet Adviser. His men had lined them up alongside a slit trench and Sheriff was moving down the line, firing a forty-five slug into the back of each man's head." Spain felt his back stiffen as he relived it. "I stopped the slaughter for a few minutes, after a shouting match with Sheriff and his chief shooter, Harmonica Pete." For a long time, Spain averted their steady silent gaze, staring out into the wet blackness masking the Pacific.

Suddenly, Spain crossed the line. He was there, rolling back the years, remembering Harmonica Pete, playing taps and laughing a deep guttural animal sound each time Sheriff squeezed the trigger, snapping the prisoner's head and body into that lousy mud ditch. Harmonica Pete. Always playing "God Bless America" and "When the Moon Comes Over the Mountain," asking Spain insistently, if he'd ever met Kate Smith. Jesus, what the hell did he know about Kate Smith?

"—Benny?" Harumi was next to him, holding his face with her long, slender fingers. "You were there, not here," she said softly.

"Yeah." He nodded. "Anyway, at one point in the shouting match with Sheriff and Pete, I heard someone yell at me in a thickly accented English. I turned because it just sounded different. And it was. It turned out to be the Russian adviser, speaking to me in an educated tongue, struggling against the ropes binding his hands behind his back. I made my way down the death line and found a man of very dark complexion, jet black hair, and almost Oriental features. In a panic he told me he had a son and wife back in the Soviet Union."

Spain frowned, then shivered. " 'Don't let them kill me', the Russian pleaded over and over." Spain gulped a mouthful of coffee, then looked over at the elder van Horn, wanting him to understand.

"He had that thousand-yard stare, Erik. That look of a man who had crossed over the line." Spain shrugged. "It could have been me, or you for that matter, in a different war. He had the numb, frightened eyes of a child."

Spain looked at both Harumi and her father, but couldn't read their silence. Maybe he was trying too hard to justify himself. But it was true—all true in a far more intense way than they seemed to want to understand. Slowly, Spain made his way back to the large sofa.

"What happened to Sheriff?" Harumi pulled her long legs up under her.

"Sheriff started killing again, watching me, watch him, as he moved closer to us, the grime and sweat glistening on his smiling face, loving every moan and feeble plea for life. 'The longer the wait,' he shouted over to me, 'the greater the pain and the greater the pleasure.' He'd fire off a round and shatter a man's life, then turn to me in defiance. 'El Viejo said to do it this way! Fuck the red and black of the Sandanistas! Fuck you! El Hombre knows the score and he is my leader, not you!' " Spain's words ran him down.

"I was even stone-cold sober on this one, Harumi," he whispered, "just in case you were wondering."

Spain searched her tear-filled eyes and the soft hurt now touching him. "That was cheap, Harumi. I'm sorry. You don't deserve that, but I wasn't exactly telling a bed-time story."

"Who's El Hombre, Ben?" Van Horn swirled the ice in the bottom of his drink.

"The famous Commander Zero, Eden Pastora, founder of the Contra movement. Also called the Monkey Man. Legend says that everytime he killed a Sandanista, the monkeys in the jungle rose up and howled with delight." Spain held up a hand.

"I couldn't go against the word of Pastora. I was just a lousy adviser."

For a long time they were all silent, then the old man finished off his drink and pushed at Spain again. "What'd you do?" There was a surprising softness in his voice.

"I reacted with total, uncontrollable anger. I cut the ropes on the Russian's hands, put my Kalasnakov on full automatic and emptied a full banana clip into Sheriff and Harmonica Pete." Spain pointed a finger at his head. "I guess I'd stepped over the line. The men in Sheriff's squad were so stunned they just looked at me, while I took off with the Russian for the darkness beyond the lights of the compound. It all happened very quickly, in the space of a few seconds. Then they opened up on us and I caught two slugs. By that time we were in the high bush, then suddenly the Russian was pulling me down into a small sewer hole for cover, up to our eyeballs in shit. A few minutes later I passed out and when I regained consciousness again, the Russian had stopped the bleeding in my right thigh and had given me a shot of morphine from my field pack. He told me he was honor bound to me and would see that I would live." Spain finished off the coffee and rubbed the tired flesh beneath his eyes.

"The next week and a half was a blur, but Captain Gregori Ovsyannikov, commando and adviser in the Soviet army, described later how he smuggled me as a fellow Russian officer to the Caribbean Coast and from there south, with a great deal of difficulty."

"Where the hell's this leading, Ben?" Van Horn rubbed his thick face. "I don't see — "

"You will, damn it, if you'll give me a chance!" Spain was surprised at his own anger. "Christ, like father, like daughter! You wanted the missing pieces, didn't you?"

Erik van Horn nodded with a brittle movement. "You're right. Sorry I interrupted."

"I remember him carrying me on his back at one point and being given food and shelter by a band of Miskitos Indians. I'm still not sure how he pulled it off." Spain slowly rubbed his mouth.

"Captain Ovsyannikov found a nurse to remove the bullets and treat an infection that had set in and festered. In the next week or so, we moved only at night in and out of the villages, always heading south." Spain dropped his eyes from Harumi and her father's steady gaze. "Ovsyannikov moved with the purpose and grace of a large cat. I've never seen anything like it."

Suddenly, Spain laughed nervously. "I kidded him about looking Oriental and gave him the nickname Hac Qui."

Harumi cocked her head in her funny way. "Vietnamese?"

Spain nodded. "It means black ghost. That man pulled, carried, and finally drove me in a stolen van more than two hundred fifty kilometers south to a shabby port called Bluefields, at the mouth of the Rio Escondido and the Caribbean. One night he ran out of money and robbed a damn bar and cafe for a lousy five hundred cordoba, equal to about fifty bucks."

"I still don't understand." Van Horn arched his sun-splotched forehead. "As a Soviet officer he had access to money, equipment and transportation."

Spain nodded. "Sure he did. The Sandanistas and Cubans would have loved to get their hands on me. I was a real prize catch. The minute he would have walked in, I would have been meat on the table." Spain looked out into the blackness. "He was honor bound to me," he whispered.

Harumi moved to him and gently touched his stubbled face. "How did you escape?"

"Ovsyannikov hitched a night ride for us on a fishing boat to a place called Little Corn Island about six hours out into the Caribbean, from Bluefields. He then registered me at a rundown boardinghouse called Residencia Morgan. He paid the head woman a hundred fifty corb, told her to see to my needs, dress my wound and cook for me, until I was well. The Black Ghost made his way back to the mainland and made certain that I was picked up by a Costa Rican contact, who delivered me to friendly forces in Honduras." Spain stopped and carefully searched their faces, the memories and debt still burning in his voice.

"Through various sources we remained in contact, then early in Nineteen eighty-four, someone pulled the plug. I tried all my sources and there was just a blank. It was as if he had never existed." For a long time Spain was quiet, listening to the wind push at the windows and the storm surf crash against the black lava beach far below.

"What's the connective tissue between then and now, Benny?"

Spain raised a cautionary hand to Harumi and weighed the question with his eyes closed, as if a trick was buried in her words. "At the end of eighty-four, word finally reached me that Captain Ovsyannikov had been severely wounded in Afghanistan, had been awarded the Order of the Red Star for valor, and had been shipped back to the Soviet Union to a military sanitorium in the Crimea. A few more inquiries turned up the facts that my Russian had been involved in special commando operations and his unit had been ambushed. He was wounded and lost a leg." For a moment, Spain hesitated, staring at the backs of his hands. "Ah, I also found out that he had not been able to adjust and was being held under guard at that military hospital in Saki, a small resort town on the Black Sea."

"Why was he a prisoner?" Van Horn jammed his chilled hands into his trousers.

Spain laughed darkly. "Ovsyannikov couldn't stand life in the dead zone. It's universal. Life in military hospitals, filled with human beings going nowhere. Ovsyannikov had been in the town of Saki drinking heavily one night at a bar, when one of the locals called him a cripple from across the room. A moment later, the man was dead with a crutch buried in his head, and Ovsyannikov was transferred to the prison ward of the hospital on murder charges."

Harumi moved effortlessly across the broad living room that she had known since she was a child. "And you went in and brought him out." She smiled lovingly at Spain.

"Abuse has always been mother's milk for me. I owed him," Spain offered simply and quietly.

"It was difficult, but my people in NIS offered all their resources, with the understanding that I would deliver my beloved Russian to the West. This time the shoe was on the other foot." Spain tried to rub the fatigue from his tired eyes. "I mean it doesn't sound like much now, with all the political barriers down and the Iron Curtain dead, but it was then."

"And" — the old man smiled — "you never finished this part of the story for me on the way from the airport."

"I didn't deliver him to my people. When I sprang Ovsyannikov, he was a mess. Just like I was, when Jack Scruggs found me." His voice grew faint against the outside wind. "Ovsyannikov was like a brother to me — at least I had built it up in my mind. He carried me across the whole damn landscape of Nicaragua. All the way through the rot, to the warm sands of Little Corn Island, so I could heal. What the hell's that worth?"

Harumi touched his back softly. "We know that. Why —"

"Why am I so defensive?" Spain calmed himself, forcing the knot in his stomach to loosen, wanting to retreat into his own last island of sanity. "When I finally got to Ovsyannikov, something had been burned out of him. Something I couldn't describe. Maybe it was his humanity. I understood it. The cruelty in Afghanistan was legend, but for Ovsyannikov it was more intense. His smile and words were still warm, but his eyes had grown cruel and abusive, and his movements with that damn artificial leg had turned him into a lumbering, angry freak, and he knew it."

Spain reached into the air with his hands. "Somehow he had become distorted."

"What did you do?"

"Harumi, all he wanted was to be delivered to an address in East Berlin. So after a great deal of difficulty, I dropped him on a door step at 18 Majakowskiring in the Pankow District of East Berlin. We hugged each other and the debt was repaid. Then I went home and landed on the streets of L.A., unceremoniously drummed out of the NIS, with all the respect of a bone at a dog show. I had failed to deliver the goodies. They even accused me of being a Soviet agent. Then I landed facedown in the gutter until Jack Scruggs pulled me out."

"Did you ever find out who lived at that address in East Berlin?" Van Horn moved very close to Spain, his tone unyielding.

Spain nodded. "It was the residence of Mischa Lutz. Lieutenant General Markus "Mischa" Lutz, head of the old East German HVA. I just didn't know it at the time."

"What's that?" asked Harumi.

The old man turned to his daughter. "It was the notorious Hauptverwaltung Aufkarung, the German killing appendage of the Soviet GRU, the Soviet General Staff. They did a great deal of Moscow's dirty work, before the East Germans kicked them out. Murder, assassinations, general chaos. The HVA was a direct outgrowth of the gestapo."

Harumi gazed at both men, puzzled. "I still don't see the connection to us."

Spain blew out a long breath. "I think that my old savior, The Black Ghost, is the one trying to kill us. He's the one who called you, Harumi. He's the one who named me Oboe and the only one who ever called me that!" Spain swallowed into his dry throat. "He gave me a warning, to get out. It all has something to do with the *Arizona* project of your's, Harumi." He searched her astonished face for understanding. "Next time he means to kill us and he will. I know he killed Jack Scruggs. I can feel it in my bones," he said in a hoarse whisper.

"I just don't know why." Spain turned to Erik van Horn. "I know Gregori Ovsyannikov. Even with his artificial leg, he's a swift, intelligent, deadly animal."

Spain's face was very close to Erik van Horn. "You have to somehow help us find out the why of this mess, or your daughter won't see next week alive."

Fourteen

"I didn't know who he is." The Hawaiian dental assistant, with liquid brown eyes, leaned across the dental chair, whispering into Kim Dubin's ear as the dentist replaced the small mouth mirror on the tray. "This was your last appointment for the day." She shrugged.

"Okay, Dukie, you're clean for another six months." Kim Dubin smiled down at the young surfer. "That abscess looks alot better and your gums are better." She leaned over the chair very close to the young patient's open face. "You're a lucky surf dog, Dukie. You may shoot alot of curls, but someday you're gonna ride the Pipeline without teeth. Massage those gums, hotdog, or all those little honeys won't love you anymore."

Dubin raised the chair, then nodded to her assistant, Kai, to finish up with the eighteen-year-old.

Kim made her way into the small waiting area unable to take her eyes from the man sitting calmly, thumbing through a magazine. He was striking, with dark, angular features, straight raven hair, and a dazzling smile, set off against a dimpled chin.

"I'm sorry," Kim began. "We don't have you down in the book for an appointment." She looked at her watch. "It's close to six and—"

Now the dazzling teeth smiled inside a perfectly shaped mouth. "No, no. I'm so sorry. Your assistant made a mistake. I just dropped by to see you." His large dark eyes locked onto Kim Dubin's questioning expression, her open face drawn to him.

Speaking with a slight melodic accent, the man used his long, narrow, effeminate fingers as fans, gesturing his apology. "I just took the chance. I'm new to the Islands and I was given your name and told to look you up." He buttoned his fashionable sport jacket and began to rise from his chair. "I can see I've caught you at an awkward moment. I should have called."

Kim reached out, barely touching his sleeve. "Who gave you my address?" She still couldn't believe this creature sitting next to her. He was gorgeous.

"Ben Spain, a very old and dear friend."

"Harumi's Spain?"

The man smiled, lightly brushing his fingers through his thick black hair. "Yes, Harumi's Spain. Benjamin and I have been friends for many years." He smiled, small sun lines pushing in against the corners of his deep-set eyes.

"I'm sorry." He laughed lightly." I'm very nervous. This wasn't easy for me to do, but I don't really know anyone and I'm not the most forward person, so I told myself I had to do this. Ben said you'd be—"

"I'll bet he said I was pushy." She chuckled, tossing her strawberry blond hair away from her blue eyes.

"No." For a moment, he studied her casually attractive face. "No, Ben said you were, ah, magnetic." He casually dropped his eyes to her large firm breasts. "He didn't say you were stunning."

"Well, you're a charmer. Ah, what's your name? I like the compliments but I would like a name attached to the words. Or is this a load in a deep bucket?"

"Greg Syann." He smiled shyly, shaking her hand. "I'm not good at these things. Sorry. And I meant what I said."

Kim sat down next to him, her blue eyes still drinking him in. "That's reassuring. What do you do, Greg Syann?"

"I'm a diamond trader. I spent a number of years living in Europe, working out of Antwerp, traveling throughout Europe and the Middle East. When I knew I was going to be here for a while, I called Ben. I'll be working on a project in Kauai."

Syann paused, allowing the woman to continue her physical inventory and growing fantasy. "Ben and I used to dive together, when he was in Europe. It was a long time ago. We did the Red Sea, and dove for Amphoria off the Turkish Coast."

"An accomplished water person." Kim laughed. "Now I'm really impressed."

"No, no." Syann held up a hand. "I always followed Ben's lead. He's an animal in the water." Greg Syann smoothed the green and peach paisley tie offset against a rich beige shirt. "Ben was a navy diver," Greg said proudly.

"At least you're not arrogant. That's refreshing and besides you're one helluva hunk. You and Spain. It's amazing!"

"My only arrogance is to pretend I have none."

"My God! A poet, too! When are you going to ask me to dinner?" Dubin dipped her eyes, waiting as a large

113

smile spread across Syann's open face. "Tonight?"

"Dinner was more than I hoped for." Syann was pleased with his success, standing and moving very slowly about the small office. "You'll have to show me the ropes, Kim. I mean, you'll have to pick the restaurant."

"Good night, Doctor Dubin." Kai squeezed past them both, smiled knowingly back at Kim, then closed the office door.

Syann turned around as Kim Dubin spoke to him from the other room. "You know, I've only met Spain once. An interesting man." Her voice fell as the sharp clank of steel dental instruments dropping into a sterilizer, broke the silence. For a long time, he could hear her moving about, opening and closing drawers, replacing X-rays into their stiff envelopes, and running water in her small lab.

"Sorry this is taking so long, but my assistant is careless. I've talked to her a million times, but she always leaves the place a slop pen."

"Don't worry about me," Syann called. "Take as much time as you need." He hesitated, thinking about something. "Say, you wouldn't happen to have a drink anywhere in the house? No, I suppose not," he mumbled. He looked at his watch. "The sun's almost down and this has been gut wrenching. I just thought —" His voice faded as she appeared in the doorway, dressed in a low-cut purple and white flowered sundress. Kim's long, muscular, well-shaped legs, deeply tanned from surfing, set her mood in low white pumps. Her golden hair, pulled severely off her face, was tied in a Madonna ponytail. The effect was exotic and suddenly, Kim was transformed from a clinical dentist in a white coat, with cold, antiseptic hands, into a voluptuous woman, with her firm ample breasts and large nipples pushing out against the low-cut dress.

"My God, you're beautiful!" Syann's mouth dropped unable to take his eyes from her full body. He flushed, feeling himself go hard in the groin as he started to turn away from her.

Picking up her purse, she smiled lightly, aware of her sudden effect on him. They both could feel the sexual tension arcing between them in a sudden burst of energy as they faced each other.

"We'd better go now," she whispered awkwardly, nudging him out of the office, locking the door behind her.

"Ah, I hope you can drive, Kim." It didn't really come out as a question. "I didn't hold the taxi." He glanced at her and quickly added, "I had every intention of calling another cab, after I had met with you."

Again, her intense blue eyes drank him in, searching his face to lighten the mystery and doubt that still nibbled at her. Slowly she shook her head and took his arm. "I can see this is going to be a mad night." She sighed. "I must be crazy to do this."

An hour later they sat in splendor, dining on freshly caught sweet Hawaiian Ono, mesquite charcoal broiled into tender thick steaks. The restaurant at Kahuku Point jutted out into the Pacific at the northernmost tip of the island of Oahu. Despite the dinner hour, the sun still hung stubbornly over the large bay windows of the Turtle Bay resort, a sprawling eight-hundred-acre retreat. For a long time, they both ate in silence, but Greg Syann was unable to take his eyes from the woman. After more than a few glasses of wine, he raised his hands lightly in surrender.

"I usually have more to say than this," he muttered across the small table, backdropped by a rocky point jutting out into the ocean. He drank more white Bordeaux, then delicately replaced the long-stem crystal on the table. "You're as natural as your islands," he finally said, the heat of the wine beginning to flush his dark skin. "I want to know you and what you're all about." His discomfort was obvious, but Kim Dubin only laughed at his plight, tossing her head from side to side, everytime Syann verbally approached.

"What's so funny, Kim?"

"You." She rubbed her strong bronze arms, the cleavage deepening between her breasts. "My God, you're awkward with women," she moaned. "Is Spain just like you? God help Harumi!"

"I — I apologize." The hurt burrowed deeply into his soft face. "No, I don't think Ben is like me." He raised his eyes to her. "I lost a leg in an auto accident in the Middle East a few years ago, and it's never been the same."

"Oh, Greg! I'm sorry for my mouth!" Tenderly, she took his hand across the table. "I shoot from the hip alot. It's always been a problem for me. I've got a fast mind and I'm very sure of myself." Greg, I — "

"Yes, you are sure of yourself. In the diamond wholesale business, I'm knowledgeable and confident. In fact, I've done quite well." He smiled wistfully. "But my personal life is another thing entirely."

Kim pulled her hand away from his, picking up her half-filled wineglass. "Are you married?" she asked gazing out at the shore.

He could see her swallow some unexpressed thought. "I've been divorced for five years. My ex-wife's in Europe. And we share two wonderful children." Now he watched the muscles beneath her eyes begin to relax. "But since my auto accident, my life has changed. I guess

116

you're right, Kim. I have lost confidence in myself. My right leg was severed just beneath the knee." He paused again, letting the weight of the emotional message do its own work.

"You move so well," she offered feebly. "I didn't know." Kim blanched in pain. "You just seem so—" The waiter approached, refilling their wineglasses, then felt Syann's icy stare and withdrew, his hopes for a large tip dwindling. "You seem so complete."

For an instant his black eyes caught her gaze. "I've had a great deal of practice. Does it make a difference? I feel complete inside."

Dubin took his hand again. "No. I didn't mean it like that!" She frowned, her face flickering and troubled. "I feel drawn somehow to you, not to just a part of you. I don't really know you yet, but I'd like to teach you to surf on one leg. Emotional balance is more damn important than physical balance."

Syann felt himself relax as he pulled again from the wine, sensing that any foreseeable danger had passed. "How long have you been a surfer?"

"All my life." Her usual energy suddenly inflated her features. She turned in her chair and pointed to the heavy surf chewing at the reefs below, off of Kahuku Point. "Those aren't waves, just ripples." For a moment she searched the horizon of the Pacific. "Looks like we still have an hour of light left. Good!"

"Why good?" He liked the surprise in her voice.

"I'm going to show you a patch of real surf about ten miles from here on the north shore, with a classic right-hand break that I guarantee will knock your socks off! Tube City America!"

"You mean, sock." Greg laughed at himself. God, it

had been so long since he had let go and this firm, inviting woman sitting across from him was a tonic for his soul. Slowly, he felt his last layer of self-doubt peel away.

Twenty minutes later the little navy blue BMW convertible pulled off of Kamehameha Highway at Ehukai Beach Park, with the spring sun, a fiery orange ball, still balancing on the lip of the blue horizon.

Kim Dubin pulled the white scarf from her flaxen hair and turned to her partner as they stepped from the car, walking toward the water. Carefully she pointed to her right. "Out there is Sunset Beach, with the surf now approaching thirty feet!"

Syann searched the deserted white sand beach, which he estimated at least two miles long, dominated by giant breakers, building like tidal waves as they hit the reef. Massive green churning walls of towering water, rolling in from thousands of miles of the open Pacific with unchecked energy and force. It was frightening for him to watch, let alone imagine riding down the curled belly of one of those monster waves.

"Look out there, Greg! That's my real world! It's not back there in the dental office, with fillings and X-rays." With her surprisingly powerful hands, she turned him to the left of the horizon.

"See how those breakers curl into a long tube? That's the 'Banzai Pipeline.' The most perfect curl in the world! The waves build along a shallow coral reef out there," she shouted above the crashing surf, "to create tubelike formations. God, you can smoke forever on those babies!" She rubbed her hands across his broad chest. It's almost better than sex." Kim impulsively slid her hands around his neck and pulled him down to her.

"I can't help myself," she whispered, lightly kissing his

118

mouth, nibbling at his chin, tasting him for the first time.

Slowly, almost cautiously, Syann brought his hands up to her full breast, cupping her hard, sensuous flesh as he flicked his tongue in her mouth, feeling her hips move against him again in a crush.

"I want you now, Greg Syann! I must be crazy! There's some privacy behind the sand dunes. I just can't help it with you! Please —" Her voice broke as her nails dug into him.

It was almost dark when they awoke on a car blanket. For a long time they lay, naked in the deepening twilight, locked tightly to each other, feeling the awesome power of each breaker slam into the beach sending shock waves through them. It was less awkward to hold each other than to talk. Finally, Kim pushed through their stillness, as the blackness closed over them.

"You're in great shape for a diamond broker." She smiled through the darkness and touched the tip of his chiseled nose with a finger. "A very sensitive, caring man beats inside that hard body of yours."

"My stump didn't bother you?" His voice was still ripe with some distant hurt, begging for reassurance. "Once, a very long time ago, a woman laughed in my face, calling me a freak with a body of a flamingo, who could only make love standing on one leg. Now all I get are dog bites on my one good wheel."

Kim nodded, "I see that. It looks recent."

"It is. Some damn black dog bit me the day I arrived in Honolulu."

Slowly, in the vague light, Kim watched his facial features begin to loosen for the first time. "Thanks for the wonderful gift," he mumbled, his eyes still closed. The pitch of his voice dropped even more as he felt himself let go. "Without knowing it, or even being party to it, you've provided a momentary emotional ark and the feeling is indescribable."

"I'd forgotten what it was like to be with an educated, cultured man. There's not a great deal of cerebral energy or zen when it comes to surfers." She hummed softly, laying her head on his chest. "Indirectly, I owe Harumi and Spain a real thanks." For a long moment she turned her head and studied him. Suddenly, she felt something very deep, something she couldn't touch, but could only sense inside Greg Syann. A part of his abyssal fabric that was somehow flawed.

"No, I owe Ben!" He cupped a gentle hand on her breast. "This time with you will always be with me. I'm indelibly marked." He felt her entire body shiver beneath his hand as he set the hook. "Yes, I owe Ben. Funny thing—"

"What?"

"I've tried to reach Ben and I can't. I've stopped by the house, telephoned. I just can't understand it. He's disappeared."

"Oh, they're both visiting Harumi's father on the Big Island's northeast coast. I got a call from Harumi before they left. Seems there's some sort of trouble and they left in a hurry. Harumi's gotten herself caught up in something very strange. I sensed real trouble in her voice."

"What kind of trouble?"

"They found this strange skull and asked me to help identify it through the teeth." Kim sat up and leaned her deeply tanned back into Greg. "A tickle would go a long way," she purred. "It always turns me on."

Delicately, he began to tickle and rub her neck erotically, occasionally reaching around to fondle her breasts

120

and nipples. All his movements were easy and subtle. "Did you help Harumi find out who the skull was?"

"Ah huh. Someone named Fred Noonan." She hesitated and looked back at him waiting for some reaction. When none came, she continued. "It took quite a bit of searching through all types of navy and civilian records, but I found what I wanted," she said triumphantly. "Harumi has always gotten herself into bizarre situations. The skull was apparently immersed in seawater for a ton of years. I've got the whole forensic report from Washington on it. Really fascinating stuff."

"Where's the skull now?" Syann tightened his hand around a large melon-shaped breast, his long fingers working her aroused nipple and surrounding areola.

"Harumi has all eight pounds of it, but we nailed that old guy. Actually, I'm very proud of myself. I've turned into a real Sherlock Holmes. A real hunter."

Syann lightly moved the heel of his hand down her hard flat stomach to her warm thighs, feeling her tremble and shiver beneath him. "Kim, the real hunter lets the prey do the work." His voice took on a faraway cast.

"Where'd that come from?" Kim moaned again from his touch.

"It's an old Russian proverb," he whispered, rubbing her warmth. "Instead of a hundred rubles, have one special friend. Be my special friend, Kim. Please."

"Oh, Greg!" Her eyes filled with tears. "This is happening too fast." Almost involuntarily, she turned and embraced him, then began a slow, erotic rhythm, wrapping her muscular legs around him.

"It's time again, Greg." Her voice was smoky and incomplete as she allowed him to work her body.

Slowly, Greg Syann entered Kim, working her body

121

and psyche to the outer edge of ecstasy that bordered on pain. Over and over, he held himself back, fighting every instinct for release as he moved her through a series of small but intense orgasms with surgical precision. Suddenly, in a wild frenzy, they both lost themselves in a rush as they climaxed together, each fueling the other's intense, wet pleasure with a series of movements that went on forever.

In the midst of catching his breath, Syann reached his delicate hand around Kim's neck and in a swift, practiced movement, crushed her windpipe and neck with a sickening snap of bone and cartilage, while still enfolded in her warmth.

"I'm sorry, Kim," he mumbled, staring into her puzzled, lifeless face, lost forever between sudden pleasure and death.

"I really wanted you to enjoy yourself," he whispered to the breeze and the roar of the giant pounding surf as he rolled away from Kim Dubin's body, now only aware of his own pulse beat pounding in his neck.

Carefully, he covered Kim Dubin's body with beach sand, then concealed the shallow grave with dried brush from the surrounding thicket. "Rest well, dentist. At least you died for something," he mumbled, staring at the mount of sand and scrub.

Quickly brushing off his clothes, he fingered Kim's keys to the BMW in his pocket, slowly thinking through his agenda and the satellite burst of communiqués he would have to send. "Austria and Havana are waiting," he suddenly said aloud as he slid easily behind the wheel of the little blue convertible.

Fifteen

Erik van Horn fought against the flat blackness of island night, his old eyes straining to see the road as the battered station wagon raced west on Highway 19 at close to seventy. Only Mollie, curled up in a ball in the back didn't mind the strained silence inside the wagon. Somehow the night had lost its earlier promise.

Just before midnight, they reached an obscure, dimly lit inner driveway that gave way to the Mauna Kea Beach Club on the island's west coast. An oasis in the shadow of the Mauna Kea volcano, risubg dramatically fourteen thousand feet above the island's black lava floor.

"I don't understand?" Spain gazed at the low-slung hotel, a geometric succession of five concrete waffles somehow tied together by a crescent-shaped emerald bay. "What is this place?" Spain's voice trailed off as his eyes drank in the chalk white sand hugging the bay, glowing in the central Pacific blackness from the reflection of cold, ancient starlight.

"As a child, this was my special playhouse. Daddy knew the man who built the hotel." A heavy splash in the bay forced Spain into an instinctive crouch, gun drawn, as his eyes swept through the darkness.

"Take a look, killer." Harumi pointed out to a graceful, twelve-foot whitish gray manta ray, gliding easily in large sweeping arcs across the still bay in search of plankton rising to the surface. Occasionally, she would slow her forward motion and beat her massive delta wings, straining the microorganisms into her scoop-shaped mouth.

"Time to go to work," Erik van Horn growled in the darkness, as he led them both up a long narrow flight of rock steps into the lobby, the dog trailing far behind. "Come on, sweet pea." Van Horn patted his leg and the black lab came close, obviously filled with affection for the old man.

The open lobby, filled with art objects from across the Pacific, allowed for the now sweet, storm-free trade wind to cleanse the air as they waited at the registration desk. Finally a large, soft-spoken Hawaiian woman appeared and immediately glared at the dog.

"We don't allow animals in this hotel, sir." She smiled coldly with bright, efficient teeth." If you would kindly —"

"We're not staying, madam." Van Horn steadied his gaze. "Tell the *Proprietaire Aubergiste*, Mister Robert Kay, that I have a possible broken arrow —"

Van Horn was interrupted by the shrill squawking of a large parrot echoing off of the lobby's polished slate floors. "I said we are here to investigate a broken arrow!" Now, a hard anger began to boil up from his throat. "Do you hear —"

The night manager held up a large brown hand, then cocked her head, as if hearing something for the first time, but having waited a long time to hear it. At once there was vagueness that gave way to a distant recognition.

"Yes, a broken arrow," she repeated. "I'll ring Mister Kay at once, in his home, adjacent to the hotel." She smiled weakly as Mollie squatted over an antique bronze urn, exercising her canine disdain.

The night manager watched the dog for an instant, curled her lip nervously, then disappeared into an adjacent office.

Harumi led Spain around the vast, open lobby past twin, acquiescent gold leaf and black lacquer, Thai Buddhas called *Mokala,* dating back to the eighteenth century. On the north wall hung two bronze Chinese ceremonial drums, cast in sixteenth-century China.

"Those are *chamlas*." Harumi rubbed her tired face, feeling the tension pulling at Spain as she guided his body about the floor, trying her best to distract him.

"What? What the hell are—"

She pointed to a series of three-legged brass Indian storage chests that reeked of fresh polish. Harumi lightly touched Spain's face, barely turning his head to meet her eyes.

"Thanks for telling me everything tonight," she said softly. "It means a great deal to me that you were trying to protect me."

"Yeah, some damn job of protecting you!" He rubbed a hand through her long black hair. "Jesus, we're in the shit, kid, and in case you've forgotten, people are being dropped all around us!" His voice was edgy and haunting.

"That's why I stayed drunk for so long. At least the demons didn't have such a sharp edge, swimming around like eels in my subconscious. They couldn't kill you!"

"No just the booze and the street could," Harumi said softly. "Look, I know how bad things are right now, but we'll work out of it. At least I'm gambling on it." There was a surge of strength in her voice.

"Jesus, Harumi! Gambling! A nine millimeter always beats four aces! This is no fucking poker game! No hide-and-seek exercise to make it sexy as you track down the meaning of that goddamn skull and little yellow pouch of worthless papers! Academia is a long way from here, wherever here is!"

Harumi shook her head, her eyes cold brown arrows. "Listen to me you bastard! What I started to say was that what you told me back at the house wasn't easy for you but at least now, your life fits together."

"How nice of you to approve! I know how much research means to you!" Spain's eyes tried to follow and find the sound as the parrot again began shrieking his horrid war chant throughout the lobby. "Christ, one day I'm fine, the fog has lifted and the sky is blue. Then wham! A fucking little bundle of papers sends my life back into the toilet and now you're acting like a goddamn wife!" His voice rose to meet the level of the squawking bird.

Harumi blew hair out of her eyes with an exasperated puff of air. "Well, that's a noble thought! I only meant to say I appreciated the fact that you filled some obvious holes of your life in for me." She jammed her hands in her pants pockets.

"Black holes, Harumi. Very deep holes that at any moment can suck the light and life out of me and now you!"

126

"Hey, break it up." A stern, fatherly order floated across the deserted lobby. Erik van Horn waved them back to the front desk where the Dutchman stood facing a smallish, bald man with a neatly trimmed reddish gray beard that curled up into a full, rich mustache, that at the moment was absorbing the sweat pouring from his upper lip.

Impulsively, Harumi grabbed Spain's arm. "Let's stop all this and just go home," she pleaded softly. "I'm sorry we ever started any of it." She hesitated, then turned Spain's head. "We'll sneak back aboard the *Arizona* and put back what we took. How about it, Benny?"

"You just can't stop it because you want to, Harumi! It's past that stage now. That chance is long since past. But you know all that. People are dead and probably more people will die before this thing is played out. The events have taken on their own life."

"Your Russian friend?" Her voice was barely audible. "You're certain, it's him?"

"It's him. The Black Ghost's somewhere out there, just watching and waiting for the right time to take us." Spain felt his grip tighten around Harumi's wrist. "I can feel his presence, somewhere. And I don't even know why, damn it!"

The hotel man glared at the loud approach of Harumi and Spain and seemed totally irritated at this late-night intrusion. "How can I help you, sir?" He sneered at van Horn through black-rimmed reading glasses.

"We have a possible broken arrow and Aleka needs to have his cage cleaned."

For a long time the manager steadied his small, watery, animal brown eyes on the trio, especially the elder

127

van Horn. Finally, his lips made a little looping motion, blowing invisible smoke rings. "I see. Well, he sleeps until 9 A.M., then the cover comes off his cage." The manager stood insect still, waiting.

"That will give us enough time to mend the broken arrow. We've brought our own tools for the job."

The manager nodded brusquely, with a stiff Prussian bow, as the bizarre conversation ended. "Very well, please follow me and please no talking." The manager arched a thin eyebrow, staring at Harumi and Ben.

"I don't want to draw attention to you, nor do I want to disturb our guests." His contempt dribbled around their feet as dirty engine oil.

Following the manager at a respectable distance, they were led through the garden level, across smooth black-rocked ponds stocked with giant *koi* of every possible color. The ponds were linked by wooden foot bridges and the lush foliage suggested a deep Indonesian rain forest. Finally they reached a small wooden cabana, bordering a plush garden dominated by a giant stone buddha, keeping watch.

"Welcome to the north garden area of the hotel," the manager announced with a snobbish dignity that made Spain want to bash in his skull.

"That Buddha is incredible," he announced arrogantly. "We dug it up in northern India, near the Tibetan border. It is dated as of seventh century A.D."

Before them, guarding the north garden of tightly manicured lawns, slate paths and raised concrete planters, squatted a massive eight-foot stone Buddha, gazing softly through blank eyes out to the black Pacific below and the gardens above. The statue had been positioned carefully to give the impression of guarding every-one within eyesight, including the tall palms, wafting in the trades. The teak cabana, with white linen curtains, was carefully isolated from the main garden by thick tropical foliage growing up and around its stone steps.

"Must the dog stay with you, tonight?" The arrogant voice was still jostling them. "These gardens are impe-rial. There's a bronze plaque commemorating the unique royal visit by Japanese Emperor Hirohito in Nineteen seventy-five. He offered special prayers, while communing in our north garden."

"The dog stays," van Horn said flatly, narrowing his eyes. Harumi glanced at Spain, her eyes choking on the irony. Somewhere off in the distance environs of the lobby, the parrot had taken up his familiar chant, maybe sensing their mission.

They entered the isolated cabana and switched on the interior lights revealing a large cherrywood desk sur-rounded with simple stick furniture including a rattan couch and matching loveseat. Silently the inn keeper brushed by them, then bent over the desk and inserted a brass key into the right side. Tentatively, he opened the wooden door and carefully pulled out a large, high-speed computer terminal and keyboard on a deep roller tray. Now beginning to work efficiently, Robert Kay pulled out the small printer unit, then hooked up a series of thick cables. When he finished, Kay quietly turned to van Horn.

"May I see your hard card?" His arrogance had soft-ened into something mechanical and almost frightened.

Van Horn handed over his plastic card with an im-printed microchip, then waited while the card was in-

serted into the computer. In a flash, the computer screen
came alive with a bright green electronic haze:

00 2345 ZULU

0110 KAUNAOA BAY STATION
NATIONAL COMPUTER SECURITY
CENTER/BETHESDA

AUTHENTICATION CODE:
   FLYING DUTCHMAN
AUTHENTICATION VERIFIED TO LEVEL
TWO.
LINKAGE TO INTERNET ACTIVATED.
SATELLITE LINKAGE ACTIVATED/64273.
ENTER MENU REQUIRED.

The manager rose from the chair and smiled nervously. "Your hard card has been approved, Mister van
Horn." This is the only time I've activated the system.
I've never experienced a broken arrow." He raised his
hands in some vague gesture, pointing at the live computer screen, his tone now respectful.

"We appreciate your cooperation." van Horn smiled.

"You have until 9 A.M., then I can no longer guarantee
your security in these quarters."

"Are your security guards armed?" Spain moved close
to the small man.

"No!" He was suddenly startled, but quickly masked
it. "No, they just carry two-way radios. We've never had a
problem like that before."

Spain smiled. "You've never fired up this computer

before either." He thought of the Russian somewhere in the islands and then shivered visibly.

Then the hotel man was gone and van Horn raised his eyes defensively to Harumi and Spain. "This whole system was put in place just in case I could make a contribution. Over the years, they've continued to update it."

"I can see that." Spain smiled. "You're still an old dog, with new tricks and sharp teeth, Erik. There are many layers beneath that thick crust of yours. You're still in the business," Spain said quietly.

"No one ever gets out. Look at you. After all these years, it's all over you like a virus. And yes, you're damn right, I can smell trouble and this is trouble!"

Van Horn turned his back for a moment, peering out through the thick teak plantation shutters. "Maybe I can use all these years of experience including this goddamned computer to help save your lives!" He glanced over his shoulder at his daughter. "I don't have a choice here, do I?"

"Where do we begin?" Harumi asked, sitting down heavily at the terminal.

Van Horn reached into his bush jacket and pulled out a small leather notebook. "These are my instructions based on a week I spent at Fort Meade last year." Placing half-reading glasses on his thick nose, van Horn carefully thumbed through the notebook.

"I think we should tap into OPTIMUS."

"The Department of Defense data banks?" Harumi's voice rose to a shrill. "You can do that? Classified, no less!"

"It's not very deep material, light classification, but it's a place to start."

"I know my way around computers and government information networks pretty well." She eyed her father with a new respect.

"I'll be right back," Spain interrupted.

"Where are you going?" Harumi widened her eyes.

"Just to the bathroom. There's one over by the fish ponds that I noticed on the way in." He held up his hands in supplication. "Be right back and I won't have a drink unless it's water." He laughed, closing the door.

"Look, Harumi, this little crisis goes far beyond academic research and your old man still does know a thing or two." His old gray eyes widened with a twinkle at her dumbfounded expression.

"My God, a classified Defense Department computer right out of the starting gate! Yes, Dad, I'd say it goes beyond my research by only five or ten light years!" For the next few minutes they both studied van Horn's leather notebook to be certain they didn't make any mistake. A gross error would draw an instant response from the Defense Communications Agency.

Quietly, Spain entered the cabana, smiling. "Feels much better. How you doing?"

Erik nodded just as Harumi typed in OPTIMUS. The response from the computer was instantaneous:

0015 ZULU
ACCESS/FLYING DUTCHMAN/VERIFIED
OPTIMUS FILE OPEN/
PLEASE REQUEST DATA

Harumi looked back at her father, the tension turning the creases in his old face, dark. "Now what do we ask?"

"I have a place to start, I think. There was an operative I worked with toward the end of the war, near the Siegfried Line, on the German frontier, in the spring of Nineteen forty-four. He was German-American and unlike most agents, we became pretty chummy."

"And?" Harumi rested her fingers on the keyboard.

"And he told me a story about the Pearl Harbor raid and about a dead Luftwaffe pilot who had been found in the wreckage of one of the few Japanese Zeros shot down that day. It was all very hush-hush and very sensitive at the time. That's why your story peaked my interest right away. This operative was sent to Pearl right after the attack, to help look for clues that other Germans might have been involved in the raid or at the least helped in preparation for the attack."

"Nothing surprises me anymore," Spain grunted. "So what happened?"

"Nothing. The operative never said much more, although I got the feeling there was more, a great deal more. Kind of like a very still, deep pool of water. Hard information about you or your missions was a death ticket, so we all said as little as possible. We were strangers, acting like friends, on a very intense life and death, but superficial level. It defies explanation."

Van Horn paused thinking something through, peeling back the years, searching his past. He closed his eyes and squinted, forcing himself to concentrate.

"What was his name, Dad?"

"I never knew. It could have been a death sentence. I only knew field codes. Damn! The Germans used physical torture and scopolamine, the gray twilight truth drug; and you just couldn't hold back. So—"

He stopped in midsentence. "Try beads. Ah, one hundred and nine and something else. Damn it! It's been so many years. Harumi, try 'One Hundred Nine Beads.' "

Harumi typed in the numbers and the word code:

INSUFFICIENT DATA FOR A RESPONSE.

"Oh, Christ, what was it!" The elder van Horn paced the small room in silence for more than ten minutes, his eyes focused on the floor and Mollie, her brown eyes watching his every movement.

"Can we help jog your memory?" Spain nudged. "Sometimes when I have a problem, it helps to talk it out. Ask Harumi. Otherwise I don't have a damn prayer."

"What? Ah, that's it, Ben!" "Harumi try 'One Hundred Nine Rosary Beads! I think that was the other half of his—"

Harumi shrieked. "Bull's-eye!" as she entered the code name into the computer, her long fingers flying over the keyboard. The response was readily forthcoming:

NO INFORMATION AVAILABLE.
THIS NETWORK AIR GAP SECURITY.
NO ACCESS TO 109 ROSARY BEADS CODE.

"Damn it!" Van Horn went back to his book, carefully searching each page.

"What about the Advanced Research Projects Agency, Dad? I use it all the time. It's linked to military records, historical information, and basic research."

Disappointed, van Horn nodded as she typed in AR-PANET, to reach another computer network hooked to the national archives and more than six thousand university computers across the United States.

Quickly FLYING DUTCHMAN was brought on line, but the results were the same.

"What about this 'air gap' business?" Van Horn looked at them both. "What's it mean? It might be significant."

Harumi shrugged. "Air gap is a basic security system. It means that access codes and authorizations have to be entered at the computer station being used. No telephone, modem, or microwave hookup is possible. It prevents what they call diddling, or a virus being implanted in someone's program."

"It also prevents stealing high-level security information." Spain's voice was steady. "I have an idea that—" The phone rang, taking them by surprise.

"Room service. Maybe a bone for the dog," Spain mumbled reaching for the receiver.

Suddenly, Harumi watched his face blanch and that special sick hue wash over him, as he nodded and listened. "When did it happen? He looked over at Harumi with a hopeless expression on his face, then he slowly hung up the receiver.

"That was Mister Kay and he was very upset."

"What about?" Van Horn moved closer.

"They just found a security guard with his neck broken on the northern boundary of the hotel. He thought we'd like to know. He's now calling the Hawaiian State Police, Five-O. They'll be here in less than thirty minutes." Spain slumped in a nearby chair and shook his head.

"It could just be a coincidence," Harumi said hopefully.

"Not a chance, daughter. Not a chance."

Spain pulled himself up and moved to the computer. "Let me sit there and try something, Harumi."

"We don't have a helluva lot of time, Ben!"

"I know that, Erik!" He snapped.

Tentatively at first, then with more authority, Spain tapped his message to the computer as Harumi and her father moved behind him.

"When I was working for the Feds, they're was a deep black computer linking system that—" One finger at a time, he typed in DEFENSE ADVANCED RE-SEARCH PROJECTS. Then:

DARPA NETWORK UTILIZE
SL ONLY.

"What's that?" Van Horn asked

"The satellite link. Sometimes it can be used to bypass air gap security.

Suddenly the screen came alive.

ENTER ACCESS CODE.

"Good," Spain mumbled. "We're in." Spain motioned Harumi to sit down and take the keyboard.

"Okay. How do I access this operative friend of yours?"

"Ask the computer what 'Beads' real name is.

"Hurry it up!" Spain urged. "We've got to be gone from here in the next few minutes! I don't want to get hung up with Five-O and the local police. Or our friend—" His voice trailed away.

Harumi's fingers moved across the keyboard, but the screen remained blank. Finally it began to flash:

ONE HUNDRED NINE ROSARY BEADS/
CODE NAME/OPERATIVE RUSSELL
WITTEN.
OPERATIONAL STATUS REMOVED 1946/
OFFICE OF STRATEGIC SERVICES.
WORKED DIRECT CONTROL OF OSS
DIRECTOR WILLIAM DONOVAN.

"Russell Witten." Jesus, how the mind plays tricks on you. Russell Witten. He sure as hell didn't look like anyone with a name like that! He was a big, tough guy. Harumi, ask the computer about Witten's involvement with the Pearl Harbor raid!"

Quickly she typed in the request, while Spain nervously watched the door, wanting to be gone. "Come on, damn it! You've got about ten more minutes, before the State Bulls begin asking a shitload of questions here!" He pulled the Czech automatic and chambered a round, carefully screwing the old battered silencer into the gun's barrel.

OSS OPERATIVE RUSSELL WITTEN
HEAD INVESTIGATOR FOR
PANDORA'S BOX 12-8-41 THROUGH
3-26-42.

"That's one of your keys, Ben! Pandora's Box! I don't know what the hell it means but —"

Harumi was already tapping in another request. "I asked the computer to tell us about Fred Noonan, the *Arizona,* and secret documents sent from Emperor Hirohito to President Roosevelt." She smiled as Spain placed his hand on her shoulder.

"Come on, sport," Ben said softly. "Time to saddle up and move out. Those events I talked about before are catching up with us. I can feel it, Harumi. It's time to go."

"Not yet, Benny, please —"

The computer began to print:

THIS ACCESS LEVEL DOES NOT
PERMIT INFORMATION RETRIEVAL
PANDORA'S BOX. NEED SECONDARY
CODE SEQUENCE.

"Now, Harumi!" Spain was exasperated. "For Chrissakes, Erik, talk to your daughter! If you want to save her

138

life, tell her about how it really is!"

"He's right, honey! You and Ben have to leave the islands now. I want you to go to the mainland."

"Just a sec!" Harumi was waiting for a response from the computer.

Spain reached over to grab her just as the computer began another run:

OPERATIVE RUSSELL WITTEN
IS LOCATED AT COORDINATES
41 30' N 123 10' W

"What the hell is that?" Harumi stared at the screen, then looked up at Ben. "Please look at this! Both of you!" She glanced angrily at her father.

"What do these numbers mean?"

Ben glanced at the screen. "Way to go, Ms. Brainpower. They're map coordinates. Simple latitude and longitude. Find a map and that's where we'll find this Witten guy."

Quickly Harumi scribbled the numbers down, then tossed a sharp look at Spain. "Dad, how do we get out of here without being caught?" she whispered.

"I can get you to Hilo and then the mainland. From there, you're on your own. I —" A sharp rap at the door interrupted; Spain put a finger to his mouth as he slid next to van Horn. "I'll get Harumi out of here. Can you take care of this end?" he barely whispered, his heart pounding like a jackhammer.

"See Willy Ashmore. He runs the airport in Hilo. Tell

him you're traveling for the Flying Dutchman, and it's a matter of life and death!"

Spain stared into van Horn's eyes. "It is life or death, Erik."

"I know that. Now get moving, take the car and I'll take care of the local heat and Mollie." He grabbed Spain's shoulder fiercely. "Find Witten if he's still alive and see to my only child!"

"I love her, too, Erik," Spain whispered, as they quietly slid out the back window of the north garden. "Keep in touch. You know what to do." Van Horn held up two fingers as he watched them disappear into the night.

Sixteen

The woman, worn softly by age and politics, but still carrying an exotic, intense beauty blurred by the passing years, gently placed the pen on her neatly kept leather-topped desk. For a moment, her black violet eyes came alive with a smoldering obsession as she swiveled in her chair and stared out the window of her fifth floor office on the Malecon, in old Havana. For a long time she watched intently as the rust-stained Soviet tanker *Argun Kalingradneft*, with high boxy lines, was slowly pushed into her berth along the waterfront on the canal del Puerto, her oversized hammer and sickle flag flapping like a laundered shirt in the stiff morning breeze coming off the Gulf Stream.

Senora Hilda Castillo Soria, the Cuban Minister of Finance and more importantly, the sister-in-law to Fidel Castro, mashed her jaw, the brilliant violet eyes suddenly burning dark and troubled. How many more shipments were coming? How long could the Soviet Union be depended upon to send anything of importance when they couldn't even care for their own. Sugar cane was no longer enough to substitute for badly needed rubles, pesos and God forbid, dollars. The Kremlin could no longer carry their debt. The Warsaw Pact had ceased to exist and now her beloved Cuba was being forced to sell herself as an island tourist paradise. A damn Eastern Block island hotel for the new capitalists that had turned the once proud Marxist Revolution into a laughable shambles! A communist whore in the Caribbean! *Condenación perdición!* The buzzing of her interoffice phone brought the minister back from her nightmare.

With effort she pushed herself away from the large window, facing Havana Harbor, reaching for the phone.

"Yes?" The irritation had carried over from her black daydream.

"Senora, your luncheon date with the Soviet ambassador has been confirmed."

"And?" Her security director and chief aide, Sed Cruz, had served her for more than twenty-three years, and it was this former artillery commander, a hero of the Bay of Pigs, for the Cuban people, who had become her eyes and ears, when her back was turned. He vacuumed up nuance and subtlety and all those hundreds of voice inflections that had given *Ministra* Castillo Soria her unique edge for all these many years.

"And he knows precisely what you want. He quoted me the standard Kremlin line that sugar cane is no longer a viable trading option and that the thirteen point three million tons of crude oil that was supplied to Cuba last year will be halved this year. He was desperate enough to mention their continuing exportation to us of light bulbs, sanitary napkins, and even caviar for your brother-in-law. It was more than a veiled threat. Moscow is tired of accepting worthless pesos."

"Meaning?" Senora Soria turned in her chair, watching the morning haze drift in small pockets of batter over the old Havana section, the small enclave of some sixty thousand, surrounded by two million of the faithful and unfaithful followers of the regime. Out of the corner of her eye, she watched a black-hulled Soviet grain freighter riding high and empty, slide past the Punta Sotavento Light, out into the Straits of Florida, heading toward the open, aqua-blue sea on the morning tide.

"Simply stated, Minister, we are reaching the end of the line with the Soviet Union. Our credit is no longer welcome. But he has agreed to meet you very discreetly for luncheon today for further discussion." Sed Cruz, hesitated, feeling ashamed that he had not been able to do more.

"Dos mio, Sed! You have done your best and I know that!" A genuine affection bubbled up in the woman's throat. "Where have you set up this clandestine economic rendezvous?" She laughed darkly.

"At fifteen Obrapia Street, a few blocks from Talcon Street and the old seawall."

"I don't understand, Sed?"

"I hope not, Senora. It is the *Casa de Africa.* A small restaurant, *La Mina,* just opened, catering to the upper-crust Canadian and European trade. There is small back dining area, overlooking a restored patio of cobble stones, white storm shutters, and red hibiscus. Your privacy has been guaranteed." Now Sed was pleased with himself, knowing that Senora Soria would be pleased. "Your security is also assured there."

"La Mina," she repeated. "You continue to amaze me, Sed."

"Senora, may I join you in your inner office for a few moments?" Suddenly his voice was laced with gravity.

"Of course, you may enter." She hung up the phone receiver, watching idly below as an old yellow, beaten-down 1951 Chevy convertible, with black trash bags stretched over what had once been the cotton top, chug along the Avenida Antonio Maceo, commonly called the Malecon, white smoke billowing from its exhaust pipe.

A smallish man, with fierce, pale eyes, carrying a deep limp, entered the office quietly, and smiled with steel-filled teeth. "I wanted to speak to you away from the phone. We received a scrambled communiqué, via satellite, from *Espectro de Negro* about ten minutes ago." He nodded his long, wrinkled face down at a pink sheet in his hand. "May I read it to you, Senora?"

Minister Soria smiled with white even teeth. "Will you never stop this formality with me, Sed? You owe me nothing. I have never been too busy for you. You are family." She waved a strong hand in small circles in front of her face.

Indeed, Sed Cruz owed this once stunning, but still beautiful Cuban woman, his life and his dignity. The debt would never be paid. Just after the Bay of Pigs victory over the United States and the infamous CIA Brigade 2605, Castro jailed his senior commanders, including Cruz, for failing to push the insurgents in to the sea during the first assault. It was then that Castro, the great *caudillo,* personally took command of the successful counterattack. Despite the fact that Cruz had joined with Castro and his family early on in the cane fields and mountains of Oriente Province, he and his fellow commanders were sent to the Isle del Muerta, the dreaded Isle of Pines Prison, where people went in, but never came out. Devil's Island in the round, where guards forced him to stand for days in liquid excrement up to his lips. If he wavered, he would drown in the horrid brown tank, but he survived with the nickname Plantados — the one who dug his heels into the earth and would admit to no crime. They even tried to dress him in the blue uniform of a common street criminal, but the former major in the People's Liberation Army stood firm and naked, like an old Cuban pine.

After two years, and close to death, he was rescued by this woman, Senora Soria, married to Castro's brother. She hadn't forgotten the early days and the morning he shielded her baby from a strafing Batista jet fighter in a flat open field. He had been wounded and bled into the rich brown Cuban earth, protecting this woman's child with his own body. It took her years, but she found him, rotting in a tiny cell, stripped of everything but his soul, living off his spirit, with his body already beginning to eat itself, his skin the texture of paper, and the deadly sweet rot of human beings everywhere.

But she found him and then sheltered him from the all powerful *caudillo* with her body and her raw power, as she nursed him to health in her own *casa*. Yes, he owed her.

"Damn it, Sed! Talk to me!" the senora's violet eyes were alive with black fire. "Stop daydreaming on me! Read it to me, *por favor!*" she asked again, softening her tone.

"Yes, Senora." He cast his eyes down to the pink sheet, reading to her:

TO: MIDWIFE
FROM: BLACK GHOST
SUBJECT: ARIZONA
IN HOT PURSUIT. MUST

VACATE PRESENT LOCATION.
CONTACT WOLFMAN IN AUSTRIA,
THAT THE HUNT IS ON!
BLACK GHOST

For a long time, Senora Soria closed her eyes, thinking about the message that her friend had just read to her. Could it be real? Could she even allow herself to hope? Her beloved Cuba was shriveling right before her eyes and if this man, this Russian maniac and his East German accomplice, the wolfman, Misha Lutz, could really find the lost bullion, Cuba's economic woes would be past. The amount was so great.

"Sed," she heard herself whisper in a dreamlike state, "prepare a secured message for that old Nazi bastard in Hallstatt, Austria, and his murdering *ex-Stasi* companions. Tell him we have heard from the Black Ghost and that he has not yet found any evidence of the bullion in Hawaii."

Slowly she looked up at Sed, a soft lovely smile parting her still well-shaped lips. "Cuba first, Sed. Cuba always."

She quickly turned her attention to the lunch meeting with the Soviet ambassador and his terse, threatening comment the last time they had met. "Havana, after dark, without our oil, will eventually resemble a campsite. A forty-watt town that is doomed to smolder and die in the mist, the only light coming from the little string of orange lights on the Malecon, the boulevard separating the city from the sea." Soria rubbed her mouth in thought.

"We may not have to deal, after all with that crazy Saddam and his band of Iraqi pirates, for oil." She smiled faintly at Sed. "Cancel my appointment next week with the Iraqi ambassador. Hold him off just as long as you can, Sed." She turned her back, staring down at the filthy, oily water of Havana Harbor.

"Very well, Senora." Cruz moved toward the door as her final words stopped him.

"We will see, Sed. I intend on making a liar out of our comrade Russian ambassador."

Seventeen

"Did you get it?" Harumi looked up hopefully as Spain sat heavily next to her in the small out of the way cafeteria, at San Francisco International Airport, that was weak on taste but strong on the local french bread.

Spain sipped from a streaming mug of black coffee, then slowly unfolded a map of California. "We'll have to stop and buy some clothes and basic things, but I want to get the hell out of San Francisco."

"We weren't being followed, were we?

"I don't think so, but did you see the way that cop looked us over? They were looking for someone. I've never seen a cop at a boarding gate at seven in the morning. He made my skin crawl."

Harumi nodded, finishing up her scrambled eggs and toast with a vengeance. Finally she sank back in her seat, squeezing out a deep sigh. "God, I feel human again." She smiled and pulled her long hair up in a mock ponytail. "I must look a sight."

Spain arched an eyebrow. "Youth never tires." He

reached over and kissed her lightly. "You look great," he said softly, "and I'm impressed with your grace under fire. Without your strength, I wouldn't have made it this far."

"I guess vulnerability creates drama. Don't sell yourself short, Benny." She smiled again, dark bags dragging under her almond eyes.

Quickly, Spain scanned the open map. "I know that the longitude is somewhere in California," he mumbled. "What are the numbers, Harumi?" Spain, using a table knife as a ruler, waited while she read the coordinates.

"Forty-one degrees, thirty minutes north, latitude," he translated as he found his mark, "by one hundred twenty-three degrees, ten minutes west, longitude." For a long time he squinted at the map, his finger at a point where the two light pencil lines intersected.

"What is it, Benny?"

"I don't know. The lines cross right in the middle of the Klamath National Forest, on the north fork of the Salmon River." He looked across the table at her, puzzled. "It's smack in the middle of a national forest! A damn wild-goose chase! This guy, called 'Beads' has to be in his late seventies by now, if he's even still alive! How the hell can he live in the middle of nowhere?"

Carefully, Harumi studied the coordinates, then the map. "You missed something." She pointed down at a tiny hamlet, the typeface barely visible on the map. Look, Ben, a place called Sawyers Bar. Your pencil lines cross right on it," she said hopefully.

Spain let out a long breath. "Jesus, talk about grasping for straws! It's a goddamned ink stain!"

"You have any better ideas?"

"Why the hell would this guy turn into a mountain man, hiding in the frigging deep forest."

"Sometimes you aren't very smart, Ben. He's hiding from something. What better place to go, than an ink stain. Look how far my father got away from Europe after the war."

Spain rubbed his graying hair. "That was forty-five years ago! Hells bells, well, we sure as hell don't have any other place to go. Let that bastard Gregori try and find us there," he mumbled.

"Speaking of my father, I'm going to call him, Benny. I want to be sure he's all right." She watched his face slide into disapproval. "I know, the line could be tapped. I'll stay on the wire for no more than half a minute."

Spain nodded sullenly. He knew he couldn't talk Harumi out of it. He couldn't talk her out of anything, once her mind was made up." Okay. I guess I'll go downstairs and rent a car. Meet you back here in fifteen." Painfully, he ambled off, Harumi watching the fear and tension eating at him.

Carefully, following Spain's instructions, Harumi called her father direct, letting the phone ring only twice before breaking the connection. It was the signal Ben had arranged. Then she punched in the Hawaiian number again.

"Dad! Are you okay?"

"Yes, Harumi." His voice was taut and guarded.

"What is it? What's wrong? Mollie okay?"

"Mol's fine. I had a helluva time though, with the State Police. They want to talk with you and Ben."

"We don't know anything about the guard's death at the hotel!"

"It's not about that." Van Horn hesitated, then Harumi heard him swallow across an ocean three thousand miles away.

"I'm running out of time, Dad! What is it?"

"Ah, Kimmy Dubin's dead!" he blurted out. "She's been murdered over on Oahu's north shore."

Harumi burst into tears, holding the phone to her mouth. "Oh my God! Oh my God!"

"Harumi, can you hear me? Harumi, for Chrissakes, talk to me!"

"What—" Her sobbing was on the verge of hysteria.

"Five-O has put out an all-points bulletin for you and Ben! They almost nabbed you in Hilo, but my friend stalled them. He's damn good at his job. He always has been! But he had to tell them eventually."

"Why? Oh, God, this isn't real—"

"It is, honey. Too damn real. They want you and Ben for questioning about Kim's murder. They think you did it. There's a warrant."

"Oh no!" she cried. "Why would we kill my best friend?"

"Harumi," her father shouted, "I want you to hang up in ten seconds. Don't tell me where you are. Otherwise you'll be traced and I'll be an accessory. Get lost somewhere, anywhere you can and stay there! Disguise yourselves. I had to give them a photo of you and they already had one of Spain. I know they're listening right now! Screw 'em! Just get lost!" he yelled into the phone. "Please, honey," he begged. "Please do what I say. Go tell Spain. Do it now! Be careful. They're looking for you, everywhere!" Then the line went dead.

Turning numbly in slow motion, she dropped the

phone, her body and mind reeling from the emotional shocks of both Kim's death and that they were being hunted for murder.

Stepping out into the moderate, early morning foot traffic of the main terminal building, Harumi moved mechanically toward the small airport cafe where she was to meet Spain.

"Ben!" she gasped. "Oh my God, he's renting a car! He'll be traced for sure on the computer!"

Racing blindly, Harumi ran down the moving escalator, hoping to reach Ben before it was too late. "What the hell was the place he said!" she talked to herself, half crazed, moving among the car-rental counters.

"Ben!" she screamed, spying him talking to an agent at the green car-rental counter. "Ben, stop!" she shouted again, this time grabbing his attention. It was the hysteria in her voice that forced him to turn. "Ah, we don't need a car!" Then she was on him, tugging at his arm.

"Harumi, what!"

"Don't!" she commanded quietly. "Walk with me, quickly," she said, now whispering, hot tears streaming down her face.

Finally, Harumi pushed him into a dark corner near the baggage claim area just as she spotted a uniformed policeman moving quickly toward them.

"Don't move, Ben," she ordered in a whisper. "Turn your back and listen carefully," she moaned, trying to regain control. "Kim Dubin's dead. Murdered and they think we did it! Everybody wants us! A policeman's coming right now. If you'd given your name, the computer would have flagged the warrant, for sure."

"Kim? What warrant?" Spain was aghast as he watched her begin to shake.

"Murder, Ben. Ah, we've got to get out of here, now!" she repeated, her voice breaking as she watched the cop out of the corner of her eye. Instantly, Spain looked at the flight board, then drew Harumi to him, burying his tongue in her mouth in a bone-crunching squeeze.

"God, our honeymoon was great!" he boomed into the baggage area, just as the policeman came within earshot. "Hey officer," Ben called, "take your wife to England. It'll be the best sex you ever had! God, I promise." He laughed heartily, shaking the policeman's hand. "Can you imagine! Great sex with your own wife!"

The large, red-faced cop studied them both for a moment, then embarrassed and completely distracted, moved quickly away.

Without missing a beat, Spain and Harumi slid into a herd of passengers heading for their luggage from the English flight that had just landed and cleared customs.

"Jesus," he moaned, trying to calm his shaking hands. "That was damn close!" Moving quickly now, they emerged on the street level of the crescent-shaped San Francisco International Airport, just as the sun began to emerge from behind the massive hand of roiling gray fog, hanging as an early morning robe over the soft, tan hills of South San Francisco. With a certain flair, Spain jerked Harumi into a waiting taxi.

"Union Square, fast!" he commanded the Pakistani cabbie. "There's an extra twenty, if you move your ass!"

"Yeah, sir," the dark-skinned man answered with a thick accent. "Luggage, sir?"

"No, damn it!" Spain turned and watched the same policeman emerge from the exit not more than thirty yards from the cab, his gun drawn. He was looking for them all right, now Spain was certain. The cop had been knocked off balance but that had bought only a few precious seconds they would need to try and escape.

"Step on the gas right now!" Spain said loudly, cutting off the cabbie's opening pitch. "Do it slowly, and don't draw attention to yourself, or I'll kill you. I have a gun in your back right now!"

"Yeah, sir!" he pleaded as the cab pulled slowly into the line of traffic. Instinctively, they both crouched down as they passed the patrolman, now carefully examining everything that moved. Spain popped up his head, for just an instant, watching the cabbie's eyes in the rearview mirror.

"Don't make a head move or a nod toward that cop! Don't even blink or you're dead! Just relax and do your job and maybe you'll live out the night! Understand, man?"

"Can do! Please, can do! I have children!"

"Shut up and drive!" Spain felt the car jerk uncertainly into the roundabout leading to the airport exit as he swallowed into his parched, dry throat. He glanced over at Harumi, crouched next to him, on the floor of the back seat, her eyes heavily glazed with shock and disbelief. For the time being, it was up to him to save their lives and he didn't even have a gun! Willy Ashmore, old man van Horn's friend, had made him leave it behind when they boarded the San Francisco flight.

For a long time he closed his eyes as the taxi swung onto the Bayshore Freeway, heading north into the heart of San Francisco. If they were going to survive, they'd need a gun, cash, and a way out. Now every damn cop, snitch, and bum on the street would be casting an eye their way. He knew the Black Ghost and the ways he operated. What he didn't kill, he bought or manipulated. Somewhere in that all-points bulletin for their arrest was a caveat that they were armed and dangerous, meaning they would be shot on sight. Suddenly he was aware that the cab had come to a complete stop on the freeway!

Eighteen

The old man slowly adjusted his glasses and raised his eyes to the leaden clouds, still thick and ripe with snow. It was going to be a very late spring this year. Toshiyuki Mizutari dropped his wrinkled face to the dirty white snow still covering his beloved rock garden, sadly shaking his head. This was going to be another spring, whenever it did arrive, without his beloved Emperor Hirohito.

Carefully he slid the paper *shoji* screen back until he felt the full snap of the cold-gripping northwestern Honshu on his thinly garbed body. The stirring behind him forced his face into a pleasant smile.

"Grandfather, *kesa?*"

"Yes, this morning, child." He looked into the clear brown, expectant eyes of his seventeen-year-old granddaughter, Katsuko. "First I must go to the greenhouse to check on our green and brown children. This cold inhibits the normal growth of new spring roots." The young woman bowed, knowing the conversation had ended as she watched him step into his wooden sandals and then into the snow, padding across the rock garden to the greenhouse.

At the entrance to the greenhouse, Toshiyuki looked out past his garden to the bent junipers and brooding fir trees that grew out of the steep black granite cliffs. Cliffs that guarded the deep, isolated inlet of the Bay of Tsugaru, leading out into the cold blackness of the Sea of Japan that reached east to the Korean coast four hundred miles away. Usually, the wind howled up the rock cliffs, turning and twisting anything living before it, but this spring morning the cold front, still choking the area of Japan known as the Alps, smothered the river symphony rushing through the trees. For a long moment, Toshiyuki froze, listening intently for a sound he rarely heard from high on his mountain retreat.

Suddenly his mouth opened into a gentle laugh. The heavy, resounding sound of the old massive bronze bell echoed from the nearby Jogu Shrine atop Mount Baijo. For a moment he closed his eyes, envisioning the priests pounding the huge rough suspended log into the worn flank of the captured Korean bell, as a call to morning prayers. It was music for his *Samurai* soul as he thought about the countless days he had spent long ago, especially after the surrender in 1945, climbing and hiking above the Jogu Shrine. Then farther west, around the Five Mikata Lakes, experiencing the many steep mountain trails and pure, glacier-fed streams in an effort to wash away the personal stain of dishonor and shame he felt for losing the war to the Americans and for breaking faith with the pledge of honor to his beloved Emperor Hirohito.

Slowly, the old man was back, staring lovingly at the racks of *bonsai* trees, waiting for their morning attention. Yes, these little trees, pruned and sculpted by his hands for more than forty years, were his serenity and joy — his children, especially after the death of his wife five years ago. Rubbing his hands for warmth, Mizutari made his way to his favorite, a two-foot Japanese *ume,* an apricot-plum tree, with a deeply marked trunk, a sure sign of its age of one hundred twenty years.

Carefully, he turned the base, intently studying his ancient child from every artistic angle before daring to snip one tiny branch from its trunk. He turned to the sound of the greenhouse door opening.

"Granddaughter Katsuko, you were supposed to wait until I said my morning devotional to these children." He laughed, feeling proud of her desire to study the art of *bonsai* and begin the process of learning to master the concept of the upright.

"I would not disturb you, until summoned, Grandfather, but there is a telephone call for you from a place named Hallstatt, in Austria. The man speaks Japanese," she said, the surprise still in her voice. "He sounds very upset and when I pressed him for the reason for his call, he said something about 'opening the *Arizona.*'" She bowed her head, feeling her grandfather's eyes boring into her, despite his outward calm. "I did not understand—"

"He is still on the line?"

"Yes, Grandfather. He said he would wait for as long as it took to rouse you from your 'little plants.' He grew very insulting, then said it was now a matter of life and death!" The young woman bowed her head again, this time indicating she had nothing else to tell him.

"The *Arizona!*" he whispered in shock. He had not dared to utter the name of that sunken American battleship since the attack at Pearl Harbor.

He cupped his hand under his granddaughter's chin

and raised her eyes to meet his. "What is his name, Katsuko?"

"Mischa Lutz and he spoke Japanese with a very thick German accent. He is waiting now, Grandfather, and he sounds very angry, yet very frightened."

"He has reason to be frightened." The old Japanese *Samurai* closed his eyes, listening for the soothing sound of the ancient bell on Mount Baijo, just once more, before taking the call that would probably mean the end of his life.

"Grandfather, may I ask you if the *Hatsukaze* is protected well enough in the cove?"

Toshiyuki jerked his head, shocked at the insight and understanding this young woman possessed. She knew him better than he knew himself.

"I don't know, but we will guard the old royal yacht with our lives. I will not break that part of the pledge to the emperor." He glanced at Katsuko, watching the fear claw itself deeply into her beautiful young face. "Your perceptions are strong, Katsuko, but remember —" He bowed his head as the final distant chime of the bell rang gently in his ears.

"Remember what, Grandfather?"

Toshiyuki let the notion and thought dance through his mind for a while, before saying it aloud and giving it life. "For the *Samurai,* and you are *Samurai* blood, Katsuko, there are no elaborations, we only aim our sword at the true nature of things. There are no ceremonies, no rewards. The prize of *Samurai* is essentially personal. The end point is the beginning and the greatest virtue is simplicity."

This time he smiled at the fear still dancing behind her eyes. "*Ai-Uchi.* We will cut the opponent, just as he cuts us, but first we treat this enemy as a formal guest in our home. Now I will take the phone call, Katsuko, but we will never let him see our true spirit, or our intentions."

Nineteen

Bogged down in the morning traffic crunch on the Bayshore Freeway, north, it took the blue cab an hour to reach a downtown parking area behind the San Francisco Tennis Club on Brannan and Fourth streets, in the shadow of the ancient brooding China Basin.

"Okay, okay," the dark-skinned cabbie chanted over and over, hopefully watching Spain's face in the rearview mirror. "I get you here to Mission District, now you go, huh?"

Without answering, Spain surveyed the upscale tennis club surrounded by shabby, antediluvian clapboard row houses, on old narrow streets that had survived the Gold Rush and the quake and fire of 1906.

"Lean your head back, man," Spain hissed, the darkness rising in his voice.

"Don't kill! Please, God, don't kill! Small boys," the cabbie pleaded in choked phrases, his mouth rasping like a leaky bellows.

"Lean back, damn it!"

The cabbie tentatively laid his head on the seat, faint whimpering sounds evaporating from his mouth.

Quickly, Spain moved forward, grasping the man's sternalmastoid muscle from behind, then quickly found the weakness in his neck, jamming his thumb in the vital pressure point just beneath the carotid artery. The cabbie expelled a sharp gasp, like a dying balloon, then passed out into a thick blackness.

"Oh my God! Benny, did you kill him?"

"No, I just put him to sleep for the next fifteen or twenty minutes." Spain tossed a twenty-dollar bill next to the cabbie on the front seat. "Maybe he won't even call the cops so they can begin to trace where the hell we're going. But at least we'll have a few minutes. He turned to Harumi and tenderly touched her face. "You're the expert on San Francisco from your Cal days, what now? We need money, food, clothes, a car, and a helluva lot of luck while dodging San Francisco's finest. Other than that, we're fine." He laughed.

"How are we going to rent a car, with everyone looking for us?" Harumi slammed the cab door on her side and walked around to meet Spain. "We're computer fodder right now!"

"We're not going to." Absently, he appraised the filthy street, scowling at the grungy environment, then his eyes finally settled on the parking lot of the tennis club.

"Stay here, Harumi, I'll be right back."

"The hell with you, sport!" she snarled. "I'm not going to be some wino's lunch today!"

Casually they glided past the security booth of the tennis club, waving at the guard, who was distracted by a personal telephone conversation. "Great security," Spain mumbled. Once inside the confines of the club, they ambled slowly down into the parking structure, walking the rows of new and late-model Porsches, Mercedes, and BMWs.

"Mind telling me what you're looking for? My God," she said bitterly, "Rome's burning and you're fiddling!"

"Ahah, whatever you —" Suddenly, he stopped in front of a dirty black, five-year-old Ford Bronco. "This will do fine." Satisfied, he ducked between the parked cars, gently rocking the body of the four-wheel drive vehicle, to see if it was wired. Holding his breath, Spain waited for the alarm, then after ten seconds laughed in his throat. Reaching around, he tried the door. It wasn't even locked! Spain jumped up and inside and within ten seconds, he found the ignition wires from the engine and the starter, then twisted them tightly together, closing the circuit. With a deafening roar, the V-8 engine burst into life.

Fifteen minutes later, with the gas tank registering one-quarter, they passed the Moscone Convention Center and crossed Market Street, the lifeline of San Francisco, heading to the northwest, up a steep hill on Stockton Street.

"Pull over into that parking space," Harumi commanded as light, misty rain began to spot the windshield. She checked her watch. It was close to eleven. "I know San Francisco and how it breathes. Actually the city is very small. We have to wait for dark, another six hours, before we make another move, especially with a stolen car. I've got an idea where we can wait it out."

Spain raised an eyebrow. "It doesn't take long to develop the criminal mind." He smiled sadly at her through his fatigue. "So much for your highbrow academics. It doesn't take long to fall into the sewer. Well, Al Capone, where to?"

"Just make a left at the corner of Bush and head west until just before we get to Golden Gate Park."

Spain swung left into Bush Street and inched his way in heavy traffic west, slowly crossing Leavenworth and then Van Ness.

"What went wrong, Benny?" Harumi rubbed her hands through her hair, forcing herself to relax, as best she could. "Two weeks ago our lives were sane."

"That was my line, lady! Life was just fine in the slow lane. Now, thanks to the *Arizona*, we're what's called high profile and every damn cop and killer wants a piece of us!"

"Those papers, the whole Pearl Harbor business and all the killings—"

"Hopefully the mountain man in Sawyers Bar will provide some answers."

"If he's still alive, Ben."

"Well, that's a pleasant thought."

"Make a left up there at Divisadero, when you cross Alamo Square, then slow down. It's been awhile, but I'm sure it's still here." The mist increased into a spring torrent as Harumi searched the old but neat neighborhood, through the thumping arc of the Bronco's wiper blades.

"This Sawyers Bar mountain man has to be alive," Spain uttered. "He probably has great genes, eats cold soup, has humble habits, and very tame dreams."

"There, Ben! Turn right here into the lot! It's perfect."

Spain stared at the blue and white sign:

CALIFORNIA DEPARTMENT OF MOTOR VEHICLES

"You out of your mind, Harumi!" Then he thought about it as he turned and pulled into a spot in the sparsely filled lot. "Fact is, it's brilliant." He laughed. "Damn brilliant! Who'd look for a stolen car in a DMV lot." For a long time, they sat in relieved silence, listening to the heavy rain pound against the roof of the four-wheel drive.

"Hungry?" Spain reached into his wallet to check his cash.

"A little. Just tired."

"That's natural. Fear does that. Ah, I want you to do me a favor. When we passed Alamo Square, I saw a small beauty shop on the corner."

"So?"

"So, I want you to get your hair cut, curled or whatever it takes."

"What?" Her voice rose to an angry pitch as she glared at him. "Why?"

"Harumi," he interrupted softly, "the whole world knows what we look like. They have our photos. Remember the phone call with your father?" He took her hand, still speaking quietly. "Your hair or plastic surgery." He laughed. "I only thought that your hair—"

"Okay, Benny." She held up a hand.

"Here I've got seventy-five bucks. Will that be enough?"

"Plenty, in this neighborhood. I'll probably smell like that old beauty shop and perm solution when I get back." She laughed, stepping from the Bronco into the rain, pulling her jacket over her head.

Harumi sat in the old green operator's chair and stared at the uneven white stucco walls washed with yellow stains, while the gnarled owner and stylist worked on her hair in the empty shop.

"Glad you came to me, honey," the woman rasped, her silver-purple hair bunched around her used face. "Name's Vera. God, you women today! Look at your hair, I'll bet you've never had a perm. Well, I'll fix that, all right!" she said with determination.

"No, I don't want a perm, Vera! Just a real short cut and maybe a little frost at the tips." The iron in Harumi's voice cut the conversation short while Vera shampooed her shoulder-length hair. For what seemed an eternity, Vera held the long, sharp scissors in her hand, staring at Harumi in the mirror.

Harumi closed her eyes as she felt the first layers of hair come off, the smooth squeak of the shears tugging at her, the mint breath of the woman very close to her. Finally she opened her eyes and stared at her new look, beginning to take shape and suddenly hot tears streamed down her cheeks. Cutting her hair was cutting off her mother's values and her traditional Japanese ways. She had always been true to her mother's beliefs and her mother had always loved her long hair.

"Oh, they all do that, honey, when I first cut it off," the purple-headed woman chirped, leaning into Harumi's side. "Go have a good cry. Well, hell, we all need that. You know, the gals got to stay together!"

Harumi just gazed into the mirror, thinking of Ben and Kimmy Dubin's murder. If only she hadn't pressed Spain about the find on the *Arizona*. If only.

"—dear, how much do you want tipped and streaked?"

"Ah, I don't know, just enough to—to give me a different look." Again, Harumi closed her almond eyes, the hot tears leaking out of the corners. What had her life become, away from her beloved Hawaii, because she couldn't or wouldn't control her own damn ego! What

166

terrible process had she set in motion by pushing Benny? *"Wa dokodesuka asa?"* Harumi mumbled aloud through her tears.

"What's that mean, doll?" Vera, now popping jelly beans into her mouth from an old cigar box, had donned rubber gloves, as she worked at streaking Harumi's cropped hair.

"Ah, it's Japanese for 'where is tomorrow?' My mother always said it when she was down in the dumps." Even Harumi felt the great distance in her own voice.

"Hon, a word of advice. Want a few jelly beans? Anyway, as I was say'en, if I had your youth, good looks, and a bod like you're carry'n around, I'd be a happy little horny toad!" Then Vera broke into a uproarious laugh as she gripped Harumi's head with those rubber gloves, forcing them both to peer into the large mirror before them. The clanging of the bell above the door of the small, empty shop forced Vera to turn.

"Be with you in a sec." Vera dropped a used cotton ball to the floor, as she grimaced. "What's the law want?" she asked guardedly.

Out of the corner of her eye, Harumi watched the uniformed policeman, covered with a wet rain slicker approach the chair.

The young, suspicious patrolman looked about the musty shop before answering. Holding onto his wet night stick, the San Francisco policeman carefully inspected Harumi in the mirror, with a deep squint and a few little grunts.

"Well, there's an all-points bulletin out for a couple that we think are somewhere in the downtown area. They're armed and considered real dangerous, Mom."

"I'm not your goddamned mother!"

The even nose and pinkish features of the cop locked on Vera for just an instant, then the face and eyes relaxed into a grin. "No disrespect, ma'am." The officer touched the wet plastic cover on the bill of his cap.

"Well, you seen them in here, Officer?" Vera stopped and moved very close to the large man, refusing to give ground. "Look around if it pleases you. I can't take any more time away from my regular customer here. She deserves the best. All my customers deserve the best."

"Where are they hiding?" The cop laughed, after nosing about the shop, his eyes still uncomfortably locked on Harumi.

"Oh, a wise guy! Well, chief, if you've done your peepin'?"

The cop raised a hand, grinning with even teeth. He then pulled out a fax sheet with two photos and names. "I'll leave this on the table, just in case you see them come by." Then casually the officer walked over to Harumi and cocked his head, gaping at her blanched face in the mirror. "What's your—"

Vera, nudged him out of the way as she moved around the front of Harumi, adjusting the tissue wrappings on her bangs. "Take a hike, chief!" Vera snarled. "The fun's over, or is this a case of police harassment? Stop hustlin' this student, or I really will call a cop! San Francisco isn't even safe to walk around in anymore, because guys like you aren't doin' your job! Go find your criminals somewhere else!" Vera stood up straight, her face now flushed with rage.

"Okay, ladies. We'll find these two, don't worry. The whole world wants them!" The cop bowed stiffly, then left the shop, slamming the glass door behind him.

"Goddamn bastard! Say, you okay, hon?" Vera scrutinized Harumi's frightened face. "You look like you're gonna faint or somethin'."

"No, I'm fine," Harumi lied. "He just scared me, that's all." She closed her eyes and held her breath, trying to regain control.

"Well, that's what those street-patrol bullies do best. Can't stop the dope, or the shootings, or the gay bashings, but they sure know how to push people around!"

Harumi closed her eyes, trying to calm her roiling stomach as she put her hands on her shaking knees to keep them from banging into the sides of the chair.

"Well, that's you all right!" The words pierced Harumi with the intensity of a searing harpoon. Vera, holding the photocopy, looked up at Harumi, still afraid to move. Then Vera laughed. It was a strange laugh that came all the way from her old, soft belly.

"Relax! I don't give a damn what you've done, or they say you done. They can go fuck themselves! No damn heat's gonna roust me, dearie!" Vera patted Harumi's shoulder, talking to her in the mirror. "Did two years in Vacaville for armed robbery. Fifty-five, fifty-six. Got mixed up with a real bum. He carried a piece, they catch me and before I can convince my family I didn't do nothin', I'm in the slammer with a bunch of bull dikes and guards right out of the movie *King Kong Rapes Bambi!*"

Vera stepped back, then came around the front of Harumi, slowly examining her work atop Harumi's head. "You do what they said? Murder and such like that?" The question was hard and piercing.

"No, Vera," Harumi tried her voice, in a cracking rasp. "We didn't do any of it! I'm a teacher in Hawaii and the man in the photo is a diver for the National Parks Service. I've never done a dishonest thing in my life, until

169

this morning, Vera, and that's the truth! My God, this isn't real!"

"Well, you look like you could use a cup of java and an umbrella. You came to Vera for a good reason. It ain't no fun lambin' it. Christ, it turned my life upside down." She pulled off the gloves and gently touched Harumi's forehead. "I'll do whatever I can for you, but I know those dicks and you don't have alot of time before they come back with their howling dogs. That dumb fuzz was only the beginning!"

Harumi smiled for the first time that she could remember. A smile of affection and appreciation. *"Shibui,* Vera. *Shibui."*

"What's that mean?"

"It means you have a great appreciation for life and a wonderful, kind soul. There's no direct translation from English to Japanese that works. For your trust, I consider you a work of art."

"Well, ain't that somethin'! No one ever called me a work of art," she said laughing as if she didn't have a care in the world.

Twenty

"Glad, you're back." Spain helped her up into the front seat of the Bronco as the rain, now pushed by an icy wind blowing off the bay, created its own wet art on the DMV parking lot.

For the next few minutes, Harumi told Spain about the police, finally showing him the fax copy with their photos and descriptions. In large bold type at the bottom, the copy read:

ARMED AND CONSIDERED EXTREMELY DANGEROUS!

Spain brooded, staring straight ahead into the rain, the old fears washing over him in shuddering waves.

"Well, you haven't said anything."

Spain turned to her. "About what?"

"Thanks. I cut my hair for almost the first time in my life, into something approaching a waitress cut, then I streak it and—"

"It looks, ah, different, Harumi. That's what I wanted, I guess," he mumbled, staring down at the sheet again. "What the hell is this? Damn it! What the fuck does Gregori want that we have? A goddamn skull and some worthless papers?" He turned to Harumi. "We're gonna die and not even know why?"

"The hell we are, sailor boy!" A resolve suddenly gripped her. "Benny, when the cop was in the beauty shop, ready to break my skull with his night stick, while raping me with his eyes, I was never so frightened, but now I've had time to think about it."

Spain pushed out a long breath, shoving himself down in the seat, not wanting to hear her amateur dribble. What the hell did she know about death and killing? What did she really know about long-term fear that turned your stomach to hundred-proof bile and your knees to decayed jelly?

"Did you hear me, Ben?" she said softly. "We have nothing to lose, so let's go find out why they want to kill us. Let's solve it and you know what else?" Now Harumi was talking rapidly, jumping over subjects like she always did, when she was frightened and her mind outraced her mouth.

"Know, what?" she asked as Spain rolled his eyes. "I don't just think it's your Black Ghost alone! This is all too organized for one man, an outcast, disabled, Russian killer at that."

"Don't underestimate his resources, Harumi! Don't ever do that!" Spain said angrily. He hesitated, then grunted. She had brought him back from his dark abyss. She always did.

"Now, let's get organized," he heard her say as he shook his head, almost forgetting to tell her his good news.

"Let's get a report, mister, or whatever they say in the navy!" She reached over and brushed his lips. "Together we have great strength, my love. No one can beat us. Soon we'll be home in Kahala with our Mollie," she whispered, gently biting at the tip of his ear, the fear still in her throat.

"Benny, you've done this tracking business before. What do we have to do to elude the police, get to Sawyers Bar, and get on with saving our lives?"

"Jesus! We're doing it, half assed, but doing it." He laughed darkly, looking into her deep eyes. "After you left to get your haircut, I went through the Bronco and didn't find much, except for this." He held up a wad of twenty-dollar bills, with a sheepish grin. "I found it under the seat, along with a few tools. A little emergency stuff, I guess."

"How much?"

"Two hundred, which gives us a little working capital." Spain looked out at the rain still coming down in sheets. "I hate to do this, but we're going to have to put that umbrella of yours to work."

"Why?"

"You'll see. The rain's a great cover right now." Then Spain opened the door, taking only the newly found screwdriver. They began to walk slowly in the rain, checking out all the cars that remained on the DMV lot.

"It'd be nice if you told me what we're looking for!" Harumi shouted, the rain pelting the top of her umbrella.

"A new license plate. We take that Bronco out of here, we'll be meat within half an hour." Grunting, Spain led her over the half-acre parking lot, the rain soaking them both to the skin, until finally stopping before a station wagon, near the entrance.

"That's what we want," Spain announced. He pointed

173

down at the powder blue Oregon license. Quickly he bent down to unscrew the front plate, at one point going flat to his belly to unthread the bolts.

"Hurry, Benny! There's a guard coming over here!"

"Damn it!" The screwdriver slipped from Spain's wet hands, the plate no more than two turns away from dropping free. Spain glanced up, his eyes locking onto the .38 service revolver attached to the thick leather duty belt of the guard. Turning slightly, he knew the man would be on him in a matter of seconds and he was ready, with that old helpless feeling in the pit of his stomach. Carefully, he rose to a crouch, gripping the screwdriver as a commando knife. If he had to, he would stick the knife into the man. It was Nicaragua and he was out of choices.

"I'll do the talking," he whispered up to Harumi, who probably wasn't listening anyway. Damn it! he thought. Please don't say anything. Suddenly, the cop, a very large state policeman was on them. He was extremely light on his feet, meaning he was in great physical shape.

Then he squatted, staring into Spain's face. For an instant, Ben turned his body, gripping the screwdriver in just the right way, so when he turned, he could thrust into the cop with one lethal movement. Nothing would be telegraphed.

"Damn nasty weather!" the officer shouted above the rain.

Spain tensed, holding his breath, not wanting to smell the man after he was stabbed and bleeding. "Yeah, I'm trying to—"

"I can see the problem," the policeman smiled. "I try to help folks get the old plates off, if they seem to be having a problem. This registration business can be difficult." Then he put his large fingers behind the last bolt and held the nut. "Now try your screwdriver, friend," the voice said helpfully.

Spain held both hands on the tool to keep from shaking to pieces, then rotated the final two turns, the tin plate finally dropping harmlessly to the wet blacktop with a dull clank.

Spain and the guard rose to their feet together, the rain still pouring down. "Thanks for your help," Ben offered meagerly. "I can manage the back plate myself."

"Be certain you bring both plates inside to change the registration. Those bureaucratic jockies inside won't give you California plates, unless you give them both plates in return." The guard shrugged, squeezed Spain on the shoulder, started to move away, then turned again and stopped. "Oh, by the way, good luck in California. Not often we get Oregon people coming south. Guess you brought the rain with you. Everyone wants to get the hell out and live up with the trees, fresh air, and the ducks." Then he was gone, his waist-level slate raincoat and the .38 fading as the low-slung building swallowed him up.

"God, that was close!" Harumi grabbed onto Ben.

Five minutes later, the Oregon plate was on the rear of the Bronco, with the California plates tucked neatly into the large glove compartment.

"What about the front license?" Harumi asked, climbing in.

"Don't really need a front plate, so the Oregon guy won't even say anything about it missing, unless he's registering today, and we won't have a problem."

"I think we should get off the lot, before Captain America decides to come back!" Harumi added. "We need to sleep, Ben. We can't fight all this," she said, moving her long fingers in the air. "We're wet, freezing, and tired, and I need a place to work on you."

"Meaning?"

"Meaning, I've got some hair dye for you. Let's get rid of your gray and you can start to grow a mustache. I think I'll like that."

Spain started to protest, but Harumi only smiled. "Good for the female, good for the male, huh, Spain? There's two people on that wanted sheet, not just me."

"Okay. Now what about this place you have for us to stay? What do you know about it?"

By early afternoon, with Vera's help, they were registered at the Welsh House, a curious little Victorian cottage hotel across from the Cable Car Museum, on Mason, in the heart of Chinatown. But the price wasn't cheap, taking all of their cash for a small but comfortable room with a view down the steep hill to the bay.

Harumi turned over and finally closed her eyes, listening to the clanging bells of the open cable cars, sliding down Mason toward Fisherman's Wharf, while a foghorn moaned a sympathetic beat. From the small window in the room she could see Alcatraz Island off in the mist deep in the bay, the massive fortress walls of the abandoned prison burnished silver in the deep mist. She guessed the rain had let up, otherwise the ancient cable cars wouldn't be allowed to make their runs up and down the steep hills, precarious enough for loyal riders and tourists, even when it was dry.

For a time she listened to Ben's deep rhythmic breathing as he slept next to her in the small double bed. Then slowly she allowed herself to cuddle into his warmth. Although deeply troubled, it was the first time she'd felt safe since the evening Ben had brought home the yellow pouch. Now all that she had worked for at the University of Hawaii was in jeopardy.

She knew that a short, shallow note, addressed to the department chairman before they left the Big Island, exercising an emergency family leave, wouldn't carry much weight. The old wasp bastard had never wanted to grant her tenure to begin with and now she was just feeding his male insecurity. A woman breaking new ground in a man's manure pit wasn't all it was cracked up to be. More than anything, it was wearing and relentless. Her teaching life had really never been normal as she often went overboard to prove her superiority with those other six male drolls, who taught from yellowed notes and had forgotten the true excitement of real teaching and historic research.

Harumi laughed darkly at the thought of the beast within her, fighting to get out; wanting to solve this mystery of Fred Noonan's skull found aboard the *Arizona*. Ben had no idea of the significance or links involved. God, she couldn't even begin to conceive of the scenario that must have taken place. Suddenly, she shivered at the thought that her fantasy of a wondrous discovery, to show those bastards what a qualified woman could do, had become a hideous nightmare.

"Who's winning?" she heard Ben say as he turned over.

"Was I talking out loud again?"

"Ah, huh. Listen, Harumi, I need to tell you something, but I need to have it penetrate, without you being defensive, so just drop your shield for a second. I mean, I know what you've been up against."

"No, you don't! You're not a woman!" She felt

her voice rise, but Spain wasn't the enemy.

She reached over and kissed Spain, his muscular hardness and special scent forcing her stomach to quiver. "I'm sorry, Benny. You've never treated me as anything but an equal and that's all I've ever wanted."

"Can I say something? Stop trying to smother me with your mouth!"

"Yes," she offered, the edge in her voice gone.

"If you want us both to survive, you have to really listen to me." He held up a hand, knowing she was about to interrupt. "Killing and hunting is a practiced business. Something you don't know a damn thing about! Unfortunately, I do. Whoever wants us, is close. I can feel it and that intuition has kept me alive for many years, in all the cruddy places of the world, from the river ooze of North Vietnam and Nicaragua to the sewers of Los Angeles. We have to work as a team and you have to trust me, damn it! Stop trying to one up me, to prove you're better. You are, damn it!" Spain felt the anger boil up in his throat.

"The next few weeks are going to be the worst of your life, you hope."

"I don't understand?"

"It's simple, Harumi. A real pro wants us dead. If it's bad, it means you're alive. We don't have squat for resources to survive right now. We're going to have to live like hunted animals just to see the sun rise. Right now, I've got exactly ten bucks left, a stolen car, and a partner who thinks she can outthink our enemy. It's a toxic mix! It won't happen, my dear! He wants us dead! There's a million ways to kill and we don't know what direction it's going to even come from, let alone when! Do you understand what I'm saying!"

Harumi nodded sadly.

"You've got to learn to live with this fear."

"Yeah, like you, in a bottle!" she lashed out. Then she looked over at Spain with his eyes closed, the pain arcing like an electric charge through his face.

"Damn it, Ben, I'm sorry. Yes, I'm scared. Yes, I don't want to live like this and I don't know if I can do it for the next four minutes, let alone the next few months! I'm sick with worry about my father and Mollie!"

"I know that, Harumi. I know. But you are right! To survive, we've got to go underground and find a way to solve this thing."

Now she was holding him tightly, talking into his rough cheek. "I'll try, damn it. I'll try. I'm so scared, Benny."

"So am I, Harumi, and it's okay. The fear will keep us going." He tried to smile, then he felt her long, delicate fingers begin to work on his chest.

"I need you, Spain. I need you now!"

Slowly at first, then with more force, she moved over his nakedness with a smooth, natural precision, working him until the reality of the moment was light years away.

Easily, Spain lifted Harumi's thighs, rousing her large dark aureole and nipples into the coolness of the San Francisco afternoon. For a long time, Spain kneaded her body and her wetness until her writhing told him she was ready. Slowly, ever so slowly he entered her as if for the last time, forcing her to respond to him in a way that Spain had never known; their life currents streaming between them.

Harumi met his sharp movements with her own, telling him in the only way she could that she loved him and trusted him like no other. Then in the white hot distance,

179

she felt him and knew they would climax as one. If she couldn't tell the man, she would show him how she felt.

Later, Harumi laid her head on his chest. "If we do live through all this, I want us to have a child together. I didn't think I could ever say that." She laughed freely and Spain liked that. "I wanted it now, but —" her voice trailed away as she emotionally descended into that back bedroom on Mason, the opaque light of day finally giving way to a clear spring evening.

"We start tonight, Harumi."

"With what?" There was a wariness in her voice.

"I noticed a sports and gun shop a block away on Clay Street." He drew a deep breath, waiting.

"So?"

"So, tonight, we're going to rob it," Ben stated matter of factly. "I need a gun and we need clothes for the mountains. We're starting from scratch."

Harumi closed her eyes and swallowed, knowing that Spain was right and that now she wanted to vomit.

"If we have a little luck, we can get what we need and be on our way to meet the Sawyers Bar connection in two hours."

"And if we don't have any luck?"

"We could get killed and then it won't matter."

Twenty-one

Spain checked his watch in the fog, then glanced up, barely making out the vague, illuminated presence of Coit Tower off to the north atop Telegraph Hill. One more time, he slowly ambled past the brightly lighted Chinese Recreation Center on Clay. Quickly he turned the corner onto Powell, just as the last cable car, with only two passengers, glided by on its way down to the bay, before heading for the barn. Swirling thick fingers of fog had created their own white silence and surreal mask and Spain was grateful for the shred of cover. Somehow the fog had softened the hard edges of his task.

Again he checked his watch. 11:30. Harumi would be in position now with the Bronco. Instinctively, he brushed his left hip, feeling for his old Czech pistol, just as a foghorn brayed its agonizing plea from out in the bay. Then he remembered and froze, feeling that special tightness cramp his belly, as he thought about the locker at Hilo Airport, where he had been forced to stow the gun for safekeeping.

At 11:35 P.M., the same green and white police cruiser that he had been watching for the past hour sailed past, this time at speed. The cop inside was getting tired as Spain marked his speed at about thirty. It should have been ten miles per hour if he had wanted to really see anything, but the wet Chinatown streets were empty and quiet and the cop inside the warmth of the car didn't want to know; at least not tonight.

One last time Spain checked his meager arsenal — all the tools from the Bronco. The screwdriver, small flashlight, a pair of large wire-cutter pliers that he covered with black electrical tape, and a small hacksaw, with a questionable blade.

Walking past Robbie's Gun and Sport Shop on Clay, Spain looked through the steel bars protecting the large plate-glass window, into the shop's interior. Atop a file cabinet, a small night light glowed its amber warmth as a small beacon for his survival. During the pass, he noted the old-fashioned hard wire system laminated to the bottom of the window. At least it wasn't radio frequency. If he tripped a hot wire, the whole damn Chinese neighborhood would be awakened, as well as the police. Slipping into the narrow alley, choked with old dirty brick buildings and the stench of garbage, Spain found the main electric junction box behind Robbie's, then traced the three thick electric power cables back to where they started their climb up to the utility pole. A sharp cough brought him up short as he glanced up at a small window across the alley, where someone had just pulled down an old stained shade. For a moment he crossed his arms to ease the trembling in his hands.

"Come on, killer," he taunted himself in a whisper, "get it on! Time to rock and roll!" At least Harumi wasn't involved. If something happened, she would have some kind of a chance, if she could make it to L.A. with the name of an old and trusted friend that he had given her. But only if he didn't come back in the next half hour. Then she would know he wasn't coming back. Maybe she'd be better off if he didn't make it.

In the dim light, he gingerly separated the three cables; if they touched, he'd fry, taking all that direct 220-volt electrical current into his hands. Holding his breath, he gripped the cutters around the first cable, closed his eyes and snapped down, waiting for the lethal bolt of current, but nothing happened. Pushing his heartbeat down his throat, Spain slowly curled the cable back, to make certain it didn't come in contact with the other two, then proceeded to cut through the remaining links, killing all power to the narrow two-story building. The alarm was now deactivated, he hoped.

Moving quickly now with the screwdriver, he pried off the rotted termite-infested jamb, holding the tin-sheathed back door, then quickly gained entry into the building. Sitting on the old hardwood floor, exhausted, Spain took a deep breath, then hooded the flashlight over his watch. Christ, it had taken fifteen minutes! Harumi would leave if he didn't meet her by midnight! She had promised him!

"Okay, hotshot," he prodded himself, "get off the fucking floor and do it!" Moving uncertainly, he found the glass case displaying a variety of automatic pistols. Moving down the aisle, he spotted an ancient Colt .45-caliber automatic. The damn thing looked clean, but must have been fifty years old. Carefully, he pried off the lock behind the case and lifted out the two-pound pistol. Looking in the old wooden drawers behind the case, he found three boxes of illegal, Teflon-coated ammunition designed to easily penetrate bulletproof vests.

"I don't feel so damn bad, you bastard!" Spain hissed. "You sell this shit to cop killers!" Quickly stuffing the boxes into his jacket pocket, he played the narrow beam around the area, looking for something he knew was close. In a moment, he found a small drawer, pulled it open, revealing five long and short silencers. "I knew it! A real charmer, this merchant and bastion of the community, with a large gold San Francisco Chamber of Commerce sticker emblazoned on his front window. Fuck you, cop killer!" he hissed again. The shells he'd taken were probably hot-loaded.

Spain then found the cash register behind a waist-high wall. "Just make sure I get fifty bucks," he prayed aloud. "We need gas and some food money —" Forcing open the cash drawer, Spain found a hundred and twenty in small bills and two white bags of powder that he guessed were heroine, probably taken in by the merchant for guns and hot shells.

Ten minutes later, Spain carried a duffle bag stuffed with warm hunting clothes, then reached for the back doorknob.

"Take it easy, mista. You ain't goin' nowheres!" Spain felt his knees go weak as he slowly turned to find a large security guard standing over him, in the darkness, with his gun drawn. The man was obviously nervous, continually shifting his body from side to side.

"Okay, put it all down and just take it easy," the guard commanded. "I'll shoot you, if you don't!"

Whirling quickly, Spain brought his foot up into the man's crotch, and knew that the sound of air gushing from the man's lungs meant he had scored a bull's-eye. As the guard began to slump, Spain grabbed for the gun with his left hand, then brought the flashlight with the other hand down on the man's head with a savage crack. The guard was out before he hit the floor, probably badly hurt, with blood spurting from the wound, but that couldn't be helped as Spain closed the door behind him, a cold panic strangling him. He was drowning, again inside the *Arizona,* trapped with all that ancient death.

Blindly, Spain ran down the alley heading for the spot where Harumi was supposed to be. Half a block of running uphill on Powell left him breathless with the duffle bag, then he finally saw the dim shape of the Bronco ahead in the fog.

"Hurry!" he screamed, out of breath. "Get the hell out! Just drive! I think I killed a guard back at the store!"

He glanced sideways at Harumi as she nodded stiffly, putting the Bronco into gear, heading for Highway 80, and east to the Oakland Bay Bridge.

Twenty-two

Capt. Gregori Ovsyannikov, late of the 318th Motorized Infantry Division, 13th Carpathian Army, slid silently into the richly brocade cardinal and gold wing chair in the far corner of the ornate lobby of the Palace Hotel in downtown San Francisco carefully balancing a small glass in his hand. For a long time he stared at the telephone sitting on the small green marble table, waiting for the hotel operator to complete the connection with the Schlosshotel Klessheim in Salzburg, Austria.

Slowly Gregori sipped a strong, opaque liquid, slivovitz, a potent Austrian brandy distilled from plums. For a moment he stared at the immense high-domed stained-glass ceiling inside the dining room, across from the lobby of the hotel, opened in 1909, at the height of the American Victorian movement.

As the slivovitz burned his throat in a strong, pleasurable way, Gregori reviewed his progress since arriving at the Market Street hotel. He knew from studying Spain's movements that a certain panic had set in. He was certain that Spain and the woman he was traveling with, had left Hawaii without much of anything and the pressure was taking its toll. Another pull of slivovitz from the small crystal glass turned his thoughts to Spain's path. Suddenly, he frowned without realizing it, then shivered as his mind drifted to visual image of Spain. Something painful and confusing bothered him that he couldn't touch. Some dark and ultimately sinister element as he inadvertently thought of Spain, not as an enemy, but as the man who had long ago cared enough to save his life. That was the soft and brittle aspect of this hunt that Gregori couldn't resolve and it was unsettling. A middle ground between light and shadow that wasn't clean and simple and Ovsyannikov didn't like it.

Three short rings of the phone brought him to the moment as he reached for the receiver. "Mister Syann, your party from Salzburg whom you requested is on the line."

"Thank you, operator. Hello."

"Kahk pagoda sivodnya, Gregori?"

"The weather is fine today," Gregori responded, with obvious irritation. "You don't have to speak to me in Russian, especially with a Spanish accent! English is preferable and we don't need code. No one is tapping this line Minister Castillo Soria. We can speak in the clear."

"So you say, Comrade," she snapped in a thick Cuban accent.

"Don't call me Comrade, damn it! This is an international line and the American government has better things to do than listen to a few old moth-eaten communists talk treason, Minister!" He was growing angrier by the moment. This Cuban monster, who he was ordered to report to as a surrogate midwife to the operation, made him sick. Even her officious voice, from halfway around the world in Austria, sounded like a broken promise.

"Besides," he said deliberately, "no one knows I'm here—"

"Your gifts are that profound, ah, Captain?"

"What do you want, Minister?" he cut her short.

"How close are you?" she pressed coldly.

"This operation can't be pushed. I'm following and being patient." Gregori heard his voice break slightly, then he downed the last of the plum brandy, trying to drown the hatred he felt for this Cuban man-eater. "I'm following the instructions of my control, Herr Lutz."

Minister Soria laughed at him bitterly. "There are no more controls, Captain! There is only the new order, whatever that is, and the need for the gold to survive."

Gregori shivered at the mention of the gold. He had tried to face this operation without thinking about its consequences, thinking only of Spain and the abstraction of what it meant. Channeling his energies only to the hunt and the prospect of matching wits with Spain as a contest of skill.

"—did you hear me, Captain?" The irritating voice was driving at him again. "Don't wait any longer. Send in your team and finish this man Spain off! We'll pick up the trail. You've done a great deal and the remainder should be well within our reach now."

"Only Herr Lutz can make that decision," Ovsyannikov insisted. "I must hear it from him, if there is to be a change!"

Gregori shifted the phone to his other ear, then rotated his large, experienced black eyes around the nearly empty lobby to be certain no one was within earshot. "Thus far I have been forced to kill three times, to stay close to Spain! The poor bastards didn't even know why they died! Now you want him dead!" He worked to keep the seething hate in his voice from rising above the high-backed chair.

"You will do what is expected and what is expedient! Is that clear, Captain? Your compensation will be great. Do you have any complaints about your percentage?"

"No, Minister." Gregori dropped his chin to his chest, allowing the phone to rest on his shoulder, wishing he could choke her with his bare hands.

"Captain, are you still there?" He listened to her voice evaporate into the high-ceilinged lobby.

"Yes," he said quietly.

"Good. It is three in the morning now in Austria and at first light, we will travel a narrow, icy road up into the forbidding Salzkammergut region to visit with your Herr Lutz at his isolated hideaway in Hallstatt, a place you know well." Then she laughed darkly. "So much for the power of his notorious Hauptverwaltung Aufkla-rung, the East German State Security, once the Berlin Wall came crashing down. Now he hides like a rabbit in the high forest at ten thousand feet!"

Gregori sighed, waiting for the Cuban to finish her usual dogmatic prattle, always pretending that her brother-in-law, Castro, was on the other end of the line. "What do you mean, 'we,' Minister?" Gregori probed.

"My assistant, Sed Cruz, of course. I thought you knew?"

"Yes, of course." Gregori recovered his even meter.

"In any event, Captain, by the end of the day, we will have arrived at our final operative timetable. Be certain you find out as many details as possible. Remember, the elimination of this Spain will be at the top of my agenda with Herr Lutz."

"You already said that," Gregori muttered flatly.

"Oh, by the way, what is your evaluation of Spain's current condition? Herr Lutz will ask."

Across half a world, Senora Hilda Castillo Soria heard Gregori Ovsyannikov sigh with obvious pain.

"I believe he is out there feeling very much alone."

"Good. That is important," she replied. "That will make it easier."

"Right now, Spain has the feeling he can't come in and that there's no place for him, just like me."

"Perdon?"

"In the new order of things there isn't a place for people like Spain and me, Minister. People like you don't need us anymore." His voice was suddenly dark and tired. "But you know that, don't you, Minister? This is a Faustian bargain for me. I'm trading the life of an old fellow warrior for my soul and a bag of fucking gold! But God Almighty, Minister, I didn't know Spain was involved in the beginning!"

"What matters, Captain, is that as long as you do the job you were thoroughly trained for, all will be well. But we must hurry! There's more here than you could possibly realize. The fate of nations rests with you." The last statement was a test.

"Minister, what's at stake are billions! This—this treasure has remained hidden for half a century. We must unravel this slowly, a layer of old cloth at a time, otherwise it will tear and we will end up with nothing."

"Will you do your duty, Captain?" she repeated slowly.

"Yes, damn it! I will do my job," he snapped menacingly. "I've done it too long and I'm too frightened to die poor and I want to leave something to my ex-wife and son, who have been exiled from my life! Just know that your heroic, melodramatic mumblings don't mean a damn thing to me!"

"As you wish." Now the Cuban woman's voice was laughing again. "We will be in touch, Comrade Captain. I will send regards to Herr Lutz." Then the line went dead.

Ovsyannikov sat on the edge of the brass bed, carefully fitting the prosthesis to the fleshy stump that was once his right leg. Something else besides Spain was troubling him as he finally pulled up his cotton bush pants. The hot shower had left him refreshed but still mentally drained. It was something that Senora Soria had said, but what? For a long time he let his mind drift, fitting all the pieces together as he finished dressing. He peered out of the window at the fog-bound night, his mind now somewhere in the Alps, visualizing the final meeting between Minister Soria and former East German Lt. Gen. Markus "Mischa" Lutz, head of the HVA, the internal killing arm for the Soviets when they roamed Germany east of the Brandenburg Gate.

Lutz was a complex man, no doubt, but he had taken in Ovsyannikov, when Spain had dropped him on Herr Lutz's doorstep in Pankov, East Berlin, so many years before. Lutz had slowly nursed him back to health, given him back his dignity and seen to it that the murder charges against him, for the killing in the Crimea, had been dropped. Suddenly, Herr Lutz had given him back his life and his freedom, from a Soviet firing squad.

"But what about Spain?" he heard himself mutter aloud, staring into the large bathroom mirror at this dark, brooding, still strikingly handsome face. Well, at least all debts had been paid. "Damn, why Spain." He shook his head as he clinically reviewed Spain's progress since arriving in San Francisco. Putting the police onto him had been easy, as had been the interrogation of the old woman at the corner beauty shop. He wasn't certain, but he felt that the gun-shop robbery last night and the beating of the security guard had been Spain's work.

Gregori stuck out his tongue at the older image staring at him in the mirror, then laughed somberly. "That's what I would do, Benjamin. I would need a gun, ammunition, and mountain clothes, if I was running for my life." Then the broad smile soured as he thought about killing Spain.

Twenty-three

Through the night and early morning hours, they pushed north through the wine country of Sonoma and Mendocino, the rolling vine-covered lowlands throwing off frightening spider shapes in the faint moonlight. Reluctantly, the vineyards finally gave way to a lone colony of giant two-thousand-year-old sequoia redwoods, somehow holding firm in the sandy soil of the jagged Coast Mountain range that collapsed precariously into the Pacific along the desolate northern Humboldt coast.

Spain stared blankly out the window as the sun finally pushed its heatless light over a vast, moving, green carpet of firs and pines. Slowing at the salmon fishing hamlet of Arcada, Harumi pulled the Bronco into the gravel parking lot of Erik & Andrew's Motel Diner, just off Highway 101.

"Benny, we've come more than three hundred fifty miles and I can't go any farther. I'm exhausted! I can't even see anymore. We need to eat something and get some sleep. How about it?"

She turned and touched his angular nose, studying his

silence and an emptiness in his face she had never seen before. Since leaving San Francisco, Spain had hardly spoken, grunting at Harumi's banter, nervously rubbing his sprouting mustache, while staring for long periods into the passenger side rearview mirror.

"It's all right, Ben," she said softly. "Maybe you didn't kill that man."

Spain shook his head, his eyes peering into the uncut, early morning light. Finally he whispered, "I turned his head into Jell-O. I swore I'd never hurt anyone, again." He turned to Harumi, tears streaming down his face.

"I, I'm coming unglued. I'm back on the fucking streets of L.A.! I've got the warm, sticky blood of all those young kids in Nam on my hands, trying at the same time to hold onto a brown paper bag, filled with rotgut wine. I don't know where the hell I am! I'm out here running on empty, damn it! My horizon's collapsed. Nam, Nicaragua—"

"You're with me!" Harumi said firmly, turning his face to her. "We're going to be fine, Spain. You told me before that the Russian, this Black Ghost is working us. We can't let him do that anymore! First we eat and sleep, okay?" She heard her own voice crack.

"Hi," came a high cheery voice as they entered the old truck stop diner. For a moment, they looked around the fifties-style interior, with a row of wooden booths next to the large window, highlighting an old-fashioned Bakelite counter, with a long row of aluminum swivel stools topped with red leatherette seats. The diner was immaculate. A real time warp, with a few customers sprinkled about the room. An old Wurlitzer jukebox adorned with bulbous orange-red plastic fenders moaned softly with the 1950s hit "Smoke Gets In Your Eyes," by the Platters.

194

"What can I get you?" came the happy voice again.

Harumi searched the face of a pixie, with gleaming brown eyes and a smile as inviting and strong as the coffee. The pixie waitress, with a short apron wrapped around the firm body of a dancer, floated back around the counter and dropped an open menu before them in one swirling motion.

"Let's see, this morning, the special is the logger's feast—"

"It's the same every morning, Rona," came a deep laughing voice from across the diner.

"Ha, ha, ha!" Rona put her hands on her hips and cocked her attractive head. "Don't pay any attention to them. Coffee?" The waitress continued to chatter incessantly as she poured coffee and placed the orders with the cook.

"Ah, we also need a room," Harumi finally squeezed in.

"Oh, sure." Now the brown eyes narrowed, for just an instant, evaluating the couple in front of her. A quick approving nod, then she added, "looks like you could use the big suite, no extra charge. I mean, it's got a fireplace, pine paneling, the works. Name's Rona Kaufman," she added. "My husband does the cooking and runs the motel, next door. We're originally from Los Angeles."

Quickly she turned and shouted into the opening between the kitchen and counter. "Jack, got a couple who looks like they could use a room right after I feed them. Give them the big suite." She turned and grinned. "We're kinda informal around here. How long you gonna be and where are you from?" Rona machine gunned the questions.

Harumi held up a hand just as Rona placed two full

plates stuffed with large thick steaks, fried eggs, and hash browns on the Bakelite counter.

"Just today and tonight. We're on our way—"

"We're on our way north to Gold Beach," Spain interrupted, trying his best to look and sound civilized. Watching the question in her eyes, Spain continued. "I'm from Oregon. Coos Bay. Also spent alot of time in Eugene."

"That so. Well, that explains your Oregon license." Then Rona's smile rippled across the counter. "Don't like it much, north of here. It rain's enough here. Up there, everyone grows web feet in the water. Besides, the logging business is worse than here. Anyway, when you're finished, Jackie will register you and take you up to your room." Then she was gone, zeroing in on another incoming customer.

Hours later, Harumi and Spain lay on the thickly carpeted floor, staring into a fire blazing in the huge, smooth-rocked fireplace, the crackling embers popping with a special, life-giving cadence. "Feel better, Benny? It's almost dinner time. You must have slept for eight hours." She rested her chin on his bare chest, watching the flames dance over and through the split logs.

"I feel like we're home in Kahala, right now, with Mollie roaming around and eating the hibiscus in the backyard in the shadow of Koko Head."

"Well it's not, damn it." Spain's eyes were transfixed on the fire as he gently cupped Harumi's breast in his hand. "Gregori Ovsyannikov has us in his sights. I can feel it in my bones. The bastard knows every move we make."

"Why do you say that, Benny?"

"Because we know each other. You can't carry each other wounded and half dead across half a world and not climb into the other guy's skin, with the other guy's blood all over your back." He smiled philosophically. "I don't know if he knows about your father's contact in Sawyers Bar, but he won't be far behind. He's a real hook-and-ladder guy."

"A what?"

"It means Ovsyannikov can do it all, even dragging a wooden leg behind him."

"You sound very sad, Benny."

"I've got to kill him, Harumi! This isn't a game of trivial pursuit or a dammed academic exercise. Look at the fear in my eyes." Then Spain thought about Ovsyannikov's eyes and shivered. Their blackness had a piercing quality unlike anything he had ever seen before. They were the eyes of a fierce circling bird of prey, the pupils no more than a dot in their imperious center. They were the eyes of an experienced killer who had always tracked down his quarry.

"— you're not even with me. Benny!"

"I'm sorry."

"Do you want to stay here another day, to rest?"

Spain laughed darkly. "If we did that, we'd be able to rest for eternity. We travel tonight. Hopefully, we'll have rain, fog, or hopefully no moonlight. From now on, we only travel at night, wherever this nonsense takes us."

Just at daybreak, the Bronco skidded to a halt on an obscure gravel and mud road, or at least what passed for a road, that ended at the swiftly rushing Windler Creek.

"Hang on a sec, Harumi." With the flashlight in hand, Spain carefully studied the detailed map of the Klamath National Forest. With a pencil in his mouth, he looked out the window to the west. Slowly, he looked up at a sharp granite pinnacle rising two thousand feet above the forest floor.

"What are you looking at?"

Spain pointed out the window. "Chimney Rock. That's what I was looking for. We're only about five miles, as the crow flies, from Sawyers Bar."

"Then what?" Harumi rubbed her long fingers through her hair. "God, I'd love a hot shower right now."

Spain eyed her, raising an eyebrow. "Good luck. Right now, we're on the point. Gunfire could come at us from any direction, at anytime." Spain felt for the old Colt .45 resting in his belt.

"Head for the east very slowly now. Up ahead there's an old quarry road that will take us down to the North Fork of the Salmon River. A gravel road parallels it right into Sawyers Bar."

Slowly and with great skill, Harumi maneuvered the four-wheel drive across the deep creek, then down a steep embankment until they ran into the narrow mud road that was really an old mule pack trail. Turning farther to the east, Harumi followed the trail as it meandered along the banks of the roaring Salmon River, swollen by the melting winter runoff.

After another half mile, Spain told her to stop. "Up ahead there's supposed to be the old abandoned Red Hill gold mine, according to the map. We'll hide up there for the day and then move into Sawyers Bar tonight."

"Ben! Jesus! That's ridiculous! No one followed us here. I was careful to watch all the way. Let's just go into that little town and find Russell Witten, if he's still alive and talk to him!"

"You're out of your league here, Harumi. You helped

me before, now let me help!" he said coldly. "For once, damn it, just do what I ask, without having to have a frigging seminar about it!"

She twisted up her mouth, ready to verbally unload, when Spain cut her off. "Do you want to unravel this mystery and live to tell the world about it?"

She nodded stiffly.

"Good! Just pull up to that mine and leave the rest to me." Spain then slid the .45 out of his belt and screwed the stolen Beckny silencer into the barrel. Next he pulled the magazine clip from the bottom of the handle making certain that it still carried the full load of seven Teflon-coated shells. Carefully he checked the clip's mainspring compression, to be sure it could push the shells rapidly into the firing chamber. Then in one quick motion he rammed the magazine up into the butt of the automatic, then pulled back the steel slide stop, chambering a round.

"Be certain, Harumi, that when you pull up to the mine the Bronco is in full view of the river." Spain grunted. "Then I'll set up a perimeter and take the watch, while you rest. Then tonight, we'll move upstream into Sawyers Bar and find the house of Rosary Beads, or whatever the hell his name is." Then Spain drew Harumi to him. "Keep your expectations low. We might only find a gravestone or a bullet."

Twenty-four

"What the hell are you doing?" Harumi whispered. "This is the third building we've broken into!"

Avoiding the question, Spain slipped them into the tiny unlocked frame building with a raised wooden porch, in the hamlet of Sawyers Bar. There was a scattering of cabins, a one-room schoolhouse, a general store, and a Town Hall, all clustered in the deep palm of thick forest wilderness.

Moving cautiously in the darkness on the wood-planked flooring, Spain used his small light to finally find the cluster of old-fashioned postal boxes, with the names neatly printed in small brass windows.

"Did you hear that?" Spain doused the light, his body shielding Harumi as they listened in the darkness to a cold mountain wind rustling through a million trees. For a long time, he barely drew a breath, trying to become one with this strange environment.

"I swear it sounded like a large animal, Harumi," he whispered again.

Nodding in the blackness, Spain switched the flashlight on again as the narrow beam crisscrossed the wall of postal box doors.

"I don't see any Witten on these boxes."

"Maybe there's another post office."

"Oh, Good! God, you do belong in the classroom — wait!" The beam settled on a small box in the lower left-hand corner, the name smudged and almost obscured. "What about Wittenberg in house number six?"

"All I know is what the computer said. Russell Witten," she whispered in his ear. "My father said —"

Wittenberg is close enough. It's got to be him."

"Thanks alot, pal!" a gravel voice shouted, followed by a hideous snorting laugh. "You've made this whole damn thing alot easier for me. And don't touch that pistol in your belt, or I'll kill you where you stand!"

Then a blinding light flashed first in Spain's, then Harumi's eyes. "I'll make it quick and painless," the faceless, gravel voice taunted. "You folks are pretty good. Had a hard time tracking you down here. Hey, Spain, you musta been in Nam, huh? I liked your defensive perimeter of tin cans, next to the cave. A few grenades would have helped. Easy shit, though." The gravel tumbled in the man's throat as he laughed, just as the door was blown open by a cold Klamath wind, howling down the hamlet's only dirt road. "Very carefully, put the gun on the floor with your left hand!"

"Who are you?" Spain turned, trying to block the painful light from his eyes as he placed the gun on the floor. "What the hell's this about?"

"The Black Ghost sends final greetings to the Oboe." The rusty laugh howled in harmony with the freezing wind.

201

"Leave him alone, you big, dumb shit!" Harumi tried to push Spain out of the way, her voice turning hard and clear, a deep rage fueling her anger. "I've had it with all this childish crap! We haven't done anything to you, or your damn Black Ghost! Just get the hell away from us!" she screamed uncontrollably. "We don't even know you, damn it!"

The voice laughed again, the large figure just a dim starlight silhouette in the open doorway. "You're a tough chick. I like that," the voice snickered. "We'll mess around after I put a slug in your boyfriend's ear!"

Then the snicker gave way to a mechanical snarl and Spain knew it was the "Sheriff" pumping life-shattering bullets into helpless Sandanistas with their hands tied behind their backs. "You Benjamin Spain?" The proper death label before the execution. "Yeah, you are!"

Instinctively, Spain began to press Harumi toward a darkened counter for protection.

"Hey, where you goin', Spain? Tryin' to crawl outta here?" the presence laughed cruelly. "All right butt face, I'm out of time! Slide away from the chick, asshole! I don't want to damage those goods yet!"

In the dimness, Spain and Harumi watched helplessly as the monstrous, shadowy figure raised a thick, cumbersome-looking black weapon that sucked in what little background light seeped through the open door.

Slowly, the man began to move toward the couple, now huddled for their lives on the cold, worn floor. Suddenly, he stopped and with an experienced eye that was now adjusted to the vague dimness, raised the weapon, gripping the wide black handle with both hands.

"Move out of the line of fire, honey." The voice was strangely mechanical and cold as death as the killer went about his business of lining up the dark form squatting on the floor.

"Get out of the way, Harumi," Spain heard his own voice mumble thickly. Spain closed his eyes as he shoved the protesting Harumi to one side, her shrieking bordering on the insane. "Make it quick, you bastard!" Now Spain could smell the foul, stained odor of the man as he began to bend, the gun coming quickly up to Spain's right ear.

"The Ghost said to tell you before the hit that it was a mistake. He didn't want this to be personal. You just got in the way of something very big." Now the man squeaked like a shaggy ship rat, the squat, cold gun resting against Spain's temple. With his free hand, the man deftly pulled up a small aerial atop a tiny satellite transmitter, then toggled the first of two switches. "Now, they know I've got you. The second switch will tell them you're dead!"

"I—I love you, Harumi." A whining thump exploded with blinding force against the side of Spain's head, slamming him brutally to the floor. For just a millisecond, time froze. Spain waited for the final blackness to end his life, but the only vision was a nightmare of a large one-hundred-fifty-pound cat with sanguine blue eyes and wet luminescent fangs, digging into Spain's killer.

"Roll out of the way!" Spain heard Harumi scream from miles away, the silenced shot ringing painfully in his ears, his cheek and head throbbing from the heat of a powder burn.

Then Spain felt Harumi's hands struggling to pull his numb body away from the hideous screams and sounds of crunching bones, coming from the middle of the room. Spain tried to speak, but couldn't. The surrealistic images turning in slow motion, defied reality. He should be dead. Maybe he was, in the black chaos that surrounded and pulled at him, but he refused to let go. Maybe that's what he needed to do, just close his eyes and die quietly.

"Ben!" Harumi was crying softly, her slender body splayed across him as a protective shell. "Ben, you're alive. A cat, a big tan mountain lion," she whispered, "came through the open door and jumped at the man, forcing him to fire early." She felt the warmth of sticky blood, matting the side of his head. Then instinctively, Harumi cradled him as she dragged him from the edge of the killing.

Suddenly, Harumi froze as the sleek mountain lion raised her massive white and tan head from the fleshy pile that was once a human being. A death-rattling growl smothered the post office as the cat, her mouth dripping with blood and tissue, turned and moved toward Harumi and Spain.

Instinctively, Harumi waved her arms and began screaming. For a moment the cat froze, raised her magnificent head again in a bellowing roar, then slowly ambled out of the open door.

In the darkness of the moonless night, they found a small creek where Harumi cleaned the skin-deep wound in Spain's temple, caused by flying wood chips from the bullet when it struck the floor next to his head.

For a long time they sat huddled together in the cold, while Spain examined the gun that had almost killed him.

"That's a strange-looking thing. I never saw a gun that looked like that before, Benny."

"It's a state-of-the-art terrorist job. Lightweight, deadly at close range and made entirely of carbon fiber, so it passes airport security and X-ray machines." He stared at the barrel in the beam from the flashlight. "It's a *Hammerlie* two-eighty, with a built-in silencer." For a moment Spain let his mind drift to something he couldn't touch. I think it's Austrian. Looks like a remodeled target pistol, firing twenty-two shells. Just perfect for the classic ear shot. Somebody finally perfected the old *Glock* plastic model."

"That's charming."

Spain held up a finger to his lips. "I know. I'm making conversation to calm myself down." Spain drew a breath of cold, sweet mountain air and surveyed the small one-street village. He was surprised that the wild racket caused by the mountain lion in the post office hadn't drawn attention, then he looked more critically at the small houses with dim, flickering light filtering through the windows.

"This place doesn't have any electricity! They're all burning real fires for heat. Crackling logs and a roaring fire masked what happened out here. They probably even use oil lamps for light. I don't hear any electric generators." Spain rubbed Harumi's shoulders. Despite their warm down parkas and ski gloves, the first sharp knives of cold were beginning to sap their body warmth.

"We can't stay out here all night, Ben," Harumi said softly.

"Let's find house number six and see if Mister Wittenberg is aka Russell Witten." Spain threw the stealth pistol down the mountain into the trees, then checked his .45 automatic, pulling back the slide stop.

"What's that for?"

"A talk and some hot food."

"Oh, Jesus, Ben! You can't strong-arm an old man! Violence isn't the answer!"

Spain touched the open cut on the side of his head and winced from the pain. "Want to bet on that! I've been shot at, hunted by the law and accused of murder. I'll do what I damn please to get at the truth! Now let's go! If you don't have the stomach or don't care about some answers, then stay here and freeze those little buns off! I didn't come all the way to Elephant's Breath, California, for the sights!" Then he pivoted and began to move toward the houses, searching for number six.

Twenty-five

Spain touched his foot to the raised worn rotted porch of house number six, gingerly testing its strength in the darkness. For a moment he paused, turned to Harumi and waved her back around the corner of the small cabin, her face in a pout. Slowly, he pulled the Colt from his belt as he crept along the porch toward a small front window. Its shallow, amber light flickering weakly.

Peeking his head above the sill, Spain slowly adjusted his vision to the one room, the round rock fireplace, scorched black from eons of daily use that framed a roaring fire; the rough-barked pine furniture that passed for a couch and chairs, backdropped by piles of old magazines that cluttered the floor. Off in one corner of the cabin, lighted by two kerosene lamps, stood an ancient cast-iron water pump sitting atop a wooden counter and a hollow that must have been a crude sink. At least I can steal some hot coffee, Spain grunted to himself.

Slipping past the window, Spain felt his way to the door, a fragile collection of roughly sawed boards tacked together with weather-stained cross members, while a crude wooden door handle stuck out of the center of the door like an old welcome mat. The shuffle of soft feet forced Spain to his knees as he trained the .45 to the source of the noise. An old man, standing ramrod straight, his shoulders wrapped in a blanket, stared down at Spain from behind deep frown lines, apparent even in the dimness.

"Who the hell are you, sonny?" The sound was human, but it was strangely alien and mechanical. The voice wasn't human, but the old face certainly was, topped with a thick shock of white hair. "Who you gonna shoot out here sneaking around in the dark with that popgun? There's a damn old bitch of a mountain lion that's been raisin' hell at night for weeks now. Too bad. We've all grown to like her. You damn State people! You here to take her out?" Then an old steady hand slowly extended itself from beneath the blanket and gently pushed the .45 aside, a broad smile spreading the old man's mouth.

"Whoever you are," the robotic voice droned, "you don't need that? The lioness isn't inside my place."

"I'll trade you the gun for some hot coffee and some talk," Spain tried, staring up at the man.

For a long time the old man gazed at Spain, somehow studying his silence and awkwardness. "Sure. You can also bring in your friend, hiding over there behind the house." Then he laughed mechanically, shaking his head. "Around here, sonny, we're pretty open." Then the old man shifted the small cylinder he was holding to the other side of his throat as he led them into the warmth of the small cabin.

Twenty minutes later they were all nestled close to the roaring log fire, red hot embers flying out of the hearth. The old man was obviously happy for the company.

"So?" the old man asked. Then he noticed them staring at the device pressed to his throat.

"Ten years ago, I had my larynx removed because of throat cancer. Smoked all my damn life." He pulled back a small cotton patch, revealing a red, fleshy hole at the base of this throat. "My new nose. They rearranged things, but my voice box is gone. The electronic stick picks up the sounds and vibrations in my throat and allows my speech to be understood. When I first got back from the surgery in San Francisco, I scared the hell out of all the kids here in the Bar." The man's faded liquid eyes narrowed for just an instant. "Any other questions?"

Spain and Harumi shook their heads as they sipped the steaming black coffee.

"Well, if you're not here to shoot that mother lion, what then are you doing in this no-man's land?" The old man turned his head toward the fire, his wrinkled hawkish nose pushing his face into a curious, frail pose.

"You're Russell Witten?" Harumi stated quietly.

Suddenly, the benign eyes, even in the opaque light turned hard. "Who the hell are you?"

Harumi slowly made her way to the old man, then lowered herself before him. "My father is Erik van Horn. I think you knew him during World War Two as the Flying Dutchman. You both served as operatives in Nazi Germany, for the OSS, before the war ended."

The old man stared into the fire, sometimes nodding his head, carrying on some silent dialogue, laying back the years in his mind. "I might."

"Your code name was One Hundred Nine Rosary

Beads." Spain added gently.

"Jesus! The Dutchman." he suddenly mumbled. "God, we had some times, we did! That crazy Dutchman. The whole fucking German army, on the Siegfried Line, was scared shitless of your father." He suddenly gestured into the air with his old, white hands, casting shadows of shapeless animals against the log walls of the cabin. "He could take any man he wanted, from any unit. His intelligence spread all the way to Berlin. He was the grim reaper to those bastards! A living nightmare!"

The old man surveyed Harumi's angular face. "He had more Nazi contacts and networks set up than the bastard fascist Pope in Rome." He closed his eyes, remembering, his face twisted into an old, distant smile. "He killed more Germans than Patton's Eighth Army, for God's sake!"

Then the old man came alive. "Christ, the Dutchman had a toast every time we drank! Oh what the hell was it?" He slapped his forehead, then grinned. "Ah, 'should your liquor be smooth, your woman hot, and may all your problems roll off like snot!' "

"My father sends his fondest regards, Mister Witten," Harumi whispered.

The old man paused, moving his aged face close to Harumi. "My name *is* Russell Wittenberg," he finally admitted, staring into the fire. Then his mood turned dark. "My parents were German nationals, so I was a natural for behind-the-lines work for the OSS. Bill Donovan shortened my name to Witten, then I changed it back when I came here to escape the world and people like you." Wittenberg's nose wrinkled, his eyes narrowing into tiny, suspicious steel dots.

Then he looked at the strange couple sitting in his

210

mountain cabin. "I'm an old man now. Whatever you want, or the Dutchman wants, forget it."

"Did you forget Pandora's Box?" Harumi asked.

"What do you know about that?"

"Enough for us to track you from Hawaii!"

"Look, young woman, I don't mean to be rude, but I can't tell you anything."

"You mean, won't!" Spain pulled out the .45 and gently placed it on a table close to him.

Wittenberg laughed for the first time. "Go ahead and put a slug in me, sonny? You think I care at my age?" He looked into Spain's eyes. "You couldn't do it anyway." There was a note of dismissal in his voice. "When I was your age, I could kill in cold blood." He glanced over at Harumi. "So could your father."

"Look, you're right, but our lives are in real danger and people have been killed because of what's on the *Arizona*. Mister Wittenberg, I dove on the *Arizona* recently and stumbled across something."

"We found the skull of Fred Noonan and a pouch that was supposed to have been delivered from Emperor Hirohito to President Roosevelt, before the Pearl Harbor attack," Harumi said in a slow, haunting voice. "I'm an historian, sir. I need to get to the truth of Pearl Harbor."

"The truth!" the old man bellowed. "What the hell is truth! Leave it alone, young woman! Leave it buried with those people at the bottom of Pearl Harbor!"

"We've got blood on our hands. Someone tried to kill us right here, not less than an hour ago!"

"Look, Spain, we all have blood on our hands!"

"It's time the secrets were opened to the world," Harumi said, leaning close to Wittenberg.

"What?" The old man laughed bleakly. "Young lady,

211

haven't you learned yet, that the greatest secret of all is that there are no secrets!" Wittenberg shuffled to a cabinet and returned with a bottle of Scotch. "Drink anyone?" Then he pulled directly from the bottle.

"So, in other words you won't help us." Harumi sneered.

"That's not it, Harumi." Spain touched her shoulder gently. "He's playing with us! A little sport for the tough old Nazi killer. He's bored in this burg, hiding out from life! Come on, there's no secrets or answers in this place. Just memories." Spain stared at Wittenberg. "This old guy doesn't give a shit about anything!"

Spain forced Harumi to the door, then turned to face the old man, still sitting close to the crackling fire. "Take it all to your grave old man! I'll tell the Dutchman you whimped out!" Then he opened the door.

"Wait!" Wittenberg shouted. "Just wait!" Suddenly the remoteness dissolved. "Please don't leave! I can't answer all your questions, but maybe I can help." Then he waved them back inside the warmth of the cabin, the spookiness gone from his face.

"I guess you young folks could use some food. We'll eat and talk. I got files I can show you that may help explain some of Pandora's Box."

"This is great!" Harumi sloshed the last piece of dark meat in the hot, flour-rich *roux,* then popped it into her mouth before settling down to finish another cup of day-old coffee. "What was that?"

"Venison." Wittenberg's eyes sparkled with pride. "Shot and cured it myself."

Harumi screwed up her face. "I just ate a deer?" Then

212

she quickly gulped a mouthful of coffee, to wash away the animal taste. "May God forgive me!"

"If I didn't kill the old buck, then it would have starved this winter here in the high forest." Wittenberg shook his head defensively. "Damn Bambi freaks! Maybe it would have been better if that mother lion, prowling around out there on the road, would have eaten our deer while he was still alive! She would have eaten his ass, then left him to bleed to death!"

"Okay!" Spain glanced sharply at Harumi. "She'll tough it out, Russell. It's just a long way from her tofu burgers and Hawaiian sunsets!"

Wittenberg grunted, then motioned them over to the long couch, reasonably lighted with a large kerosene lamp. A moment later he appeared with a forty-year-old cardboard Blatz beer box. "Been carrying this thing around, since — well since the end of the War Crimes Trials in Tokyo, held by General MacArthur's staff in Nineteen forty-six. I should have burned this shit!"

"What's in it?" Harumi's tone changed instantly.

"You asked for Pandora's Box, didn't you? Well, here's my old beer box that has pieces of Pandora's Box in my files. But I think I should tell you what I remember first, then you can paw through it." He winked at Spain.

"Within a week of the attack, I was sent by the OSS to investigate the rumor of German collusion with the Japanese at Pearl Harbor. I spent four months tracking every lead from Sand Island, the Japanese and German Consulate offices, then all the way to the dirty end of Waikiki at Lousy Lui's bar, where every damned Honolulu whore deposited her short curlys."

"My mother was Japanese by birth, American by choice, and interned at Sand Island until the war ended.

Her mother died on that damned sand bar! That's how she spent her teenage years," Harumi said bitterly. "Sitting right off Honolulu as a criminal spy! Assholes!"

"I'm truly sorry, Harumi," Wittenberg took her hand. "That bastard Cordell Hull panicked in Washington and convinced Roosevelt to drop a net over all Japanese, whether they were American citizens or not. The tragic thing is, we never turned up one spy who was *Nisei.* Anyway, the general story, as I pieced it together, was that indeed the fix was on. Even MacArthur in the Philippines knew, everyone except poor old Admiral Kimmel and his sailors." Wittenberg stared into the fire again.

"Didn't think I'd ever tell this story to anyone. Most of the people who cared are dead now. The world's passed it all by with countless wars and desert fighting," he assured himself.

"Not everybody's passed it by," Spain added. "As I said before, there's more than a few deadly souls out there in the night, just waiting to blow our brains out because of Pearl Harbor, the *Arizona,* or some damn thing associated with it all! There's a piece of human dog meat on the floor of your post office to prove that point!"

"What did you find in your initial investigation?" Harumi probed.

"That the Nazis were involved, up to their eyeballs." He swallowed another gulp of whiskey straight from the bottle, Spain watching his every move. "Let's see." Wittenberg thumbed through the box, finally pulling out a thick, old dog-eared manila file that he spent a few minutes reviewing. "Yeah, that's right." He nodded. "Christ, I can remember my fifth-grade teacher, but nothing else. We captured a German Abwehr agent, who was also working and sharing information with the Imperial Japanese Navy's Third Bureau, who had been living in Honolulu for a year before the attack. In fact, he admitted to the FBI that German Admiral Wilhelm Canaris, head of the Abwehr, German Naval Intelligence, sent him to Honolulu to assist the Japanese."

"So? Can we focus down on what happened?" The edge was back in Harumi's voice.

"Sorry. Forgive an old man his sins. The agent's name was Otto Kuehn, who had set up an elaborate radio intelligence operation in Pearl City, adjacent to Pearl Harbor. He picked off code signals from navy warships and shore installations. The American navy got sloppy and he broke the signal code and sent that ongoing information back to Owada, Japan, the center of Japanese naval intelligence cryptanalysis during the war. The code name he picked off was called Brilliant Fire." The old man closed his eyes trying to remember the small details that weren't in the file.

"For some reason, when the *Arizona* was sent on a secret mission in mid-November Nineteen forty-one, he changed the cipher call to Japan, to Brilliant Fire Manila. The fact is the Germans and Japanese knew all our movements! It was the navy's own code for some operation—"

"Where was the *Arizona* sent?" Harumi dropped her voice, drinking in every sound in the cabin.

"There were a few parts to the *Zona*'s secret mission. I know that they rendezvoused at Johnston Island on the instructions of H.H., after having been in Far East waters for a period of time."

"Who was H.H.?"

"Harumi, H.H. was Harry Hopkins, who in reality,

215

along with Cordell Hull, ran the government in Nineteen forty-one. He was FDR's special assistant. A prehistoric Henry Kissinger."

Harumi rubbed her hands through her now short, blond, streaked hair. "I know who he was, damn it! How did you find out about the *Arizona* going to Johnston Island?"

"I knew the special White House agent who went along." Wittenberg took another drink from the bottle, mashing his face from the bitter taste of whiskey.

"What was his name? Is he still alive? Can I talk to him?" Harumi's questions came in her typical rapid style.

"You sure as hell have your father's energy." He turned to Spain. "I feel sorry for you, sonny. You can't win with this one."

Spain smiled awkwardly, sipping from his mug of hot coffee.

Wittenberg moved his long fingers into the air as he talked. "The last I heard, he was alive, living in England."

"I want to see him," Harumi interrupted.

"Might be kind of difficult." Wittenberg laughed. "He lives as a monk in a monastery, on the Welsh Coast, on a rock called Caldey Island. I was told his sandals were a little light these days, though."

"What's that mean?"

"He's not all there," Spain grunted.

Wittenberg nodded. "A real spook when he was hitting on all his cylinders. His name is or was Alvin Dvorak. He was the man who ordered and sailed with the *Arizona* on its special operation before Pearl Harbor. There were always rumors that Earhart and Noonan were alive, but how Noonan ended up on that

216

death ship, is anybody's guess. FDR was capable of anything! Ask Dvorak. He was there for Chrissakes!"

Harumi was still agitated and started to speak.

"Let Russell continue," Spain urged. "Stop pushing noise at him and let him give you the big picture, then he'll answer whatever questions he can."

Harumi blew out a long subdued breath.

"Let me say that I have a half-century perspective and additional information that wasn't available at the time. In Nineteen forty-six, while listening to secret testimony from the head of Doro Nawa, the Japanese secret clandestine operations section, I was told that in the spring of Nineteen forty-one, Emperor Hirohito really wanted peace, to restrain his military, and he hoped that if he could establish a personal cable writing friendship with Roosevelt, the administration would lift the oil embargo, leading to a real Pacific peace."

"I don't understand? What did oil have to do with it then? I mean, now, with the Middle East and all I —"

"You don't know your history, do you, sonny? By early Nineteen forty-one, when Roosevelt embargoed all exports to Japan, they were importing ninety percent of their petroleum from the U.S.! That was the military clique's great pretext for war." He glanced sideways at Spain. "What the hell changes? We're still fighting over oil and money. Now they call it petro dollars!"

"What happened then?" Harumi asked soberly.

"Well, according to the head of the Doro Nawa, who was bound by secrecy to the emperor, a series of letters changed hands between the emperor and FDR and the man swore to me, before he was hanged for his war crimes, that Hirohito sent Roosevelt, by special courier, a copy of the Yogeki Sakusen, the Z plan. It was damn hard to believe at the time! In fact, the Doro Nawa man said that a special teletyped copy had been sent directly on a secured line, to the White House, followed sometime later by an actual copy of the Z plan. The man told me with his own lips, without lying! A deathbed confession."

"The Z Plan?"

"The Pearl Harbor attack plan, Harumi. Yogeki Sakusen translates directly to Ambush Operation. The Doro Nawa general even insisted that the emperor had sent an actual Z signal flag to Roosevelt as a gesture of his sincerity and honor. There were only two flags like it. Those flags had flown from the masts of Admiral Togo's fleet in Nineteen hundred and five when he defeated the Russians at the Battle of Tsushima." Wittenberg paused and pulled another long drink from the whiskey bottle.

"The other Z pennant was flown by Admiral Nagumo from the mast of the carrier *Akagi,* for luck, during the actual Pearl Harbor raid." The old man was beginning to slur his words as the alcohol was taking its toll in the thin mountain air. "That flag went down with the *Akagi,* when she was sunk during the Battle of Midway, six months later."

"That's the flag that I've got!" Harumi whispered to Spain. "It was inside your yellow pouch."

Spain closed his eyes, the wild speculation of Harumi back at the house in Honolulu now being verified by this old, drunk operative, sitting in the middle of the wilderness.

"Why the hell would Hirohito give their archenemy their battle plan?" Spain asked again. "It's a goddamn cliché!"

"Good boy, sonny! The old sixty-four-dollar question!

218

We asked our Doro Nawa man, over and over. It was all somehow tied up with face, honor, and the emperor's naive view of the world to achieve peace." Then Wittenberg turned to them, his tone dropping almost below the snap of the fire. "It was all so simple to him."

"So there's no doubt that Roosevelt and his staff knew about Pearl Harbor in advance?" Harumi asked the old man slowly. "Not the slightest doubt? I have to be sure in my own mind."

"Jesus Christ! Even the goddamn American Matson liner *Lurline,* en route from San Francisco to Honolulu, as early as November thirty, Nineteen forty-one, picked up a shitload of radio signals, with mysterious operators blasting away on the lower marine frequencies in naval code from station JOS, Tokyo. With the help of RDF, the target of those signals was the Kido Butai, the Japanese Pearl Harbor attack force, en route across the north Pacific. The roofers —"

"The what?" Harumi was writing it all down in the dim light.

"The roofers. The 'on-the-roof gang' at Pearl. The ears of radio intelligence stationed at Pearl and at Station N or Negat, the old Navy Department building, in Washington. Christ, the second deck knew it all, at the Navy Department! The real problem was covering it up with 'it was all a failure to communicate!' We even had a special electronic crew monitoring powerful radios on Market Street in downtown San Francisco, who followed the Kido Butai all the way from Etorofu, in the northern Kuriles, when their fleet was still forming! We had more info than Chuichi Nagumo, the admiral who led the attack!"

Spain shook his head, gazing into the flames, licking

at the black round rocks of the hearth. "I still can't believe it!"

"Why?" the old man said cynically. "The fix was on then, just as the Desoto Patrols in Vietnam were a setup by President Johnson to mix it up! Dishonesty is a way of life in America!" The old man wiped his mouth with the back of his old, discolored hand.

"Christ, the emperor virtually gave us the war on a silver platter, without even realizing it!"

"Explain yourself, please!" Harumi demanded.

"Well, daughter of the Flying Dutchman, the advanced information that Hirohito provided Roosevelt allowed him and Admiral Betty Stark to send our only carriers in the Pacific, the *Enterprise,* the *Saratoga,* and the *Lexington,* out to sea on bogus missions, out of harm's way, before the raid. Christ, some damn school-bound historian you are! Shit, this real history never gets into the books. If those carriers had been sunk at Pearl, the occupation of Hawaii would have followed. FDR would have been forced to sue for peace in the Pacific, right then! Instead, the Japanese sank a bunch of worthless, overaged, slow as shit, obsolete battle wagons; that focused every ounce of American hatred on the Japanese and finally gave FDR his reason for entering the war. Besides, six months later those carriers helped sink all six Japanese carriers at Midway! Do you know —" Wittenberg raised the bottle almost straight up, chugging down the remaining whiskey, his head resting at a precarious angle against the back of the couch.

"Do ya know that the Niponese missed the carriers and something just as important! Ya know what that was, Miss Textbook Historian?"

Harumi shook her head.

"I'll tell ya, kiddies. Oil. Our oil in the tank farm right next to Pearl. That was all the bunker oil we had in the entire Pacific! If they had taken out that farm with a few well-placed bombs, then we wouldn't have been able to fart our way back to San Francisco or San Pedro with what was left on the fleet! It would have taken a year to replace it! No Midway, no victory! Battleships, Jesus!" The old man rattled on. "They sank a fucking bunch of scrap iron that was old when Hoover was President! But the carriers! Hirohito saved the carriers and inadvertently allowed us with that air power to kick their asses halfway back across the Pacific to the mandates. I—" Then suddenly, he was snoring, loud waffing sounds coming from his nose and open mouth, the file dropping to the floor.

Gently, Spain picked up the old man and carefully laid him on his bed, while Harumi covered him with two blankets. Standing back in the flickering light of the fire and the kerosene lamps, they held each other without speaking.

"You okay, Benny?" she finally asked.

"Yeah, I guess so. Where's all this leading? Have you put any pieces of the puzzle together yet?"

"A few. He's got more to tell us though." Then she shivered in his arms. "Do we have the time?"

Spain shrugged. "I don't know. The Ghost isn't done yet. The operation to take us out is too pro for them to just go away. There's heavy bucks behind it all." Spain looked over at the snoring old man. "He's got to help us. It's all we have left." Then he drew a deep breath. "Get some sleep and I'll stand watch. Just maybe we'll be okay for the night."

"You're a lousy liar, Spain," she whispered, kissing him

221

gently. "Professionals don't work alone, not this far from the beaten path."

"Sleep, Harumi. You're the one who's got to figure this all out. I'm just the meat, carrying the heat, riding shotgun, before the wheels come off our wagon."

Twenty-six

The cold April sun of the Salzkammergut swelled over the jagged lip of the brooding Dachstein Massif, with the same inspiring early morning force that had once influenced the creative energies of Franz Schubert and Johannes Brahms. The massive nine-thousand-foot limestone roof of the alps showed off its craggy face, riddled with deep caves and massive blue glaciers just as the black armor-plated Mercedes limousine reached the tiny Western Austrian village of Hallstatt.

"Dos Mio! How quaint this devil's playground of Nazis!" grunted Hilda Soria as she did her best to disregard the startling beauty of the high forest and sharp, snow-capped peaks that surrounded them on the narrow highway, still laced with deadly black road ice. The driver slowed cautiously to take a narrow hairpin, which set off the Cuban minister again. "Hitler's Jewel!" she spat out, trying to stay warm. "Where the hell are the palms and sweet trades of my island?" she moaned aloud just as Hallstatt revealed itself, with its small chalets of dark woods and round stones, all stepped crazily up the side of the Dachstein Massif.

Off to the minister's right, as the car slowed to a controlled roll, a lusty glacier-fed waterfall sliced the village in two as it rushed down the mountain, contained only by a deep canal. Suddenly, a large stone building appeared across the narrow road. "What's that?" the minister asked.

"Oh, that!" the Salzburg driver responded cheerfully in perfect English, from the front seat. "We call it the bone bin."

Minister Soria glanced sideways at her aide, Sed Cruz, and cynically rolled her eyes. "My God, bone bins, Hitler, Nazis, and a running dog gang of damned Aryans still running around with their right arms up in the air. And here's Herr Lutz, hiding out in the high forest!"

Sed Cruz let out a long, slow breath as he watched the deep blue eyes of the driver in the rearview mirror. "There is a certain odor."

Soria parted her lips and laughed silently at her companion's understatement to make a point. "Tell me, driver," Soria continued, "what is the bone bin?"

Now the blue eyes in the mirror came alive, carrying out their mandated function. "Well, the diggable land is so modest here that there is not space enough to bury Hallstatt's dead. So, bodies are interred in the one church-side cemetery for only a decade, then the exhumed remains are stacked in that stone charnel house, or ossuary."

"God!" Soria bellowed into the cold. "Gaily decorated Aryan skulls sneering at the civilized world in the half light of a sputtering candle!"

The blue eyes in the mirror narrowed, then refocused on the winding road ahead.

For a long time, Soria stared out the window at the

rich, expansive forests, then pushed her head back against the leather seat. "I don't know, Sed," she whispered, "maybe the Russian, Ovsyannikov, is right!"

"About what?"

"That we have struck a bargain with the devil."

"You mean General Lutz?"

"Yes," she said wearily. "I mean the old Nazi wolf, in Lenin's clothing."

An hour later, the Cuban Minister of Finance Soria and her aide, Sed Cruz, hero of the Bay of Pigs, sat facing former Lt. Gen. Markus "Mischa" Lutz, former head of the notoriously brutal East German secret police, Hauptverwaltung Aufklarung (HVA), and his lawyer, a fat bulbous Austrian with a pink sweaty face, who had trouble breathing at the high altitude. Surrounding the eighteenth-century Swiss chalet-styled estate, were security men whom Cruz could not see that were planted on the vast rolling grounds and throughout the dark, mahogany-ridden mansion, squatting on a plateau just east of the village.

"Does the coalition still stand together?" Minister Soria probed harshly, finally allowing herself to sip from a bone china cup of dark, bitter Austrian coffee. There wasn't the slightest pretense of warmth in her voice.

General Lutz, a careful, political man, ran his fingers over the smooth patina of the old dark serving table. For a moment he turned his head, breathing a steady rhythm as he gazed out at the soft gentle curves of the Echern Valley off in the distance.

"For as long as we want it to be, Comrade Minister. In the last forty-eight hours, I have spoken with Toshiyuki

Mizutari at his home in Japan. He is willing to share."

"What is this, a child's game of trading toys!"

"Yes, Minister, in a way it is. This cannot be rushed. We must let it all unravel itself." Then Lutz rubbed a hand through his smooth, dyed black hair. "It has been fifty years. A half century."

"This sounds like some damn *Samurai* exercise!"

The general smiled. "True enough, Minister. It is just that. Former Japanese Navy Lieutenant Toshiyuki Mizutari taught me a great deal over the years about waiting. He taught me without even knowing it."

"What have you been taught?" Sed Cruz, sitting near Minister Soria, kept his voice even.

"You don't have to answer any of these questions, General!" the sweaty attorney advised sternly. "None of this rationale is necessary. The terms of your agreement with the Cuban leadership call only for resources in exchange for fifty percent of the gold bullion, when it is found and then recovered in a reasonably and timely manner."

Lutz smiled brilliantly, then held up a large hand, his fingernails carefully manicured. "None of this is necessary. We are not adversaries here. We all want the same things, don't we?" he said smoothly. "This secret has been part of my files since they came into my possession in the early Nineteen fifties. Before that, the secret was kept by Reichsfuhrer-SS Heinrich Himmler, who appropriated it from Admiral Wilhelm Canaris, who headed the German Intelligence group, the Abwehr."

"General, this isn't necessary."

"Oh, indeed, I believe it is, Minister." He paused, his voice maintaining a certain pleasant benevolence. "Eastern and Central Europe are in economic ruin. Communism has been repudiated on every level. Only Germany will emerge as a healthy economic entity. The Soviet Union is no longer even a union, it is a collection of starving cultures held together by common and age-old hatreds." Lutz watched the anger boil in Minister Soria's black eyes.

Then suddenly the general laughed. "You don't understand yet, do you?"

"No!"

"It is simple, Senora. Cuba is an economic joke! The Russians can no longer feed and clothe themselves, let alone your island nation. Your brother-in-law, Fidel Castro, has taken Cuba past economic ruin into something that borders on mass starvation and deprivation. It is a fourth-world country, if that's possible!" General Lutz screamed at her. "You spout dogma and angry slogans, and put everyone down! Yet you want the gold to save your beloved Cuba." Lutz rose from his chair and walked around the table to face the Cubans.

"And now the time has come to pay. You waltz in here, like you are doing me a favor!" The general slapped himself in the chest. "It is me who is doing you the favor, damn it! Fidel was a friend of mine. He did me a number of favors over the years and I always liked the women he gave to me!" Lutz intentionally studied Soria, waiting for her female protests. "I'm not helping you, Frau Soria, I'm helping an old friend keep his ship afloat!" General Lutz sipped his coffee, carefully replacing the slender china cup in its saucer with a rock steady hand.

"This lost treasure has a real market value today of close to one hundred billion dollars, American! One hundred billion," he repeated slowly. "I have spent years cultivating and putting the pieces in place, all the way from Samurai Mizutari, to the keeper of the sunken *Ar-*

227

izona, at Pearl Harbor, to Captain Gregori Ovsyannikov, now operating under my strict orders and control in the United States." Lutz adjusted his horn-rimmed glasses.

"We know all that," Sed Cruz said, filling the silence.

"Then if you know all that, why do you give errant signals and information to Captain Ovsyannikov!" His voice rose to the octave of betrayal. Then he stood tall, his wiry frame staring down at his two guests. "How dare you counter my direct orders! I spent years rebuilding the psyche of the Russian captain, a former professional stalker with the vaunted Aquarium, the killing arm of the GRU, the Soviet General Staff." Lutz calmed himself as he walked across the old, high-ceilinged room.

"The captain will move cautiously and slowly, is that clear?"

In unison Soria and Cruz nodded silently.

"It has taken me years," Lutz said softly, "to nurture our Samurai in Central Japan. He is in essence the new keeper of the privy seal for the old, dead Emperor Hirohito. I have nurtured his anger that Japan's warrior class has been denigrated into historic fools. But most importantly, I have waited for the time, with the crowning of the new emperor, his son Akihito. "Today," Lutz continued, "the emperor is no more than a corporate marionette. He is no longer a God. He no longer adheres to the warrior code of *Bushido.*" He is a corporate P.R. man. While Hirohito was alive, I couldn't touch his devotion or his old promises, but now I can and I have! He feels a great dishonor for his beloved emperor and is ready to move!"

"What does he have to do with the treasure?" Sed Cruz inquired, holding his gnarled hands together in a prayer.

"When it was clear to Hirohito that the war was lost, he

228

entrusted our *Samurai* with an imperial rescript. An order if you will, that details—"

"Those details are not important to this discussion," the lawyer wheezed, with difficulty. "My client must protect his interests." The lawyer gazed across the table, his weak eyes suddenly focused and strong. For another moment he regarded the Cuban mission, their dark skin, piercing eyes and Indian features something he found chilling. "The point is, General Lutz is now handling, with my assistance, all these delicate negotiations with his Japanese contact and he—ah, we expect a very fruitful outcome that will be of benefit to everyone at this table." Exhausted with the monologue, the lawyer slumped back in his chair, trying to catch his breath.

"So it would seem," Senora Soria said, smiling coldly, "this entire operation is contingent upon an old racist Japanese warrior, out of the middle ages and the successful elimination of all of Captain Ovsyannikov's targets in the United States."

General Lutz slowly removed his glasses and then again moved his long fingers in little circular patterns on the table. "It seems to me that you have taken complex issues and simplified them to a point where they lose their meaning and importance." He held up a hand to silence the Cuban minister.

"I must continue!" he added, his voice rising.

"The Russian now operating in the States will do what I say to do, when I say to do it. It seems his prey have come across some vital information that we must learn about!" He then swept a hand before his face. "That requires great patience on all our parts. The captain is an intelligent hunter. He only kills when he has the information that he has been sent to retrieve or when I say it is appropriate." He smiled quickly, then his lips dropped into cruel pout. "And I will tell you when it is appropriate! I will tell you what is important or not important! If that does not suit you, then you are free to leave my home and all aspects and rewards to be gained from this operation! Is that clear?"

Sed Cruz leaned forward at a familiar angle and Minister Soria knew instantly that he was ready to kill both men with his hands.

Soria laughed, shaking her head, then told Cruz with her eyes that the time was not right. "You are right in correcting our methodology, General." She bowed her eyes in supplication, hoping it would hold the old Nazi for just a while longer. She glanced at Cruz and knew these men would be dead sometime before they left the chalet.

General Lutz rose from his chair, and smiled broadly at his guests. He walked to an antique wooden cart and poured another round of acrid coffee from an ornate silver coffee service.

"Please know," the general eventually continued, "that our Japanese contact needs us to retrieve the bullion. He needs us for a variety of reasons including the fact that the American gold bullion of the preworld war two variety is formed in bars each weighing seventy-five kilograms, which is equal to one hundred sixty-five pounds. Multiply that out to one hundred billion dollars in weight." Then the general laughed heartily, followed by a triumphant grin from his lawyer.

"It will take organized manpower, engineering, and a great deal of up-front money as well as total secrecy to remove the treasure, once it is found. Plus the fact that our Japanese *Samurai* wants his fifty percent share as a foundation to rebuild the *Samurai* class in Japan."

General Lutz raised his eyes to the high, dark ceiling of his Austrian chalet. "A *Samurai* will never go back on his word or promise, once he has committed himself to it. The only question now is when."

"There is still another question," Minister Soria said flatly.

"Yes?"

"When will your Russian captain eliminate his prey?"

General Lutz pushed out another breath, amazed that this woman was still grinding him. God help Castro and his people, he thought. What a sharp, poison thorn she is.

"Maybe this will help. I have already instructed the captain to kill the male traveling companion of our target couple. We think that will force a faster conclusion to what might be revealed."

"When will this happen?" Soria pushed further.

"We have already had word, via satellite signal, that the pair have been located." Lutz watched her eyes, waiting for them to soften, but they continued to hold his stare. "When our target has been killed, I will receive another satellite signal. It is only a question of time." General Lutz smiled evenly again. "More coffee, Minister?"

Twenty-seven

The clatter of heavy pottery dishes brought Spain out of a deep, troubled sleep, where his dreams had taken him back to his bloody riverbank in North Vietnam.

"Morning, sonny!" Russell Wittenberg, none the worse for his drunken stupor the night before, smiled down at them, laying on the bare wooden floor wrapped in blankets.

"You put me to bed last night?"

Spain nodded, sitting up, the smell of brewing coffee and frying steaks rousing his senses.

"Christ, I do that alot of nights, only I wake up the next morning where the two of you are sacked out."

"Terrific." Spain stood, stretching his sore body. Then he tensed, remembering that he was supposed to have stood guard, waiting for another of the Black Ghost's team to pay them a visit. Quickly he made his way to the front window of the cabin.

"No one out there except the trees and a few kids on the way to the schoolhouse." For the first time, Spain examined Wittenberg's countenance in the bright morning light that filled the cabin with what warmth existed. It was an odd, oval-shaped face with the texture of a slag heap, traversed with gullies on either side and below his nose that passed for eyes and a mouth.

"Relax, sonny. During the night, when you and Miss Question over there were sound asleep, I stood guard. Even saw your mountain lion cruise by once, then go down the mountain." He slapped his belt, holding an old leather holster and the narrow, curved pearl handle of an ancient .38 double action Enfield pistol.

"I guess all that conversation tired you both out last night." He laughed. "I've got some more steaks frying in the pan if your historian can get my junk food down." He turned and looked at Harumi now awake and sitting up.

Harumi rolled her eyes and moved to Spain, sliding her arms around his middle. "Tell this man I don't eat animal, Spain."

"Well, Harumi, you can have an old can of evaporated milk or half a box of soggy crackers, without the caviar." Wittenberg, more confident and happy for the company, served up the plates of venison in that thick brown *roux*. Hot black coffee sat next to each plate at the round table.

"It's not the Four Seasons, but what the hell," the old man called. "Room service is a bit iffy these days, so I serve the same thing everyday." He laughed, pointing a fork at Harumi, then her plate. "I must confess I lied. It isn't deer, it's a slab of roast beef that a friend brought up to me this past winter." He waved his arm to her, reluctantly drawing her to the table, the lie playing on the hunger squeezing her stomach.

233

After eating and cleaning up, they sat around the table, the flames roaring in the fireplace. "When I was up last night," Wittenberg said, "I relit one of the lamps and thoroughly went through all the files, thinking about what could be so deadly about what you found on the *Arizona*."

Wittenberg, rubbed a hand over his stubbed face, then peered at Harumi. "I just don't know and how the hell Fred Noonan ended up on the *Arizona* is a real shocker to me. But as I said last night, before the actual Japanese raid at Pearl, Roosevelt's administration played alot of games."

"Without being found out by some hawking media person?"

"Spain, compared to today there was no media. It was controlled news that came out of the White House and most damned editors in this country bought the big sell. Today's electronic media is far different. For years, Roosevelt had a mistress who visited him regularly in the White House and the press corps knew about it. Everyone in Washington knew about it. Can you imagine what would happen today if President Bush had something going on the side? Could you see a media person sitting on that story?" The old man shook his head.

"The point is?"

Wittenberg gazed at Harumi, a twinkle in his eye. "The point is, FDR played extraordinary games and pulled off deals in secret that we never knew about, obviously including Noonan's head on the *Arizona*."

Harumi touched her fingertips together. "We have a packet of historic documents that I think, with proper narrative, should be released to the American public," she said, frustration nibbling at her voice.

"Well, there are a couple of things that came back to me. If you remember during our conversation last night, before passing out, I mentioned a FRUPac agent in the Philippines."

Quickly, Harumi reviewed the notes she had taken. "No. No, you didn't mention—a what kind of agent?"

Wittenberg raised his hands. "Sorry, I thought I did, or at least I gave it alot of thought. Anyway, a FRUPac agent, a Fleet Radio Unit Agent, snooping electronically against the Japanese, was stationed on Corregidor. His name was Navy Lieutenant Ed Severin. My own Pearl Harbor investigation diary notes tell me that he had information about operation Brilliant Fire, when the *Arizona* went out on her secret mission. Christ, the White House even gave Severin's unit a magic machine to decode the Japanese purple diplomatic code. What a joke!"

"Go on, please," Spain gently urged.

"When Corregidor Island fell to the Japanese siege in May Nineteen forty-two, Lieutenant Severin was captured and then proceeded to give it the M.M. treatment."

"The what?"

"Like you, Harumi," Wittenberg said, laughing bitterly, "the motor mouth treatment. That bastard Severin sang like a bird about his whole operation to the Japanese. They even captured the magic code machine, intact. He used it all to barter for his life!"

Harumi looked up puzzled. "I don't see the connection with us?"

"Well, I'm not sure, but this guy knew alot. We had to change all our operational codes, techniques, signal procedures, spy networks; the whole works. After I closed the Pearl investigation, I received word from a source in Japan that Severin had somehow ended up in the protective custody of the emperor's own administrative staff. We all thought it was unusual, but we never could connect it with anything of importance."

Harumi shrugged, the frustration still in her eyes. "It doesn't help one damn bit!"

"Well, it might," Spain interrupted. "Begin to think like an operative thinks, Harumi. Begin to slowly piece the puzzle together. This Severin and his connection with the emperor is just one more piece that will eventually fit into the puzzle."

Tenno Heika Banzai," Harumi mumbled.

"Long live the emperor," the old man helped Spain out. "I like your sense of humor, daughter of the Dutchman. Even after Hirohito's death, he's still alive!"

"Tell me more about, ah, Brilliant Fire?"

"I can't, Harumi, I don't know anything else. Just that the German Abwehr agent picked it off when the *Arizona* sailed out of Pearl into the Western Pacific in November Nineteen forty-one, and sent that info to Japan."

Spain shook his head. "What the hell have we let loose that has marshaled a killing team?"

"The ghosts of those kids laying in the bottom mud of Pearl," Harumi offered.

Spain slowly shook his head, a deep sadness growing in his eyes. "I almost want to believe you. I think it's something a little more earthly. I just can't believe a few

236

musty documents and the skull of an old flier is worth just one life."

"What happened to Lieutenant Severin? Did he survive the war?"

Wittenberg shrugged. "War is chaos. He never turned up on any POW Red Cross lists, or Missing in Action reports."

"What about after the war?" Harumi pressed.

"I was in Japan for the War Crimes Trials in early Nineteen forty-six, and I tried to track him down. Tokyo was a mess then," Wittenberg recalled. "It was almost personal for our group of OSS investigators. He was a bad apple. Your father even spent a short period of time in Tokyo helping out. The navy commission had been a cover. He had been trained by the OSS. Severin was one of us and then he turned on us! General MacArthur's staff at SCAP—"

"What?" Harumi interrupted.

The old man laughed. "Supreme Commander Allied Powers. It was always a one-man show. MacArthur's show. He became the new dictator of Japan and he wanted us to find Severin. MacArthur's massive ego was at stake here. My team went through the entire Imperial Ministry and Household, with a fine-tooth comb, but it was a shambles. We even found out that Hirohito's favorite breakfast was English kippers, eggs, and bacon! He loved everything English. A *Samurai* who ate bacon and eggs!"

"How tough was the search?" Spain asked.

"Good question, if you didn't know. Emperor Hirohito had build a small military empire of his own, from household staff to army and navy personnel under his command. He even had his own air force transports and a navy sea plane. It was all nicely protected by imperial elements of the supersecret Doro Nawa. Hirohito even had his own intelligence unit called the Third Bureau, a spin-off from the navy ministry's own operations."

"How many people were involved?" Spain asked, carefully pulling back the checkered curtain in front of the window. Satisfied, he turned around, raising an eyebrow. "I mean, how big could his staff have been?"

The old man laughed. "Oh, we estimated about eight thousand people who were called retainers. Hirohito, the god, had a frigging army protecting and serving him. Christ! Some historian you are!" He pointed a finger at Harumi. "What the hell do you teach?"

"Apparently not the right stuff." She laughed. "Now, what about Severin?"

"Like I said. He just vanished. We only found one small reference to him that he had been transferred in the summer of Nineteen forty-two from a Japanese Prisoner of War Camp in Shanghai, to a special holding prison at the Imperial Ministry."

"And?" Harumi looked up from her pad.

"Into the night. Gone. *Puuff.*" Wittenberg snapped his fingers. "If he survived a firing squad, or wasn't starved to death, as was often the case with prisoners that ratted on their fellows, he slipped through our fingers, when we, ah, liberated Japan. His trail didn't stop, it just vanished into thin air."

"Could he have survived?" Spain moved close to the old man.

"Sure, he could have. The Japanese didn't keep

records of the prisoners they shot. Only the Germans were that stupid." Wittenberg shook his head. "I'd still love to get my hands on the bastard! His singing cost us alot of innocent lives, during the war. Yeah, he could have easily slipped through us, without a trace."

Then Wittenberg picked up the file. "It's yours. You know, I like you." His voice took on a strange cant.

"Oh. You sound surprised," she responded.

"I was. In all candor, your father was a real bastard. I mean he treated me well, but he had a real cruel, selfish streak in him."

Harumi bowed her head, an emotional pain arcing between her eyes. "I know that, but all that's changed, now, especially with the death of my mother which hurt him deeply." She closed her eyes to repair the damage to her consciousness.

The old man nodded sympathetically. "Well, good." Then he handed the file to Harumi. "It's for you and real history," he said softly. "We come with the dust, we go with the wind."

"We've got company!" Spain whispered loudly, that awful heavy tension back in his voice.

Wittenberg quickly checked the window. "It's the county sheriff! Damn!" Then he pulled back the dining table, then the old throw rug, revealing a trapdoor. "Quick! It's a tiny store room. Get down there, now!"

"Thanks, Russell!" Spain touched the old man's narrow, bony shoulder.

"Don't thank me, damn it! Just get down there!"

A moment later, they scrambled down into the musty dampness of a rough cement coffin that passed for a storeroom, with barely enough air to breathe. The only light came from a dim flashlight they found next to the bottom of the steep wooden steps.

In the cold, stale darkness, they held each other, listening to the clump of heavy boots and loud conversation coming from above.

"Russell, what happened to that couple you had in here? Your neighbor saw them come in last night." The regional sheriff from Siskiyou County, Peter Paroli, with a middle-aged open face, squinted at Wittenberg with knowing eyes.

"They left before sunrise this morning, Pete. Nice kids. Why" The old man dropped his voice. "They do something?"

"Well, we found what we think is their car up the road, right before town. We're dusting for fingerprints right now."

"Fingerprints! What the hell is this?"

"Suspected of murder in Hawaii and San Francisco. They might even have had something to do with a body in your post office, although it looks like that rogue mountain lion did some forest beggar in. Not much left—but that's later today. Anyway, the fax came over the wire late last night that they would be heading this way." The sheriff then showed Wittenberg photos of the couple. "That them, Russ?"

For a long time he studied the dark fax pictures, thinking it through. "Yeah, I think so. But they look different now. God, I didn't know they did anything! They banged on my door last night, half freezing to death. Said they were lost and asked if they could sleep next to the fire." He raised his hands into the air. "It was

240

no skin off me!" He smiled earnestly at the sheriff, watching his eyes.

"What's different, Russ?"

"Ah, let's see. The woman's black hair is a lot longer now and has kind of a curl in it. The man's hair is now cut into a butch. Real short, like he was in the service or something."

Satisfied, he watched the sheriff take it all down in his report.

"What about their car?"

"Stolen," the sheriff said matter-of-factly. "Smart killers."

"How so?"

"They stole Oregon plates off another car to put on their hot four by four. I want you to watch it, Russ?" He squinted down at Wittenberg.

"Watch what?"

"They could come back and they're armed and dangerous. We have orders to shoot to kill if they resist arrest. That came directly from the FBI office in San Francisco. That gun loaded?"

Wittenberg shook his head, deep in thought. Then he slapped his leather holster. "Hollow point thirty-eights." He looked down at his feet for a moment. "They really kill those people?" His voice took on a new seriousness.

The sheriff closed his notebook, his eyes expertly taking in every corner of the room. "You got alot of dishes in that sink for one person, Russ?

"Oh, I fed them last night." He shrugged. "I didn't really know they were killers." Now his voice was uncertain.

A moment later Wittenberg caught Sheriff Pete Paroli outside the cabin. "I need to tell you something else, Pete. I just remembered. It could help you catch those killers!"

Twenty-eight

"Oo menya bol'ert golovnaya!" Gregori moaned aloud as he looked up, the telephone still in his hand. Now he did have a splitting headache! He knew inside; deep in the softness of his gut that Spain wouldn't be easy to take down. In a way, he was glad that his old friend was still alive. Still resourceful, yet—

"Hello, are you still there?" came the deep voice on the other end of the phone.

"Yes, damn it!" The artificial agitation grew. "There are four of you out in the field! You *Stasi* bastards! In the Aquarium I would have burned you alive! Goddamn German shit! What do I tell General Lutz?" Inside, Gregori was growing more relieved by the moment that Spain had escaped.

"There are only three of us left," the German voice corrected timidly. "Somehow, Spain killed Prien—ah, he is mangled almost beyond recognition. I saw what was left of him myself." Now there was real fear in his tone.

"So, Spain has killed the best and strongest of the lot of you!" Gregori swallowed into his dry throat, bringing himself down as he picked away at the operative.

"Where is Spain right now? Is he still traveling with the van Horn woman?" Ovsyannikov demanded, his voice growing low as he gazed out the window of the Palace Hotel facing a busy midmorning Market Street, in downtown San Francisco.

The long silence on the other end of the line from Eureka, California, along the North Pacific Coast, far to the west of Sawyers Bar, told the Russian everything he needed to hear.

"Goddamn arrogant German *Stasi!*" Ovsyannikov bellowed again into the silence of the phone. "Clandestine operations! You and your team are a disgrace! It doesn't even matter to me how you lost them, what it means now is that I've got to again become directly involved, or Spain will eat all of you!" He rubbed the freshly healed dog bite on the calf of his one leg as a reminder.

"We will find his trail, Captain, then carry out the assignment." There was a resurgence in the telephone voice." I will then contact the general in Austria and report our error."

"No, you will not compound the felony, otherwise you'll get us both killed!" There was a sudden vulnerability in Gregori's voice that made him genuinely angry. "Can you find their direction and pick up their trail?"

"Yes," came the firm reply.

"We'll see. I expect a telephone call to this number by early this evening, telling me that you are actively tracking the couple, otherwise I will hang your balls from the Golden Gate Bridge before pushing you over the railing!" His mind was now a bottomless black pool. "If you are careless for the next six hours, it will be your last six hours! What Spain doesn't finish, I will!" Then his voice smoothed into a spurious lightness. "I know you will not let General Lutz or me down."

"Yes, sir!"

"Oh, incidentally. You will not use your satellite transmitters again until I give you the proper signal. It that clear, Herr Staven?" Gregori paused, letting the man digest the friendly spin in his voice.

"There is one other thing I want you to do, Herr Staven?" Now Ovsyannikov was overtly friendly, even brotherly, to his team leader.

Ten minutes later, when he finished giving Herr Staven his instructions, the former Soviet captain paused again. "I want to hum a little song that I learned years ago in my training days with the GRU and the Aquarium back in Sevastopol. I think it will make my point." Then Gregori began to half sing with a rapping beat:

We wage a war with no rules,
a killing snowstorm with no
end.
We share a bottle with a foe,
then always shoot a bullet into
a friend.

"Right this moment, Herr Staven, you are my friend. You have six hours in which to change your status and your death sentence," he said, taking a deep breath, his voice once again flexible and light. "To your health, old friend! *Zha vashe zdarovye!*"

Sed Cruz leaned over the bed staring down at the still firm and voluptuous breasts of Hilda Castillo, rising and falling in a peaceful rhythm of a light, relaxed sleep. Despite the chill of the air in the cavernous bedroom that raised her oversized brown nipples into the thin air, there was still a wet warm gloss on the woman's chest and face.

Cruz shook his head, slipping into his underwear. They had been passionate, adulterous lovers for more years than he could remember, yet she still roused him into a grunting wild animal before allowing his sexual release. Her muscle control might have lost a bit of physical strength over the years, but she had replaced it with an uncanny sense of timing and such a complete domination of his body, that it frightened him. She had reached a point of knowing when he was ready, even before his own body told him of the pleasure that was about to rise and boil over.

He turned, gazing out the large window at the incredible sight of the snowcapped Alps, rising into red and purple smudges of sky that marked sunset in Hallstatt. Slowly, he felt her still supple hands move around his buttocks, gently stroking him from behind with her long fingers.

"Hey, Cruz," she said softly, "you want to show these Nazis again how real Cuban love sounds echoing against these cold sterile walls?" Then she laughed, squeezing him in just the right place and with just the right intensity that roused him again.

"Come on, Sed, we may be slower, but the beat is steady and the music is just as intense!"

Cruz turned and then she smiled up at this thin pencil of a man, who had survived so much and had loyally guarded her all these years. "So, Minister," he whispered, "if I service you this time, will it be enough?"

"It will never be enough!" she shouted at the naked walls. "Not with you, Cruz. I love every part of you!" Then she tenderly pulled him down to her large breasts. "It's time now Cruz. I need to feel you inside me again."

Later, when the sky had turned from cobalt to black, they both sat facing each other at a small table, still in the privacy of the bedroom.

"Are we really alone, Cruz." The minister rolled her eyes around the room.

"Yes, I've already checked for audio and video equipment." He nodded slowly, his long, sinewy hands waving about the bedroom. "But there could be a sound dish in some other part of the house, listening, but I doubt it."

Tenderly she took his hand, the light of the small table lamp playing off her dark, deeply lined face. "What can we do?" she whispered. "I don't think we

247

have a choice with the control that Herr Lutz has exercised."

"You don't believe then, after our meetings, that Lutz will honor his agreement with the Cuban Government?"

The minister shook her thick salt-and-pepper hair, then drew a long breath. "I have to think here, not on a personal level, but on a State level. I represent the people of Cuba in a moment of great need! I cannot afford to trust the guile of this East German strutter. The fate of Cuba's immediate economic future is at stake! With the Soviet pullout, we need to make up a five-billion-dollar, American, shortfall, annually!" Her voice was almost pleading for his understanding.

"Still and again"—Cruz eyed Minister Soria—"Lutz and his people understand all aspects of this gold business. Do you believe we can effectively carry on with Lutz and his Austria people out of the way? This is all very complex. General Lutz also has a highly dangerous group of operatives out in the field. How will you control them?"

Minister Soria tossed her head to one side, then squinted. "I'm not an amateur, Sed. The fact is, ah—" she paused and studied Cruz's melon-shaped face. "I slept with Lutz to gain his confidence." Instantly she saw the hurt in Cruz's face.

"Sed," she said tenderly. "I love you. I have for many years, but this goes beyond you and me." She took another deep breath, wanting desperately to reach this man. "Sed, please. It was over very quickly and it didn't mean a thing to me." Now tears welled

248

up in her eyes for the first time that Cruz could ever remember. "Like you, I'm a prisoner of *El Commandante* and this economic mess that threatens to strangle our Cuba! How many acts did you commit that violated your personal code to survive your years on the Isle of Pines? You are my soul mate for life. We are locked together for life. Please, Sed, help me!" she begged.

"I will, Hilda. I understand what you did and why." Yet his entire body remained tense as he paced back and forth in front of her. "My question remains unanswered. Do we know enough to control this operation, with Lutz and his worldwide connections? What about the operatives now working in the United States?"

The minister laughed, the leather back in her tone. "I have been in contact with the Japanese agent Toshiyuki Mizutari and the Russian, Gregori Ovsyannikov, now operating in America."

"And?"

"And they will do whatever they are told. I already have Ovsyannikov off balance. He is rigid and overtrained."

"Do not underestimate an operative with his experience and special gifts. I know of him. His talents are the great arbitrator in his business. Lutz chose him for a reason."

"Oh, damn it, Sed! Lutz brainwashed him over a period of years. It isn't skill that allows the Russian to move freely about, it is loyalty to Lutz and his criminal band of Aryans in this post-Cold War era!"

Cruz maintained a steady gaze on Soria. "Your public words don't move me."

"Then why the hell did you want to kill General Lutz yesterday? You tried to put your teeth into his groin, for God's sakes! I don't see a great deal of trust in that kind of an act!"

"True enough, Hilda. I lost my head and they are arrogant and vain and everything you say! But can we go it alone?"

"If we don't simplify this Austrian connection, Cuba will never see an ounce of that gold," Soria stated flatly. "And yes, Cruz, I can manipulate his operatives to work for us. Don't forget this is no longer ideology and flag-waving for these people, it is personal greed. The Russian and his people will be paid fairly for what they do." Soria paused and once again took Cruz's hand across the small table. "Can you do it here, Senor?"

For a long time, Cruz stared down at his hands. "Yes, I can do it here. It is very risky—" Then he smiled coldly. "Since Lutz now knows you, I will need your direct help. Let me explain."

Twenty-nine

"Keep your damn head down, sonny!" The mechanical voice droned above the engine noise. Russell Wittenberg dropped the artificial larynx device on its cord and turned his attention back to the road as he weaved the white Chevy van through light traffic.

"Okay, let's see." Wittenberg stared at the lighted green overpass signs on the Santa Monica Freeway. "Stay down and talk to me! I just passed the Harbor Freeway exit, How far?"

"The San Pedro Street exit, north," Spain instructed from the floor of the empty van. Spain tried to smile at Harumi laying next to him in the flashing darkness of downtown Los Angeles at night.

"Scary damn place. I haven't been here for years. Now I know why. Christ, it's dirty! What the hell way is north?"

"Just turn left under the freeway. Listen, Russell, thanks for risking it all to get us down here to L.A. You don't owe us a damn thing." Spain kept Harumi from sliding across the bare mental floor as the van banked sharply to the left and bounced to a halt. Wittenberg, still showing amazing reflexes and presence for a man in his seventies, accelerated onto San Pedro just as the van hit a series of potholes, punched into the worn-out blacktop.

"Welcome to L.A.," Spain grunted as the van snaked its way over the uneven street. "You don't visit this place, you're swallowed by it!"

"Where now, Ben?"

Spain looked up at the eerie red glow from a stoplight that cast an alien reflection off of the old man's face. "Any signs of a tail, Russ?"

"No, I've watched most of the way. Looked for relay cars, trailers, anything that stayed within fifty yards of us. I've been changing lanes every three or four minutes." He shook his head. "But it doesn't mean someone's not back there, waiting for the right time! Well, at least you can be sure it isn't the police."

"How so?" Harumi asked, fear choking her throat.

"Just before the County Bulls left the cabin in Sawyers Bar, I told them you were traveling north into the virgin country of the Rogue River National Forest, eventually hoping to make it to Grants Pass, Oregon. I said you had family there." Then Wittenberg allowed himself to laugh. "Dumb shits! Local cops. When I was still in clandestine ops for the CIA, we really had some fun and games with those local lugheads."

"I thought the CIA couldn't operate on American soil."

"Well, historian, at least you know your federal law. But forget it. The CIA has conducted domestic spying and clandestine operations for years, right here in the good ole U S of A. You ought to teach that to your students! It would kinda give them a sense of the real world, Harumi." Then he laughed again with that haunting robotic sound. "Ah, I just crossed Eighth Street! Now what?"

"Slow down and when you get to Seventh, turn right, if you see you're not being tailed, then pull over in the dark."

"Christ, the whole fucking place is dark! My God, look at those street urchins. God, Spain, the place has the feel of bombed-out postwar Europe and Japan. Just the homeless and filth!"

"I guess I just couldn't stay away from this sewer."

A moment later, Wittenberg pulled the van over to a spot where the sidewalks were littered with hundreds of large cardboard boxes in the sour darkness.

"Keep the engine running and turn off the lights, Russ."

"What the hell!"

"Welcome to the Cardboard Gardens, Russell. There's a city of Home Boys sleeping under those boxes. A kinder and gentler society. Hello, LaLa land," Spain laughed darkly. "Well, it hasn't changed much since I escaped."

"Where we goin', sonny?" Wittenberg rasped.

"About two blocks from here. An old hotel on the corner of Kohler Avenue, called the La Peer. A real skid-row flopper."

"Why this?"

Spain sat up between the seats and rubbed his face.

"Two reasons. One, the whole damn world wants us. The Hawaiian cops, you say the FBI, and a bunch of damn well-heeled thugs led by someone I knew a lifetime ago. All these people will be searching for us anywhere but as streeters in the Gardens. It will give me the time I need to sort all this out." He drew another deep breath. "I couldn't care less about the *Arizona,* Pearl Harbor, or that damn smoking-gun skull of Noonan!" He glanced over at Harumi in the darkness, sensing her disorientation.

"I'm tired of it all! Now, I've got to revert to gutter type. I spent three years on these crummy streets. But there's a certain peace here, if you know the rules. It is a chance to hide from life. Even the cops won't come down here." He paused and stroked Harumi's short hair, then shuddered in the dark. "When I'm here, in this forgotten stinkhole, I always find a way to survive. This cesspool sharpens my will to live!"

Wittenberg turned and handed Spain a small envelope. "It isn't much, but it's all I have. A thou in cash. I know you need it, so don't say anything, Spain." He held up a hand in the light of the windshield. "This cash is for Harumi to find a way and the courage to fit this puzzle together and finally close the book on it. We didn't have the guts to make it right in our time."

Wittenberg leaned back in the driver's seat and paused, watching the few shadowy figures still moving about on the sidewalk, looking for a place to lie down. "Maybe you can make all this right, too," he said softly, pointing to the sea of cardboard boxes. "Anyway, don't let them take you down, historian! Find out the truth, despite my own cynicism, and then tell anyone who'll listen, before they shut you up!" His old fingers moved slowly over his speaking stick, then over the large steering wheel. "In the OSS and later at the agency, we had a dirty little motto we lived by: 'the CIA has the right to lie to protect itself.' In our world, Harumi, lies have become the truth and in a very insidious way, the truth is laughed at as a lie."

"I know that, Russell. I'll try!"

"Just do it, damn it!" He paused, adjusting the speaking device on his throat. "I forgot to mention, that when you get to England, Alvin Dvorak's handle during World War Two was Linch Pin. If he's still alive or even half sane, he can put it all together for you. He can tell you why the powers-that-be want you both taken down, if anyone can. It sure as hell isn't because of a few damn imperial scribbles on parchment!"

Spain took the ten hundred-dollar bills and shoved them in his socks. "Thanks for the loan, Russ. I'll pay you back."

"I hope you try." Then he made a funny gurgling sound, dropping the van into gear. A minute later he pulled up at the La Peer, a 1920s brownstone and brick two-story tenement that passed for a slum hotel, the bottom floor dominated by a Laundromat, emblazoned with a large yellow sign: LAVANDERIA.

"Well, it isn't the Dorchester."

"Maybe not, but it's gonna hopefully save our tender butts," Spain said, sliding open the panel door.

Harumi turned and grabbed Wittenberg's hand.

255

"Thanks for saving our lives!"

"Yeah, tell your father hello. Now bail out that jump door and get your ass wet with a little of Spain's reality. Someday your students will appreciate it."

Then Wittenberg reached out and touched Spain's arm. "Take care, Hamlet," he rasped. "Something does stink here!" He pulled his hand away. "Remember Linch Pin, if you get that far." Then he stood and leaned back into the rear, slamming the panel door shut with a bang. Then he was gone, the squat rear of the white van disappearing into the night, their last lifeline now irrevocably broken.

Harumi began to adjust her eyes, peering down the deserted street and then up at the small rundown apartment hotel, painted in tones of used mud. "Oh, Spain, this is awful!"

Spain took her arm painfully. "Listen up!" There was a dark stain in his voice. "Keep your eyes down and never make eye contact with anyone on the street here! It could mean a quick knife in the belly. Two, keep your mouth shut! You don't need to talk here. Just let me handle this end of it. This is a world of bottom feeders and nightmares, fast mouths and faster knives! So save yourself for when it counts or they'll saw you in half!"

Then unceremoniously Spain picked up a handful of scum from the curb and rubbed it all over Harumi's clothes, despite her writhing protests.

"Spain! Damn you, you bastard!" she screamed. "Get your damned hands off me!" Then she began to sob, looking up at him with fear in her eyes. "Damn you," she sobbed. "I can't do this!"

"Yes you can!" He finished brutalizing her ego by rubbing the smelly muck on her face, then turned and rubbed himself down with the questionable ooze. "We're street people, Harumi! This is how we hide out in the open, until I can make contact with my friend. Clean clothes can be a death sentence! A good pair of shoes is worth more than life here and a smart mouth is a blood debt!"

A moment later, then stood next to the front door of the La Peer Hotel, a strange noise of running water piercing the thick, urban quiet. Harumi glanced up at the sound, watching a man urinating out of a second-floor window, then she suddenly laughed, breaking the tension.

"I thought it was Trump's Castle in Atlantic City! Well, a waterfall's a waterfall!"

After paying three hundred in cash in advance for a week, Spain insisted on the front corner apartment, so he could easily watch all incoming traffic.

Carefully, Spain punched in the numbers on the steel touch pads on the pay phone down the hall from his room. The wide, dimly lighted hallway, crumbling and reeking of urine and cheap wine, dipped precariously in the middle, somehow waiting for a swift jolt from another earthquake to send it crashing to the ground. He touched the .45 in his belt to reassure himself.

"Parker Center. How may we help you?" came the

257

mechanical voice on the other end.

"Ah, Detective Lieutenant Danny McBroom, please. He's in Homicide."

"I'm sorry, sir, he can't be reached—"

"Damn it, I need to speak to him!" Spain bellowed, a sickening panic rising in his voice.

"Sir," the labored voice continued, "Lieutenant McBroom has been relocated to South Bureau, Homicide. I can transfer you, if it's an emergency."

"It is," Spain replied, calming himself, praying that McBroom would still be around despite the fact it was eight-thirty at night.

Waiting, Spain changed the phone to his other ear, his eyes now adjusted fully to the dingy hallway. For a second he thought he heard something. Maybe he felt it, the hair rising on the back of his neck. Jesus! Even the phone smelled of bile.

"Yeah, McBroom here," came a low, dour voice, with just a wisp of a Southern drawl.

Spain held his breath watching the dark corners of the hall. Suddenly, he sensed a presence as he pulled the old Colt from his belt, chambering a round with a sharp metallic click.

"Damn it!" the voice smoldered, following a deep breath. "It's too fucking late at night for this! This is the Los Angeles Police Department and if you don't answer this call, you're in deep fried shit!"

"Hold it, Soprano Maker," Spain croaked. "I've got some big bad monster sliding up on my flank and I think I'm dinner!"

"Who the hell is this! Some fucking roach? Soprano

258

Maker?" His voice took on the meter of sudden surprise, even shock. "Only one guy ever—"

"It's Spain, butt head," he whispered pushing the hard lump of fear back down his throat. "I'm dropping the phone, McBroom. Don't flush yourself or anything stupid. This asshole here really has me on his dance card!"

Spain allowed the phone to slide through his hand as it swung below the pay phone. Barely moving, he flattened himself against the crumbling wall. Suddenly a shadow flashed silently past him, a powerful, calloused hand found Spain's neck with incredible speed. Quickly, the hand pulled him down by the neck, just as Spain brought the Colt around reaching for the stranger's head. A lightning jolt of pain shot through his right wrist, the automatic dropping harmlessly to the floor. Now even the dim hallway grew fainter as Spain began to swim desperately for a sailor floundering helplessly in the fast muddy current of the Red River near Haiphong. Something was terribly wrong. His legs grew heavy as lead as he felt himself fall, but where was the water? The hand was still crushing the life from his throat, when he finally gave into a distant warmth. Abruptly, the feeling was pulled away with the shattering of glass crashing over skull bone.

The next thing Spain knew, Harumi was holding his head, massaging his throat. Quickly, he tried to sit up, but slumped back, a terrible pain still choking his windpipe.

"Easy, Benny." She was smiling down at him. "Just

259

breathe, honey. Please, just breathe."

Finally he sat up, and glanced over at the huge man laying unconscious next to him. "Christ, his hand was like steel. What did you do?"

"Well, hero, I hit him over the head with an empty whiskey bottle, before he sawed you in half." Slowly she helped Spain to his feet. "You better watch out for all those bottom feeders."

Spain rolled the giant of a man, with a week's growth on his face and rags that passed for clothes. The man's half-open toothless mouth was laced with blackened diseased gums, which only served to highlight the deep cut on the back of his head.

"One of the Black Ghost's folks?"

Spain felt the man's pockets, coming up empty.

"Don't think so. It couldn't be. Not even Gregori knows where the hell we are. Eventually, he'll figure it out, but not yet." Spain stood up, looking down at the pathetic giant now moaning on the floor. "He looks like a draft reject from the Knicks or Celts."

"What?"

"Nothing." Spain found the .45 and brought the thick cold barrel up the man's cheek. Then he wedged his elbow hard against his Adam's apple. "Okay, home boy, rise and shine! You stepped on Superman's cape and he's real pissed!" He then jammed the gun barrel in the man's ear.

Now the bloodshot, mucous-stained eyes of the giant stared at Spain in disbelief. "Ooh, man. What you be doin' that for?"

"Breathing is a bad habit of mine, home boy!"

"I only wanted some jingle, man!" The giant tested Spain's elbow, then fell back moaning as his Adam's apple felt the pressure of Spain's elbow.

"Well, man," Spain hissed, "you pass the fucking word in the Gardens that this dude's gonna kick some ass, if you go messin' about with me and my woman! Can you dig it, hands?"

As fast as lightning, the giant bucked Spain into midair with ferocious energy. Spain landed with a thud just as the giant reared back to thrust a foot into his rib cage. A strange laugh erupted from the man's throat. "Shit, I ain't gonna take no honky crap!"

Just as the old leather shoe came around, Spain grabbed it and twisted with all his strength, sending the giant tumbling to the floor. Spain rolled quickly to his right, then came upright into a firing stance, the .45 aimed with both hands at the giant's face.

"This honky's gonna splatter your face all over this hall!"

"Ben!" Harumi shouted, "God, don't!"

"Too late! I mean to kill this asshole! I wanna see his blood!"

Now the giant was frightened as he slowly sat up, his mammoth arms raised tentatively into the air. He tried to speak with that toothless pink mouth, but fear stopped the words in his throat.

"You got it, home boy," Spain said slowly, moving toward him with the automatic raised to kill. "I've been havin' a real bad time the last few weeks, butt face, and I need to see some blood." Then Spain lashed out with the .45, viciously whipping the side of

261

the giant's face. The blow sent the man down to the floor, with a sharp cry, as Spain followed him down, the gun shoved into his soft belly. "This isn't a race thing, home boy, I guess we just have bad chemistry!" Then Spain again slammed the gun into the man's gut with the sound of air rushing from a dying balloon.

"You tell the other home boys and especially the rabid dogs like you, that next time anyone ever comes near me again in the Gardens, I'll off him, then I'll find you and put a manhole cover in your face! Got it, friend?" Spain smiled coldly, trying to hold his anger in check.

The giant fighting to catch his breath nodded slowly as he rose to all fours.

Spain backed up to the pay phone, finally picking up the receiver, the weapon still aimed at the intruder now staggering off down the hall. "You still there, McBroom?" He heard background voices, then he called McBroom's name again. Finally the dour voice said hello.

"I'm sorry for the delay, Danny. Some crud *borracho* decided to separate my body from my head and it took my roommate to save my ass!" He glanced over at Harumi and winked. "How's Helene and the kids?"

"She's fine and James started Howard last year. Jesus, you're really something, Spain! Hey you okay?" Suddenly, McBroom's voice changed pitch. "Where the hell are you?"

"I'm back at my old haunt?"

"In the Gardens at the La Peer? Oh, Jesus, Spain!

You back in the shit?"

"No, I haven't touched a drop, since Jack—" his voice cracked. "Since Jack Scruggs pulled me out. No, Danny, I've got a bigger problem. And you're all I have, to help!"

There was a long silence on the phone. "I owe you, Ben. You know that. If I can help, you know I will."

"I need to meet you and talk." Spain dropped his voice, and turned his back so Harumi couldn't hear. "Hey, man, I'm scared. Really scared. Meet me at the usual. Will you do it? We can get lost in the Nickel for an hour?"

"Yeah, Ben, I will. Let's see. We'll meet at the corner of Crocker and Fifth streets at ten." Then McBroom paused, something indefinable in his silence that carried through the phone.

"Ah, Ben, we've got a major problem here."

"What?"

"There's a big fat All-Points Bulletin out for you." Spain could hear the pain in his friend's voice. "It came in three days ago. Ah, you've made the top ten. Murder, armed and dangerous. The works. It seems everyone but the Nazis wants you, Ben."

"Give me an hour of talk. No cuffs, no slammer, no custody!"

"Jesus, Ben! I'm a peace officer! I've got a sworn obligation!"

"I don't have a choice! Help me!"

263

Thirty

The sun began its final slide behind the brooding limestone of the Dachstein Massif, quickly turning the brilliance into a thin, restless twilight. Slowly, Sed Cruz made his way from the window over to the bed lamp and switched it on.

Turning to the task at hand, Cruz unzipped his large, soft-sided suitcase and carefully pulled back a thick rubber padding in the lining. He then pulled back a Velcro seal, revealing a wide carbon border that traversed the entire perimeter of the case.

Feeling her presence, Cruz turned and watched the Cuban minister watch him as she dressed in the adjoining bathroom. "Are you certain, Hilda? There are forces here we may not be able to control."

Soria pulled the low-cut black silk bra over her full breasts and stared at herself in the bathroom mirror. "I don't believe we have a choice, Sed." Pleased with herself, she turned and faced him, stepping lightly into silk panties, her legs still muscular and well shaped. Then she smiled knowingly. "There is nothing here in this

264

alien place that we can't control," she offered, pulling the tight-fitting red silk dress over her head.

"Are you going to be with him tonight, Hilda?" Cruz shuddered visibly, turning back to the suitcase. For a moment, he hesitated, then ran his long, slender fingers on the underside of the carbon border until he found the opening. Working carefully, he peeled away the top half of the carbon edge, revealing high-powered .22-caliber shells.

Cruz felt Hilda's hands slide around his sunken midsection as he dumped a hundred gleaming brass shells on the unmade bed. "I don't really have a choice, Sed."

Angrily he whirled around. *"Dos Mio!* This is your choice! You don't have to let him touch you!"

Soria pushed out a deep, heavy breath. "I do," she said tenderly. "I need the recall code for his field team. I don't want them at our backs. I've thought about what you said about the agent Ovsyannikov. He is highly dangerous!"

Cruz laughed crudely, picking up a handful of long-nosed shells. "And what makes you think you can get that code from General Mischa Lutz?"

The woman gently touched his face. "Can you keep anything from these hands?" Then she shook her head sadly. "I would have hoped you would have understood what I'm doing. This is not about desire, it's about control."

"I understand! Just another sacrifice for our beloved Cuba!" he spat out. Cruz turned back to his work, next pulling back another Velcro flap hiding a three-inch-deep compartment in the bottom of the case. Slowly he removed a six-inch-long black polymer helical cylinder, and began loading the shells. Silently Soria watched as he then unscrewed the large post handle from the top of the suitcase.

"What's that?" Her voice was still loving.

"The combination stock and grip made of glass-filled resin. It's extremely light and functional."

"Is it Czech?"

For an instant he turned and glared at her. "No, Minister," he seethed, "it's not Czech, it's American, called the Calico M-900P! The Czechs no longer have it in the high-tech department, as much as it might pain you!" Still angry, Cruz then turned the suitcase upside down and with a sharp pocket knife cut through the thick nylon and cardboard surrounding a shallow dog-leg impression. Using the knife with a surgeon's skill, Cruz deftly cut around the shape that also acted as a wheel strut on the bottom of the case. Removing what now appeared to be a very narrow gun stock composed of high-tensile aircraft aluminum alloy, Cruz finished assembling the assault pistol by snapping the helical magazine atop the stock.

Soria shook her head, still fascinated with and needing this man. "You amaze me. What does it weigh, Sed?" She hugged his back, trying to reach him.

"About six pounds, fully loaded with a hundred rounds."

"And you're sure General Lutz's X-Ray machinery picked up nothing?"

"Yes. The machinery would just pick up the aluminum wheel struts on the bottom of the case and a hand search wouldn't turn up the resin components buried in the structure of the case."

"Two and a half kilos, fully loaded! Where did you find it? With the suitcase disguise and all?"

"From a mail-order house in Chicago." He laughed darkly. Then he walked into the bathroom and bathed his face in warm water, trying to dilute his growing tension. He dried his face in silence with a thick hand towel.

"I only intended to bring the weapon into this place in case of an emergency, not to murder these people." He turned to her, his tired eyes pleading with her.

"These aren't people, they're corruptors of our way of life. Modern day Neo Nazis!"

Cruz held up a hand in surrender. He had had enough. There was no way to reach this powerful woman, who one day would probably become prime minister of Cuba, when Castro could no longer hold his crumbling empire together. For a long time he stared at her, his face filled with both dread and poignancy as he studied her now passive face. He laughed to himself. The only thing that would ever give this woman away were her eyes. They were raven pools with flecks of light gray in the pupil that had the incredible piercing quality of white hot steel. They were the misplaced eyes of a circling bird of prey, both fearless and magnetic and at the same time fierce.

Suddenly Cruz burst out laughing, finally touching the emotion deep within himself that he had been long searching for. This woman could play the big poker hand and eventually she would, using this gold business as a stepping-stone to becoming the Pope of Havana.

He finally reached out and curiously touched her face. "They say, Hilda, that if you live long enough, what's in your heart will show up in your eyes. Now, you had better tend to that Bavarian pastry of yours." He smiled somberly. "I will do your work in the morning, Senora. No, excuse me. I will do Cuba's work," he whispered, holding the pistol in his warped hands.

"The morning in Hallstatt, Austria, always brings its own hope, with its clean air and crisp temperatures," General Lutz murmured as he stood by the large double front doors waiting for his guests to come downstairs, his lawyer hovering by his side. Slowly the general smoothed his blue regimental tie, thinking about last night. Indeed, he had never been with an older woman of such firmness and overall talent. Her muscle control was something to behold and for a man in his late sixties, this Cuban fireball had been a tonic. He smiled inwardly, staring at the sickly body and complexion of his counselor, now making funny little gestures with his chubby pink hands. In fact, General Lutz was very pleased with himself as he turned to his lawyer. "Be patient, Otto, we only have to drive them down the mountain to Salzburg. Last night, the minister even tried to wheedle the code from me—in a moment of compromise."

"General!" Now Otto Krestmier was beside himself, that awful purple hue flushing his nervous face with a lack of oxygen. "I don't trust these brown bastards!" he hissed. "The code!"

Lutz touched his shoulder with a perfectly manicured hand. "I gave her the discarded code. It's our insurance. Believe me, Otto, all is well. You wait here for me, then we can talk." He smiled with perfectly square, dazzling teeth that reflected his mood. "Now we have the ground-level mules and muscle we need to make the necessary transport of bullion."

"You are playing with fire with that woman!" Krestmier warned.

Lutz laughed, tossing his head to one side just as the houseboy bodyguard made his appearance at the top of the landing, carrying two large suitcases. "She is fire, Otto," he whispered. A moment later, Minister Soria, with Sed Cruz trailing respectfully behind, descended the long stairway.

"Ah, you look ravishing, Minister!" Lutz bowed curtly, bussing her extended hand. "I trust the new suitcase is to your liking."

"Thank you, Mischa," she chortled. "In Salzburg, at the hotel, someone must have taken a knife to it. They even stole the handle, looking for God knows what— only a few nonessential items were missing."

"You know, Hilda, it's strange we didn't notice the damage when you arrived."

For a long frozen moment, Cruz watched Soria stand silently, staring at the general. Not being able to stand another moment, Cruz stepped easily forward, his eyes bowed. "I hand carried the damaged luggage in myself. You would not have noticed, General Lutz." Cruz momentarily made eye contact with the general, then respectfully turned away waiting for Lutz, with Hilda on his arm, to move to the old Cadillac.

Five minutes later, the spotless 1965 Cadillac stretch Seville limo inched over the gravel driveway, finally passing through the electronic gate onto the narrow mountain road. The burly driver, his chest bulging with a shoulder holster, was fully occupied negotiating the second sharp hairpin turn, almost a mile down the mountain from the chalet, when Cruz was seized with a sudden fit of coughing. Finally recovered, he stared over at the arrogant blond driver and smiled helplessly. In the back seat, Minister Soria was moving her restless hands over General Lutz's growing hardness as he hoped for another moment of pleasure with this incredible woman.

The loud moaning and pleadings of the general were unsettling the driver as he tried not to stare into the rearview mirror at the general's erection, now exposed to that crisp alpine air. Shaking his head, the driver refocused his attention on the road as the cumbersome Cadillac slowed for another narrow hairpin at nine thousand feet.

Turning slowly in the seat, Cruz reached into the right pocket of his overcoat that had been cut away to accommodate the Calico. Carefully, Cruz inched his finger over the safety, flicking it off, then he coughed again. A moment later, he whirled and at point-blank range, brutally sprayed a burst of .22 bullets into the bodyguard's face and upper torso. Acting quickly, Cruz reached over, smashing open the driver's door with his boot, shoving the dead man out onto the road. Grabbing the wheel and jamming his foot on the brake, Cruz turned, just as General Lutz, his eyes fogged in ecstasy, began to comprehend the moment.

"General Lutz, do you understand?" Cruz screamed at him in thick German. "I want you to understand that I'm going to kill you!"

Gen. Mischa Lutz forced himself into the back of the seat, shaking his head as his eyes began to clear, his lips trembling. "No! No, you bastard! Not here, not like this!"

Sed Cruz laughed. "Good, now you're awake and you understand!" Then he laced the general's heaving chest with a sharp burst of fire, the angry tears already hemorrhaging onto his tan camel hair overcoat.

For an instant, Soria watched the intensity in Cruz's face and she was suddenly frightened, the smell of gunpowder and death permeating the Cadillac. Then he smiled at her as he turned and set the emergency brake.

Suddenly overwhelmed with waves of heaving nausea, Soria stepped from the back seat, then began to vomit uncontrollably. "Oh, Sed," she finally gasped, wiping her mouth, "it was terrible! I've never been that close to a man, shot to death!"

Grimly Cruz held her shoulders. "I have." For a moment, he turned his back staring out at the sharp icy peaks across the valley. Then his eyes wandered down as he spotted a familiar building, then he shook his head. In silence he dragged General Lutz's blood-smeared body from the back seat and rolled it off the steep cliff, into the thick clouds that formed below.

"Well, Minister, there's another body for the bone bin." Then he turned Soria's face to him with those gnarled, used hands. "This was the easy part. Now, because of your decision, this will all become very difficult and deadly!"

Thirty-one

Spain stirred the oily black coffee with a questionable spoon and looked about Spider Webb's diner in the heart of the Nickel in downtown Los Angeles. The whole shabby place was still painted in hopelessness and tire eyes, and Spain shuddered inside from the thought that he'd never again escape this place, alive. He closed his eyes, but when he opened them, the small cafe was still overrun with the homeless, moving from table to table mooching whatever change was available. He shuddered again, the raw, bone deep memories pushing over him. Tips left on an empty table were a symbol of territory and worth a knife wound or a deadly finger in the eye. Spain forced himself to watch a middle-aged man, his left eye now gone, replaced with a pulpy growth of flesh and fungus, move quickly to the next booth, snapping up the small tip before the waiter could make a move.

"What the hell did you do!" The massive black man, dressed in an old blue sports jacket and a shirt that was clean two days before, shook his perfectly shaped head.

Then his intense police eyes followed Spain's every move as he reached into his pocket.

"Easy, Danny. I'm clean."

"Jerk off!" McBroom moaned. "What the hell am I gonna do with you? Where's your gun moll?" He slowly rubbed the filthy red-and-white-checked tablecloth with his huge square fingers.

"I haven't seen you in three fucking years, and you treat me like I'm ready for old smoky at Sing Sing!"

"You are, damn it! Then again electrocution is too quick!" Then McBroom lowered his head and pushed himself back in the booth.

"I love you, too." Spain tried the coffee, then mashed his face from the taste. "How are the kids?" He tried to smile, a large, angry bruise growing on his face from the fight at the La Peer Hotel.

"The kids," McBroom repeated softly. "The kids—"

"What?"

"You don't know, do you?" Suddenly McBroom's suspicious eyes slumped at the corners, his face turning to soft brown custard. "Jon's dead."

Spain's mouth dropped in shock. He'd played kid games with Jon McBroom when he lived with the family in Baldwin Hills, a black middle-income suburb of Los Angeles, while he was drying out and lacing his life back together.

"What happened?" Spain felt himself shiver from deep in his soul.

"He was in the reserves and when the Gulf War started, he was activated, with the Eighty-second Airborne. They pulled the kid right out of UCLA. He had only a year to go until graduation." McBroom rubbed a hand over his fatigued face, searching for the right words. "It's good talking about Jon with you, Ben. It really is. When Jon died, everyone who knew me tip-toed around, like my kid never existed. I like saying his name. I like—" For a long time, he held his words, biting down on his upper lip. "Jon," he whispered. "Jon was my first born and was killed when they pushed a special ranger combat team into a place in western Iraq, Qasr Amij, to take out a Scud missile site at a base called H-Two. Now all we have is a Silver Star and a flag. I—"

Spain pulled his eyes down, staring at the checked ta-blecloth and the old, stained coffee mug. "Oh, God, Danny! I'm so sorry! Christ, now we've visited war on our children!"

McBroom took a gulp of coffee, shaking his head, his eyes refocusing. "Thanks for listening."

"What about Helene and James?

"Helene has a picture of Jon on the mantel, a Silver Star in a fucking little blue box and a folded American flag that she holds like it was her newborn baby." McBroom raised his hands in the air. "James and I are on our own. Helene's in her own world and so I work all the time." A wisp of a smile crossed his face. "I investi-gate homicides, check the vics laying on ice in the morgue and have a shitload of blue murder case books sitting on my desk. They will probably never be solved because this place that passes for a civilized city is in fact a third-world shooting gallery for every pimp, gang banger, cokehead, and rainbow thumper in the world."

McBroom placed his powerful black hands under his chin. "L.A. is the end of the rainbow. There isn't any place to go, when the dream goes sour here, except into the Pacific. Now, what the hell's this APB and warrant shit all about, Benjamin?"

After another cup of coffee and an explanation that defied reality, McBroom sat back in the booth, slowly shaking his head. "Ya know, Ben, all I have now is my work. James is away at Howard University and Helene lives out there somewhere in her own world. When you were still practicing law, you saved my ass, my job, and my marriage on that false rape charge. I'll always owe you for that." McBroom watched a homeless woman press her purple lips up against the front window of the cafe, begging for a handout.

"I'm just a black cop who made it off the fucking street and I'm grateful to the LAPD and God, despite their bad P.R. I'm also grateful to you for being my friend, but, Ben, I'm a peace officer!" He felt the heat rise in his face, his voice rising to a shrill. "You're hotter than a clean, five-hundred-buck-an-hour hooker's pussy. Within a few days, when the world gets your scent, even the boy scouts will be down in the Gardens looking for you and your history teacher. You're so bad now, you're nationwide, sucker!"

For a long time, McBroom watched the disappointment and the crush of hopelessness eat at Spain's features. Finally he smiled sadly. "Relax, Ben, I'm still your friend. I'm not gonna cuff you to the hat rack — at least not yet. Until you prove me wrong, you're still one of the good guys and I don't give a shit what that APB says. I can't take you, if you're not in Shakytown, can I? Of course," he said, laughing, "that's off the record." Then he leaned his large head across the table drawing himself very close to Spain. "With all that you've told

275

me, what's next? You do have some kinda game plan, don't you?"

McBroom watched the fear hang all over Spain's pinched face. "No game plan. Okay, what's your next move?"

"To continue breathing and find a way to get to England, to visit that monk I told you about." Then Spain paused. "The monk, if he's alive, or sane, can supposedly pull all the connective tissue together." He looked at McBroom's funny expression. "I know it's a fool's errand, but it's all that we have."

For a long time, McBroom stared out at the grease-smeared window to a group of homeless huddling next to a fire coming from an old fifty-gallon oil drum. "You do know that if they really want you dead, there's not a thing I can do for you. It will be you against them!"

"Thanks for the philosophy." Angrily, Spain rose, dropping a few single dollar bills on the table. "I guess you were a roach, Soprano Maker! My arrogance died on these streets a long time ago! A man's purpose and conceit dies when he confronts wet feet, cold ground, and an empty belly stuffed with fear. Right now, I'm at ground zero, waiting to take the big hit and I know it, damn it! Incidentally, you don't owe me a goddamned thing! The books are clear!"

A powerful hand reached up and pulled Spain back down into the booth. "Still the fucking hobo lawyer! Shut your face and listen to me! You need a deep, dark hole to hide in, to let the heat pass on by, leatherhead!"

"And where the hell do I find that?" Spain screamed across the table. Then he slumped back, reaching for the coffee mug with a shaking hand. "In a fucking coffin, or swinging from the trees out in the forest?"

"Close." McBroom rubbed his cold nose, thinking it through. "You told me once that when you were a kid your old man taught you to live off the land. Was that true or some lawyer bullshit?"

Spain nodded. "True. Basques are always very independent. My father trained me, but it's been alot of years."

McBroom shifted his large body in the hard, torn seat. "There's a street slicker who makes a living as a pusher, snitch, and trader of goods here in the Nickel. Name's Boxcar Willy."

Spain shook his head disgustedly. "I don't know any Boxcar Willy on these streets!"

"Hell, he's half snake oil salesman, half moon man, or whatever you want him to be. Anyway, he owes me a big one."

"So?"

"So, he bagged a great big sailboat in a drug deal that soured last month. One of those ocean jobs. That's all I know. My folks aren't supposed to be able to swim or go near the water," he said, laughing, "but you were a navy boy. I used to hear you talk about sailing at dinner."

Spain shook his head. "I sailed years ago, when I was flush. What are you going to do? Nail this Boxcar guy and take his boat?"

McBroom smiled for the first time that night. "Exactly. He doesn't know a sail from a tit. For the right price, he'd be happy to sign over the title."

Spain groaned. "I've got exactly six hundred bucks and change. You're talking thousands, Danny!"

"No, I'm not! We're talking his freedom. What do you think that's worth, Ben?" Then he smiled again.

"Let's go roust us a street admiral. Time to do some trading."

The massive, single-span Vincent Thomas Bridge arced its towers out of the fog and shadows as a menacing primordial beacon, guarding the Port of Los Angeles, in San Pedro, twenty miles south of the city. A loud foghorn from somewhere off in the distance brayed its warning of dangerous shoals and of the almost invisible rock breakwater that rose to guard the huge port facility from the open Pacific.

A wave of fog swirled past the breakwater, then over the abandoned Cavanaugh Anchovy Company as an unmarked navy blue Ford, with its telltale blackwall tires, rolled slowly through the mist on an adjacent wharf.

"I can't see a damn thing," Danny McBroom mumbled as he pulled the car to a stop, trying to take some kind of reference fix. Slowly, his trained eyes cautiously swiveled a one-eighty as he fought the squashed light and muted sounds that fouled his keen senses.

"Where is it, Willy?" McBroom turned his head and found the man's nervous eyes.

"Take it easy, Lieutenant." The voice was clear enough, but something was wrong with the tone. It was tinny and shallow, like half of a vocal cord had been somehow cut from his throat. "See that blue neon haze. That's the water taxi sign. Let's see." For a long time, the once handsome man, now run down by gravity, rotten teeth that eroded his jaw line, and two stretches at San Quentin, listened to the fog with an animal's cunning. "I was down here yesterday to make sure everything worked."

"How the hell would you know? Shit, Spain!" he said to the back seat, "Boxcar Willy here is a fucking admiral! He wouldn't know a rope from a limp dick!"

"Sheet," Spain corrected.

"See there, Willy," McBroom thundered, pounding Willy on the arm, "that man back there is a real sailor!" Then McBroom squeezed Willy's shoulder until the man winced in pain. "You're really doin' the right thing, Willy. I mean being the kind of professional associate you are, to give title of this sailboat to my friend here." McBroom's voice took on a deep, false warmth.

"Give! It's a fucking heist! You got your foot on my balls!"

McBroom slammed on the brakes and smiled again, staring at Willy as he spoke to Spain and Harumi in the back seat. "You know, Ben, the world's full of lizards, sitting on the rocks, just warming their hides, watching the world go by. Willy here likes to live the good life! New Mercedes. You know, Ben, one of those little two-seat jobs, expensive wine and women with heaters built into their mouths and thighs. But Boxcar Willy, the great skid-row trader has one problem. He doesn't like to work! He spent his formative years in the slammer."

"Come on, Lieutenant! You're jacking me off here! It's a false rap. I'm innocent! The warrant—"

"So is Saddam Hussein! The warrant's real and even if you cop a plea, you'll be a three-time loser, on a heroin bust! You can kiss your nuts goodbye, except for some of my folks in the big house just waiting to take a shower with you! You'll do five to seven, if you last that long!" Then McBroom laughed.

279

"Let me run it down for you, mudrat! You scored this sailboat in exchange for two kilos of China White that you were pushing. Christ, I've got enough on you that it might be easier if we implant a license plate stamping machine into your hands right now! You shouldn't have put the word out on the street that you had a sailboat for sale. You thought you scored, but you went down for the count, instead!"

"Okay!" Willy held up his hands, smiling at Harumi in the back seat. "You like to sail, honey?" He tried his best smile, his eyes sliding over Harumi's firm body in the dim light.

A large hand cuffed Willy in the ear, forcing him to cry out in pain. "Hey!"

"Hey nothing," McBroom said gently. "Don't talk to her. She's too smart for you. You ask me the question first, then I'll see if she wants to answer it!"

The squawk box in McBroom's car suddenly hissed: "This is ten Whiskey twenty-four, calling nine Yankee seventy-two."

"This is Yankee. What's up, Whiskey?"

"Ah, I just talked with a guy on the horn who said he was federal heat. You said you wanted to know if any Feds came sniffing around."

"Yeah, I did. What'd he want?"

"Well, he starts running down the description of two people, the same two that came over the fax on that APB from Five-O in Honolulu last week. He was real curious. Ah—"

"What?" McBroom squeezed down on the car mike.

"I don't know. Ah, he didn't sound like he was really FBI. At first I thought it was a cranker, but he had too much info. Refused to ID himself."

"That's Gregori," Spain said faintly. He shuddered, taking Harumi's hand.

"Look, Whiskey, you got a number for this guy? Where is he now?"

"On his way down to Shakytown?"

"Where's that?" Harumi pushed forward in her seat.

"It's here," McBroom answered. "L.A. is called Shakytown. The earthquake capital of the world." Then he depressed the speak button. "Whiskey, see if you can track him down. Where'd he call from?"

"Santa Barbara."

"My, God! He's right behind us!"

"Take it easy, Harumi," McBroom said, keying the mike, again. "Ah, Whiskey, the second this guy makes noise in your ear, I want to know! Just keep it loose, no friction as far as this guy is concerned. Apparently he's a real pro, and I can't track him, if he's the least bit suspicious. Offer him some help if you have to."

"Ten-four, Yankee." Then the hissing radio faded into the special San Pedro dampness.

"There it is!" Willy almost jumped out the window of the police car, he was so relieved. "Damn it, Lieutenant!" Boxcar declared, a fragile confidence suddenly rising in his voice. "I told you it was straight and you made me feel like common street dirt."

McBroom shrugged. "Sorry, Willy. I don't know what came over me." Then he grabbed Willy again by the shoulder with his free hand as the car rolled to a stop at a small gate leading down to a narrow, rickety wooden boat slip. "Just doin' my job." Barely able to make out the dim shape of a boat's hull through the fog, Boxcar Willy led the way down the steep ramp.

Ten minutes later, Willy anxiously stepped down into

the cabin and tentatively approached Spain, who was carefully checking the bilge for water. Great ocean goin' ship, huh, Ben?" His curved smile had the shape of a possum's mouth.

"It better be!" McBroom interrupted, bending his head to make it down the short flight of steps into the crowded cabin.

"So, what do you think, Ben? This tub good enough for an ocean cruise?" he whispered out of earshot of Harumi and Willy.

Spain narrowed his eyes. "She's sound. A good thirty-foot coastal cruising boat," he answered evaluating the boat. "Newports are solid craft. Self-furling jib, strong main, four-cylinder diesel inboard, responsive rudder to wheel." Then he laughed darkly. "It depends where we're supposed to be cruising. I wouldn't want to try for Hawaii this time of year."

McBroom waved his large hands in front of Spain. "No, no!" Then he reached into his topcoat and pulled out a folded chart. "Take a look." Then he put his finger to his lips, nodding his eyes in the direction of Boxcar Willy.

Spain spread the chart out on the navigation table, switching on the special gooseneck light. After a moment, a slight smile spread across his face.

"You always talked about the times you spent on Catalina with your father, tending the sheep of the Wrigley family out in the back country. It's the only thing I could come up with that would bury you for a few weeks and still keep you close to me."

"What about getting out of the harbor? Everyone's watching for us." He looked down at the chart, detailing San Pedro Harbor, the Catalina Channel, then finally the narrow, almost primitive neck narrow, twenty-eight-mile-long island, some thirty miles west of the Southern California coast.

Turning quickly, McBroom blocked Boxcar Willy's view as he peered between them at the chart. "Get up on deck, Willy! Jesus! What do I have to do to get some respect from you? Freeze dry you and drop you in the evidence locker for a few weeks?" Then he grabbed the thin man by the throat and smiled his unique, menacing smile. "Get your ass up on deck," he said softly. "As far as you're concerned, this meeting, this boat, never happened. Go wait by the car and don't sell it! You understand, mudrat?"

Quickly, Boxcar Willy backed up the stairs and disappeared.

"I don't know, Danny. Look at this. I've got to get by the Coast Guard station, the harbor pilots and then the army at Fort MacArthur, right here on the point. If they see a sailboat sneaking out on a foggy night, it's a red flag!" For emphasis, Spain tapped the chart.

McBroom moved his hands in front of his face. "I've done the best that I can, with some contacts, and I've built a little agenda for you." He looked at his watch. "I'm no sailor, but you've got half an hour until the tide goes out and you're going with it." He turned to Harumi and smiled.

"You got some bullets for that ancient heater stuck in your belt?"

Spain shook his head.

"Good! You might need them, for close-in work." Then McBroom stopped smiling.

Thirty-two

After instructing Harumi, Spain checked his watch with his old flashlight that had seen him through the gun store robbery in San Francisco. It had been only a week! He couldn't believe it, then he shivered, remembering what life on the street was like, where time had a very distorted meaning. Maybe if Einstein had spent time on the street it would have helped him with his Time Unification Theory.

"What now?" Harumi whispered as they both hunched in the narrow cockpit of the blue-hulled sailboat, dominated by a large chrome helm, anchored by a lighted compass. The soft, muted thumping of the four-cylinder diesel engine exhaust was the only sense of movement as the sailboat glided silently down the dark, narrow inlet toward the main channel of the Los Angeles Harbor.

"Give me a time check every minute, starting now!" Spain ordered.

"Ah, ten twenty-six."

"Damn!" Spain dropped his head under the main boom, searching behind him. For another instant, he watched the main channel, fast approaching. Disgusted, he swung the boat's bows hard over to port, barely missing a seawall before completing the full turn.

"God, Ben! What are you doing?"

"Trying to save our worthless lives by sneaking out of one of the busiest harbors in the world, just in case you didn't notice!" For an instant Spain squatted, his shaking knees on the fiberglass bench of the cockpit.

"What are you looking for?"

Half listening, Spain watched the mouth of the channel approach again, marked by the fog-smudged blue and white neon beacon:

RAE MOUNTAIN WATER TAXI

Pressing on in the shrouded blackness, Spain slid past the rust-stained hull of the tuna trawler *Santa Maria,* her massive seiner net strung up from her mast below the crow's nest.

"Time! Damn it!"

"Ah, ten twenty-nine."

"Come on, baby, come on!" Spain coaxed the empty channel.

"What are you looking for?" She repeated.

"Some luck, Harumi!" He turned his focus and concentration back to the channel, looking east toward the faint amber lights of the Vincent Thomas Bridge. Maybe he could somehow will their survival. Maybe he should pray, something he hadn't done since Vietnam.

"We've got red lights coming up fast from the bow!" Harumi's voice rose to a shriek.

285

"Jesus!" Spain turned his eyes for just an instant, watching the low-slung, sharp bows of a harbor patrol boat racing toward them. By the look of the rooster tail wake behind the police boat, it had to be moving at close to twenty knots! In a matter of minutes, the patrol boat would be on them.

Suddenly out of the indistinct horizon a mountainous, slowly moving tower appeared, decorated with green and red lights. "Get me the field glasses from the chart table!" Quickly he scanned the massive 20,000-ton cargo-container ship, looking for her five-story-high black bows. A moment later, he spotted the ship's name, a dull light shining down on it:

KIM PUSAN
Pusan, Korea

"My, God, that's it! You lovable old bastard! Danny McBroom, I could almost kiss your ass!"

"That's what?"

"Maybe our way out of San Pedro, alive!" Again he squinted into the glasses. "Christ, she's moving like a snail. That, Harumi, is a cargo-container ship, probably a drug runner, and we're going to ride her like a pilot fish, close up on her starboard flank, using the energy of her bow wave to get out of here into the fog!" He turned the glasses gauging the fast- moving police boat and its course.

"That ship is filled to the gunnels with pineapples bound for Hawaii that were grown in Hawaii, but are cheaper than if you picked them out of a field in the islands. Then this mother of all ships steams into Rangoon, picks up a load of China White Heroin and sails back into San Pedro. Free enterprise! I love it!" he said sarcastically, helplessly watching the police boat draw closer.

Spain leveled the gun at the approaching boat, gauging the range.

"Don't, Ben!"

"Jesus, Harumi! Give me a fucking break! We give up, we're dead! Maybe I should kill that boat with my spit!" Then she was next to him holding him tightly, feeling his thick warmth against her. Spain shook his head, turning back to navigating the bow wave of the *Pusan*. "Christ, it's Willy Peter fear all over again. Your skin gets hair that stands straight up, whether you have it or not!"

Now they could hear the police boat's siren as it drew closer. "Willy Peter fear?" Harumi was making conversation, to fight her own fear and helplessness.

"In Nam and Nicaragua and I suppose in the Gulf War, both sides used white phosphorous incendiary artillery shells that exploded, pushing white-hot burning shards of steel into skin and bone. It was real neat stuff. When a barrage would start, we'd just bury our heads in our knees and shake. We called 'em incoming Willy Peters. It could turn anyone's dick into a useless string!"

"No wonder you ended up in the Nickel." Harumi touched his face. "My life was so different."

Spain grunted. "Well, our lifelines have crossed now, kid!" He nodded to the police boat, her deep powerful engines even piercing through the thrashing beat of the *Pusan*'s propeller. "You're down in life's little sewer with me now, where the first casualty is always the truth!"

287

He shook his head watching the police boat. He could now make out three figures holding rifles.

"Jesus, Danny McBroom set us up!" he mumbled. "A sewer without truth, Harumi." Spain shook visibly. He closed his eyes in defeat, slowly putting the Colt back in his belt. "It'll be over in another five minutes. We might as well enjoy the scenery."

Spain momentarily refocused his attention to the tricky matter of sailing a close-hauled course with the massive cargo vessel. A wrong move and they would be smashed to bits against the *Pusan*, then sucked into the prop wash. Off to their left they could only see the massive black of the steel hull, while to the right they slid past the gasoline tanker *Star George*, being eased into her berth by a squat, churning tugboat. Unexpectedly, they were both overcome with a stoic calm as they watched the fog dance over the narrow pier and office of the Los Angeles Harbor Pilot's House.

Suddenly it didn't matter. They were finally released from the hunt. Spain knew, from studying the chart, that the *Pusan* was protecting them from the Coast Guard station that would now be passing on the left. "What the hell difference does it make now," he mumbled.

"Ahoy, sailboat, *Bonnie,*" came the metallic voice over the loud hailer. Now the police boat slowed, running a parallel course with the *Pusan* and the sloop, matching their speed, maybe thirty yards off the *Bonnie*'s beam.

"Fuck 'em," Spain said defiantly, focusing the field glasses through the thick moist air. Slowly, the dark shapes in the police boat became human, especially the men holding up the assault rifles. "Heavy artillery!"

"At least Gregori can't get to us." Harumi slapped her thigh, angry at herself. "Damn it, Benny, I'm sorry! It's all my fault. If I'd listened to you, we'd be home!"

Spain smiled and kissed her deeply, careful to keep a hand on the helm. "What the hell!" Then he laughed into the fog, flipping the police boat the finger. "Gregori set this all up, for Chrissakes! The bastard beat me." Then he shrugged, looking up at the dirty white Dacron main sail, fastened tightly to the boom. "When there was real trouble, my father always said that 'we are promised today and nothing else.'" Then he scowled. "Shepherds have alot of time to think about life and make up stupid sayings." Spain threw the winch handle to the teak deck of the cockpit, overcome with a rush of anger.

"Sloop *Bonnie,* this is the Los Angeles Police Boat running on your starboard beam. Please turn on your radio to channel number six. Tune channel six for instructions," came the loud hailer again.

"Take the helm, Harumi."

Spain slowly stepped down into the cabin and tuned the marine radio to the proper channel, then reluctantly picked up the mike. "This is *Bonnie,*" he whispered. "We have an open channel—"

"*Bonnie,* standby—" the radio hissed.

Spain looked out at Harumi, bundled in her dark ski parka, expertly steering the large chrome wheel. "Love you," he called up to her.

"Me too, Benny." Then she smiled, her almond-shaped brown eyes dancing over him, tears flooding down her cheeks.

"Spain, ah, you okay? Over," the radio blared.

Ben stared at Harumi, who also heard the voice. "Yeah. Who is this? Over."

"Admiral McBroom, you fucking honky! The real stealth cop! Who the hell did you think it was? Little Black Sambo! Ah, over."

A wave of relief flooded through Spain. He was completely astonished. "I thought it was the cops!"

"I am the cops, you conehead! Listen, sorry for the unexpected visit, I'm sure it scared the hell out of you, over."

"Oh, nothing like that, Danny." He rubbed his mouth with a shaking hand. "The *Bonnie's* fine. She's a great little sloop. Over." He raised a questioning hand to Harumi.

"Ben, after you left the dock, we got word that your Russian hit team is now somewhere in L.A. They called the office again. That's why I came out here. One of my guys, Detective Connick, inadvertently told the Russian you were in L.A. Boxcar Willy's name was also mistakenly mentioned. Over."

"Thanks for the great news. Over."

"If I can get to them, I will, Ben! You know that! But this Russkie is a pretty smooth dude. Just watch your devil dog ass! I want you out of sight of everything on that frigging island for the next ten days. Clear, pukehead? Eat bugs if you have to. I don't want any trace of you, not even a fart, *hombre*. Understand? In the meantime, I'll work on getting you guys out of there. Over."

"Thanks, Danny. Over."

"God's Speed, Shepherd! You'll need it to make it out alive! Over and out." Then the radio went dead and the police boat veered away.

The dark-haired man slowly straightened his tie, his eyes taking in the busy deli in the late morning. Finally he focused on his target.

A moment later, he stood at the booth, thrusting a warm, firm hand into the outstretched grip of Boxcar Willy. "William Chicki?" He smiled openly. "Greg Syann, FBI." For a moment, Syann stood over Boxcar, allowing the weight of the words to do their work. He then reached into his suit jacket and pulled out a double leather wallet, flashing a dull federal shield at Boxcar.

"Hey, I'm a good American!" Willy smiled that hungry possum smile and eased back in his seat. "I pay my taxes."

"Do you?" Syann cut him short. For a long moment he stared at this man, with a funny, oblong head and fearful yet defiant eyes that couldn't seem to focus on the reality of the moment. His thin neck, which seemed to act as a swivel for his head, was punctuated with a large walnut-size Adam's apple.

Finally, Willy brought his eyes back to the table of the Nosh Box Deli in Brentwood, a wealthy suburb of West Los Angeles. "How'd you get my name and number? I mean, I travel around alot, know what I mean?

Syann shook his head. "A detective at South."

"Christ, you mean McBroom's lackey Connick, don't you!" For the first time, fear cracked in Willy's tin voice. "That prick!"

"Slow down, Willy!" Syann touched his arm and smiled with those perfectly squared teeth. "I don't want

291

you. At least I don't think I do!" He smiled again, then furrowed his forehead as if the statement was a question.

Willy blew out a long, stale breath, smiling weakly. "Glad to hear that." He held up his hands feebly. "What can I do for you? I mean, I got my ear to the ground here in Shakytown. I know alot of the players."

"Do you? How about a man named Ben Spain?"

Willy shrugged, his face blank. "Should I?"

Syann sensed the waiter's presence, looked up and smiled. "You wouldn't happen to have any Austrian liqueur, would you?" The blank expression on the deli waiter's face quickly ended the discussion. "Beck's Light. Willy, what about you? I'm buying."

"Got any malt liquor?" The tired waiter nodded. "Good. That'll do for a start."

"Okay, Willy." Something in Syann's voice seemed to shift imperceptibly. "Back to Ben Spain."

"I said—"

"You answered my question with another question. That annoys me, Willy. I simply don't have the time. I'm on a very tight schedule." Slowly Syann reached over the table and drove his thumb into a pressure point in Willy's shoulder muscle, until he turned beet red. The round of beers saved him momentarily.

"You got no right to touch me!" Willy rotated his arm, trying to rid himself of the pain. "You're just like McBroom!"

Syann held up a hand. "You're right. Sorry, Willy. Now what about Spain?" he asked again softly. Syann pulled a crisp fifty-dollar bill out of his inside jacket pocket and carefully placed it on the table. "Spain," he said again, almost whispering.

"The name's getting closer, Mister Syann."

"No it isn't, Willy! Take the fifty and talk to me or you'll spend the night in a federal lockup!" Syann took a sip of beer and smiled brightly. "Are we communicating, Willy?"

"Well, I guess I know him. He's a buddy of that asshole McBroom! They stole my boat, damn it! It was a straight, legal deal and they stole my fucking boat, Syann!"

"Where's Spain and this boat now?"

"What's in it for me?"

"Your boat of course. I'll see you get it back. Now, once again."

"Okay, okay! I'm not totally sure, but I saw them workin' over a map of Catalina Island. Somethin' else about gettin' lost for a while. I think the high heat's on this guy Spain and he's got this fucking sweetheart deal with that ape McBroom!"

"What kind of boat, Willy?" Syann looked past Willy to the large street window, gauging how many hours of daylight were still left.

"Sailboat. A real damn yacht! They muscled me to sign it over! You take care of that?"

"Sure will, Willy. I'll take care of you. Oh by the way, I want you to come out to the car for a moment, so you can identify Spain's photo."

"No problem. You must want him pretty bad, huh?"

"Pretty bad, Willy. And I'll get him. If he's on that island, I'll get him this time, make no mistake about it!" Then he shivered, fighting his own repulsive instincts.

293

"Hey, you okay, Syann? You look real sickly, all the sudden!"

Syann nodded sullenly. "Let's go to the car now, Willy," he repeated mechanically.

Syann opened the rear door to the unmarked black sedan, motioning Willy in. "Okay, what you got for me?"

Syann climbed in next to Willy, closing the door. "Like you to meet my driver. Boxcar Willy meet Herr Pete Staven."

A large burly man sitting in the driver's seat turned and smiled politely. "Herr what?" Willy's animal eyes glistened with panic. "Hey, what the hell is this! Herr! There ain't no German FBI."

Syann touched Willy's arm lightly. "You're right, Willy. Herr Staven is a member, or should I say, a former member of the East German FBI. We call it the *Stasi*." He held up his hands and smiled brightly. "What's the difference for people like us, Willy? I have a few more quick questions for you, then you can go. Where did Spain leave from and who was with him?"

Willy's eyes darted from Syann to Herr Staven and back again. "Ah, San Pedro and he had this honey with him. Real exotic-looking fox. A great piece."

"That's fine, Willy," Syann said patiently. "When did they leave?"

"Ah, last night, right in the middle of the fog." Suddenly, Willy's voice rose to match the fear in his eyes. "You all done with me, now?"

Herr Staven, cocked his head and nodded silently,

then raised a .22-caliber Webley revolver, with a long bulbous silencer screwed into the barrel. "You vant to die in da forehead or das ear, Villy?" His thickly accented voice was very clinical.

Willy bolted for the door as the copper-jacketed slug smashed into his skull just behind his right ear, with a whining bump, tearing only a pencil-size bright red hole in his head. The low-velocity bullet ripped into his brain tissue, killing Willy instantly, his dead eyes staring up at the grim Gregori Ovsyannikov. Even in death, Willy's gray empty eyes looked cheap.

"Good hit, Staven. I hope you do as well tracking Spain on this Catalina Island, wherever the hell it is."

Staven raised his eyes cautiously. "Ya. Count on me, sir."

"I will and if you don't take out Spain, I'll kill you!" Ovsyannikov shook his head disgustedly. He stared out the window at the now passing noontime foot traffic, totally oblivious to what had taken place in the back seat of their car. Now he only felt an overwhelming sadness, knowing that Staven would find and kill Spain.

He looked at his watch, thinking about Spain out there somewhere in the Pacific, fighting to survive, then shuddered again. Why did he pick an island?

"When will you be in contact with General Lutz?"

"I'm sorry, Staven." He smiled vacantly. "Yes, General Lutz," he repeated, sucking in a long breath. "Not until early next week." Then his mind wandered again to Spain, and how their relationship defied explanation. Maybe, after all, it wasn't a relationship but a lifetime of shared emotion. A companion and fellow traveler from the dark side, who understood what their lives really meant. Soon he would be alone, never able to share his nightmare again. With Spain dead, he would never complete the task of defining himself or being complete and the thought made him sick to his stomach.

Thirty-three

Through the night, the *Bonnie* drifted in the fog-corrupted ocean, her sails flat and lifeless against the dense unclean air that sailors dread. Afraid of being run down by Gregori Ovsyannikov, Spain shut down the inboard diesel and used the fog's silence, drifting west in and out of its soupy tides that washed over the Catalina Channel.

By the first light of dawn that broke yellow and murky, the *Bonnie* had run by controlled drift, only ten miles from Angels Light, at the San Pedro Breakwater. After a restless night, with both Spain and Harumi riding an emotional and vigilant roller coaster, they were exhausted. As the dirty light washed the boat, Spain rested his frame against the bright yellow life ring and *Bonnie's* stern backstay as he watched the dirty air push feebly at the main sail and genoa jib, forward at the bows.

"Hi, Admiral!" Harumi came up through the hatch and handed Spain a cup of instant coffee and a handful of soggy soda crackers. "Don't ever say I never gave you breakfast in bed." Harumi leaned over the side, idly

297

watching a colony of yellow green kelp slowly drift by. "How can you tell how far we've gone?" Harumi watched his eyes, still heavy and dark with worry.

"We're in the weeds. You can even smell it. It's called the Horseshoe Kelp, a massive band that arcs south halfway to San Diego, paralleling the coast."

Harumi shook her head. "How do you know all this?"

"How do you know all the history that you do? You had the sophistication to recognize those imperial seals inside that yellow pouch in *Arizona*, didn't you? Where'd it come from?"

"I spent years being a student of history."

"Well, for the first part of my life, I was a student of all this. And I never should have left it." He moved a hand across the horizon. "My father and I migrated each winter from the high western Sierra meadows to Catalina Island. Before that, my grandpa, originally from Spain, brought my father here. We had to eat. Shepherds don't have expense accounts."

"I don't understand."

"The horseshoe kelp beds are filled with fish. Halibut, barracuda, white sea bass, and sand dabs. We'd stock up on fish before spending months on the island. At least it used to be filled with fish, before they crapped up the water with mercury, DDT, and too much untreated sewage from half the world living in Los Angeles now. God, they sure ruined it. You could see the towering San Bernardino mountains off the east filled with snow and you could really smell the damn orange blossoms, even this far out at sea." He rubbed his firm stomach, feeling suddenly hungry.

"I guess that's why everyone wanted to be here."

"I don't know, Harumi. Did you know that writer Zane Grey lived on Catalina for years and did some of his best work there? My grandpa met him when he'd come up into the mountains on his hikes." Then Spain's face lit up and he chuckled.

"What?"

"Ah, my dad would tell me grandpa's stories about how Grey hated the Wrigley's, the chewing gum people, who owned the island. The irony was that Dad tended to their flocks of sheep, but Grey and my grandpa became great friends and would sit out at night by open camp fires telling stories that my father passed to me. Stories are a great Basque tradition."

Harumi watched his features lift and Spain's warmth reach out to her. "The subject was fish, I thought, but I got the whole shaggy dog." She laughed, then lightly rested her hand on his arm. "I feel so damned protective of you, Benny." She met his eyes. "I don't want anything ever to happen to you."

"This is a helluva time to be telling me that, bobbing around out here in the Pacific, with old vodka breath stalking us!" Then he raised his eyes to the top of the main mast, watching the wind vane beginning to swivel. "Look's like we'll be getting some wind pretty soon. The fog's starting to thin out."

"Fish, Ben? What about the fish?"

He grinned. "Well, Grey, a great fisherman of his time, used to show my grandpa photos of what they'd catch. Right where we float, all the way to the island, you could drop a line and pull out five-hundred-pound black sea bass, hundred-pound tuna, and giant sunfish as big around as a family hot tub. It was really paradise. Ask the Chumash Indians who lived on Catalina for fifteen hundred years."

"What happened?"

"Everyone started mucking up the waters and that, combined with those millions of new folks fishing out all the anchovy schools and puff, it disappeared. Now it's a desert." Spain squinted into the brightening haze, the clean breeze beginning to stir the clanging halyard atop the main mast. "Sorry. I didn't mean to sound preachy. Christ, I still can't even wipe the warm sticky blood of all those kids in Nam off my hands, all these years later! I don't have the right to criticize anyone."

Harumi stood next to him for a long time rubbing his back, quietly beginning to feel and understand the special rhythm of the sweet air beginning to fill the sails of the *Bonnie,* now heeled over, her rudder and keel vibrating responsively to the rising wind and sea.

Spain went below and studied the chart that Danny McBroom had supplied. "Harumi," he called up, "your new heading will be one eight two degrees, true."

"Aye, sir," she called out, "the new course is one eight two, true, on a heading of south by southwest. Why don't you stay below for a while and get some sleep."

Spain popped his head up in the companionway. "You sure?"

"Yeah, macho man. I can handle this female boat just fine. You know that. Remember I grew up sailing in the islands." She smiled affectionately. "Ben, you're all in. If the Russians descend on us, you'll be the first to know."

For a long time, Harumi sat behind the large chrome wheel, steering her course and setting her own special track with the wind, within the fine seam of full sails and the ocean current, as *Bonnie* picked up hull speed to eight knots. The Southern California sun finally burned off the remaining fog and within an hour, Harumi had stripped down to her breasts, the sun baking her white skin and large dark nipples in the privacy of her own ocean.

Slowly at first, then with more focus, Harumi began to piece it all together. Thus far, answers had eluded her. The yellow pouch, the skull of that round-the-world flyer, and finally the *Arizona* itself. What had she missed? Something was so close, she could almost reach out and touch it. Now, occasional whitecaps began to appear in the blue-green ocean marked with a strong southeasterly roll, as the *Bonnie,* heeled over far to port, knifed through the growing seas. Staying her course, Harumi watched the large compass rocking crazily in its alcohol womb, but steady on a heading of two hundred and two degrees, south by southwest, as she guided the sloop out into the Pacific.

Thunderous splashes drew her attention as three bottle-nosed dolphin danced and leaped close to the bows, forcing Harumi to laugh at their playfulness. Then suddenly, the laughter twisted into tears as she thought about her father back in Hawaii and his firm, searing instructions not to phone and not to make contact for their own protection. She still wasn't sure what he was trying to accomplish, but he didn't give her the time to debate the issue. But God, she missed him and his warm, fatherly counsel and strength.

Now a rare school of silver flying fish, responding to the growing surge of the waves, glided from whitecap to

301

whitecap, the sea-green foam beginning to push over the bows of the *Bonnie*.

A lone flying fish had somehow lofted itself into the cockpit, helplessly flapping its narrow wet body. Carefully, Harumi bent and retrieved the fish, then gingerly released it over the side, its doubtful, transparent wings taking flight as it skipped and glided into a distant wave.

Watching the sun glint off the fully extended wings of that fish, Harumi suddenly touched the missing piece that had eluded her. Why hadn't she seen it before! When Spain came topside she would tell him!

She turned her naked upper body in the warmth and freedom of the sun and peered through the cabin, watching Benny's face, finally at peace, in sleep. She shivered for no reason as a large rogue-green comber roared over the *Bonnie* amidships, spilling cold seawater on the floor of the cockpit.

Harumi adjusted her course to the rising gale force wind, beginning to howl as it strained and heaved against the sails, searching for the slightest flaw or weakness.

Now, massive waves were pounding over the *Bonnie* with frequency and Harumi had difficulty climbing back into her soaked T-shirt and sweater, with the cockpit water up to her ankles. She stared up at the wind vane at the top of the main mast, the red arrow pointing hard to the southeast.

Heeling more sharply to port, the *Bonnie* nosed precariously into the deepening troughs of the angry green seas. Pushing out a deep breath, Harumi slackened on the main sheet, pulling the *Bonnie* more to an upright stance, yet still her speed strained at nine knots.

"What's up?" Spain had difficulty standing in the cockpit from the force of the waves smashing into and over the bows. For a moment he studied the growing maelstrom and the howling winds. "How long's this been going on?"

"About an hour. It just came out of nowhere!"

"They do. This channel can be a real killer! It's a spring northwester!" Spain winced, watching the gale force winds slamming into the sails in waves of freezing air. "I've got to reef the main! It won't take the wind pressure!"

"Get a lifeline on!" Harumi warned as a wall of freezing water swelled over the open cockpit, drenching them both.

"No time!" Spain called, climbing atop the cabin. Laying flat on the cabin deck, Spain waited for the next giant wall of water to crash over them, then crawled to the foot of the mast to lower the main. It was the only hope of saving the sail from ripping and from capsizing the *Bonnie* as the velocity of the wind increased to almost cyclone force. With great difficulty, Spain raised himself on the bucking deck, grasping his arms around the mast like a monkey hanging onto a swaying branch.

Harumi helped, swinging *Bonnie* into the face of the waves and wind, trying to take the tremendous pressure off the sails. Slowly, Spain began to lower the metal sail head on its track toward the deck. "Got it made, kid!" Spain shouted above the whistling wind. "Just keep her pointed into the—"

Suddenly a tremendous wave, with an angry foaming crest, rose almost to the top of the mast, hesitated for a moment, then crashed down on the *Bonnie* with sickening force. For at least a minute, the *Bonnie* was completely on her side, then slowly the proud *Bonnie* rose to the surface, and righted herself, tons of seawater pouring off of her superstructure.

Now flooded knee-deep in water, the open cabin filled with floating debris, Harumi hung tightly to the helm as *Bonnie's* rudder faithfully responded to her commands. Then a lethal chill squeezed her throat, as she searched for Spain on the deck. He was gone, vanished into the storm!

"Ben! Ben!" she screamed on the verge of panic. Swiveling her head she talked herself down. "Easy, take it easy! Look for him, damn it! Just put your eyes down in a three-hundred-sixty-degree arc and find him! No panic, no hysterics. Just look for him!"

Slowly, she scanned the empty, heaving sea. "Oh, God, Spain! Don't you go and die on me, damn you!" Then he was there, a bobbing cork already fifty yards behind *Bonnie's* tern. "Okay, lady," she said to the sailboat, "we're gonna save that man's life!" Judging the distance and direction of the waves and wind, she came about, careful to keep her head down as the loose boom, with the useless flapping main pulling on its tack, whipped viciously over her head to meet the wind.

"That's it!" Gauging her speed, Harumi used the wind-filled genoa jib to maneuver toward Spain. "Hang on, Ben! Hang on, Benny!" she called out to the storm. Slowly, *Bonnie* reversed her course, inching up on Spain. A wrong move or the force of a large wave would crush Spain against the hull or the huge, deep keel.

Then she was alongside, tossing the bright yellow stern life ring to Spain. Tightening the wheel to its course, with a clamp, she drew Spain to the boat on the lifeline. Finally, Spain was able to pull himself up the short steel ladder of the angled stern.

"Van Horn, I owe you my life!" Spain smiled, cold and wet. "That was the fanciest piece of sailing I've ever seen! I thought I was dead! I sure as hell couldn't have maneuvered this boat in a goddamn gale without running you over!"

"You all right?"

Spain nodded as he surveyed the boat. "What a mess. I better see if I can get the bilge pump going!" Another wave slammed into them, pushing them back down into the cockpit.

An hour later, with the storm still raging, the water level in the cabin had receded back to the bilges as Spain climbed back out into the cockpit, field glasses in hand. "There's ship rock!" He looked out in the distance at the mountainous brooding land mass of Catalina Island. Then he pushed out a deep, troubled breath. "I hope we make it."

"What's wrong?"

"The force of the waves has separated some of the keel bolts from the hull."

"Meaning?"

"We're leaking and eventually we're going to sink. If we lose the keel, we'll capsize! There's nothing I can do. The real question is, can the bilge pump keep up and for how long?"

Harumi squinted, assessing his face. "How much

305

time do we have?"

"In this weather? Three, maybe four hours."

She gazed out at Catalina Island, now clearly in sight. "We can always swim for it."

"I want to try for the backside of the island. It's very isolated. We're in the shipping lanes here," he said, examining the scrub and sage-covered coastline. "The Isthmus is close by, but every yachtie in Los Angeles knows it. That's no good!" he said again, shaking his head. "We've got to get around to the backside of the island, where we can put down the boat and escape into the island's interior." He thought about Gregori Ovsyannikov and quaked inside. "It's all we have," he said softly, ducking another foaming wave that roared into the cockpit, soaking them again.

Once the flood of seawater had drained through the cockpit scuppers, Spain opened the cabin hatch and went below, checking on the keel and bilge pump. The water was now ankle-deep in the compartment and satisfied that he had done everything possible for the moment, he found the now soggy navigation chart and plotted his new course.

"Harumi," he called through the closed hatch. "Make your new course two eight five degrees, right. That will parallel the coastline, heading northwest, and put us into the face of the waves. It'll be rough, but we shouldn't take on half as much water.

"Turning right to two eight five degrees now," she called down.

Now back on deck, Spain wenched in the jib to a quarter of its normal capacity, so the storm winds couldn't blow it out, then cut some torn sheets with a pocket knife he found below. He then set about starting the inboard diesel engine that finally fired on the fourth try. Now the *Bonnie* was moving on a smoother course to the storm waves at close to ten knots, the wash across the rudder giving them far more steerage and control. An hour later the proud *Bonnie* rounded the west end of Catalina, then passed Eagle Rock on a southeasterly heading for Little Harbor.

Harumi glanced at her watch, her stomach growling. It was now 4:30 in the afternoon, the early spring sun starting its final dive below the vast horizon of the Pacific.

"How much longer, Benny?"

Spain checked the isolated coastline with the rubber-coated field glasses as they glided down the jagged, mountainous coastline, with towering breakers crashing on the deserted beaches. "Little Harbor is down on the chart as a protected cove."

A large ground swell rolled under *Bonnie,* and she groaned markedly.

"Ben!" The sound of sloshing water grew louder from below.

"I know! It's her death rattle!" He went below and checked the water level, now almost to the port windows. "We can't stay with her much longer, Harumi! She's all broken up and I think her keel's busted! If we lose the keel, she'll roll over before we can climb off!"

Again, Spain squeezed his eyes back into the field glasses, debating how much longer they could wait. Then he saw the high sandstone peak protecting Little Harbor. They were maybe a hundred yards from shore.

"That's it, Harumi!" Spain went below and brought

up two flotation cushions. "It's all we have!" He glanced up at the growing darkness, tying the field glasses around his neck. "I want to be on that beach before it's pitch black out here! Get over the side now, Harumi!"

A moment later, she splashed into the cold water holding tightly to the flotation cushion. After he opened the sea valve next to the bilge, allowing a final, lethal flood of seawater into *Bonnie,* Spain walked over to the side and together in the growing darkness they swam for shore.

Thirty-four

"Something is wrong," the old warrior concluded, with a deep shiver from within his sinewy body. He had to give serious, focused thought to this Cuban woman who had just telephoned. How different were her objectives from those of General Lutz? She was not unknown to the old *Samurai,* having been told by Lutz about his association with this Cuban government official. He shook his head, trying to polish his dim memory of her, all based on second-hand information from the general. Now that the general had met an untimely death through a heart attack, she had moved to fill the vacuum. Sometimes perception is strong and first sight is weak. Yes, in the end his trusted instincts would dictate a course of action.

"Grandfather, watch your step!" his granddaughter Katsuko shouted as they both descended the narrow wooden steps laid precariously into a deep scar in the black-green granite cliffs below their home. Carefully Toshiyuki Mizutari placed his foot, draped in a thick white sock and traditional wooden sandal on the "loose one." Gingerly he pushed the weight of his body onto the next old weathered plank, then continued down the cliff toward their private boat dock a thousand feet below, in the isolated deep inlet of the bay of Tsugaru.

"How did you know I had forgotten the 'step'?"

The young woman smiled, her dazzling white teeth and highly defined face chiseled from snow stone. Just coming into womanhood, Katsuko's hard, muscular body strained against the simple blue cotton dress and wool coat as she lithely jumped the errant step. "You always miss that plank when you are deep in thought, like now."

"Ah, youth!" Toshiyuki resolved to think hard on the issue of the Cuban, once the morning chores had been completed at the yacht. For an instant he wondered how the Russian felt about her? Slowly he turned and stepped quickly down to the dock and surveyed the archaic vessel that was launched in 1903. Climbing the steel gangway, Toshiyuki pulled up a thick, varnished teak rail piece, set on brass hinges, finally stepping down to the snow-covered wooden deck.

Out of habit, his eyes took in the high steep cliffs surrounding the single dock and yellow water on three sides. Only his friends, the weather-twisted firs, and the ever constant breeze, stood silent guard for the ancient royal yacht *Hatsukaze* that had belonged to Emperor Hirohito. Thank God, some things never change. In the cold, leaden sky, the naked auxiliary sail masts stood out as a dead fossil skeleton of something long since past.

Toshiyuki turned and almost fell over a man dressed in dirty overalls. "Ah, Takada, prompt as always!" Impatiently, Toshiyuki fluttered his hand as a sign for the

310

mechanic to rise from his usual deep bow. As skilled a craftsman as he was, Takada sometimes took the old traditional ways too far.

"What have you to report? Good news, I hope."

"Better than we could have expected, sir. I discovered a small family foundry in Nagoya that has experience with old marine engines?"

"You did not tell him what boat it was for, did you?" Toshiyuki widened his *Samurai* stance, ready to draw an invisible sword.

Takada's eyes twitched in pain. "No, sir. I have been in your employment for more than thirty years and never once have I ever revealed the true identity, location, or name of this sacred imperial vessel."

Toshiyuki patted his shoulder. "I have a great deal on my mind. The error was mine for having even a thought that such a loyal friend could make that kind of mistake." The *Samurai* smiled gently. "Now, you began to tell me about our old, tired engine."

Together they slowly walked out to the graceful clipper bows, carefully surveying the thick hemp sail rigging, that despite the frosting of snow and ice looked fresh and ready to use. Even the long, sharply pointed bowsprit was properly secured with all lines neatly coiled and ready.

"This small foundry, based upon my drawings, is fashioning a new cylinder head for that old beast fourteen-cylinder *Miyabara* engine. It should be ready sometime next week and then I can begin to reassemble her. They will send the part by Bullet Train. We will be right on schedule for our spring cruise."

"Wonderful news, Takada! Wonderful news!" Toshiyuki cast his eyes back toward the stern, drinking in the ancient ship, her tall sail masts, high narrow smoke stack, and beautiful narrow lines leading back to the mizzen mast. During the war, the emperor had summoned him once again and assigned him the task of hiding the one-hundred-twenty-three-ton royal yacht, while maintaining the *Hatsukaze* to a state of readiness. My God! That was 1943, he thought, and even today, with the stipend arriving the first of every month, he was still bound to his pledge. He thought about this second and last imperial rescript from the dead emperor to secretly guard this yacht and his special *daisho:* The three-foot-long fighting *Samurai* sword that Emperor Hirohito had inherited from his grandfather, Mutsuhito — The Emperor Meiji; the "sacred one," who was God incarnate.

"Later in the summer, as routine, her bottom and seams will need recaulking." The mechanic was no more than a foot from his face, but Toshiyuki wasn't focused. He nodded affirmatively, but his eyes narrowed impatiently and finally Takada bowed deeply and withdrew down into the bowels of the engine compartment.

Toshiyuki found his granddaughter in the grand salon, sitting quietly in a thick leather chair surrounded by rich ornate, turn-of-the-century mahogany decor, with kerosene lamps adorning the bulkheads.

"I love this place, Grandfather. When I was young, I would sit here and think about the old times and these walls would always speak to me." She lowered her narrow eyes.

"Of what?" The old man smiled broadly, always surprised and pleased with Katsuko. Her insights and perspective were always so refreshing and clear.

"They would speak to me of your life, as a descendant of a fighting shinto *Samurai* clan, your days as naval officer and *bonsai* master, but mostly—" She paused, not certain she should go on. In a moment she raised her eyes and stared over at the *Dojigiri* sword on its *tachi* stand, which she knew belonged to the late emperor when he was *arahito-gami*, God incarnate.

"So that's it." Toshiyuki made his way to the glass and wood case, examining the graceful arc of the three-foot sword, its red lacquered wood scabbard inlaid with bone, and the all-important hilt, or handle, made of wood, and overlaid with the skin of a brave, fighting shark and bound with silk braid. Even the *Tsuba,* steel sword guard, with its chrysanthemum design, was unique. Indeed, the *Dojigiri* sword was a lost national treasure which she deserved to know about. She had waited since childhood for his story and suddenly he knew that he had to tell her, especially with the death of General Lutz. Her trust and Shinto loyalty to him and Imperial Japan was without question.

"Come here, Katsuko. I need to show you something that is secret." Fumbling in his pocket he found the key chain and then the key, opening the front door to the chin-high case.

She had never seen the case opened before and the excitement grew within her as she watched the old warrior slowly lift the sword from its wooden *tachi* stand. She knew a lesson was forthcoming before the reason for this act was unveiled to her. What would her life be like without a valued lesson from her beloved grandfather?

Pulling back the red wooden scabbard, the sword's blade revealed itself to the light of day, taking on its own presence in the ship's salon; the old *Samurai* acting only as midwife to the act of rebirth. "This blade was given life by the sword smith Yasutsuna, during the Heian Period of Japanese History, about 850 A.D. It had been signed by the smith and was created in the fires of hell, in which bars of iron and steel, after being hammered and welded together, were repeatedly folded over and forged no less than twenty times." With precision, the old man ran his thumb down the living razor sharp blade. "It is an emperor's sword!"

The dark, smoldering fire behind Toshiyuki's eyes frightened Katsuko. "Grandfather?"

He shot an open hand into the air before her, his face glazed and fierce. "Katsuko! Don't interrupt me!"

She bowed, refusing to let the shock within her become known. "I am sorry, Grandfather."

The old man pivoted on his right foot, developing a feel for the sword and its point of balance. In reality, the sword belonged to him now. Hirohito's son, Emperor Akihito, didn't care. Slowly, he brought the sword back to the upright and smiled. "Do not be afraid, Katsuko, but in my hand this blade is alive and I feel the thousand-year-old presence of every *Samurai* who ever carried a *daisho* into combat! This blade consists of thousands of layers of iron and steel and these hardened crystals can easily slice through armor."

"Why is such a sword here?"

Toshiyuki met his granddaughter's eyes. She was truly ready, always asking the cogent question. "There is great symbolism here. My dead emperor now called

314

Showa, during the dark days of World War Two, feared that the Imperial Throne would come to an end, once it was realized that Japan could not win the war. A bargain was struck with the American President Roosevelt, but he died before it could be implemented."

He reached over to the gracefully curved hilt of the sword, unscrewing an almost invisible cap in the end of the sword's handle. For a moment he peered inside, then slowly withdrew a tightly rolled scroll of rice paper. It was just where he had placed it, some forty-nine years before in the presence of the emperor within the Imperial Palace. Warily, he pulled apart the rolled paper and read from it. Then he looked up, his gaze steady and sure.

"We hold the future of Imperial Japan here, Katsuko." Then he handed the paper to her. "I want you to commit the contents of this imperial rescript to memory, now!"

Dutifully, Katsuko read the entire rescript, then looked up at her grandfather, expecting more. "Is that all? A series of coordinates and Calauit Island?" She seemed deeply puzzled.

"Did you commit this scroll to memory?"

"Yes, sir."

"Good. Whatever happens, remember those numbers and Calauit Island!"

"Is Calauit Island the same as Giraffe Island?"

"Yes, but you are now my navigator. It must be formalized and never spoken of to a living soul."

"I have always loved Giraffe Island during our yearly visits."

"Then you must protect it always, Katsuko." Then he

315

took the scroll and walked out onto the cold deck, where he lighted a match, quickly destroying the rice paper. Immediately he returned to Katsuko in the comfort of the salon. After a few moments, the sacred ninth-century sword was once again locked securely in its case.

"Do you know why I do *bonsai*, Katsuko?" He moved to a leather chair next to her, dragging his square wooden sandals over the thick carpet.

Slowly, she shook her head, aware of his darking mood.

"I thought not. How could you." He nodded. "The *bonsai* and the *Samurai* carry many similarities. *Bonsai*, like the *Samurai*, symbolizes the struggle of the tree and warrior against the forces of nature, growing in character as the tree and the human being grows older. A good *bonsai* is not explicit down to the last detail, it is spare, abstract and impressionistic, just as is the life of a *Samurai*." Uncharacteristically, the old man took his granddaughter's hand, feeling her great youth and warmth.

"For me, as with all honorable *Samurai*, to die with your intention in life unrealized, is to have lived uselessly." He then pointed over to the *Dojigiri* sword. "The sword is the soul of a *Samurai*. It is a way of life and the natural path of the sword blade is a natural movement associated with natural behavior."

Katsuko frowned. "I don't understand?"

"We are descendants of the Fujiwaras, one of the foremost *Samurai* clans in all of Japan. Our family dates back a thousand years. That sword is a moral teacher for me. Its life is based on the simple premise of aiming

316

at the true nature of things and—" He watched her eyes and realized it was too much for one sitting. It had taken him his entire life to understand that one had to reduce life down to its simplest form and that the beginning and end point in one's life were the same.

"What does this sword of the dead Emperor Hirohito *Showa* symbolize, Grandfather?"

Toshiyuki Mizutari slumped deeply into his leather chair, gazing at Katsuko. "I want you to close your eyes and walk for a moment with me in your mind's eye." Suddenly, his voice grew deep and hypnotic as he began his short narrative.

"We are now crossing the pristine Isuzi River on a narrow bridge built of bare cypress wood. It is night and our pathway is lighted by pink paper lanterns, holding flickering candles. Once we leave the bridge we walk down a broad smooth rock path guarded by towering cryptomeria trees and suddenly, at the end of the path, we behold the most sacred spot on earth for a Shinto loyalist: the Grand Shrine of *Ise*."

"I can see it in my mind, Grandfather. It is clear!"

"Let me guide you, child," he coaxed gently. "At *Ise*, we encounter a tall gate and behind it, we come to a simple thatched-roof shrine, holding the ancient *Yato* mirror, the embodiment of the Sun goddess, *Amaterasu-Omikami*. It is here, Katsuko, that the ritual of *Daijo-sai* takes place, where the true emperor will enter *Ise* alone, face to the southwest and engage in sexual intercourse with the Sun Goddess."

"I know, Grandfather, it is called *Amaterasu*. But I still don't understand the connection of this sacred ritual to the sword?"

317

"This sword of Hirohito is the Shinto connection with the living God, incarnate, during his *Daijo-sai*. His son, Akihito, despite performing the ceremony at *Ise*, will not proclaim himself the living God, incarnate!" He felt his voice rise, betraying his control.

"So, this sword and its contents of the rice scroll are symbolic of the true Shintoist spirit that does not live in modern Japan?"

"Yes, Katsuko, this is precisely correct. But the contents of the sword will allow us to bring back the old ways. Destiny is destiny!" There was a black chill in his voice that forced Katsuko to shiver.

Thirty-five

The Black Ghost raised the collar of his leather jacket against the thunderstorm. Carefully, he looked out to the horizon of the Pacific, beyond the Santa Monica Pier, watching the brilliant flashes snake across the brittle, parched-gray evening sky. Nature's flares, lighting the coming battlefield, he thought to himself, as he slowly climbed the wooden steps to the small room he had rented the day before above the cavernous pier restaurant, Sinbad's. The rickety wooden barn was built in the late 1920s as a watering hole for wealthy patrons waiting to take water taxis out to the gambling ship *Rex*, in Santa Monica Bay past the three-mile limit.

Gregori Ovsyannikov only knew that meaningless footnote, because the owner of Sinbad's had insisted on a long drink and the useless history, after Gregori told him he owned a similar seafood grotto on the *Nevsky*, in the Delta of Leningrad. Sometimes it was so easy, he couldn't believe it. But the distraction was necessary and the location was perfect.

Finally, he opened the door to the small, musty room, and shrugged just as a frigid blast of storm air pushed

319

through the open window. Removing his wet jacket, he stood at the large window, watching the storm fanning in from the west, piling the surf against the old wooden pier. Another jagged bolt of lightning ripped across the sky, clearly revealing Malibu way off to the north end of Santa Monica Bay.

Reaching behind him, Gregori grabbed a half-filled bottle of Jack Daniel's just as another thunderclap exploded almost dead center over the pier. Slowly, he removed his shoulder holster, tossing it on the small bed.

For just an instant, he forced himself to visualize Catalina Island, which he now knew was some thirty-five miles to the southwest from where he stood. What a place to die! Damn, Spain! Why did he have to get in the way? He took another drink of the bitter whiskey, then laughed nervously. "Spain, I'm tired! *Ya oostal! Ya nyeh poneemayyoo!*"

He shook his head and drank from the bottle again. He really didn't understand any of this. Then he felt his entire body shudder, like that of a child, frightened of the dark. "I tried to warn you in Hawaii, old friend," he mumbled aloud. "But, I know you are like me and that damn dog of yours, that bit me! You grab ahold and just don't let go." The artillery duel between the thunder and lightning grew more intense as the storm center approached.

Maybe the rough sea and weather conditions would delay Herr Staven. "Screw fate!" he shouted through the open window out into the wet blackness. But in his belly, where all true Russians buried their souls and their fiery peppered vodka, he knew the truth. Spain was a dead man! He had warned Staven, after his failure in Northern California. Staven, the monster, was too good at what he did. He was too German, too efficient, and too well trained like a mindless stalking pit bull. The Kraut loved the wet work, the killing and the explosion of violent death in front of his eyes.

He looked down at the almost empty bottle of Scotch. Spain had even taught him how to drink this stuff over vodka, when he had been rescued by Spain from that death sentence in the Crimea. Just as brothers, they had carried each other on their backs. Now he was a Judas! He slumped down in a wooden chair next to the window, talking aloud to the bottle, the rain now whipping through the yellowed lace curtains. *"Ya zabluzhen!* I'm lost!"

He struggled to his feet, feeling that he had just rinsed his ego in Spain's blood. The blood of one of the only men who ever cared about him. "God, Spain, I'm sorry! You pulled me from the darkness, when no one cared, not even my wife!" His voice dissolved into a tormented wail of a graveyard whistler as he fell back onto the bed, closing his eyes to the violence all about him.

It must have been two hours before Gregori was startled awake by a brilliant ribbon of lightning punching through the wind and the cold sheets of rain pushing against the old frame building. With his skin soggy and mildewed from the rain, the Black Ghost slowly focused his eyes in the darkness, tasting the waste of Scotch and saliva in his mouth that had thickened into cotton. He checked his watch. It was nine o'clock already! He reached over and switched on the small wicker table lamp, making certain the portable shortwave receiver was a reality and not just the stuff of more bad dreams. From off in the distance, he heard the old merry-go-round, at the head of the pier, thumping its joyous, monotonous beat against the night.

Now he would have to wait another hour to find out what updates and further orders awaited him from General Lutz in Hallstatt. The message would come via his midwife, Senora Soria, in Cuba. In a way he was happy he didn't have to talk with her directly, or her chief goon, Sed Cruz, head of the infamous Directorate MC in Havana. Instinctively he disliked them both, but it was Cruz who forced him to show his teeth. Maybe they were both too much alike.

At 2200 hours, Gregori carefully extended the telescope aerial and tuned the shortwave receiver to 10.4 meters, to reach the nightly English rebroadcast of Radio Havana's Industrial Workers' Hour. Finally, the announcer, his shallow voice echoing in a steel tube, began his nightly harangue against the capitalistic exploiters in Washington. It took another fifteen minutes for the intelligence housekeeping announcements to begin. Ovsyannikov was told his message would come in the form of a short nursery rhyme, sung in English. Then it was on:

All my duckies, swimming on
the pond. Heads deep in
water, tails to the sky . . .

The Black Ghost suddenly sat up, clearing his head as he listened again. Three times he heard a haunting off-key voice singing the lyrics.

Something was terribly wrong! General Lutz had changed the code a month before! The old code, the duckie tune, had been discarded and was only to be played if there was real trouble! Now fully awake, Gregori could feel his heart pounding in his neck as he paced the room thinking it through. He would be forced to defy orders and telephone the general directly, bypassing that Cuban bitch. If he took the meaning of that tune's message literally, it was a cry from Austria for help! Something terrible had gone wrong. Instinctively, he pulled the *Steyr* automatic from its worn leather holster and checked the ammo clip in the butt of the gun's handle. Another bolt of lightning punctured the sky right before his face, revealing his deep, brooding eyes, staring west toward Catalina Island.

"I'm truly sorry, Spain," he suddenly shouted at the empty room, knowing that Spain and that woman were getting close to the truth, if they hadn't already discovered it. It was only a matter of time, he told himself. It had to be this way, with Herr Staven doing his work, he mumbled to himself, finishing off the last of the Scotch. "It's all chocolate sauce on horseshit, Spain!"

For a moment he stared down at his right pant leg, visualizing the fleshy stump below the knee attached to the prosthesis, his gift from Afghanistan. What was it Spain had said to him, during a drinking bout one night, before he was special delivered by Ben to General Lutz in Berlin? My God, then it was East Berlin, filled with intrigue and filth. Now it was just part of the new greater Germany! Herr Staven's Germany! Ovsyannikov closed his eyes. Spain had said, half kidding, half drunk, that they didn't belong anymore. We were an embarrassment, along with a million other cold war professionals. Christ, we all couldn't join the French Foreign Legion, Spain had growled. Hot wars, like the Persian Gulf, were better left to the young lions. Gregori aimed the gun at the open window. "Damn you, Spain! I can't help you any longer!"

Thirty-six

Spain blanched, his eyes screaming with pain as the lightning struck just to the right of the shallow sandstone overhang. Off in the distance, past the roar of the surf and the wind, he swore he heard the shriek of a wild animal.

"Ben, I'm so cold," Harumi whispered, her teeth chattering as she tried to pull her wet, cold body closer to him.

For the past two hours, since making it ashore in giant sand-busting breakers, they had been unable to move in the storm that had fed itself into a savage killer. If they had waited another hour, they would have drowned in the monstrous surf, but now the problem was warmth. Spain could tell that Harumi had lost far too much body heat. She was slipping into hypothermia and would soon fall into unconsciousness. Their survival would be an illusion if they couldn't find heat and soon.

Again, through the confusing roar of surf, rain, and

wind, he heard the faint anguish cry of an animal in pain. "Harumi, we've got to move into the hills to find some warmth and shelter," he gently coaxed.

As Spain lifted her freezing, limp body over his shoulder, he felt his own hands and feet going numb. He had to hurry now. "Come on, hon, tough it out," he called up to her as he began to slowly and painfully move inland away from the beach into the rough, muddy scrub of Catalina Island.

Then the terrible wail of that animal startled Spain, forcing him to slip on the side of a rock, sending them both tumbling into a patch of prickly cactus. Harumi caught the brunt of the sharp, delicate needles, crying out in pain as the agonizing shriek of the animal grew louder, accompanied by an awful smell. Ben helped Harumi up, just as another flash of lightning ripped across the peaked hills, revealing a massive shaggy brown buffalo lying on its side, ten feet from them, its hugh diaphragm pushing out in troubled, labored breaths. Cautiously, Spain approached, the animal severely injured and in pain. In a moment he found the bull's large triangular head with arced horns, his large brown eyes bulging in fear, his nose snorting painfully with each breath.

"Be careful, Ben!"

"Of what?" Pumped with adrenaline, Spain momentarily circled the animal, hoping to help, but found a deep, angry wound in his thigh, blood gushing out with every beat of his heart. Suddenly, the proud four-thousand-pound animal tried to rise, lifting its regal head into the darkness, knowing that to live, he would have to stand. Spain pushed the bison from behind the neck, hoping to help, but it was a futile effort. "Come on, Buffy, sit up, Damn it!"

With a thud and snort of his flared nostrils, the animal's head fell back to the wet earth. "Come on, damn it! Help yourself!" Now Spain's hands were covered with the animal's thick hot blood, as the wound continued to hemorrhage.

Not even sure why he was crying, Spain bent his head in the mud, next to the frightened animal's face. "I'm sorry, old friend, I think you're done for. Just let go and the pain will leave you!" Spain placed his hands on the buffalo's magnificent face, to calm him in death, but the animal wouldn't let go, blood now foaming from his black nostrils.

Despite her own weakness, Harumi crawled through the mud to Ben. "Oh, God, Ben! Do something! He's in terrible pain!" she pleaded.

Despite the pouring rain, Ben touched his forehead to the broad face of the horribly smelling buffalo. "May God have mercy on your magnificent soul, old friend!" Then he reached into his pocket, pulled out the large pocket knife from the boat and plunged the blade repeatedly into the animal's heart just above the breastbone. At last, the fear and agony left the large brown eyes, replaced by the dull, unfocused sheen of death.

Cold and exhausted, Spain squinted up at the leggy bolts of lightning striking at the mountainous terrain with a vengeance. "The lightning is now your soul and I will carry it always!" he railed at the storm. Disgusted with himself, Spain knew what he had to do. They were out of time. He glanced down at Harumi, her freezing face now blue against the wind and rain.

Slowly he crawled around the animal's body to its tender underside, talking to calm himself. "You're going to save us, old friend. Your body will give up the warmth and protection that we need to survive. You didn't die without a reason. I will always keep you alive," he grunted, hoping his father and grandfather would be proud of him.

Working from just under the breastbone, from the jagged series of puncture wounds that he had inflicted on the buffalo, Spain cut as deeply as he could into the animal's gut, sawing at the still hot flesh and muscle back toward and through the intestines. Losing more strength to the butchering, the stench, and the cold, Spain finally gave up and dragged Harumi around to the long, jagged open rift.

"What are you doing?"

"We've got to get warm and our friend here will serve us."

"Ben, I can't—" she weakly protested.

"Watch." Carefully he pulled the rift apart in the intestines making a pocket. "Crawl in, Harumi!"

"I can't. The smell!"

With his last burst of strength he shoved her into the hot softness of the animal's gut. "Damn it, I'm past your civilized sensibilities! Without heat, we'll smell like that in the morning!" Then Spain crawled in next to her, his teeth now chattering uncontrollably. Suddenly, the buffalo's heat was now pushing in around them as he felt himself slipping into a warm unconscious sleep, thanking the animal for its life.

* * *

From out of the high blue pink dawn, a red-tailed hawk, her long wings and salmon-hued pinion feathers guiding her direction, swooped low over the shallow gully carefully scrutinizing the large dead buffalo lying on its side. A field mouse raised its nose to wind, next to the dead animal, when the first ominous shadow passed over his head. Suddenly, the hawk broke right, spilling altitude, with her wings tucked to her long narrow body. In a blinding instant the controlled dive brought the bird down, her talons extended, just as Ben Spain crawled out of the dead carcass of the buffalo. The huge shadow and smell of the man destroyed the hawk's precise geometry and rhythm as she broke off the run, climbing into a thermal with her five-foot wings.

Spain glanced up, startled by the sudden blur of the diving hawk, soaring back up toward its cliff-side nest, hidden from view by a rare grove of red barked ironwood trees and giant silver-green buckwheat.

The dead bison must have been some animal, Spain thought, his eyes taking in its twelve-foot bulk. "A proud bull," he muttered aloud. Harumi stirred, lost except for her head in the still warm innards of the animal. Slowly, he walked around the bison, finally spotting the mortal wound that must have occurred when the animal was spooked by a ground strike of the lightning. Spain could see where he must have stumbled down the boulder strewn gully, a sharp outcropping of rock tearing into his thigh and femoral artery with lethal force.

"You saved us. Thank you, again," he said humbly. "You live inside me now." A stirring in the nearby scrub

328

caught his attention. A fresh, dead animal as large as this bull, was a waiting meal for the island population of wild boar, eagles, mule deer, mountain goats, and foxes. Necessity had turned natural hunters into scavengers and the scent of this bounty would draw animals from all over this part of the island.

"Come on, Harumi," he grunted, helping her from their belly pocket. She was weak, but the cold had not caused any permanent damage. The cocoon had saved their lives! The warming spring sun, just rising to the east, would give them the warmth and energy they would need to find shelter and food before nightfall. Thankfully, the storm had passed to the east, leaving the island damp and fresh. Before the morning was out, they'd have to find a place to hide, although this time of year, the rural part of the island was totally isolated from tourists. A small gray fox darted from behind a patch of prickly pear cactus, across the gully into a thicket of manzanita.

"There's the cactus that nailed you last night. How's your arm?" he asked, pulling up her sleeve, still wet from the foul-smelling waste of the buffalo's intestines. In the intense morning light, the small puncture wounds from the cactus needles weren't as bad as he first thought. The shafts hadn't completely broken off and he quickly pulled the tiny sharp barbs from her upper arm, despite her wiggling and bitching, forcing him to laugh.

"What's so damn funny?" She pouted, jerking away her arm. "God, I smell awful! So do you! We smell like death!"

"You're wrong," he said gently. "We smell of life because of that bison! Jesus! Pretty soon you'll tell me you're hungry, too."

"I am." She smiled, the sun beginning to draw the color back into her exotic face.

For the first time since diving on the *Arizona*, Spain felt truly free. He pulled the knife from his pocket and gingerly sliced off two purple fruits from the top of two large ears of cactus. Cutting off all the sharp needles from the purple-hued fruit, he sliced it in two and handed the halves to Harumi. "Breakfast with a view."

"What's it taste like?"

"Like pears. Look, Harumi, I know this place and a long time ago, I knew this land and what it could do. I've forgotten alot, but hopefully I've remembered enough to keep us alive." He swept an arm west across the gully down toward the vast Pacific, growing serious. "We have to stay alive, one hour at a time. That's what it is now. Food and shelter. Real basic stuff. Later, when we feel our way, and we know it's safe, we can plan for a future, but not now. Last night we came close to freezing to death."

Spain prepared another cactus pear and devoured it immediately. "Fiber, protein, and lots of water. Sorry there's no tofu around." He smiled, patting her rear end.

Finally, she began to eat, finishing off half a dozen pears as she watched Spain cut into the rear flank of the bison with his knife. For the next hour he carefully cut the blood-red muscle and tissue into long strips, laying them out on a high flat rock to dry in the sun.

"Is there anyone else out here, Benny?"

"A few Island Company employees, scattered about.

330

But there's alot of virgin canyons in these mountains that we can get lost in, this morning. I just have to find out exactly where we are." He watched her finish off the pears, knowing that the cold of last night drew off hundreds of vital calories.

"What are you doing with that?"

"Making strips of dried jerky. In a few days, I'll come back for it, if the animals don't get it, and we'll have some protein that we'll need." After cutting enough strips of bison to cover the entire rock, he covered it with a thin layer of dried scrub.

They collected enough cactus pears to fill their parkas, now serving as baskets, then took off into the mountains. "Don't ever walk a ridge line, Harumi. If people are out there, you'll be picked off immediately. Always walk five or six feet below the ridge. The scrub colors will mask you. Animals do it all the time."

Approaching the summit of a high peak, they stopped to rest in the absolute quiet and warmth of the sweet early morning, a light sea breeze moving the air. Scattered about the hillsides were an assortment of spring wildflowers, including brilliant orange poppies and fluorescent red mariposa lilies.

"What a place, right across from Los Angeles! I can't believe we just left the Nickel and all that living hell." Harumi laid her head in the damp grass, her exhausted body beginning to uncoil.

Spain nodded, ashamed that he had thought Danny McBroom had set him up. He shivered, pushing down the thought that this haven with its bounty, wasn't the end, just the eye of the storm.

For a long time his eyes drank in the vaguely familiar

craggy mountains and scrub canyons and slowly, from his past, something stirred deeply within him. A past that was born and nurtured in the deep impoverished rocky pastures and rich grasslands of the High Sierra, where his father Mike and his grandfather before him, had joyfully lived off the land all their lives. Always alone, resourceful and optimistic, as they tended the endless flocks of sheep and goats.

Spain watched a silent flight of husky ravens land in a seventy-foot ironwood tree that over the years had been shaped by the wind into a neatly trimmed poodle. No, he thought, Mike and grandpa, Francisco Zufiourre, originally from Vitoria, Spain, in the heart of the western Spanish Pyrenees, had carefully given these special Basque gifts to him, only to have him push it all away for a university education, and the professional life of a gentleman. His eyes danced over the wet cool grass to Harumi, soaking in the warmth and momentary security of the sun.

Spain flashed on the obsidian eyes of Gregori Ovsyannikov and shivered. Now, after all these years of torment and pain in the civilized world, he was back in the mountains, alone with this woman, needing to call upon something deep within himself to survive. Back on this island where he had spent his summers as a child.

"What is it, Benny?" Harumi was next to him, stroking his face.

"The whole damn thing comes full circle." He pointed over to a deep scrub canyon, with a herd of wild goats hanging precariously to its edges. "My old man, Mike, said it would. I haven't been here since I

332

was a high-school kid and here I am, with you, a flock of one, trying to make it happen, after all these years!" He laughed darkly. "Mike's snickering in his grave, pointing a hairy old hand at me."

She shook her head. "Meaning?"

"When I abandoned my Basque traditions, Mike said on his deathbed, no less, that my test of fire on the land will come someday." He raised a hand toward the west. "I thought I'd already passed the test!" He shrugged, then closed his eyes trying desperately to re-call all the vivid memories of his father's lessons, some now only dulled childhood dreams and skeletal images.

Spain stood and faced the rock canyon. "So it finally came around to this, you old bastard!" he shouted, toss-ing a rock down the cliff.

"Nik zu behar zaitudaneon, non ondoia zaude?" he called.

Harumi dipped her eyes in a brittle, questioning movement. "What the hell is that?"

"Basque! You hear that, Mike? It's Basque! After all these goddamned years, I still remember and I still love the animals," he answered quietly. He saw the puzzle-ment in Harumi's eyes, still at half-mast. "It means where the hell are you, when I need you?"

"Not only are we going to make it, but we're going to solve this damn mystery!" Now she raised her eyes to him. "This must really be something!"

Spain nodded. "In the meantime, we need shelter and heat for tonight. No more Buffy's. I couldn't take it."

"Who is Buffy? You called that animal Buffy, last night."

"For the five summers I spent here, there was one domesticated buffalo the shepherds and rangers had named Buffy. Until last night, I'd forgotten. She was orphaned as a calf, and made her home with a herd at Middle Ranch, hopefully not too far from here. Every year she went off with the herd during the rutting season, and always returned to us at the ranch with her new calf." Tears welled up in Spain's eyes. "She was my summer pal. Like a pet dog, only she was the size of a Cadillac. I'd even roll in the dirt with her, to brush off the mosquitoes. I don't know what ever happened to her, but killing that bull last night brought it all back," he said, wiping his eyes.

Spain turned his back, throwing another rock down into the canyon. *"Mendietako bihotza gogoratzera laguntzen nauzu, zuk madarikatua!"* he called out. He glanced at her and smiled. "I said, 'help me remember the soul of the mountains, you bastard!' I always called Mike a bastard behind his back. I guess it's an endearment now." He took Harumi's hand. "Until we can find a safe way off this rock, we've got to live like Stone Age people, literally off the land. The damn island is twenty miles long. That should be enough land! The Chumash Indians did it for a couple of thousand years, I guess we can."

She searched his face with that relentless stare. "What else?"

"I lost the gun, when I went overboard. I'm going to need to find a way to steal a gun." He turned his head and surveyed their isolation. "We have to be invisible. There are people about this island, not alot, but enough with rifles and two-way radios. We can't leave a trace. No smellables, or garbage from us. We leave

334

everything just as we found it." He kissed her lightly. "We are now in Navajo parlance, *Naahwiibiihi*. Those warriors who always win." Then Spain's eyes searched the land and all its immediate possibilities. There was a real purity in these mountains that defied the corruption he knew surrounded them, just waiting for a vulnerable moment to strike. He drew a long breath, watching the white-laced clouds roll steadily to the east in the deep blue sky. Then his eyes traveled the ridge lines surrounding them and knew from his past that they were in the midst of an invisible groundswell of life in the scrub-brown mountains.

Silently, Harumi picked up her jacket, holding a dozen or so cactus pears that would have to serve them for food and water. "Time to go find a new house!"

"Yes it is. Once I get my bearings, I have a plan of attack."

"Oh God, Spain, no more gun shops!"

"No, just an airport."

Harumi thought of the *Arizona* and the potential of their historical find. "I wonder how far we'll really have to take all this?" Then she grew sullen. "I have a question for you, Spain. Maybe it's for me, too. When does the dancer become the dance?"

Thirty-seven

"You're kidding!" Then Harumi van Horn watched Spain begin to fill the old gunnysack they had found at the unused line shack called Eagles Nest, belonging to the vast Middle Ranch spread.

"God!" Harumi bent down and gingerly began to pick up the piles of dried buffalo excrement that littered the grassy plain as soft land mines, in the shadow of Mount Banning.

Spain mashed his face in silence, then moved toward her. "This will work!"

"I just can't wait to barbecue my dinner over a roaring fire of aged bison shit!" Exasperated, she continued to harvest the chips. "You sure—"

Spain nodded. "I found a dry pack of matches at Eagles Nest."

"Why can't we stay there, where we'll at least have a roof over our heads!" She knew the answer before the words finished tumbling from her mouth. "I know the risk of being seen!"

"We can't freeze tonight, damn it! We need warmth

and that small cave we found will work! Chips burn damn hot and the smoke is negligible." He watched her jaw drop as she thought about it, almost ready to give herself up for a hot meal and warm bed.

"Hot but smelly! In a cave no less! What about that shack?" She ran her fingers through her scraggly, bleached hair, disgusted and tired.

We've been set up, Harumi! Keep it in mind! We only have one friend right now and that's Danny McBroom! If we stay just one night in that shack we'll leave a trail that a pro can find!"

"We have my dad!" Tears welled up in her eyes.

"True enough. But he's a helluva long way away and doesn't even know where we are! He's out of reach now!"

"I need to talk to him, Spain." The pain in her face matched the ache in her voice. "Look at us! You're face is still cut and swollen from that fight and I look and smell like a—a buffalo!"

"I know that!" He watched her body sag as she squatted in the warm, noonday sun.

"Tell you what. After we drop the bag back at the cave, we'll wait it out and find you a phone tonight."

"Not that airport thing, again!" She shook her head doubtfully. "You're some criminal." .

Spain's voice turned grim. "We need foodstuffs and a weapon."

"We've got plenty of those pears."

Spain raised his eyebrows, watching her work it through. "We need to survive," he repeated again. "We're back to the Stone Age."

"When do you want to do this airport thing?"

"From that faded cold tourist guide we found at the line shack, we're probably about four miles southwest of

337

the airport. We'll get a fire going, then hike over so that we can get there at sundown."

"What about people and planes?"

"By three in the afternoon, this time of year, the place is deserted. All the private pilots have flown back to the mainland and the lounge is closed down."

"How the hell do you know all this?"

"It was like that, when I was a kid." He smiled lamely.

"When you were a kid! Jesus, Spain, airplanes still had two wings!"

Spain slung the bag over his shoulder as they began to hike across the hilly meadow toward the small canyon cave, about a mile away.

The shallow cave was only accessible from the west, facing a small arroyo. The climb up the rocks was tricky, through the rounded sandstone boulders and cactus patches, offering sporadic, but dangerous traps. From the mouth of the cave that was almost invisible from the floor of the canyon, they had an unobstructed view of the Cape Canyon reservoir. The security was perfect and Spain gravitated to the shelter because there was a small fissure in the rock ceiling that he knew could be used to vent the smoke in a slow, wispy fashion.

As they approached the cave mouth, Spain looked back at the sun, now beginning its slow downward arc. He checked his watch. It was already after three. When they lost the sun, heat would again become the primary need.

Slowly, he raised his index finger to the sun, then began measuring its width down toward the ocean horizon. "We have about two hours over the horizon sunlight," he finally announced.

"How do you know that?"

Spain laughed. "It's an old Basque trick. The thickness of your finger represents ten minutes in time, from the position of the sun in the sky down to the horizon."

Harumi shook her head, tousling his dyed curly black hair, finally smiling. She took a deep breath as they climbed the narrow path to the cave, which was undoubtedly used by the ancient Chumash Indians and later by Russian fur trappers, when they needed to take refuge on the Island from their otter hunting, at the turn of the century.

Carefully, Spain arranged a kindling mix of dried twigs and leaves in a round pit he had fashioned from small rocks, then emptied the massive pile of pungent buffalo chips next to the ring. Looking up to be certain he had positioned the material just below the natural rupture in the rock ceiling, he then struck one of the precious matches, giving life and warmth to the small pile. For a long time he studied the updraft of the infant fire to be certain the smoke cleared the cave, yet was dispersed well enough rising through the rock opening.

He turned to Harumi and grinned proudly. "Just like a frigging shepherd!" Then he placed a few chips on the crackling tinder. For a while they watched as the dung began to burn, throwing off thick waves of heat and enough fire to light the dark corners of the cave. Spain then placed a pile of chips on the flames. "That'll see us, until we get back here." He watched the doubt dancing in her face as the light flickered from the fire.

"If you can't do it, stay here," he said, suddenly angry. "I'll get what I can and be back when I can! At least I won't be slowed down with any problems!" For the first time, he was sorry she was with him. Her doubts and continual critical judgments were now taking their toll.

Maybe he had overestimated her. Maybe he had no right to expect anything and maybe she was doing the best she could. God knew how frightened he was most of the time.

"What's it going to be? Staying or going?" He glared at her.

"I'll go, but I want to call my father, if it's possible. Is there something I can carry? I need to do my share!" she said defiantly.

Just before sundown, they crossed over the deeply rutted mud fire road without having seen another living soul, except for a lazy herd of black and white goats eating the growth of a vast hillside down to the soil. Their walk across the top of the island was slowed every fifty yards or so as Spain piled rocks into small mounds to mark their way. He knew the danger of leaving a visible trail but he had no choice, if he wanted to find the cave again in the dark.

With less than half an hour of sunlight remaining, they approached the bottom of a steep oak-covered hill, a four-story adobe-styled control tower with thick wooden balconies rising up to meet their view. Carefully, Spain's eyes swept the area, then he studied the terrain with the field glasses he had taken from the *Bonnie*, before she sank. He paid close attention to the tower, but it looked empty, he noted with a flood of relief.

"It'll be dark in a few minutes," he whispered to Harumi, the fear back in his battered face. Motioning her to lay flat against the belly of the damp hill, Spain glanced up, just as the deep-throated roar of a piston engine filled the heavy air. "Get your head down and don't move!" A moment later a single-engined Beechcraft, dragging its famous V tail, easily lifted off the runway and circled low over their heads, its red-and-white fuselage gleaming in the layered Pacific sunset.

"They see us?" Harumi turned her head and checked the sky, answering her own question. "Of course they did! Well, so much for the invisible approach."

The airport had been quiet for half an hour now. Spain checked his watch. It was close to five-thirty, the last shades of pink and red fading to black, the cold beginning to seep back into their bones. "Stay here. I'll check it out."

Suddenly, Harumi was on her feet. "Nice try. We go together!" she proclaimed. "Someone's got to bail you out of trouble. I don't want you to bump your head on a wing from one of those old biplanes."

Slowly they made their way up the hill to the edge of the now deserted airport, finally emerging onto the back patio of the main lounge.

"God, Spain! This is breaking and entering!"

She reached for the double-glass doors to test the lock, when Spain caught her hand. "Let me check it! There could be an alarm!"

"Against who?" she whispered. "We're the only two thieves on this whole island."

Spain ran his fingers around the jamb of the door, then peeked in the large window. The large room and snack bar were dark and empty. "I can't find a thing." He laughed nervously. Spain then pulled out his pocket knife.

"What's this for?"

"Ah, to jimmy the lock."

Harumi shook her head. "It's not locked." Then she simply opened the glass door and entered the lounge.

"It's like at home in Kumuwela. The small airport is open for anyone who needs it." She smiled and brushed past him into the lounge, heading directly for the snack bar area.

For a moment, Spain took his bearings, assessing what they could take. Slowly he walked into the souvenir shop heading for a rack of backpacks. Then he found a long row of sweatshirts. In a moment he was next to Harumi, then he smiled, handing her the backpack. Then he put his finger to his mouth, when he thought he heard something. Shrugging they made their way into the small kitchen, behind the lunch counter.

Quickly Spain took a small frying pan, and a few stores including bacon, flower, instant coffee, and some powdered milk. "I'm only taking a few things. Nothing they would notice right away." He smiled again, shoving a few candy bars into the pack, then an entire box of matches. "Thank God for these!"

Out in the small gift shop, Harumi found a map and a box of thick sweat socks, which she held up to Spain. He nodded and then made his way over to a large open stone fireplace that squatted next to a large case of Indian artifacts.

Carefully sliding open the case, he removed a large bow and a number of long wooden arrows, tipped with what looked like flint arrowheads. "That the gun you came for?" Harumi was next to him, shaking her head.

Spain shrugged again, picking up a long flint knife blade from the display case, his hands shaking visibly. Proudly, she pulled two pairs of souvenir sweatpants from behind her back. "What about these? They've got warm written all over them."

Spain nodded impatiently, ready to move out. They'd

really stretched their luck and it was time to vanish back into the thick blackness, now wrapped tightly around the island.

Spain disappeared into the kitchen again, emerging a moment later with a small flashlight. "I want to be able to—"

The unmistakable approach of an aircraft stopped Spain short. For a second they glanced at each other in fear, then made their way to the window facing the dark five-thousand-foot landing strip, built on artificial fill between two mountain peaks.

"See anything?" he whispered.

Harumi pointed to the east, a tiny red wing strobe light blinking every few seconds. Then the ominous, primordial shadow of a twin-engined Cessna closed the runway, dropping flaps, as it flared for a landing. Just as the wheels bumped down with a sharp squeal, they watched the twin headlights of a van pierce the mountain night, moving swiftly up the main road from Avalon, onto the apron of the runway.

"Get down!" For an instant they were blinded in panic, squatting under the window. Cautiously, Spain raised his head, the lounge now filled with the idling crackle of two Lycoming engines. Cold beams of light from the van's head lamps froze on the cockpit as the pilot cut the switches, the propellers slowly winding down.

"A closed tower and a dark runway without lights," Spain whispered to her. "Pilot's wearing infrared night goggles." Then he pushed down a horrid thought. "Probably running drugs into the island." Now they watched, their eyes just above the bottom of the windowsill; fascinated and frightened, as a very large man emerged with difficulty from the passenger seat of the cockpit, no more than fifteen feet from the lounge window. Harumi shivered when the stark beam of light caught his face as he reached for his bag. The huge man had the eyes of a hungry shark, cold, remote and slightly out of focus. Slowly, the passenger reached up and touched his bald forehead, highlighted by a cluster of dry blond hair that clung to his wide scalp as wildflowers fighting for life on a cold rock.

Mesmerized, Harumi couldn't take her eyes from the man as he climbed down the wing and moved ponderously to the van. "I have this horrid feeling, Benny," she suddenly muttered, her whole body shivering. As the man turned to step into the van, his hungry eyes swept the dark lounge, making invisible eye contact with Harumi. The focus of his eyes burned with laser intensity through the night, into her chilled body.

"He's trouble," she said with finality, as the van's lights disappeared down the mountain. A moment later, the Cessna's pilot, without lights, revved his engines to full power and hurried down the short runway into the night.

Totally drained, Harumi rose and stared at Spain in the darkness. "I don't know who he is, but it's trouble for us," she repeated, tugging at his jacket. "I can feel it in my bones and on my skin!"

"That's crazy! He's a scary-looking guy, but it's not our problem. It couldn't have anything to do with us! It's a drug thing, probably." He motioned to the pay phone over by the large fireplace, reaching into his pocket for a quarter. "Call your father and let him know you're alive and well. I think we'll both feel better."

"You mean, alive," she quipped, as she dropped in the quarter. "Operator this is a credit card call." A moment later, her heart racing, she listened to the familiar ring of the phone in her father's home on the Big Island. Then she heard the warm voice of the Japanese-Hawaiian maid who had almost raised her.

"Euphemia! Hello, it's Harumi!" she shouted excitedly. "Can I speak to my father!" Then her face dropped, as she nodded, staring at Spain. "I see. How long has he been gone?" Then she nodded somberly at the answer, her voice growing very quiet. "How's Mollie?" Then she laughed. "Good! If she gets into the garbage, she's feeling fine. Ah, Euphemia, tell my father hello and that I love him. Tell him I'm well. I love you, Euphemia." Then she hung up.

"He's out of town on some business." She felt crushed by the isolation from her father.

"Harumi, it means he's out of town. He's allowed, for Chrissakes! Just because the world is chasing us, doesn't mean he's in trouble. He can take better care of himself than we can. He's a real tough guy! Come on! Lighten up!" He patted the filled backpack and the bow and arrows he was holding. "Besides, maybe he's trying to help us. I know he wouldn't let anything happen to you."

Slipping out of her funk, Harumi nodded. "You're right, of course. About all of it. Only McBroom knows where we are, right?"

"Right!"

"By the way, Ben, I have a plan of my own. When we get off this rock, I need to find a way to get back to Hyde Park, New York, and for you to go to England to see this monk."

Spain wrinkled his face as they headed back down the backside of the airport, the flashlight guiding the way past the rock markers he had placed on the way up. For a long time they were both quiet as they walked in the cold island air, occasionally glancing up at the night sky,

345

crowded with constellations and the faint wisp of a Magellanic Cloud that laced its way through the bright star fields.

"What's in New York?" he finally asked.

"The Franklin Delano Roosevelt Library. All his private papers are located there on his family estate. All his wartime journals are also there. I have to go through these documents! I know the answers are buried there somewhere. They have to be." She turned to Spain and kissed him lightly. "I know how you feel about all of this, but we've been through so much. It would be a crime not to really know the answers."

Spain drew a long cold breath as they approached the dim glow of their cave across from the small reservoir. "I have a feeling the real crime hasn't been committed yet." Then he slid past her, dropping more buffalo chips onto the fire. "I'll take the first watch, while you sleep," he said, munching on a candy bar. Then he notched a long arrow into the bow, feeling the precious warmth of the fire at his back, as he hopelessly peered out at the black-on-black night that he knew in his gut couldn't really hide them.

Handing Spain a peeled pear, Harumi sat next to him at the small mouth of the cave. "What do you expect to see out there?"

He glanced down at her angled beauty, apparent despite her ragged appearance. "I hope I don't see anything, but I expect to see the building blocks of bad dreams."

Thirty-eight

"Don't be a goddamn fool, Captain Ovsyannikov! The fact remains that General Lutz is out of the picture and I've assumed the reins of direction. It is not an enviable task, but I am willing to be responsible for all of us!" she said in thick, angry English. For a moment, she swiveled in her chair, searching the flat cloudy horizon of Havana Harbor, trying to calm herself. She wasn't used to blatant resistance. My God, she thought, why is this stupid Russian pig so stubborn?

"Gregori," she said gently this time, "I can raise your fee to a flat twenty percent of the gold bullion that is recovered. That is a hundred percent increase over your current fee with General Lutz," she reminded him. "As I said before, I used the old code so that you would contact me! I need your help. We all do!"

For a long time there was only the static of background cosmic radiation as the hissing from the satellite connection continued to fill the vacuum. The Russian was cut from the same cloth as that crazy suicidal bastard Saddam Hussein, when he took on the Allied Coalition. My God, it was advisers just like this mad-dog Cossack who pulled Iraq down. He just hung onto old facts and old loyalties without a perception of the real world. But Ovsyannikov was intelligent and very dangerous to her personally and to the mission she forced herself to remember. He knew all the elements and he was totally schooled by that Nazi, Lutz. She laughed darkly to herself, thinking about the reaction, if the Russian ever found what had really happened in the shadow of the bone bin in the Austrian Alps.

Minister Soria swept her eyes from the naked, sooty view of the green-watered harbor around her office, to the official party portrait of *El Commandante* Castro, his deep-set maniacal eyes peering down on her, those clown ears listening to the potential treason she was talking. Defiantly, she blew a black kiss to the portrait, thinking how Castro had aged severely since that photo was taken. Now his muscular athletic frame was stooped and the kinky black hair on his head and face had decomposed to gray wire. "It's no longer guns that matter, Comrade, but butter. And billions of pesos to run the island," she said firmly.

"Minister Soria, I will think it over," she heard the distant, smooth voice finally respond, free of any emotional cues.

The bastard was playing for time! She could ill afford the Russian backtracking the murders to Hallstatt. She had to neutralize him now. Suddenly she felt a deep quiver of fear in her stomach, like nothing she had felt in years. And that fear excited her. She couldn't afford to make an enemy of this man.

"Would it help if I faxed you the official Austrian Government's death certificate indicating heart failure?" She held her breath. It was her last card. "The autopsy indicated coronary disease had narrowed his arteries for years."

"Yes it would help me, Minister," Gregori answered cryptically, seemingly tuned into the conversation for the first time, yet there was something vague and malevolent in his voice. "I must be certain. As you say, Minister, it is only business."

A matronly female secretary quietly entered the minister's office and carefully laid a neatly typed note on her desk:

YOUR DINNER WITH RAUL IS
CONFIRMED FOR TONIGHT AT
THE FORTRESS EL TORREON
DE LA CHORRERA AT 7:30.

Suddenly, she felt the challenge and the warmth in her thighs as she instantly changed tacks. "You know, Gregori, you have been out in the field for a long time now. You have performed your assignments under a great deal of pressure. I want you to come to Havana, to relax as my guest, so that we can iron out our differences and build a bridge." Her voice took on the same thickness as the smoldering haze that choked the harbor below her. She knew Ovsyannikov's sexual appetites. She had carefully read his GRU file, courtesy of the Soviet KGB Charge de Affaires in Havana.

For a moment, she looked down at her muscular legs sheathed in dark nylons, and stylish two-inch blue pumps. Yes, she could easily leave footprints in his back and a hole between his eyes, if necessary.

Gregori was stunned and off balance. On his last visit to Havana, at the request of General Lutz, Minister Soria, a strikingly handsome, intelligent woman had been appointed his midwife; his control, despite her denial of that fact. She was aloof, demanding, and arrogant. Suddenly, General Lutz, his mentor is dead, and she is purring like a wet kitten. Christ, maybe he should dump the Scotch and go back to peppered vodka. For an instant he thought of Spain and their heavy drinking bouts in the Crimea, then shivered.

"I know a spot, Captain," she continued into the phone. "A little spot when Havana turns to dusk, on the seafront's Malecon. We can drive out to the headland where there is a wonderful and elegant water grotto with a private cupola surrounded by a garden of great beauty. We can talk and walk and eat and drink as we face the Boca de la Chorrera. We can have the entire Eighteen thirty restaurant to ourselves! What do you say, Gregori?" she pleaded softly.

Ovsyannikov quickly surveyed the dingy surroundings of the bar at Sinbad's on the Santa Monica Pier, three thousand miles away. The smell of urine and cheap wine was a stench that offended his senses. Now this powerful Cuban woman with hard breasts was offering him more money than he could possibly even imagine and extending an invitation to share her favors in Havana, away from this bloody storm and Spain's death.

"Gregori," she hesitated. "I like you."

"Yes, Minister. I'm flattered by the meaning of the gift."

"It is not a gift, damn it! Lions must mate with lions, not mice!"

For a time he was awkwardly quiet. Then finally: "I will call you at the same time tomorrow with your an-

swer." Then he quickly hung up before she could continue to weaken him.

He sat listening to the wind and rain pound at the
building and the faint, sad strains of the merry-go-
round as he played with a double Scotch at the old, tattered bar. He was now alone except for a few Latin
types hovering over a pinball machine in a corner of the
bar.

Suddenly, an exceptionally large sea slammed into
the pier, forcing Sinbad's to sway like a ship in a storm.
Gregori looked up and gazed at himself in the long mirror behind the bar, doubt nibbling at him as he thought
through the minister's offer. He closed his eyes, but the
fog wouldn't lift. Now he only felt confusion and sadness. In a dark corner of his mind, he was beginning to
unravel.

Hilda Soria replaced the phone in its cradle, then in
a quick motion, almost as an afterthought, picked it up
and punched in the private number of the director of
the dreaded secret intelligence Directorate MC.

"Sed! My love," she said, lowering her voice. "I am
happy to hear your voice. I need a favor. I have invited
our Russian captain of murder here to Havana so that
we can resolve our differences. I want you to arrange to
have an Austrian death certificate drawn up and faxed
to Ovsyannikov in California. I'll send over the details
to you."

She looked down at her legs again. "When the time is
right, I want Gregori Ovsyannikov shot between the
eyes, but only when we're finished with him!" She re-
crossed her legs, hanging up the phone, her dark eyes

suddenly growing tired and drawn as she thought about facing off with Fidel in a power struggle.

A moment later, having drawn new energy, she pressed down on the intercom. "Maria, place a secured call to Toshiyuki Mizutari in Japan. Then begin to make arrangements to secure an aircraft for a flight to Tsugara, Japan." She laughed at her secretary as she slowly spelled the Japanese name in Spanish. Then she picked up a copy of the latest Politburo memo projecting how quickly the Soviet Union would halt all financial support and stop its annual loan of five billion dollars, American.

Then her thoughts drifted to the scarcity of Cuba's international credits and the projected need for oil that Baghdad was showing signs of backing away from. Iraqi oil was cheap, but with the Soviets no longer supplying arms to Baghdad as part of the old sweetheart deal, Cuba was now being forced out onto the open market, or worse, having to deal with the Japanese to obtain their oil with anything but a discount.

The minister tapped a pencil against her chin. Yes, the Japanese were masters at racking off the discounts for themselves, while forcing their secondary customers to pay through the nose.

Well, no matter, she thought. Soon, if Baghdad wanted only dollars, they would have them to secure Cuba's petroleum needs, which had been a tricky supply problem, at best, since 1960. Again her eyes swept Havana Harbor. Her Havana, which she had known all her life, from the days of the wild 1940s with the casino life and that butcher Batista, through the halcyon days of the revolution with the Castros. Her eyes fell upon the scene of the off-loading of massive sacks of wheat

352

from a Hungarian freighter, with thick rope nets strung from two large cranes. She enjoyed allowing her mind to move to weighty problems of state. It was excellent mental training for what was to come.

Thirty-nine

Harumi leaned back staring at the small but hot fire bounce shadows against the cave's rock walls. "You know what I think, Benny?"

Spain turned his head as he finished emptying the contents of one of the backpacks. "Christ, I'm afraid to ask."

"Seriously, I've played it out in my mind a thousand times."

"Played what out?" He pushed the flashlight into the backpack. "What are—" His ears picked up the distant beat of helicopter rotor blades. For a long time, he stood very still in the mouth of the cave, watching the blackness, as if it were a violent curse. He rubbed the hair standing on the back of his neck. Then the noise dissolved into the night.

"What is it, Benny?"

"I heard a chopper out there somewhere." He glanced back at her questioning face. "Sometimes they bring 'em into the ranches." He shrugged. "It was pretty far away. Sounded like it went somewhere into the Salta Verde, near China Point."

Spain pushed out a long breath, then smiled nervously at her. "What were you saying?"

"I was thinking about Fred Noonan and Amelia Earhart. I think that along with all the plans for the Pearl Harbor raid and the warning to get the carriers out to sea, Emperor Hirohito was offering back the lives of those fliers as a gesture of peace and sincerity."

"You mean, you think Earhart was also aboard the *Arizona?* That her skull is also still floating around that compartment?" She watched that troubled expression wash over him.

"That's right! But I don't know the whys."

"And Roosevelt somehow knew in advance? How the hell did they get into the *Arizona?* By magic? You just don't waltz into a battleship of the line! Maybe FDR was hiding them out there. Maybe they'd been there for years!" He raised his eyebrows. "How's that for a theory?" Then he laughed.

"Lousy!"

"Why? If Roosevelt somehow got his hands on those fliers while they were alive, could he have afforded to tell the American people they were spys, sniffing around the Japanese mandates as well as taking pictures? I don't think so! America wasn't ready for warmongering. Until the raid on Pearl Harbor, they wanted nothing to do with sending men to fight the Axis, whether in Europe or Japan! Revealing the fact that Earhart was a spy would have been political suicide for FDR!"

"I'm impressed, Ben. You know some history, all right!"

"Do you want to hear what's on my mind, Harumi?

It'll be poaching into your professional territory." He studied her face and her intense, piercing eyes.

"Sure."

"You've really been trying to distill this whole thing, like it was an academic exercise, not based on the reality of human beings. You saw those skeletons inside *Arizona!* Maybe you've never had to approach it that way before, as a real time, living event, so close at hand. It's called reality."

"Reality?" She felt the shrillness of her voice echo in the small cave.

"Yeah," he said tentatively. "I'm no historian, but I know about war and the international chaos of that time. My God, Harumi, there'd been war since Nineteen thirty-nine, with alliances, massive death-dealing maneuvering, invasions and spys under every bed! It's been called the fog of war stuff. Random events of death and destruction that cause emotional distortions at that moment in time."

"What are you trying to say, Ben?"

"That life is not as well ordered as you're trying to make it out to be. A little isolated freeze frame. Christ, look at us! We're a random happening. A bird shit stain on history. We're emotional, scattered, and not really centered on things that are probably staring us right in the face. A survival crisis does that to people! Look, hard admissible evidence in court is difficult enough to discover a few months after the commission of a crime, then add to it a fifty-year passage of time. This whole thing, in human terms, is at best a faded color snapshot out of the early Nineteen forties!"

He eyed her uncertainly. "You want me to continue?"

She nodded. "I can use all the help I can get!"

"From day one, Harumi, I've asked a question, starting the night that someone shot out our den window, back home. Why would Roosevelt allow all this to happen with such sinister intent?"

For a long time she thought about it, watching the white hot glowing ember chips in the fire. "Well, maybe he didn't," she finally answered. "Maybe Roosevelt, needing an honorable political way into the war, just got caught up in things, as you say, in an emotional, random way. Don't forget, Roosevelt and his inner circle, except for helping England with lend-lease, didn't have any prior experience with war. Their only learning curve had been economic issues of the depression. Harry Hopkins, Henry Stimson, even General George Marshall, just got caught up in the emotional firestorm."

Then her voice turned cold and unyielding. "But know this. History is organic and interpretative, depending on who is judging the facts, or the evidence, as you say. Once in a great while indisputable facts appear that speak for themselves and time can't change their real meaning."

Spain nodded. "And your hoping that the FDR library and that monk in Wales can give us those hard facts, to give foundation to the yellow pouch?"

"Exactly. Look, probably if the emperor did offer Earhart and Noonan back, Roosevelt didn't know what to do. As you say, the moment they would have reappeared on the American scene, it would have been a tacit admission of an act of war, in Nineteen thirty-seven!" Harumi raised her thin fingers in the form of fans, then smiled through the opaque light of the small cave.

"I've visualized the Pearl Harbor raid a hundred times in my mind the last few weeks, especially after I dove on the *Arizona* with you. Besides, there's not a native born Hawaiian who hasn't thought about it."

She closed her eyes speaking softly. "It took the Japanese eleven days to cross the storm-tossed north Pacific after leaving Hitokappu Bay in the northern Kurile Islands. The attack was led by a nervous Admiral Nagumo and his six large carriers, with legendary names like *Akagi, Kaga,* and *Hiryu,* who launched their one hundred eighty attack planes when they reached station about two hundred miles due north of Oahu."

She paused, gazing up at Spain, then closed her eyes. "Can you imagine the fear those sailors felt when they saw those Zekes roaring down through Waianae Pass into Pearl, dropping their torpedoes and bombs on battleship row? Or the blinking blue lights of the wing guns of the Zero fighters as they dove to strafe the sailors on the decks of those ships? God, Benny, can you imagine what must have gone through the minds of Earhart and Noonan, with all they'd been through, whatever that was, when they went down with the *Arizona?* I just shudder when I allow myself to really think about it! So many questions—"

"All right then, you've had time to think through the big question. "Why the hell does most of the civilized world want us dead? Is it because of Earhart and

Noonan?" Then he answered that part of the question. "For Chrissakes, most people today don't even know who those people were! The world just keeps on spinning like a damn overhead curveball."

"Maybe," she answered softly, "this was and still is a real embarrassment historically to the American and Japanese governments. What we've already uncovered and hope to uncover, certainly won't help to reduce the economic and political tensions that have developed between the two countries. In many circles these are delicate face-saving, matters that could cost billions of dollars in trade. At some point when we go public, both sides will be very unhappy."

Spain shook his head violently. "You're back to your sanitized argument again, looking for that neat little box answer." He shoved the long flint Indian knife taken from the airport into his jacket pocket, then changed his mind and dropped it next to the fire pit. "It doesn't wash, for Chrissakes!" He moved very close to her. "This whole thing's got the reactive smell of drugs and big dirty bucks all over it! There's something obviously very compelling and very important behind that skull and those yellowed rice papers! But historical arguments just don't do it here! It's apples and oranges."

He felt an angry heat rise in his neck. "Damn it, I don't want to be here anymore in this stink, fighting every second for our lives and a few crumbs of food!"

Harumi watched the frustration in his face sour into anger. "Maybe it's fate, Benny. The skull, the pouch, this place."

"Don't give me that metaphysical crap! Screw fate!

Some good people have died in this! I just want to go home!"

"What the hell do you want me to do, damn you!" she shouted back. "I can't solve your damn puzzle yet! I need more information! What the hell do you want?"

"Want? I'll tell you what I want! I want my dog, clean sheets, and the right to eat a fucking slider and fries, without the fear that I'm gonna be shot!"

"A what?"

Spain looked down, his anger dissipated into the warmth of the cave. Now he was sorry for venting his frustration on her. "Ah, a slider is a cheeseburger."

Harumi cocked her head. "Jesus, a cheeseburger!" Then she burst out with laughter, reaching for him. "God, Ben, this is awful," she said softly. "That's why we have to get out of here and go to New York and England and talk to that crazy monk." She glanced up at Spain's bruised face, now a crooked dark alley. "I think we're closer than we realize, to finding out how this whole web is interconnected."

"You better hurry up, before they kill us! I just don't give a shit. I never did! I'm too old to be this hungry. I'm a lousy Basque!"

"Have another cactus pear. They're really not that bad."

"I can't stomach it! Old Tonto is gonna hike over to where we left Buffy and see if those jerky strips have dried out yet. When I get back we'll whip up some coffee with that can of water I brought from the reservoir and I'll make some skillet bread." He smiled.

"Then we can bed each other down and pretend we're home." Slowly, he rubbed his hands over her hips and the tightness of her body, then kissed her lightly; his bruised face beginning to turn purple and yellow. He picked up the ancient bow and quiver filled with arrows, shaking his head. Then he was gone, in the blackness, slowly descending the narrow path from the cave to the arroyo below.

For more than an hour after Spain left the cave, Harumi jotted down as many details of their conversation that she could think of in a small notebook she had taken from the airport. Totally focused on the mystery that had sucked them into this lethal vortex, Harumi lost herself in writing down a number of theories in the firelight. Maybe Ben was right. Maybe she was approaching this just as an academic exercise, rather than as a living circumstance.

She reached for another sweet pear, then settled in, watching the full moon dance its harsh beams of white light off the surface of the small reservoir across the ravine. From somewhere a coyote howled a mournful shriek, then it was absolutely still. Growing tired, Harumi leaned against the mouth of the cave, and closed her eyes drifting into sleep. From somewhere in that troubled sleep she was haunted by flashes of the man's dead eyes at the airport, then she floated along with a strange smell of men's cologne.

Then abruptly the smell was a stranglehold, from the pressure of a thick, cold hand over her mouth.

Somewhere between the seam of sleep and reality, Harumi opened her eyes to confront the worst nightmare of her life. It was the man from the airport, his head as big as a table, punctuated with those dead, unfocused, shark eyes.

Instinctively, Harumi tried to pull away, but her head was caught in a steel vise. God, this can't be happening! Again, she caught sight of his unearthly face in the firelight and shivered.

"Sind Sie allein hier?"

Harumi struggled to remember some basic German. Anything to survive! "Ah, yes, I'm alone."

"Du bist sehr hubsch!" Then the giant smiled very pleasantly. *"Sprechen Sie Deutsche?"* The man gently released the pressure on her mouth and head.

"No, no ah, I don't speak German."

"I said you are very pretty, Fraulein." His English was fairly clear, then he laughed as he climbed up fully into the cave, taking her with him in one easy motion. Then those dead eyes came to life, quickly taking in every aspect of the cave and the meager supplies piled against a rock.

"Name please?" The smile didn't fit the hostile movements of his eyes and huge body.

"Go fuck yourself!" Harumi tried to back away, before a large open hand caught her flush on the mouth. She was more startled than hurt.

"Name please?" He waved his hands in sympathetic movements, telling her that she couldn't win. He would simply beat her to a pulp to force her to speak her own name.

"Ah, Harumi van Horn, you bastard!" she snarled.

"Good," he replied smoothly. "We will be friends then." He reached out and ran his thick fingers through her short bleached hair. "You should not have

362

cut your hair. A bad disguise." Then he pulled out his .22 Webley revolver, with an ivory handle, from a shoulder holster. "This business won't take long," he chatted. Pulling the *zeiss* silencer from his field jacket pocket, Herr Peter Staven smiled down at her as he spun the cylinder of the gun to be certain it was fully loaded.

Forty

Terrified, Harumi could hardly breathe as she watched this monster, preparing clinically, to kill her. Satisfied, Staven finally focused those glistening gray eyes on her.

"Don't be concerned. I don't want you." Then he smiled. "I want the fox, Spain. We came close in Sawyers Bar, but—" he hesitated. "But it was not meant to be. But it is now. I assume Spain will return shortly." It wasn't a question.

"Are you the Black Ghost?"

"Me? No! But I can tell you he sends regards. He is out of touch for the moment, but never out of reach."

Harumi circled Staven, the panic growing in her throat. Ben would be back in a few minutes. She had to do something, despite her fear. "Why are you doing this?" she finally uttered.

"Why? I have a directive from the Black Ghost."

Then Harumi moved close to him, pushing herself each step of the way. "No! That's not my question!" she said sharply. "Who is involved besides the Black

Ghost?" Now she was very close to him, smelling his hideous cologne, as if it could hide the stench of death all about him.

Staven cocked his head. Her questions were throwing him off balance. Talking wasn't what he was paid to do.

"How did you find us out here?" She was chewing at him again.

Staven shrugged. It couldn't hurt. "A simple infrared night scope from a chartered helicopter. I checked Avalon thoroughly today and you were not there, so I hired a helicopter." He smiled evenly. "It only took a few hours of searching these hills to find the massive heat coming from the cave. Animals don't build fires in caves. Not very professional of Spain. This was very easy! Spain must be tired. It is not like him, or not like he used to be. He was very good, when he was young. Now he's dead shit!"

"Why do you want to kill, Spain? Harumi swallowed into her tight throat. "It isn't right! You can't do this to Spain! We haven't done anything to you!" she screamed at him.

"My God, how did you find us?"

For a moment, Staven thought about it, then shrugged, again. "A man named Willy told me. You took his boat. He was very angry about it."

"Spain hasn't done anything to you!" Harumi pleaded.

"His crime is existing." Staven was growing tired of her cross-examination.

"Why Spain, damn it!"

He pushed out a thin, angry breath. "Because I've been assigned to it! He is getting too close." The echo of a tumbling rock from below brought Staven into a crouch. Quickly, he waved her forward to the mouth of the cave, with a finger to his mouth. Then Staven raised his nose sniffing the chilled air like a terrier at a rathole.

"He is coming," Staven grunted, moving back behind Harumi. "I will kill him quickly with one shot. Greet him." His voice was steady and mechanical.

The sound of Spain climbing the narrow path beat at Harumi's mind, as his footfalls grew closer. Then suddenly the sound stopped, replaced with an eerie quiet of a vagrant wind pushing through the rocks below.

"Tell him to come in," Staven whispered.

"Fuck you!" she screamed as loud as she could. "You Nazi bastard!"

Then the cold steel of the silencer pushed against the back of her ear. "More accurately, my father was a Waffen-SS officer in the famous Totenkoph, the Death's Head battalion at Dachau." Then a mild smile spread from his mouth to those cruel eyes. "Now, call him in, or I will kill you, too," he whispered again. "I want this fox!"

"I'm down below," a faint voice interrupted. "I'm not armed but you'll have to come out and get me, butt-head!"

"Come in, or I'll kill her!" Staven called out.

"Belästigen Sie mich nicht!" Spain called back, laughing.

Staven shook his head. Spain was speaking German. We'll see about bothering him, the Gypsy bastard! "I'm out of time, Spain, I'm going to kill her, now," he called out.

"Go ahead!" Spain's laughter echoed across the arroyo. "Then what are you going to do? You'll still have to come out for me! Is the *Goombah* of the Ovsyannikov crime family a coward? *Viel Gluck,* fuck face!" Now Spain's laughter rose to a bellow, challenging Staven's manhood.

"Are there any children you can kill before you have to face me?" Spain shouted. "Your mother was a Nazi whore!" More laughing echoed across the ravine.

Angrily, Staven threw Harumi to the floor of the cave, next to the hot fire. His eyes bulged with rage as he paced the small cave. Then he made a decision, starting for the cave entrance when Harumi called to him. "Kill him, then come back to me," she called seductively.

For a confused instant he stood very still, then started for Harumi, just as she whipped around scooping up a handful of white hot buffalo chips from the fire, with a T-shirt that Spain had left behind. It was a perfect strike, the coals hitting him in the face, scalding him badly; the gun dropping harmlessly to the rock floor.

A deep animal scream brought Spain into the cave, an arrow drawn back on the taut old bow, just as Staven pulled his hands away from his damaged face.

"Ich verstehem nicht!" Staven screamed in pain.

"What's not to understand? Jesus! You're a cute little gargoyle!"

"Spain!" the burned man shrieked as he started for him.

Calmly, Spain raised the bow to eye level and released the flint-tipped arrow. In a split second, the feathered shaft found its mark in Staven's forehead, with the awful crack of bone, the force of the blow slamming him back against the wall of the cave.

Frozen in motion, they watched Staven stagger back to his feet, the arrow embedded deeply in his forehead above his left eye, blood pouring down his burnt face, his eyes swelling fiercely in the dim light. Somehow, Staven mustered up the animal strength to reach his large hands around Spain's neck, pulling him down to the stone floor.

"Harumi—" Spain choked. "I can't—"

Staven was atop Spain, his hands in a death grip around his neck, as Harumi jammed the long flint Indian knife, laying by the fire, into Staven's side with all her strength. Again, she was forced to stab the giant and finally he yielded, the light ebbing from his dead eyes.

Sometime later, when Spain was able to breathe, they both rolled the body of Peter Staven out of the cave down into the rocks of the arroyo. Exhausted, they collapsed next to their meager life-giving fire, hanging onto each other as life preservers.

Finally, Spain gave in to the hunger in his belly and prepared a skillet bread in the small frying pan they had stolen. Using flour, a small amount of water and fat he had cut from the dead buffalo, before coming back to the cave, Spain mixed the ingredients into a thick rough dough. From time to time, he glanced over at Harumi, sitting dazed next to the fire.

Then he took the dried buffalo jerky strips and tore them into bits, mixing them into the dough, before greasing the pan with some leftover fat. Then he flattened the dough into the pan and put it atop the glowing fire.

For half an hour, he tended to the hot pan then announced that it was finished, glancing over Harumi, who had grown sullen.

Spain broke off a piece of the pleasant-smelling skillet bread and handed it to her. "Eat something," he urged gently. Finally, she took the hot bread, which tasted like a chewy biscuit.

"Not too bad," she finally said, a faint smile nibbling at the corners of her mouth.

"Okay. What is it? I've never seen this kind of silence before."

She focused on Spain, then suddenly large tears rolled down the cheeks of her darkened troubled face. "I never killed before!"

Spain sat besides her, munching on his bread. "That's it, is it?" He leaned over and dropped a few more chips on the waning fire. "Well, I've got a flash for you. I killed him with that arrow. What you did, was slow him down a little, before he crushed my windpipe."

Harumi held up her hands. "I've got blood on them now." The remorse rolled from her with a tragic thickness.

Spain mashed his face. "I can't tell you not to feel this way. God knows the problems I've had over the years, but I need to tell you he would have killed you without blinking."

"That doesn't make it right!" she snapped angrily. She shook her head. "I should have listened to you at the house and taken the damn pouch back to the *Arizona!*"

"When a Basque has to deal with a death in this way; when it is in self-defense, or to protect his flocks, it is called killing in the eyes of God." Spain rose to his feet. "I embrace this killing as a badge of honor!" he shouted at the cave entrance.

"Do you love me, Harumi?" he suddenly asked.

"Of course I do. What kind of question is that?"

"You helped me kill a glob of spit to save our lives, damn it! We'd both be very dead on the floor of this cave right now!"

"You're right, Ben." She nodded.

"Look, this pouch and the rest of this mysterious prize isn't free. You thought you could pull it off without getting dirty."

She started to protest, then stopped herself, nodding.

"The only free cheese is in the mouse trap, but now we have a responsibility to see it through."

"To who?"

"To who? To Kim Dubin. To Jack Scruggs. To those dead fliers, to your father, who risked his life for us and finally to that buffalo, as dumb as it sounds. And the final responsibility to all those dead souls still aboard the *Arizona!*"

He took her hand and held it firmly. "I hope you never again have to participate in a killing for as long as you live." Then he smiled. "Better?"

"Yeah." Then she pointed down at the bread. "This is really good." Then she reached for another piece.

"Wait until we get home, then I'll make it again and you won't be able to stomach it. I hope we're never this hungry again."

"What about getting out of here, Ben?"

"Let's rotate some sleep for a few hours, then I'll hike back up to the airport and call Danny McBroom, before the sun comes up." Spain reached down and picked

370

up the Webley revolver, a squat silencer screwed into the barrel.

"At least we have a little protection, temporarily. McBroom's got to get us off of this frigging rock! Gregori's coming for us, next!"

Forty-one

Spain made his way into the now familiar lounge of the Catalina mountaintop airport. For a long time, he allowed his eyes to adjust to the darkness, then he searched the entire area, before making his way to the pay phone. He knew this routine was dangerous and that Ovsyannikov could have someone just waiting to pick him off, but he didn't have a choice.

He glanced back toward the back double doors leading to the patio and watched Harumi's shadow against the full moon. She had insisted on hiking along, afraid now to be alone in the cave. Spain took a deep breath and held the Webley revolver tighter in his hand, his gun finger brushing the trigger guard.

Swallowing, Spain dropped in a quarter and called Danny McBroom at home in Los Angeles. The connection was made on the second ring. "Danny, it's Spain."

"You all right, Ben?"

"Almost. We had a visitor, the size of an elephant!"

"I know," McBroom cut him off. "Ovysannikov's people got to you through a detective here in my office who told him where to find Boxcar Willy. It was a miscommunication and Willy's dead. I guess he overheard our conversation or saw the map or something about Catalina. This Russian plays rough!"

"Really! Listen, Danny, we have to get off this rock! Harumi's scared shitless and I admit, I'm doing three sixties every couple of seconds! I know the program. Gregori's coming next. Just find a way to get us off! Now!" He felt his voice rise in his throat.

"Come on, Ben! I'm doin' the best I can, for Chrissakes!"

"Goddamn it!" Ben hissed into the phone, his eyes still searching the dark corners of the lounge. "We've been given a death sentence, if we stay anywhere on this island! Help me, damn it! Don't make me beg!"

"Okay, okay, Ben. Calm down. Ah, let me think it through and do what I can. It's late."

"It's late for us, Danny!"

"Jesus, Ben! It's eleven fucking o'clock at night. I can't pull a rabbit out of a hat!" Then his voice faded.

"Danny!"

"Look, get your ass down into Avalon by eleven tomorrow morning. I'll make certain you get a package on the first Catalina shuttle of the day. They'll deliver it to the post office, and I'll make certain it's top priority."

"Can you get me out of the country? I've got to get to England and Harumi's got to go to New York!"

"I know that, Ben. Slow down, damn it! I've got your file open in front of me right now. Look, I can't

373

promise anything, but let me see what I can come up with. I'm not a frigging Houdini!"

Spain took a deep breath, ashamed of his own panic. "I'm sorry, Danny. You've already stuck your neck out further than you should have and I know what could happen if any of this ever goes public. I appreciate your back channel efforts."

"Thanks, Ben." His voice grew calm and steady. "Now look, you know how to duck. He's a major pain giver. You know what this Russian asshole can do! The word we have is that Ovsyannikov and his people have goose boxes."

"What?"

"Satellite communicators. It's a real sophisticated operation. So obviously, he's reporting to people outside the States. It's a real cozy setup. We've run an Interpol line on Ovsyannikov and he's hooked up with an ex-German, a General Mischa Lutz."

"My God!" Spain rolled his eyes.

"You know him?" McBroom sounded surprised.

"Yeah, in a way. I delivered Ovsyannikov to his home in Pankow, East Berlin, years ago. I told you the story, I just didn't name the contact. Lutz? Jesus!"

"Get off the phone, Ben!"

"Okay." Spain was reluctant to break the connection with his lifeline and friend. "You know what I want now, Danny?"

"I know what you want, damn it! But who gets everything they want in life? Watch your backside and be at the post office by eleven tomorrow!" Then the line went dead.

They hiked most of the night, crossing the treacherous Swain's and Gallagher's canyons, finally emerging, exhausted and tired at Hogsback Gate, in the hills above the city of Avalon, just as the pink sun lifted above the eastern horizon.

For a long time, they sat above the steeply built town, on a park bench across from the Zane Grey mansion, commanding a magnificent view of the hillside homes, and the boats dotting the harbor below.

Suddenly, a chime rolled like a shrill thunder across Avalon. "What's that?" Harumi painfully held her ears.

Spain pointed to the small stone tower next to them. "The Wrigley hourly bells." He pointed across the street to the low-slung structure built into the steep scrub hillside.

"That was Zane Grey's home in the Nineteen twenties. He hated the Wrigley chewing gum family, who owned the island. My father told me the story. I think one night the Greys and the Wrigleys ended up at a local gathering and Grey's wife tossed a drink in lady Wrigley's face. The next morning Wrigley retaliated by building that bell tower across the street from Grey's house to disturb his writing on an hourly basis."

Harumi rolled her eyes, not sure whether to believe him or not, then she turned and looked down at the crescent-shaped bay. "Look, Ben! A cruise ship! God, what I wouldn't give to be on that right now, heading for Mexico. God, the food, clean clothes, hot showers!" She ran her fingers through her filthy hair.

For a long time they watched the large, sleek, white liner nuzzle into the bay, finally dropping anchor close to the deep water pier.

Spain checked his watch. It was now seven in the morning. The resort town was still sleeping, especially in the off season. He still had some cash. Maybe they could take a chance and steal down into town for a real breakfast. Then he thought about the Black Ghost and shuddered inside, afraid to let Harumi see or feel his gut-level fear.

"We don't have to be at the post office until eleven." For a while he watched Harumi watch the cruise ship, a thin wisp of steam floating up from its raked funnel; its massive bows beginning to swing from an anchor chain in response to the light breeze. "Why don't we drop into town and have a real breakfast, then we can hit one of the shops for a few new duds?" He surveyed their ragged appearance. "Christ, it looks like we've been begging on the street."

"We have!" she said sharply.

An hour later, after descending into a deserted Avalon, composed of quaint cobblestone streets, rustic shops, and turn-of-the-century Queen Anne Bed and Breakfast homes; they found a small coffee shop on a back street at the Edgewater Hotel. After a sour look from the owner, Spain quickly explained their boat had run into trouble and after a few iffy nights at sea, they were finally towed into the harbor. He smiled coldly at the squinting eyes, feeling for the Webley in his jacket pocket. Finally they were seated close to kitchen and ate until their stomachs were in their throats.

Making their way to the small beach, they continued to warm themselves in the sun until the stores opened at ten, just as the passengers from the cruise ship began to come ashore.

"We are going to be okay, Benny!" Harumi searched his face, smiling, when he came out of the public shower on the pier dressed in new cotton denims, shirt, and blue deck shoes.

Silently Spain surveyed the few people milling about the mint-green pleasure pier, some waiting for special tours, others just idling in the sweet morning sun. Even in the shower, he had kept the gun within reach. His obsession with Gregori Ovsyannikov, here out in the open, was growing, yet they had to be here to survive!

"What? You say something, Harumi?" His voice was very far away as his eyes moved like a sentry to every shadow and movement.

"I'll be back." Then she picked up her new yachting clothes and headed for the women's shower, while he sat in the shadows, watching; the tension crawling over him with the weight of a dirge.

Suddenly out of the corner of his eye, he spotted a uniformed Los Angeles County Sheriff's Deputy, climbing the ramp from a police boat. For just a moment, a frozen, recognizable moment, his eyes locked on Spain, then the cop approached slowly. The closer he got to Spain, the closer his right hand moved toward the thick wooden handle of the gun on his hip.

For a blind instant, Spain had the urge to bolt, to jump over the wooden railing into the sea. At least it would pull the cop away from Harumi, still in the shower. Then suddenly, the sheriff's dark khaki uniform was offset against his star badge, now shining in Spain's face. "Pardon me, sir."

Pushing down his panic, Spain slowly moved his right gun finger over the trigger of the Webley, stuck in his pocket. Then he leaned over, carefully aiming the weapon at the cop's stomach. The peaked cap, with its black visor bent toward Spain, the right hand resting on the handle of his service weapon.

"Sir, excuse me." The young, undefined face beneath the cap smiled sheepishly. Who had spotted him! Damn, they were cursed!

Spain rose slowly, his face flushed with fear, but careful to keep the revolver's barrel aimed at the deputy sheriff. "Yes?" Spain croaked, his voice uneasy and skiddish.

"You look like a boat person. Where can I find the harbor master's office?" Then his young head dropped a bit. "I'm just out of the academy and I've got to serve a child custody subpoena."

Spain went blank, his suspicious eyes staring past the sheriff. "Sir, did you hear me?" Now the youthful, round face hesitated, beginning to look at Spain in a different way.

"You passed it," came the pleasant voice of Harumi. She pointed to the end of the pier, to a large painted sign on a two-story Cape Cod building. "The old boy here was up all night, sailing down from San Francisco. He's out on his feet."

"Sorry," Spain uttered, then smiled weakly, as the sheriff turned and moved off toward the head of the pier.

"God! I almost killed him, Harumi," he whispered hoarsely as he sat heavily on the bench. "I can't take much more of this out in the open." He looked over at Harumi's chiseled face, scrubbed clean, her wet hair combed neatly, offset against her white sailing pants and red-and-white-striped sweater. Then she did a quick pirouette.

"Well? What do you think?" She raised her eyebrows, hoping to distract him. "Wanna find a place and mess around a little?"

"Let's get out of here! I can feel Ovsyannikov's eyes watching me." He rubbed the hair on the back of his neck, as that ancient war pain washed over his face, turning him ashen gray. "God, I see him in every face that comes my way!" There was a frail pleading in his voice that frightened Harumi. "I know he's here right now, I can feel him, damn it!"

He slammed a fist against the pier's wooden railing, then rubbed his freshly shaved face, feeling the mustache that was actually growing full and bushy. "How much killing does there have to be, before all this ends? How many crucibles, just to survive, to see the next day's sun?" His eyes searched the calm waters of the harbor. Then he shuddered with an invisible cold hand on his shoulder, as he searched Harumi's face, grasping for possibilities. "I've relived every lousy part of my life these last few weeks. I'm just plain tired, Harumi. A bullet in the ear might be a relief."

"The hell you say!" she snarled. "Let's go see what Danny McBroom has for us. The post office should be open now."

"What we need is a flak vest, assault rifles, and

hand grenades; then a visit to a plastic surgeon to change our looks."

Harumi patted his thick shoulders as they slowly moved off the pier into the center of town, her face a determined mix of toughness and patience.

Forty-two

Spain tensed as he searched the old wooden shopping arcade that housed the tiny post office. He could see beyond the two people in front of him in line, his right hand still on the gun in his jacket pocket. Then suddenly, Spain was facing a young, pleasant-looking woman, dressed in mail grays. She cocked her head, waiting for him to say something. Then hc fclt Harumi's sharp elbow in his side.

"Ah, I'm here to collect a package for—" What the hell name did McBroom say to use? "Ah, I'm Jeff Light." He smiled thinly.

"Light," she repeated, turning to check the in-basket. "No, it's not there." Then she held up a finger, as he felt the heat flush his face. "Wait a sec." Then she disappeared behind a warped plywood wall. In a moment she was back, holding a large brown box, with a funny expression on her face.

"I'm sorry it took so long, Detective." There was new respect in her voice. Then she checked the large photo taped to the package, against Spain's face. "It's you, all right." She smiled, pointing to the signature line. Quickly Spain scrawled a signature and then withdrew across the lobby to a long, chest-high table.

"Our miracle has arrived." Harumi smiled.

"Don't count on it." Spain pulled the wrapping off the officially sealed Los Angeles Police Department package. On the top of the box inside was a handwritten note:

BEN:
I'VE DONE THE BEST I CAN WITH SUCH SHORT NOTICE. I AM NOW A FELLOW TRAVELER SO WHEN THIS MESS IS ALL OVER AND THE BAD GUYS ARE GONE, DESTROY ALL THIS EVIDENCE, INCLUDING THIS NOTE. I AM NOW AN ACCESSORY TO YOUR ALLEGED CRIMES. I LIKE HARUMI. DON'T FUCK IT UP. STAY CLEAN, SHOOT STRAIGHT AND BON VOYAGE. NOW I'M OUT OF IT.

DANNY
P.S. RELAX. I'VE PAID FOR ALL OF IT MYSELF. NO LOCKER FUNDS. I'M IN YOUR HANDS!

"Bon Voyage? What the hell does that mean?"

"Ben, look!" she whispered excitedly. Then she held up two oval-shaped bronze shields, with a relief of the Los Angeles City Hall etched in the background of each.

Ben shook his head, astonished.

"McBroom's a smart man, Ben. He did the only thing he could for us. He made us cops!" Then she held up two pink laminated identification cards. She then flashed Spain his card.

"My God, Jeff Light is a detective sergeant!" He glanced over at the other card she was holding with a head and shoulders photo of Harumi. "You're Arlene Lynn, also detective sergeant. We're part of a special ATU, an antiterrorist unit." She then proceeded to clip the ID card to her shirt pocket and place the shield and its wallet case in her pocket.

"Let's see what else is here." Harumi picked up a handwritten itinerary obviously completed by McBroom. "Ben, my God!"

"What?" Spain kept shaking his head, laughing.

"Bon voyage! He's gotten us on the *Azure Seas*, the cruise ship in the harbor, on police business! We're going to Mexico!"

"Let me see that!" He studied the sheet. She was right. McBroom had pushed them through the back door to beat the federal search system. McBroom knew all the national airports were flagged on the mainframe computers. They were federal fugitives now. The *Azure Seas* was scheduled to put into Mazatlan, in another three days.

"Part two." She held up two Delta ticket jackets, which she read quickly. "He's been very busy! He's got you scheduled round trip from Mexico City to London and me round trip from Mexico City to Poughkeepsie, New York, via connecting flights from Canada." Then she hugged Spain. "I told you!" Then she looked back inside the box. "This is for you."

Spain pulled out a shoulder holster and a standard police model 10 issue .38 snub-nosed Smith & Wesson revolver. "Now I've got a meat eater back!"

"That's disgusting, Benny!"

Spain drew a deep breath. "Maybe, but Gregori Ovsyannikov and the FBI and every two-bit police department between here and New York aren't going to be shooting marshmallows at us!"

She held up her hands in surrender, but she couldn't contain her excitement. Then she picked up the box, ready to toss it in the trash, when Spain touched her arm. "Not here. We'll dump it as we go." He stopped and smiled darkly, looking up.

"What is it?" Then her eyes climbed the wall, decorated with FBI Wanted Posters. There in the middle of the sheets was a large black-and-white page:

WANTED
BENJAMIN SPAIN
MALE CAUCASIAN
MURDER, ASSAULT, ARMED ROBBERY, FLIGHT FROM FEDERAL PROSECUTION. ARMED AND CONSIDERED EXTREMELY DANGEROUS. DO NOT APPROACH THIS INDIVIDUAL. CONTACT YOUR LOCAL LAW ENFORCEMENT AGENCY. REWARD FOR INFORMATION LEADING TO ARREST AND PROSECUTION, $50,000.

Spain's face stared down at them, free of the new mustache and the dyed hair, but to the trained eye, Spain was staring up at himself.

"Where's my picture?" Harumi shivered, then touched Spain's face. "We'll find a way out, I promise, Ben," she said softly.

He laughed nervously, still staring at himself on the wall. Then he tried to smile. "I've come a long way for a shepherd's kid, huh, Harumi? Jesus, I'm trying to regain my balance, trying to rationalize a healthy ending, but I'm the real problem!"

"I don't understand?"

"To make it back alive, I've got to be extra sharp and I'm not! I'm out of touch, and I've lost my edge. Like I heard that German bastard Staven say to you in the cave, when I was right outside, I'm not like the old Spain. I've lost the cunning and the taste for the hunt."

Then he glanced up again at the FBI poster. "But, God, these people play rough. Gregori and General Lutz are moving in real fast company these days." Then he shook his head. "This doesn't have a fucking thing to do with our little yellow package, like I said before," his voice growing angry and frustrated.

"Look, Ben!" Harumi opened her airline ticket jacket and pulled out a wad of cash. "There must be two thousand bucks here! Did he steal it, Ben?"

"No, not Danny. He must have used his nighttime ATM machine," he said softly. "The bastard thought of everything but wiping our behinds. He's a good, honest cop. Always was." Spain wiped tears from his eyes, then turned to her. "Now we're cops and I'm wanted for murder by the FBI." He shook his head slowly. "Life's a real comedy if you can understand."

"And if you don't understand?" There was an edge of bitterness in Harumi's voice.

"Life's a tragedy."

Forty-three

"Detective Light?" The chief purser of the cruise ship, *Azure Seas,* leaned over Spain's shoulder at the dining table in the Grand Salon of the southward-bound liner, whispering into his ear with a practiced, discreet voice. "We have a priority radio communication for you, from a Lieutenant McBroom. He's on the radio telephone from Los Angeles."

Spain brought his eyes up to the face of the freshly scrubbed ship's officer, dressed in sterile Alpine white. Spain glanced at Harumi, then followed the officer out onto the main deck of the massive ship, now two days steaming out of Catalina. It was plying through the calm seas south at a smooth twenty-five knots, a large wake churning the Pacific at the stern of the twenty-thousand-ton ship.

A moment later he was silently directed to a small private cubicle inside the radio shack, jammed with single sideband radios and radio telephones. "Ah, Detective Light, here, over."

"Light, this is McBroom, over."

McBroom was playing it straight, especially on a

call into the clear. "Your primary target has been discovered, over."

"Where, damn it?" The hiss in his ear seemed to last forever. "Ah, over!"

"We tracked him down to a room over a restaurant on the Santa Monica Pier. Unfortunately, we missed him by eight hours. Gone without a trace, over."

"As I said before, one of his Nazi goons, a Petr Staven, tried to off me and ah, Officer Lynn. You'll find his body at the base of a shallow ravine, across from the Cape Canyon Reservoir, near the airport. He's a little messed up, but we had to improvise, over."

"I copy that, Detective, over. I thought you needed this latest information, over."

"Ah, yes. Thanks for all the—"

"Not now, over!" McBroom cut him off.

Spain wiped the tension from his face with a tremor in his hand. "Any ideas about his current location? Over."

"Sorry, Detective. He vanished into thin air. Are you and your partner all set on your travel line? How's the boat ride, south? Over."

"Ah, thanks, Danny." A lump rose in Spain's throat. "I don't care who's listening. God love ya, McBroom! Over."

For a long time the static grew in Spain's ears, then: "The Black Ghost is on the move, so watch your backside! I hope you find what you need. This will be our last communication until the operation is concluded. Over and out." Then Spain heard McBroom break the connection.

* * *

The combo eased into a smooth version of "Moments to Remember" as Harumi and Spain huddled in a dark corner of the small dance floor.

"You believe this, Benny? We're clean, our stomachs are full, and we're dancing on a cruise ship. Heaven-sent."

"Yeah, heaven-sent." He looked down at her new dress, from a trendy boutique aboard the ship, that pulled itself around her tight, shapely figure. Slowly he raised a hand until it cupped her ample breast, through the silk, his fingers resting lightly on her hard nipple. "I'm kinda not into dancing tonight. Wanna mess around?"

She reached up and ran her tongue over his lips. "I guess you're feeling better. You have this thing for my breasts." Her voice was suddenly hot and wet. "We dock in the morning, then we won't be together for a while."

Half an hour later, he pulled the yellow silk dress over her head, then slowly and carefully began to kiss her fully aroused breasts. "Benny?"

"Quiet. Stop directing traffic!" With precision he moved down her hard, flat belly, finally reaching the hot fullness between her thighs. Quickly, her moaning dissolved into a withering cry as he brought her to the edge.

"God, Ben, now! God, hurry!" Not waiting, Harumi mounted him with a shudder of pleasure. "Come with me, Benny! Come with me," she demanded, as her hips and wild movements brought them both closer and closer until they exploded into a searing series of orgasms.

Later, they lay holding one another, still cherishing their warmth, feeling the gentle, throbbing rhythm of the *Azure Seas,* as it glided through the warming Pacific seas. As the ship rounded the southern tip of Baja, Mexico, she turned her thick bows almost due east heading for the Mexican mainland at Mazatlan.

"How will I contact you, Ben?"

"In two days, I'll call you."

"I don't understand? I don't know where I'll be staying."

"It's easy. You'll find the Howard Johnson in Poughkeepsie and that's where you'll check in."

Harumi roared with laughter. "There's nothing in Poughkeepsie! It's a joke! An old Jack Benny joke!" Then she looked at Spain, who wasn't amused.

"Then why don't you just advertise yourself. Take lunch at the goddamned Russian Tea Room in Manhattan and then advertise in the New York *Times* for information regarding two lost fliers, circa Nineteen thirty-seven!"

"Oh come on, Spain! Really! Your male stuff is sticking out!" She sat up in bed, staring at him.

"You like watching my guts shake apart for kicks? I did great on the pier with that cop!"

"No." She pushed out a deep sigh. "You know I don't."

"Last night, I checked out the ship's travel library. Poughkeepsie works. You'll rent a car. Excuse me, I recommend that you rent a car to reach the FDR Library that is only five miles up the Hudson River.

Hopefully, it's good security for you and we can have minimal contact. I'll find a way to call you in two nights. You understand what I'm saying to you, Harumi?" He peered at her, his eyes narrow and focused.

"What if you don't call in two nights?" she said defiantly.

"Then I'll be dead."

Forty-four

Ben Spain shivered as a blast of cold North Sea air curled around him as he quickly exited Royal British Customs in Terminal Three at Heathrow. He stood to one side of the massive swinging doors, trying to take his bearings. It had been years since he had been in London. It was still cold and blustery. Then he suddenly smiled. McBroom knew exactly what he was doing. He had been able to carry his gun on the plane and the moment he flashed his ID card and police shield at Customs, he was waved through.

Slowly, his eyes focused on a large sign:

TAXI RANK

Beyond it stood a long line of the backs of squat, round-ended black cabs. All he knew was what Russell Wittenberg had told him about an island off the coast of Wales named Caldey. An island that held a monastery and an ancient wacko monk named Alvin Dvorak, code named Linch Pin, who during World War II had been Harry Hopkins's special White House agent. Whatever the hell that meant?

"Sir? Did you hear me?" A small man, with a peaked cap marked by a bright yellow band labeled Traffic Warden, was speaking to him. "You look like a very unhappy Teddy."

"A what?" Spain pulled back sharply.

"Ah, a Yank!" came the deep cockney accent. "Didn't mean a fright. An unhappy Teddy is an unhappy soldier."

Spain took a deep breath and released his fingers from the handle of the snub-nosed .38, that rested in his jacket pocket, then sucked in a breath of cold damp air. "You've got that right!"

"How 'bout a cab, Yank? Zip you into London, straightaway, or wherever?"

"I need to get to the Welsh Coast, as quickly as possible?" Then Spain flashed his police shield. "Official business, undercover," he added with a cold smile.

For an instant the warden's eyes squinted, making some sort of a decision. "How you going to pay, mate? Sterling or American?"

"American. How far is, ah, Caldey Island from here and what rate?"

The warden scratched his head, then motioned for Spain to follow him. In a moment he was at his stand, checking his charts. "Don't get requests for taxis to Wales very often. In fact, not at all," he said exasperated. "Where exactly now, is it, you wish to travel to?"

"Caldey Island, off the coast of Wales."

Deep in thought, the warden finally found Caldey on his map. "I never studied the knowledge for that one,

392

mate. You don't want a butter boy or a face for this work."

"What?"

"Sorry. A butter boy is a new driver and a face is a driver that only is allowed to make the run into London. You need a green." He smiled at Spain's tense expression. "A master cabbie."

A woman passenger, dressed in high suede boots and stylish leather coat, banged into Spain with a large suitcase on wheels. "I'm so sorry, sir." She bowed slightly, with a pretty smile. She was young, blond, and probably Danish or something northern. "Excuse me? Do I obtain a taxi for London here?"

The warden waved to the cab in the front of the line and a moment later, the cab sped off, then the warden was back with Spain. "I've got a man in mind for you." He snapped his fingers and said something into his walkie-talkie. A moment later a black diesel cab, with a large square plate on the rear boot, chugged up.

"This is Taffy Negien." He leaned into the open window of the right-hand drive cab with the looks of a World War II armored personnel carrier. "Say, Taff, I got a fare here, who wants to go to the West, to the Pembrokeshire Coast."

Spain started for the taxi, carrying only a small shoulder tote bag. "Come on, Taff, he's a Yank copper! See if you can come to a deal with him!"

Taffy Negien, a veteran cabbie, with forearms as thick as Popeye's, cast a sharp, grim eye on Spain as he approached. "Well" — Taffy scowled to the warden — "if he won't come to my deal, I won't do it! Besides, Jack, I'm on the hook tonight with the wife."

"Christ, Taffy, get off the fucking hook!" The warden,

growing angry at the cab driver, turned to Spain. "To get you where you want to go, the man says it will take six hours each way."

Spain stepped in front of the warden. He was growing nervous standing out in the open. London was notoriously an open city, with more operatives and freelancers working, than anywhere in Europe. He was shocked he'd even made it this far without being hit. "I'll make this easy for both of us. Name your price!"

The cabbie glanced up at the warden then at Spain. "Well, mate, I got to bed down for the night, since it's that far to the west and is more than two hundred miles of English roads."

"How much, damn it!" Spain mashed his face, ready to walk away.

"Two hundred."

"Four hundred American," the warden helped out.

"Done!" Spain was already opening the rear door of the round-backed sedan. "Let's move our asses, mate!" he said sarcastically. "This is police business!" Spain flashed the badge and his ID card again. "Move out now!" He needed to sleep. Jet lag was running him down.

Taffy Negien winked at the warden and turned off the electronic fare meter to his left. "Have you there in no time, mate," Taffy welcomed. "Sorry for the delay. I would have told the warden to brown off, but when I found out it was Yank police business, I wanted to help." He pulled away from the curb and swung into traffic. Then he finished rolling down the glass partition, separating the front and back of the cab, hoping this cop would keep him company during the long drive. Then he turned off his two-way dispatch radio.

"In an hour we'll swing onto the MFour and that will take us part of the way west into Wales." He turned and made eye contact with Spain. "Now you let me know when you want to stop for the loo or grub. You can call me Taffy, mate."

Spain nodded. He almost liked this tough, street-smart, working-class Englishman. But for now all he wanted was sleep. He would need to be totally focused and ready when he reached Wales.

Spain spent a few minutes engaging in surface talk, as the flat English countryside slid by the wide-laned motorway. "Well, you've come to the right man, now. My sister-in-law lives in Saint Florence, close by to Tenby, which is our destination."

"Look, ah, Taffy. I need to sleep for a few hours." Spain smiled at Taffy's restless eyes in the rearview mirror. "Watch our backside, huh, Taff?"

The cabbie nodded as Spain dosed off.

Spain opened his eyes with a start, the sky through the taxi window casting an eerie glow of apricot orange and black, the sturdy diesel engine purring softly in the deepening twilight. For a time, he allowed himself to slowly awake from what must have been the first deep sleep he'd had in days. He checked his watch. Damn, it was on Los Angeles time.

He tried to speak but his mouth was thick cotton. "Taffy, what time is it?"

"Ah, there you are!" The cabbie's voice was even and cheerful. "It's close by six. Should be in Tenby in a few hours."

Spain looked out the window at the strange, darkening landscape. "Where are we now?"

"Comin' into the edge of the haunted Preseli Hills. Welcome to Wales. Home of coal, slate, and musical accents that have charmed the world for centuries."

The taxi slowed, as the road narrowed and then crossed over an ancient stone bridge guarding a small gentle creek. "We're approaching Carmarthen, home of Kidwelly Castle and the Landsker." His conversation was infectious and Spain enjoyed the distraction.

"The what?"

The Landsker Line. There are three Norman castles that were built in the twelfth century to guard Carmarthen Bay. The castles were built to protect the Normans from the warlike Celts who used to swarm down from the north of England."

Then they drove in silence as the cab crossed another narrow fourteenth-century stone bridge, spanning the Gwendraeth Fach, in the shadows of St. Mary's Church.

"Now we're moving closer to the home of Dylan Thomas, at a place called the Boathouse, guarding the Taf Estuary. It's damn overrun with Yanks down at the mud flats, in the summer."

Taffy stared at Spain in the rearview mirror. "I made it a point, not to ask your business, but you might want to know that we've had headlamps blinking on and off for the past hour, staying just out of range."

Spain spun his head but all he saw was the blackness of the country road behind them. "I don't see anything."

"Lamps are off now. He's back there about half a mile. I know a tail when I see it! This have a bit to do with your police business?" Taffy cast a hard eye in the mirror, studying Spain.

"Not that I'm aware, Taffy," Spain replied, thinking

about Gregori Ovsyannikov and his reach. "Don't know what it is." Then he carefully pulled the .38 from his pocket, to keep it out of Taffy's line of sight with that interior mirror of his. Now the silence in the taxi was thick and tense, as they both watched behind them, the cab moving easily through the southern Welsh coastal villages of St. Clears and Red Roses.

"There it is again!" Taffy called the alert. "Spain swung in his seat, ducking with just his eyes above the back of the seat. Sure enough a pair of headlights on low beam, followed at a distance. When Taffy speeded up, so did the twin lights. When he slowed at one point to a slow roll, the lights matched their speed.

Now Spain knew. Gregori had reached him again, only now, he was on strange turf, away from his strengths.

Up ahead, the road curved toward the vast mudflats that bordered the road. "Comin' up on Monkstone Point. You should get your first look at Caldey Island." Off in the distance, a powerful beam of light from the lighthouse at Suandersfoot played its narrow beam out into the English Channel and then he saw a glimpse of the island, standing high with its brooding, towered monastery, probably two miles off the beach. A moment later, Caldey's own powerful light answered with a powerful flash as it swept the coast.

"Bastard's still there!" Taffy called out. "He's not even turning off his lamps now. Afraid he's going to lose us," he said evenly.

Slowly, the cab pulled into the seaside resort of Tenby, an old thirteenth-century, walled Welsh town. "What time is it?"

"Past eight-thirty, mate." Taffy check the mirror.

"Bastard's gone and turned off his lamps." Following Spain's directions, Taffy suddenly pulled off the road next to a low hedge, the diesel idling in the heavy night air.

Spain carefully opened the right-hand door and rolled out to the ground, the stench of the damp, sour earth in his nose. "Turn off the engine, Taffy," Spain ordered, "and get down, now!"

"Right, mate! I don't want my cab mucked up!"

Spain moved forward alongside the passenger side of the car, his hand resting on a thick chrome signature CAR BODIES. Now, he was on the ground, flat on his belly, looking back down at the road, his thumping heart keeping pace with the sound of the distant waves, offshore. Carefully using both hands on the .38, he arced the revolver from left to right, down to a stand of old oaks, where the road curved away from his line of sight. Then he waited for maybe fifteen minutes, without even another car passing on the road.

"Where the hell's the traffic, Taffy?" he called up into the cab.

"Not this time of year. It's a bloody ghost town around here. The hobbys don't come until June, when it warms up."

Jesus, Spain thought. The guy's not even speaking English. Sounds almost like Basque. Then he bit, to reduce his own tension. "What's a hobby?"

"Hobnobbers," Taffy whispered. "Vacationers. The tourists. What'd you think?"

Angrily, Spain stood up in the damp night air of Wales. "This is stupid! Just get me to the docks, so I can find a boat out to that island."

Slowly, the London cab cruised into Tenby, easing

into the narrow, medieval streets, heading for the docks. Taffy turned into Frog Street, sliding past the closed marketplace, cobbled mews and small pottery shops. Still, the streets were deserted of people. This was the old England that existed in the travel folders. Then the cab passed the gabled fifteenth-century Tudor Merchant's House, when a series of bright flashes pushed him back in his seat.

"They're firing!" Taffy yelled. Spain knew instantly, as he dropped to the floor, pulling the gun from his jacket.

"The next three shots came over the windscreen just in front of Taffy's face. "Don't stop, Taffy! That's what they want! Don't speed up, just keep your pace!" Spain raised his head, taking in the dark shadow of a small car, keeping station to their right. The speed was no more than five miles per hour. "They're trying to kidnap me, for Chrissakes!"

Sucking in a breath of air, Spain knew what he had to do as he pushed open the door, dropped his shoulder, and rolled out of the moving cab. Then he was on his feet, the gun leading the driver's compartment of the mystery car. In that instant, he opened fire, puncturing the heavy quiet of the seaside hamlet. Now he was firing and running, aiming at the driver's compartment, bracketing where he thought the window was located.

"Look out!" Taffy called, as the mystery car veered sharply, just missing the taxi. In a moment, the mystery car slammed into a high hedge, the engine still idling.

Spain took off at a run, keeping the .38 in front of his face as he rapidly covered the thirty meters. Now his hands were shaking, as he slowly approached the door.

Then in the faint dimness, he saw three clean bullet holes in the driver's door. Standing, Spain quickly reached for the door and jerked it open, the body of a woman falling heavily to the damp ground.

Trembling, Spain bent down and turned the woman's body over, three angry red smears covering her stylish suede coat. Clenched in her dead hand was an Uzi machine pistol. It was the young blond woman who had bumped him with her suitcase in London. "Damn it! Why didn't I see it! She made me and I didn't even have a clue!"

"Know the rotter?" Taffy stood staring down at her. "You're a fine bloak. What's your name? That was a fine piece of police work!"

Spain just smiled, ignoring the question. Then he turned and reached into his pocket, pulling out a wad of American currency. Slowly, Spain peeled off seven hundred dollars. "Can you move this body so it won't be found for a day or so?" His voice was cold steel.

Taffy stared down at the cash his hand impulsively reaching for it. "Sure, mate! I can do it right and proper, no questions."

"Good, because if you don't, I'll be back." He glared at the cab driver. "Anyone hear the gunshots?"

Taffy glanced around at the heavy stillness of the Welsh night. "No one here to hear anything." He tried to smile, but was too nervous.

"Okay, Taffy. Drive me to the docks, stash her car, and have a good life." He held the driver's eyes in focus and knew he was frightened and would do what he was told. There would be too many questions and the chance he could lose his taxi ticket. A wheel man who took part in murder wouldn't sit well. Spain smiled to himself. At least that part of it was clean.

He then motioned to the cab. "The docks, Taffy. Time to visit the monks."

Forty-five

The wind, funneling from the southwest through the Bristol Channel, worked at flattening the seas, as Spain ran the small outboard launch he had taken from the old stone wharf in Tenby. He turned down the throttle of the noisy outboard, bobbing in the cold swell, carefully surveying his target.

Off his bows, Spain studied Caldey Island, crowned with a giant tower of a lighthouse that illuminated the channel every thirty seconds. Halfway down the mountain from the light, squatted a series of steeply roofed Gothic buildings. "So that's the haunted house," he mumbled to the wind. Observing only a broad flat beach in the pale moonlight, Spain idled the small wooden boat through the light surf, right up into the flats.

With his heart pounding in his neck, Spain made his way up into the monastery's compound. Pulling the gun from his pocket, Spain reloaded the cylinder with the last of the extra shells that McBroom had provided. Feeling his way now, in the moist night, Spain moved silently across the main court yard into what appeared to be the main arched building. So far his luck was holding—no locks or people. In fact, it was eerie, there wasn't a sound, just the deathly quiet of a graveyard.

Carefully, he pulled open the thick English oak door that looked like it was a thousand years old, then slowly he moved into a dark entry way. Even at night the place was a Gothic time warp. For a moment, he checked the luminous dial of his watch. It was only nine. Maybe the place was deserted. Maybe Wittenberg had run him on a wild-goose chase halfway around the world. The slap of echoing leather sandals against the damp stone floors brought him up short. In the darkness, Spain flattened himself against a rough wall, watching the shadow of a man emerge out of the distance, dressed in some sort of long apron. The man, oblivious to his presence, must have passed within five feet of Spain, without taking notice; the stench of perfume now in the air. It was a strong woman's perfume, with the distinct odor of lavender.

Spain crouched low, following the man down a narrow hallway, with whitewashed plaster walls smelling of sweet mildew. Finally, the figure opened a door, pushing a bright shaft of light into the hall, then with a thud and the clang of an ancient lock, the door slammed shut. For a long time, Spain listened at the door, the only sound, a strange tinkle of glass touching glass, with the hallway reeking heavily of that damned lavender.

"Come on, Spain," he pushed himself with a whisper. "Just do it!" For a moment he steadied himself, listening to the thump of his heart, then gripping the gun in his right hand. Then he slowly turned the old pewter door-

403

knob, finally feeling the lock catch release, against the door jamb.

He swallowed again, still not believing he was in this ancient place or what he was about to do. He gripped the gun with both hands at face level, then pushed his shoulder into the door, falling into the room, rolling over into a crouch. The gun sighted on a full bearded man sitting placidly at a chemist's bench, washed in the bright light of a laboratory.

For a frozen moment they both stared at each other, the bearded man, startled and curious, yet his eyes weren't frightened, despite the gun.

"The door was not locked," the man said, a smooth Oxford inflection in his voice. Then he smiled openly. "Do you want all our secrets? I suppose we have penetrated the market in quite a fashion."

Spain shook his head, now off balance. "What the hell is this?" He waved the gun around the sparse room, filled with test tubes, a lighted bunsen burner, and what looked like hundreds of hand-blown glass beakers. A small computer rested on the bench next to the man.

"It is the laboratory, my son." Slowly the man put the tube he was filling into a rack and rubbed his clean-shaven head. "What is the purpose of the gun? Are you hungry? Do you require a place to sleep?" The tone of his voice was totally disarming, warm, and unafraid.

"No! No, ah, I'm looking for someone." Then his voice rose to a shrill. "What is this place?"

The man approached Spain, "Please put that away. You can have whatever you need, except the formulas." Then he smiled blandly. "Industrial espionage, is it?"

Spain shook his head. "I really don't know what this is about. I'm just looking for a monk here."

"Hello, friend, I'm brother Anthony. Will I do? I'm the keeper of the scents." Then he saw the puzzle grow in Spain's eyes. "We make perfume here. Welcome to our Cistercian Order. We usually don't receive visitors here. But as long as you've taken the time to come to us—" Then he smiled, again. "Put the weapon away, my son. Our faith here is stronger than that. That's why we live only for peace and contemplation.

Stunned, Spain carefully uncocked the hammer and put the gun in his jacket. "I'm looking for a monk." He searched the room. "I didn't realize how big this place was. There must be hundreds of monks here!"

"No, my son. There are only ten of us left. But please know that our time of retirement and contemplation is seven-thirty in the evening. Who do you wish to see?" The clear blue eyes focused on Spain.

"Ah, he was an old friend of my father," he tried. "They were together during World War Two. He is an American. They were very close. My father made me promise to come to England and speak with him."

"With a gun in your hand, my son?"

"No." Spain lowered his eyes. "I—it's an old bad habit that I have."

The monk squinted. "Indeed. Well, what is his name?"

"Ah, his name is Alvin Dvorak."

The monk shook his head. "Of course." Then he rubbed his forehead. "I thought you were a pirate, here to take our perfume secrets." He glanced over at Spain. "Come, I'll take you to him. Brother Alvin tends to our wild crops of lavender and gorse that abound on our island."

405

The old man, probably close to seventy-five, sat in his small room, reading from a new copy of *Time* magazine. He glared at Spain, startled that he sat facing him. Brother Alvin was dressed in a dark brown frock, with long orange knee socks, keeping him warm. Gold wire-rimmed glasses rested on his old fleshy nose. His stature was comical. Only his eyes betrayed the laugh. Finally Brother Anthony withdrew, when he was certain there wasn't a problem.

"Now, what did you say your name was?" The accent was worn-down Ivy League.

"Ben Spain. I bring greetings from Russell Wittenberg."

Alvin Dvorak squinted. "Who?" Then he rubbed his face, struggling to fill in a blank yellow page.

"You'd probably know him as Russell Witten. Code named One hundred nine Rosary Beads. World War Two?" Spain watched his face closely as the recognition spread with surprise across his sunken mouth. Then Dvorak reached into a half-filled glass next to his chair and pulled out a lower plate of false teeth. A moment later, his jaw was full and robust, his smile whimsical.

"That son of a bitch! He sent you, huh? He still hiding out in the mountains?"

"Like you're hiding out here?" Spain moved his eyes toward the narrow leaded glass window.

"*Touché!* How is the old farthead?"

"Strong and tough."

Dvorak shook his head, then smiled peacefully. "Good!" His square face, crowned with thin strands of snow-white hair and a reddish complexion, appeared gentle after a storm. "Now what do you require? I don't have any friends left who would send their sons to me as a deathbed promise." There was a distant irony in his voice. "What do you want?" he repeated softly. "Brother Alvin is a long way from anything of importance."

"Information that Russell said you had about Pearl Harbor." Spain held up a hand, anticipating the resistance. "My life depends on what you might tell me."

Brother Alvin pushed out a long breath and rose unsteadily from his reading chair, then ambled slowly across the room to a simple table with two stick chairs. He motioned for Spain to follow.

"Now, what makes you think I know about Pearl Harbor? It's a finished chapter of history."

Spain studied his old, wise face. Dvorak looked like a monk. "I don't have time for this! I know of your connection to the White House, to Harry Hopkins, and to the *Arizona!*" Spain watched his face and telltale mouth. Then Spain gambled. "I know about your relationship to Amelia Earhart!"

Spain moved his face close to Dvorak. "You were Linch Pin and ran the whole damned show! You are my only link and my only chance to unravel this Gordian knot. My only chance to survive!" Nervously, Spain wiped his mouth, trying not to sound like he was begging.

Dvorak cupped his old hands into a steeple beneath his nose, weighing something. Then he stood brusquely, which surprised Spain. "Come with me, Spain." Then he opened the arched-shaped door, motioning for him to follow. In a moment, they entered a very old chapel, that bled gothic tranquility. It was a long, narrow, whitewashed room, with a ceiling that reached seventy feet into the air. The only visible support was offered by a series of rough-hewed oak-flying buttresses. Brother Alvin offered Spain a hard pew.

"I always take great strength in this room." Then he removed his glasses and rubbed his eyes. "I now live in a world that is simple. In our library, we have a written document from a hermit named Pyro, who lived on this very spot in a tiny cell some thirteen hundred years ago. He devoted himself to prayer and—"

"And contemplation!" Spain interrupted impatiently. "Look!"

"No, my son, you look." There was both dread and poignancy in Dvorak's voice. "I now tend to perfume crops that help this order of monks to barely survive. I help make perfume!" Now he couldn't help but smile. "This house of prayer has to be four hundred years old. They took me in, without question, without history or without portfolio. This house of God makes your circumstance very trivial! I rise each morning at three-fifteen for my first devotional of the day." Dvorak stared down at his hands, then held them up. "These hands, with the help of my head, helped plan World War Two; now these hands grow and tend life in the earth." He paused watching the anger rise in Spain.

For a moment he glanced down at the handle of the .38 sticking out of Spain's pocket. "You going to kill me if I don't tell?"

Spain shook his head, then pushed out a long stale breath of air. "No, but I'm desperate!"

"Tell me what about, my son."

For the next hour, Spain poured out the story, from his first dive on the *Arizona,* the skull and yellow pouch and the horrid deaths that stalked him. Then he told Dvorak about his feeling of something very dark behind that piece of history. Finally, Spain slumped in the pew, exhausted from the release of the pent-up feelings inside him. Then he whispered, "You can't die with those secrets."

Slowly, Dvorak rose and then kneeled before a large figure of Christ, crossed himself, deep in prayer, then rose. "This old room is an appropriate place to tell the truth."

"Thank you, Brother Alvin," Spain croaked, bathed in sweat, despite the wind now whistling through the cracks in the leaded stained glass of the ancient windows.

"It might be easier if you ask my questions, then I'll fill in anything that you missed or that I can remember."

"Fair enough." His voice was barely audible above the heavy push of Bristol wind. "Did Roosevelt know about the attack on Pearl Harbor?" Spain held his breath, waiting.

"Yes. He was warned on two separate occasions by the emperor of Japan."

"So, it's true!" Spain gritted his teeth, thinking about Harumi. God, he wished she was here. She was the architect of all this. She deserved to hear it. "Ah, were you on the *Arizona,* prior to the attack?"

Dvorak nodded, a wisp of a smile parting his lips. "You've really done your homework, haven't you. Yes, I spent two weeks in *Arizona,* at the direction of Harry Hopkins, special assistant to President Roosevelt. We had taken the *Zona* on a special mission to the Philippine Islands. When we returned to Pearl, I left the ship on the evening of December Six, Nineteen forty-one and moved to the Royal Hawaiian Hotel in Honolulu."

"Waiting for the attack that you knew would come!" Suddenly, Spain was thinking about those skeletons, and souls locked forever in the mud of Pearl Harbor.

"Don't judge me, Spain. I was an intelligence agent. There is not a day that has passed since the attack, that I haven't thought about it, believe me!" His voice was a distilled parable. "It was a decision made at the highest levels of the U.S. Government. I was just an agent of that policy."

"Just following orders," Spain growled. "That doesn't make you much better than the fucking Nazis!" Spain held his breath. "I'm sorry, Brother Alvin. You don't deserve that."

Dvorak nodded, seeming to understand. "No one ever wants responsibility!"

"How the hell could Roosevelt do that to American servicemen?" A foghorn brayed in sympathy from somewhere on the island.

"Quite honestly, I don't think Roosevelt's inner circle, including Hopkins, George Marshall, Secretary of War Stimson, and Chief of Naval Operations Betty Stark, thought the Japanese could do all the damage they did, without suffering terrible losses, themselves."

"I don't understand?"

"FDR needed the raid at Pearl Harbor to find a political way into the war. Everyone surmised that much. What was so shocking, was the fact that the Japanese so totally annihilated the American Fleet. The inner circle truly expected a better show by Admiral Kimmel. They didn't expect the loss of life or toll of ships to be that high. Kimmel went down very unfairly, because of that slaughter. They wanted a good fight."

Spain stared off into space. "How could it have been

any different. Where the hell was the airpower at Pearl? It was out at sea, very conveniently!"

Dvorak cocked his head at Spain. "It's been a long road for you, hasn't it?"

"The trouble with long roads to somewhere is that they always have bumps!"

The man closed his eyes, remembering. "Well, as you obviously surmised, the two precious carriers, the *Lexington* and *Enterprise* were ordered out to sea, to hunt for the Japanese to the south, while the *Saratoga* was sent to San Diego for repairs."

"In the opposite direction from the attack!" Spain shook his head. "That was real slick. You know I fought in Vietnam and was a victim of government lying, deception, and the waste of human lives to make a political statement, but somehow I thought that it was different in the Big One. I guess the Persian Gulf triumph whitewashed everything else." Spain shivered involuntarily.

"All the prayers in the world won't absolve you and those suits in the White House and War Department, for not clearing out Pearl Harbor and saving those lives!" His voice wavered with anger. "Someone has to stand up for those dead souls, even if it is half a century later, and ask, why? And you're a monk!" Spain's eyes searched the ancient walls. "I don't care if you pray all day and night for a thousand years, you'll never get the stains off your hands or their death screams out of your ears, cleric!"

Spain rubbed his hands, calming himself. "Just tell me why, one human being to another."

"We couldn't!" His voice suddenly rose to a defensive shrill. "We just couldn't! The Japanese military would

411

have traced it and found out that the emperor was the traitor and they would have killed him! It was in our national interest to maintain the only sane link with Japan at a state level." Dvorak's lips began to tremble.

"Bastards! You're all no better than Saddam and his butchers in Baghdad, sitting in your nice warm comfortable arm chairs, deciding who lives and who dies for the sake of a fucking policy that can change with the next fart in the wind!" Spain drew his exhausted frame close to the monk. "Just know that when you look into my eyes, I want you to see all those people who died at Pearl Harbor."

"I do." Dvorak paused, then began to speak quietly, without anger. "We've shaped our lives for generations to come. That's why I'm buried here. It's the beast within me."

For a long time, Spain was quiet. "God, I wish my partner was here to listen to this. She's an historian. A woman who believes strongly in herself and her truth." Then he smiled, his tired eyes pulling under their own weight. "I suppose I couldn't get you to put this in writing or on tape?"

Dvorak raised his eyes. "Of course not! I'm surprised you'd even ask. You will give me the courtesy of maintaining my privacy in this matter." He swept an arm around the chapel.

Spain just looked at him in silence, then he asked: "What is Pandora's Box?"

"My, oh my! I am very impressed!" For a time, Dvorak turned his head and silently studied the Christ figure, lost somewhere within himself. Finally he turned to Spain. "Pandora's Box is a phantom from another time. It is the complete file on the real events surrounding Pearl Harbor. The hard facts of the matter, including total documentation and time lines."

"You mean the secret communiqués from Emperor Hirohito to the White House, prior to the attack?"

"Including those."

"We tried to get into the Pandora's Box file, without success."

"I'm not surprised. I designed it that way." Suddenly, Dvorak was pleased with himself. "My last year with the company, Nineteen seventy-six, I pulled it all together and dropped it into the mainframe of the OCTOPUS. I suppose that subconsciously I wanted someone to find it eventually. How did you get the Pandora's Box code name?"

"Russell Witten."

"Of course." He shook his head slowly. "Old age. I'd forgotten that Beads was the wartime operative dealing with the Pearl investigation. But he had only part of the story."

"How do we get into Pandora's Box? I tried on the Defense Advanced Research Projects, DARPA network."

"I'm old. I don't have too many years left. Ah, there is an ETD with the code."

"A what?"

"An electronic trap door."

"A secondary security code!" Spain was angry at himself. "Why didn't I think of that? All right. What is the ETD code?"

"What comes out of Pandora's Box?"

Spain tensed. "No games, Brother Alvin! I'm worn out. I'm the purple testament of a bleeding war, my friend!"

"You also know your Shakespeare. Richard the Third."

"I wouldn't know. I read it off of a wall of a pay toilet once!" Spain searched the room. Suddenly he was feeling uneasy, the hair rising on the back of his neck. "What is it?" He tried to keep the warmth from bleeding from his voice.

"*Hope.*"

"Please Brother Alvin," Spain pleaded.

Dvorak shook his head. "The ETD code word is *hope.* Prometheus had confined all the evils that troubled mankind into a box. The woman God Pandora finally opened the box, allowing the evils to escape, except for the gift, hope."

"Hope," Spain repeated softly, as he slowly walked the chapel checking the dark corners.

"Something wrong, Spain?"

"I don't know." Spain cautiously moved next to an opaque glass window, but seeing out was hopeless. "I thought I heard something."

"You did. The wind. This is Wales. The wind speaks to us in musical and human tones. I've been here fifteen years and the Bristol Channel is alive with sound and spirit. There is no one out there, Spain. We haven't had a visitor since we closed down the island to tourists last September and we won't reopen until May."

Spain returned to his seat, trying to refocus. "Ah, what about Amelia Earhart?"

Dvorak bowed his head to his chest. "I was afraid we'd get to that part of it."

"Do you know about it?"

"Yes. When I worked for FDR, then the OSS and finally the CIA, we lived with a creed that one or two

414

deaths in pursuit of a goal were a tragedy, but a million deaths were only a statistic."

Spain shook his head. Maybe Wittenberg was right. Brother Alvin was beginning to stray. "What about Earhart and Fred Noonan? I found Fred Noonan's skull inside the *Arizona?*"

"I'm truly sorry for what happened to them. It was a tragedy. A real tragic footnote to the beginnings of the Second World War."

"What happened? Were they together on the *Arizona?*"

"Yes! Yes, they were! When we were coming back from the Philippines, during the first week in December, Nineteen forty-one, I received a top priority communiqué from Harry Hopkins in the White House, to rendezvous at Johnston Island, to pick up two Americans being repatriated from Japan. It came from the roofers at Pearl on the shovel runner. The Hawaiian emergency circuit."

"What was that?" Spain was suddenly on his feet, his Smith & Wesson drawn, adrenaline coursing through his body. Moving like a cat he made his way to the arched oak front doors. He held a finger up to his mouth for Brother Alvin, who watched him now, with more than curiosity. "Get down between the pews," Spain whispered across the chapel.

Abruptly, Spain turned his head pushing himself into a crouch. He swore one of the double doors was beginning to slowly open.

Forty-six

Harumi van Horn used her shoe to scatter the dirty remnants of a late snow that covered the slate walk in the courtyard of the Franklin D. Roosevelt Library in Hyde Park, New York. She was cold and worried as she stood alone in the library quad, facing a granite bust of FDR, which smirked at her with a certain arrogance she hated.

"Where is it?" she asked the stone face softly. "Give me something, damn it!" She turned her head to make certain no one saw her talking to the statue. For a time she stared at the likeness of the thirty-second President, then down at the dark polished stone base, donated to the Library by the International Ladies' Garment Workers' Union.

Discouraged and tired, she made her way back into the main library. Actually, the former estate of the President was most impressive and as she was reminded and often warned by the chief archivist, who had been assisting her with her police "investigation," that the FDR Center contained some forty-five tons of documents.

For luck she returned to the main entrance and

placed her cold hand on the massive leather-bound Dutch family Bible and prayed for just a shred of evidence. It was the same bible that FDR had used for the oath, when he took office four times. She ran her fingers over the thick, beaten cover, thinking about the last few weeks. Maybe it was all a dream and she had created something out of nothing because she was so desperately filled with herself and an ego that needed professional massaging.

She shook her head and slowly moved to a small area, where the President's desk sat, neatly appointed with the accoutrement of his White House years. A little plastic sign stated that this desk was where FDR signed the declaration of War against the Empire of Japan on December 8, 1941.

Harumi walked behind the mahogany desk, examining the small black bust of his Scottie dog, Fala. For a painful instant, she thought of Mollie back home on the Big Island, her large brown doe eyes reaching out to her six thousand miles away. It was Spain and home that she missed and the stability of a sane life. Casually, she ran her fingers along the back of the bright quilted, yellow satin chair, fraying at the seams.

She closed her eyes, trying to feel what this man must have felt, as he weighed the options of peace and war before the Pearl Harbor raid. She leaned further over the desk and was shocked to see her reflection in a cut-down polished brass, eight-inch navy gun shell casing, which served as his ashtray.

"Please give me a sign," she mumbled, trying to feel FDR's presence. "Where do I look?" she asked.

"Ah, miss, you'll have to step away from the desk!" An old security guard, who looked like a benign housekeeper smiled at her. "You can feel the man, can't you? I do everytime I get this close." He shook his head. "There was such power in his hands."

Harumi smiled. "I wanted to touch what was close to him."

The guard tipped his peaked cap. "Most people who come to the house all want to touch." He rubbed his face. "Not sure why? Maybe it makes history more real for them?" It was a question. "At least that's what the missus says."

Then he followed, as Harumi made her way back to the large room that served as the research center, where she found her small desk, covered with documents and three gray storage containers resting next to the chair. She had been at the search now for a day and a half, with not the slightest hint of a Pearl Harbor conspiracy in anything she read.

Slowly, she replaced the documents in the box labeled October 1941 and opened:

NOVEMBER 1941, OVAL OFFICE
FDR PERSONAL NOTES, MISC.
NOTES AND ENTRIES.

There wasn't any order to the notes. In fact, it looked like this box of notes, with a heavy musty odor, hadn't been opened in years. The chief archivist had told her that the library was assembled in the precomputer era and the retrieval of information was always an iffy prospect.

Slowly, she began thumbing through the carbon copies of typed letters on frail onion skin, as well as what looked like personal telephone notes. In fact, she had grown to admire Roosevelt's doodling ability. He had a real thing for faces and sailboats. The miniature scratch art was quite good. Names, half-legible sentences, words. None of it made any sense as she turned over one piece of paper after another, still careful to focus her concentration, even though she wasn't even certain what she was looking for.

Spain had more confidence in her than she did. He told her again and again that she would know instantly when she came across something hard and irrefutable.

Then, her warming fingers stopped for an instant. She stared down at a doodle of someone familiar. The baby face, the tiny, thick, wire-rimmed glasses. The half-closed eyes! Carefully, she picked up the small telephone-size paper, yellowed about its edges, the top embossed with:

THE WHITE HOUSE

Who was it? Damn. She sat back, her instincts alive for the first time in days. She didn't even notice the same old security guard standing patiently next to her desk. Finally he cleared his throat, startling her.

"Ah, miss," he whispered. "I thought maybe you would like to see the actual Declaration of War against the Japanese."

"What?" She glanced down again at the doodled face, only partially focused on the guard. My God! That was it! The sketch was Hirohito! It was unmistakable, with the head dressed in a squared military pith helmet! She had seen the pose a million times, in old newsreels, of the emperor on his white horse reviewing the troops, that arrogant pose, pushing through the old grainy black-and-white films!

"Ah, miss, did you hear me?"

"I'm sorry." She looked up and smiled. "What do you want?" Her tone was very distant.

Gently he touched her shoulder. "I know that look. I'll come back later, miss." Then he was gone.

Almost afraid, she forced herself to look down again at the small sketch. God! It had to be! It was Emperor Hirohito as a young man! War bonnet and all!

Carefully she turned over the paper to the next, her hands now shaking visibly. The next full yellowed sheet was handwritten:

HH-OVAL OFFICE — EYES ONLY
BETTY STARK JUST INFORMED ME THAT MY REGAL "FRIEND" JUST SENT ME A NOTE FROM JOS. THE DANCE IS DEFINITELY ON ACCORDING TO THE FRIEND! THE DATE IS 8-12-41. THE DANCE BAND WILL PLAY AT 26 N 158 W, 0600 LT ON 8-12-41, JOS.

FRANKLIN

Harumi stared at the short handwritten note, trying to make sense of it. She knew the numbers were coordinates. Ben had taught her that much, when they found Russell Wittenberg by latitude and longitude. Moving very slowly, Harumi moved to the copy machine in the corner of the room and ran off ten duplicates.

She had never known such professional excitement in her life. God, if only her father and Ben could see this! See what, she mumbled to herself. Translate it all out, first. Slow down and walk through it. Casually, she stopped by the archivist's desk in the center of the room and smiled. In a moment he was silently at the other side of the small counter, whispering. God! They all whispered!

"Ah, do you have any idea who has looked at the files you pulled out for me?" She smiled openly, keeping her voice vague and innocent.

"That's easy. No one. I just brought those file boxes up from the basement for you. You said it was police business. Ah, an old murder case that was being reopened in Los Angeles, that might have had some connection to the White House in the last few months of Nineteen forty-one?" He was precisely playing back the premise she had established. "That's all you would say."

"Yes, that's right," she responded officiously. "That's why I wondered why this material wasn't out in the general catalogue of information?"

He laughed sarcastically. "Because, Detective, we haven't gotten around to it! Do you realize that when FDR was President, he received more than four thousand letters a day, on the average, for sixteen years! Not to mention the sixteen million pages of documents, of which only about half have been catalogued and indexed. In short"—he raised his eyebrows, still speaking in a whisper—"we haven't gotten around to it!"

"Thanks." She smiled weakly, backing away. Then she sat with a copy of the handwritten note, thinking it through.

The note mentioned Betty Stark and H.H. She left the desk and returned a moment later with a reference guide to important members of the FDR Administrations. Thumbing through the index, she found his name. Admiral Harold R. "Betty" Stark. Chief of Naval Operations, 1939-1945. "Thank you God!"

Then she tackled the next hurdle, JOS. Now, that was familiar. She thought for a long time. Then a smile spread across her face as she checked her written notes from Northern California. Back a thousand years ago, in Sawyers Bar, Russell Wittenberg had referred to JOS as the radio "roofers" intelligence code for Tokyo. Regal friend was obvious. She shivered, forcing herself to not yet draw a conclusion.

"Okay, buster," she whispered aloud, "let's find a map of the Pacific." In short order she spread what looked like a colored high school map on her jumbled desk. Then she marked off the coordinates in the note. Finally, her hands really began to shake. The lines intersected about two hundred miles due north of the island of Oahu.

"Bingo!" she screamed, then looked around at the few scholars scattered about the library doing research. She met the chief archivist's scowl with a vulnerable smile, turning her hands over in surrender.

She sat back, her entire body trembling. "Finish it," she mumbled aloud. "Finish the note!" Then she looked down at the date and it confused her. The way it read meant August 8, 1941. That didn't make any sense. Damn! One of the key elements. She played with her pencil over the date. What the hell happened that August eight? It could finish off the credibility of the entire note! Now she felt the weight of the last few weeks squeezing her buoyant mood.

"Is everything all right, miss?" It was the chief archivist, coming to scold her for her unprofessional outburst. He stood very still, his hands folded at his belly button, a leering redheaded preppy Buddha.

"Yes." She smiled nervously. "Yes, everything is fine. I'm sorry for the noise."

Placated, he started to turn, when her hand touched his arm. "Maybe you can help me? This date here." Then she wrote down the date as it appeared in the note on a blank tablet of paper. "What do you make of that?"

The archivist narrowed his eyes at this semiliterate cop. "Well, it can be read two ways. The American way is August eight, Nineteen forty-one."

"The other way?" She leaned into him.

"European and Asian. December eight, Nineteen forty-one. Anything else?"

Stunned, she nodded, then he stalked off with his squeaky shoes.

"My God! This is really it!" She instantly felt the heat rise in her face, like she was going to faint. Then she glanced down at the note again. Dance Band is obviously the Japanese Fleet and 0600 LT is six A.M. local time.

"The very time the attack was launched!" she said aloud, trying to contain herself. Then she looked up. "We got it, Benny! We got the hard document I needed!" She looked around the room and found herself alone. Then she took the original note and carefully placed it in her coat jacket.

Forty-seven

Spain crouched flat against the cold ancient brick, next to the outer door of the chapel. From his vantage point he had a dim view of the courtyard, around which the monastery was built. Despite his fear, Spain carefully scanned the faces of each Gothic building, including the dormer eyebrow windows built into the steep slate roof. It was hopeless as he held the gun just below his eyes, watching and listening to the pace of the night. Maybe the monk was right. With the Bristol wind now howling in from St. George's channel to the west, feeling the night was impossible, the damned wind *was* alive with musical sounds, voices, and strange litanies.

"Come on, Gregori!" Spain finally screamed into the wind. "Come on! I'm ready! I can feel you, damn it! Let's get it over with, you bastard! I know you opened the damned door!"

Then for an instant he held the .38 unsteadily in both hands, aimed at a dark corner, waiting for it to move, wondering if he could really shoot. Then just as quickly, the shadow dissolved in his mind. "Face me, my brother! You owe me that!" he shouted. "I hauled your ass back from the dead, through the Crimea and the Dardenelles! Remember that fucking village of Tskhinvali, deep in the Caucasus's, where we hid after I pulled you from that State hospital for the criminally insane, on the Black Sea?"

Then Spain laughed. "Jesus, they were right! Look at us, all these years later! The truth is, we are insane!" Then in frustration, Spain fired a round into the black Welsh sky. "I taught you how to drink like a man," he whispered, emotionally exhausted. Then he slumped back against the cold bricks, suddenly aware of the monk, standing in the open, watching him.

"Come in, Mister Spain," the monk said softly. "You can't win the battle of the Bristol wind as it blows its way to Worms Head. Now come back into the sanctuary."

"I know I heard something besides the wind!"

Dvorak laughed. "When I first arrived here from the real world, I heard everything from monsters to the voice of little Harry Hopkins summoning me back to Washington. I even heard the sound of huge rolling logs and the sound of human voices speaking a dialect I'd never heard."

Spain sat heavily in an oak pew, facing Alvin Dvorak, now the perfect, kindly old monk. "What was it?" he asked, still questioning himself.

"The abbott told me it was the ghostly rolling sounds of Mabinogion lore, when the ancients moved the giant blue stones down from the Preseli Hills to the east, some two hundred miles, to form the inner circle of Stonehenge."

"Oh, God!" He stared at Dvorak. Was the monk all there? Was he filling Spain with remembered truth, or the romantic fantasies of an old man, tucked away from the world?

"I'm really quite sane, Spain. I do live in the moment." Dvorak smiled openly, his eyes clear and focused. "Do you wish to continue our conversation?" Then he folded his arms inside his frock.

"Yes. What about Amelia Earhart?"

Dvorak stared down at his hideous orange thermal socks. "When we weighed anchor in the Philippines, I received an emergency transmission, as I said, from the Shovel Runner out of Honolulu, the emergency relay circuit to NAA."

"What was NAA?"

"Washington. A direct link with Hopkins's office and the Chief of Naval Operations, Admiral Stark. I was given orders to divert the flagship of BATDIV ONE, battleship division one, meaning the *Arizona,* under wartime conditions, to Johnston Island, about seven hundred miles southwest of Honolulu. My orders were to pick up two top-level repatriates, to be delivered by a Japanese messenger, who would be flying into Johnston in a flying boat." He paused recalling it. "The *Arizona*'s code call was YTTEB."

"Did you know who the repatriates were?"

"Yes." He looked up and held Spain's hard glare. "It was a very tense time in the Pacific. Hirohito was desperately trying to regain control of the military cliques on Tokyo. He was frantic, if his direct cables to the White House are any indication, where he was trying to show good faith. But Admiral Yamamoto, despite his image as a peacemaker, was bent on the Pearl Harbor raid, to wipe out the American navy as a threat to the Imperial flank, when their war machine moved south into Indo China and the Dutch East Indies. They needed oil in the worst way."

Spain held up a hand. "What happened with Earhart?"

"Sorry. I've kept all this inside me for half a century."

"The captain of the *Arizona*, Franklin Van Valkenburgh, didn't have much use for me. In fact he hated my guts and always found a way to tell me." Dvorak shook his head. "He wasn't very political. It wasn't smart to mess with the White House." He held up a hand. "I know. This is just background. When I ordered him to change course for Johnston Island, he was a very unhappy man. He really went off the crazy scale when we returned to Pearl and I confiscated the official logbook."

Spain's eyes widened. "So it wasn't lost in the attack! Well, that explains that! Did the *Arizona*'s captain know who you picked up? What about the crew? Earhart was well known. Her photo had been everywhere!"

"No." The monk's eyes were suddenly filled with guilt and pain. "They were malnourished skeletons. Their families wouldn't even have known them." Dvorak shook his head. "Incidentally, the *Arizona* logbook is somewhere in a top security vault inside the CIA fortress in Langley."

"Or it was destroyed."

The monk smiled. "Or it was shredded."

"You were talking about the pickup?"

"Three hours after we anchored in the lagoon at Johnston, a giant *Kawanishi* sea plane flew in and landed near the ship. The scene was very hostile on both sides. After a few preliminaries, this Japanese navy lieutenant stepped out. His name was Toshiyuki Mizutari. For some reason, I'll never forget his name. He was the escort for Amelia Earhart and her navigator, Fred Noonan."

Dvorak held up his hands, in a funny mournful way. "Washington was caught off guard. They didn't know what to do with that political hot potato."

Spain came forward in the pew. "Was anything else delivered aside from Earhart and Noonan?"

Dvorak peered at him with surprise. "How did you know that?"

"Just guessing. What was it?"

"A sealed yellow pouch that was from Emperor Hirohito for Roosevelt."

Spain's eyes held the monk's face for a long time. "Did you look inside that pouch?"

"Not a chance! I was the mule for the operation. Agents don't mess with presidents and emperors. Besides, it was sealed." He smiled. "It was heady stuff, Spain. My God, it was December the third. Just a few days before our world exploded."

"Did you debrief these fliers?"

"On the way back to Pearl and in the days that followed, before the attack." Dvorak's thick voice was coming from another time. "I got to know those people. They had had a terrible time. They were sick, exhausted, but very excited about coming home."

428

"But?"

"But is right, Spain. The Japanese had taken them, when their twin-engined Lockheed Electra crashed on the atoll of Nikumaroro, four hundred miles south southeast of Howland Island, which was supposed to have been their destination. They were half dead when local natives turned them over to the Japanese." Dvorak rubbed an old hand over his pink face."

"Then?"

"Then, according to what Miss Earhart told me, they were taken to Saipan Island, where they were imprisoned, beaten, tortured, and nearly starved, in Garapan City for years." The monk shook his head, tears rolling down his cheeks. "They were imprisoned from Nineteen thirty-seven until we got them in Nineteen forty-one."

For the first time, Spain touched the old man's shoulder. "Did Washington know what happened to them, after the crash?" Spain was desperately trying to ask Harumi's questions.

Dvorak nodded painfully, his old face loosened with age. "Yes, yes, yes! We knew they were alive, we knew where, but FDR couldn't touch them because it was a political nightmare. In Nineteen thirty-seven, the American climate was based on more butter, not guns. The American working and middle class was fighting to survive. They wanted nothing to do with stopping Japanese land grabs in China, the Nazi Sudetenland steal in Europe, or Mussolini in Ethiopia. Then the navy turned this woman hero into a flying spy! Yet we all knew war was coming. We just didn't know when or how, but we needed photo information

429

on the Mandates, controlled by the Japanese."

"Ah, what was FDR planning to do about them when you got to Pearl?"

"It was ironic. There was a flight of B-17's en route to the Philippines, from the Thirty-eighth Reconn Squadron out of Hamilton Field, California. Harry Hopkins told me that two of those bombers had been detailed at the last moment, to secretly return Earhart and Noonan back to the States. They were scheduled to fly back from Pearl on December eighth." He held up his hands. "I did what Harry Hopkins wanted and didn't have the power to question him."

For a while Spain was quiet, thinking of Harumi and what she needed. "Too bad there's no hard evidence that this scenario took place."

Dvorak shook his head and yawned. "As a footnote to this discussion, in the six days that I spent in that compartment with them, I learned to care a great deal about them. They still believed in what they did. Fred Noonan, especially. The Japanese really worked him over. In fact, the fingernails on his right hand were pulled out and half his teeth were knocked out."

"I know," Spain said softly, thinking of the skull and Kim Dubin's early detective work.

"That's right. You dove on the *Arizona!* You know, ah there is something that you might want to explore, if it hasn't been destroyed."

Spain raised his eyes, watching the dim candlelight fill out the wrinkled face of Alvin Dvorak. "What's that?"

"Well, no one else knows about this."

"My God, no one knows any of this!"

Dvorak smiled. "When we started back to Honolulu, I asked Amelia to write down all their experiences, with as much detail as she could remember."

"A diary! She wrote a diary?"

Dvorak nodded. "Yes. In fact, to keep it authentic, I asked her to put something into it, which people wouldn't know about."

"Kind of like a precomputer trapdoor?"

"Indeed. We talked about it and she went for the idea, because she said her husband was a magnate in the publishing business in New York and it would be an instant best-seller." Dvorak shrugged. "Even in her weakened condition, she was very publicity minded. She wasn't shy at all and that surprised me."

"How do you remember all this? It was more than fifty years ago." Spain cocked his head.

"As it turned out, it was both the high and low points of my life. I've played it out a million times in my mind."

"What?"

"How I could have done it differently and gotten them off the *Arizona* before the attack. "I didn't believe the *Arizona* would sink and they were protected below decks." His voice was still filled with guilt. "That ship burned in the mud for three days!"

Spain pushed out a breath. "God, I know that one." He thought of his young chief, his face blown away, dying in those brown river weeds in North Vietnam, so many years before. "Yes, I know."

431

Dvorak drew a long deep breath. "Amelia and I discussed what to do, to give her diary a ring of truth. And she came up with the name, Neta Snook Southern. How's that for a name?"

"Who was she?"

"Her first flying teacher and lifelong friend. She taught Earhart to solo in Los Angeles in Nineteen twenty-one. Her father had taken Amelia down to this field, on the streetcar, where this woman pilot was giving lessons. She was very proud of the fact that a woman, even in that day, had taught her to fly, in a male-dominated business."

Spain swallowed, almost afraid to ask the next question. "What happened to this diary?" His tension sucked the air out of the chapel.

"When the Japanese messenger, Lieutenant Mizutari, turned the fliers over to me with that yellow waterproof pouch, it was wrapped in an outer waterproof purse that the lieutenant handed to me, because he didn't know what to do with it. It was empty, so all the notes she wrote were put into that second yellow pouch. I have no idea what happened to it when the attack started."

My God, Spain thought. That was the second pouch that Harumi swore she saw, when he took her down into the *Arizona*'s compartment! Suddenly, his hands began to tremble. All this historical evidence was now within reach for Harumi. He thought about her and smiled.

"Did you hear me?"

Spain looked up into Dvorak's face that had grown sallow and prunelike. "Yes. I heard you."

Dvorak cocked his head in a funny, expectant way. "I am very tired now. Is there anything else you need to ask?"

"Yeah." His voice was still troubled. "I guess from an historical point of view this is an incredible find, but is there anything here that you've told me, worth killing for?"

Dvorak slowly rose and made his way to the Christ statue, sitting atop the altar. Slowly he reached for a lighted candle, then began to touch a field of white candles before him, with the flame.

"You really don't know, do you?" Dvorak turned and faced Spain still sitting in the pew.

"Know what? Don't play with me!" His voice rose to a shrill, then he tensed again, standing before the older man. "I'm circling the damned drain, right now!" he seethed. "Living on the fucking floor, because the ceiling's too damned low! In short, my ass is grass! Pardon my language, Brother," Spain said sarcastically, "but aside from you, I've got nothing left, so, if I have hit a blind spot, help me! Show an old Basque shepherd's kid some of that Christian charity that you monks seem to grow on this little island!" Now his face was menacing.

"You never asked why the *Arizona* had gone to the Philippines?"

Then Spain remembered something that Russell Wittenberg had said about a German spy, monitoring a mission, involving the *Arizona*. He'd forgotten all about it.

"Then why don't you tell me, Brother!" Spain fought to control himself.

Dvorak gently extended a hand, motioning Spain to again sit across from him in the pews. "You are a real hot-blooded child of the Euzkadis, aren't you?"

Spain squinted. "That's Basque." The whispered name that all Basques have given to the country that lives secretly inside France and Spain.

"I know you Basques. I tried to use your resourceful people to help smuggle weapons to the resistance in Vichy, France, during World War Two. Black berets, crunchy bread, wine, and profit."

"And murder, Brother!"

"And murder. Basques don't like outsiders much. Sorry for the divergence. Through the cables that you'll find in the Pandora's Box computer program, you'll see that Harry Hopkins and FDR knew the Philippines were going to be hit at the same time as Pearl, so they deployed the *Arizona* and an empty transport, the *President Harrison*, to Manila."

"To do what?"

"To hide the Philippine National Gold Treasury from the Japanese. Philippine President Molina Quezon, FDR, and MacArthur agreed that it was the proper thing to do."

Spain shook his head. "So?"

Dvorak smiled wryly. "So," he said softly, "the entire treasury was lost to the Philippine Government. A special team of OSS operatives, working only at night, supervised the loading of gold bullion, by rural tribesmen, into the *President Harrison*." He stared at Spain. "Only a few people knew about the location of the gold. I knew, and so did a bastard by the name of Edward Severin."

"Old motor mouth?"

"You know him?" Spain watched Dvorak tense.

"Wittenberg told me. I now remember something called Brilliant—"

"Brilliant Fire, Manila. Only Severin stayed on in the Philippines and was captured by the Japanese at Corregidor, when the Manila Bay Island fell to the Japanese, in May of Nineteen forty-two. What a blunder that was." Dvorak shook his head, remembering. "A brother OSS agent who turned on us! I have only one dark passion left in this world and that is to kill Ed Severin. That bastard sang to the Japanese when he was captured and the next thing we knew he ended up in the service of the Imperial Household in Tokyo. Here was a man who knew names. A man who named those names. A man who knew our naval codes, having headed a roofers group called Op-Twenty-G, whose job on Corregidor was to intercept Japanese messages and then forward them to the roofers in Honolulu."

"What happened?"

Dvorak shook his head, his eyes noticeably very far away, even in the dim light of the chapel. "Apparently he helped the emperor locate the gold and then in early Nineteen forty-five, we received a special cable in the White House, from our friend Hirohito. He knew the war was lost and tried to bargain with Roosevelt and MacArthur. Then FDR died and Truman said no."

"Bargain for what?"

"Hirohito the God wanted to stay a God! He wanted to keep his real throne, in the postwar period,

435

in exchange for the gold that he had moved to another secret location in the Philippines."

"So Ed Severin, the double, showed the Japanese where the gold had been hidden, in exchange for—"

"His dirty life and a *geisha*. We heard through our networks that he lived under imperial protection and lived damned well, masquerading as a German, while his brothers on Corregidor, died."

"Gold!" Spain was stunned. "And that gold is still in place where Severin helped the Japanese hide it?"

"Yes. After the war, we interviewed every high-ranking Japanese staff officer we could, at Sugamo Prison, in Tokyo, looking for Severin. No one knew him, or would acknowledge his existence. He was the ghost of the Pacific."

"How much gold was there?"

Dvorak smiled. "You mean *is* there. It was never recovered. By today's value, between fifteen and twenty billion dollars of the noble metal, maybe more."

"Billion!" Spain stared at him, unable to speak, then he began to laugh. "And I thought it was a drug deal! Jesus, Harumi!" he shouted. "You hear that? Gold!" Then he began to tremble thinking about it. "But why us? We weren't anywhere near that gold!"

"But the *Arizona* was. And you dove inside the *Arizona* and asked questions. All those secrets inside the *Arizona*." Then Dvorak laughed. "There's even a small number of gold bars down in the ballast compartments of the *Arizona*, under the manhole covers. We threw some of the lead overboard. The *President Harrison* was loaded to the gunnels, so we took aboard the remaining gold bars. There must be at least a hundred bars of bullion aboard the *Arizona,* down under manhole cover number three." Then he shook his head. "I think the *Arizona* went down quickly, because the manhole covers were left open, destroying her watertight integrity, despite that great explosion. We left them open and kicked out the crew, so we could retrieve the gold, and ship it back to Washington, but we never had a chance to, before the attack."

Spain mashed his face, his eyes bulging. He couldn't believe what he was hearing. "Is that why the *Arizona* was never raised?" He swallowed into his aching throat.

Dvorak was quiet for a while, thinking about it. "Yes. All the other ships were raised, including the *Utah,* but the *Arizona* held too many secrets. Too many political time bombs."

"So the Roosevelt Administration made a national shrine of her." Spain slumped back into the hard pew as he thought about everything that Dvorak had said, trying to cut through the shock, still lost in the fear of running for so long. He thought of Jack Scruggs and his beheading. He must have been part of all this at some level. "My God, they must have watched the *Arizona* like a hawk for years."

"Now you're a keeper of the secrets. When we die, Spain, there'll be no tears shed for us. That is why I take such comfort here." The monk stared at the flickering candlelight bounding off the old, musty walls of the sanctuary. "We're the unwanted. I gather you found that out from your own experiences. We're the collectors of the darkness — the outcasts," Dvorak whispered, his voice carrying the timber of the Bristol wind.

"When I dove on the *Arizona,* I sensed those souls all about me. I know it sounds funny, but I felt the presence of those sailors," Spain said. "For me and all those families of the dead, it is a true shrine. What the government intended, to save itself, doesn't concern me, damn it! It is a shrine, despite the passing of more than half a century."

"God brought you to me, Spain. You and your historian partner will set things right."

"That's what Russell Wittenberg said. Who wants the gold now, Alvin?" Spain closed his eyes, stunned and emotionally exhausted. "Do you know?"

"He doesn't, but I do?" The cold barrel of the Makarov 9mm automatic pushed painfully into Spain's temple. The voice. God, the voice! "Don't open your eyes!"

But Spain did, glaring up at Gregori Ovsyannikov, smiling down at him with those dazzling white teeth. "Welcome home, Benjamin. You led me quite a chase." Then the Black Ghost laughed.

Forty-eight

Spain felt the sharp nose of the old Makarov pistol in his side as the car sped away from the ancient stone docks in Tenby, Wales. Spain raised his wrists, shackled together with steel cuffs, then turned his head to the sound of Ovsyannikov shifting in the seat next to him.

"How's the blindfold? Is it cutting into your eyes?"

Spain found that funny. "You fucking bastard! You cage me like a damned beast, kill half a dozen people, hang our asses out there for spit, then ask me if the blindfold is bothering me!"

"We were both victims of circumstance. I'm sorry it was you, Benjamin. There was nothing personal in it. In the beginning I didn't know."

"Nothing personal in beheading Jack Scruggs, or god knows what to little Kim Dubin! Then," Spain seethed, "you sic the fucking state and federal bulls on us!" Then his voice grew sad. "My brother, who descended into the depths of the shit. You suffer from a lacerated pschye."

439

Spain raised his head with a dog's precision, sniffing the cold air for Ovsyannikov's reaction. "Just pull the fucking trigger and get it over with, you-coward!"

"No, not yet," Gregori said quietly. "My people have watched you since you first dove into the *Arizona*. The organization is far more extensive than you realize. Far larger than the two of us."

"You mean the gold!" Spain shook his head. "Was Jack Scruggs part of it?" Spain thought of Scruggs pulling him out of the Nickel, so long ago and giving him the chance at another life.

"Yes, I'm afraid so. I knew you'd find it out. What more perfect way to keep a watchful eye on that ship. Besides, he was paid well and promised a percentage as was I."

Spain turned his blinded eyes toward Ovsyannikov. "So, you sold us both, brother, for a fucking piece of gold!"

"*Vy prah'vy*. But there are things you don't understand."

"I am right, Gregori! *Atkoo'da vy preeshlee?*"

"Still a little Russian that I taught you. Good." Regret smothered his voice. "I was desperate! I have an ex-wife and grown son back in Moscow. Once the Kremlin went to a free market economy, I didn't have a fucking kopek! My military disability pension couldn't even pay my family's rent. General Lutz sent them funds to live and cared for me, after we escaped from the clutches of the Crimea! Because I was a criminal for killing that bastard with a crutch, the government even threatened to take my meager pension. General Lutz," he said softly, "even saw to that,

440

fixing it up with the ministry through the KGB! I owed him loyalty."

"What about loyalty to me? To the memory of every damned Cold War ground pounder who died for nothing but the smell of a political garbage truck! That was our badge. Even that damned old monk, who you tied up, understood, Gregori!" Spain shouted. "Where we fought or who didn't matter! What mattered is that when it was all over, they all wanted us gone, blown back into dust. We were the real bad news! So, that's what we all owed each other. You don't sell your brothers, who tasted the murky fire!" Spain rubbed his nose with his handcuffed hands. "No quick or clean victories for the likes of us, Gregori!" Then he leaned back in the car seat.

"You are a soldier without honor," Spain said sadly. *"Mahlchee'te!"*

"Why should I hold my tongue? *Mne styd'nah za vah's!"*

"I am ashamed! I don't need you to tell me, but what's past is past."

Frustrated, Spain turned in his seat as the car hit a rut in the road. Then he raised his cuffed hands into a fist, hoping they would find the mark on Ovsyannikov's head. At the last second, Gregori jerked his head, then Spain felt the awful sharp punch of steel slamming against the side of his head as he slipped away into a blackness, his head falling like a limp rag doll against the backrest.

A dim flamingo light pierced the darkness through a narrow tunnel. Spain turned his head and instantly felt a stab of pain. Now his eyes were fully open, his mind trying to catch up as he tore at the cotton webbing clogging his mind. The pinkish tunnel was a window. An airplane window! At least the blindfold was gone. Then he heard that special whine of a jet turbine, its raw power vibrating through the cabin. Then another turbine burst into life as Spain glanced down at the cuffs still shackling his wrists.

From somewhere up front, he heard faint conversation in Spanish, then a dark-skinned man, dressed in a commercial pilot's uniform, made his way down the aisle. Then a thick hairy hand reached down and checked Spain's cuffs, before moving back to the cockpit.

Painfully he moved to the window seat and watched the now blood-red sunrise eat at the fog on the airport tarmac. He glanced out the window at the sleek-swept wing in front of him and the engine pod attached to the fuselage behind him. The small metal label on the engine read General Electric turbo fan. Then Spain looked about the expansive cabin. It was a large intercontinental executive jet, with a large round table in the center of the plushly appointed cabin. The plane was as big as a commercial liner.

Spain pushed to clear his mind. They were probably still in Wales. What was that city we passed through with Taffy, the cabbie? Carmarthen. Only place large enough for a jet strip.

Slowly, the beige flight deck hatch opened and there stood Gregori Ovsyannikov, dressed in black shirt and trousers. He nodded sullenly at Spain, then began moving toward him, yet something was wrong. It was

442

his gait. It was labored and his limp pronounced.

"*Shto' vygahvaree'te?*" Spain held up his shackled wrists.

"Sorry, Benjamin. I can't do that. Well," Gregori said heavily. "We're off." He glanced at Spain. "It's a French Falcon, in case you are wondering. First-class all the way. It will take us all the way to Southern Canada without a refueling stop. I told you it was a complex operation."

Suddenly, the twin-jet Falcon was moving over the wet concrete, then it burst into life, the whine giving way to a throaty roar as the jet lifted into the thick Welsh mud fog.

"What do they call this, Oboe? Crossing the Rubicon? Jumping over the edge, without a chute!" He turned and surveyed Spain's face. "Don't look so shocked."

"Southern Canada?" Spain pushed his head back into the seat. "You bastard! You knew where she went all along, didn't you?"

"Yes."

Spain folded his face. "Why? It's like me going after your family!"

"I know, Benjamin." There was real pain in the Russian's face. "There is no end to this."

"Like last night? A real rank job. This young Danish blonde made me at the airport, then tried to scare me off the road in Wales?" Spain shook his head. "If she'd been good, she could have offed me! Sloppy, Gregori. And I thought I'd lost steps!"

"It wasn't me." Ovsyannikov held up his hands. "She was a Cuban. It gets complicated and I can't tell

443

you things that—anyway." He paused. "It was the long reach of the Cuban Government. The Cuban Minister of Finance, to be precise. I spent a few days with her in Havana and she thought she could scare you off the road, kidnap you, and find out how much you had learned about the gold. It was a fear tactic."

"It worked!" His voice was dry and brittle.

"Ben, you are right in what you said last night, about a soldier's honor," he said quietly. "In any event, don't try and steal the plane, or kill the steward when he comes by. We have a long flight to Ottawa, where Doctor van Horn will be waiting for us, while we refuel. The Cuban Government has diplomatic relations with Canada and besides, the French Canadians in Ottawa hate the Americans."

"If your gargoyles hurt her, I'll rip out your fucking eyes with those two hands!" Spain strained at his cuffs in frustration.

Gregori smiled that easy dark smile, which had carried him through a quarter of a century of murder. Then the smile dissolved, his voice dropping below the whining engines. "We are brothers, Ben. Always remember that. The experiences of Nicaragua and the Crimea now flow as thick as blood through our veins." Then he leaned back in the rich leather seat.

"You are still very dangerous to me, Ben. You took out my whole hit team and that animal, Herr Staven, on that island." Then he shook his head. "Wasted talents. Staven was a performer. I'm still impressed with your precision and innovation, as misguided as it might be. It's hard to kill your brother, but I will!"

444

"Kill me now, damn it! I'll sure as hell blow your brains out, if I get the chance, you traitor!"

Harumi leaned back at her small desk, then rubbed her arms. Ben didn't call last night and she was terribly distracted, yet here she sat, hoping to God that he was still alive and well. In fact, she hadn't slept, waiting all night for the phone to ring in her hotel room. Then early in the cold morning she drove back to the FDR Library, to keep busy. Maybe he would call tonight. Besides it was all anticlimactic. She had her one hard piece of evidence. But maybe there was more to glean as she continued to turn over the small personal handwritten notes of FDR. She thought about the position of the Japanese Task Force, which the White House knew about. Then she forced herself to focus on the moment as she continued to slowly scan the yellowed papers that were still mostly sentence fragments without meaning.

Two hours later, with Harumi working her way down to the last five inches of the NOV/DEC '41 OVAL OFFICE FILE BOX, she stared at another handwritten note, in FDR's familiar scrawl:

12/1/41
HH—
BETTY SAYS TO GET THE TRIPLETS
OUT OF THEIR TROPICAL CRIB
PRONTO! MAYBE A TRIP SOUTH
WILL DO, UNTIL THE STORM PASSES?
SEE ME TONIGHT IN QUARTERS!

Harumi's stomach tensed. Betty was Admiral Stark! It was another of those small unimportant housekeeping notes in silly little codes that passed from the Oval Office, with a flurry that FDR was famous for. Yet, as with the last note to Harry Hopkins, detailing the co-ordinates and time of the Pearl Harbor raid, this telephone pad scribble was worth studying. In fact, this was only the second note she had found directed to Harry Hopkins. If only those male bastards at the University of Hawaii could see this!

Slowly and carefully Harumi thought the note through. Then she again pulled out her handwritten notes that she had taken at Russell Wittenberg's cabin in northern California. Thank God she had this to take her mind off of Spain.

After using the copy machine, Harumi set about the mystery of deciphering the message. Using one of the copies, she circled the word TRIPLETS. Remember the context of the note, she reminded herself. The threat of war in the Pacific was imminent. Betty Stark was Chief of Naval Operations. Could TRIPLETS be special American envoys, or Ambassador Grew in Japan? Maybe it was the Japanese peace diplomats in Washington, including Nomura and Kurusu.

For a long time she tapped her pencil, occasionally glancing across the room toward FDR's private study, and the menacing powerful eyes of FDR's mother, Sara Delano Roosevelt, staring out at her from a large oil portrait, from a tripod in the corner. There was such personal power in the room. Then her eyes fell on the pathetic sight of FDR's wheelchair, a simple wooden kitchen chair with the legs sawed off and replaced with large spoked wheels. It was such a contrast in simplicity, power, and pathos, that it made her shiver. Then Harumi noticed an oil painting of a warship behind the President's desk.

A ship? Three ships? Three of a kind? Harumi scowled, then started thumbing through the Wittenberg notes trying to spark something in her mind. There was something Wittenberg and Spain had talked about, that night in front of the fire, when the old man passed out.

Then she came across her notes that detailed Wittenberg's remarks about the great mistakes the Japanese had made at Pearl Harbor. "Overlooked land fuel tanks," her notes read. Then the next line forced her to smile. "Nagamo's Fleet missed the carriers." How many were there? Then she continued to read. "Admiral Halsey ordered to Wake Island with carrier *Enterprise, Saratoga* to San Diego and carrier *Lexington* ordered to—." The sentence stopped. "One, two, three, bingo, the TRIPLETS!" she mumbled this time triumphantly, pleased with her detective work. How about that, Spain! We did it! The carriers! The valued TRIPLETS, that would live to fight another day, six months later at the victorious Battle of Midway, which broke the back of the Imperial Japanese Navy.

Harumi reread the handwritten FDR note. It all fell into place. TROPICAL CRIB was Pearl Harbor. SOUTH was in one case Wake Island. It was really southwest, but she would take it. UNTIL THE STORM PASSES, was obviously the attack itself.

SEE ME TONIGHT, added authenticity to the note. Harumi knew, as did most modern American scholars, that Roosevelt often retired to his bed in the White House living quarters in the early evening, then held court with his inner circle, of which Harry Hopkins was always close to the center.

"Well, Spain, this is the hard evidence I needed," she said softly. Carefully she looked around, then as before placed the original note in her own notebook. "Sorry," she mumbled, feeling a bit guilty. "But this is too important. I promise I'll return it all when the time is right," she whispered to the portrait of FDR's mother.

Harumi picked up the small pack and then made her way back out into the inner courtyard. She needed a release and walking in the gardens, despite the cold that still gripped upstate New York, would help as her thoughts once again turned to Spain. As before, the courtyard was quiet, with the colonial architecture, highlighted by white dormer windows peeking down from the gray slate roof. The tan fieldstone that adorned the walls and the sides of the crisp white french windows, only added to the feeling of tranquility.

"Miss, can you guide me?"

Harumi turned to find a nondescript blond man wearing a luxurious camel hair greatcoat. "I don't know the place very well." She looked down and instantly knew, with the thick, lethal black tip of a silencer sticking out from his pocket.

"Please come with me, if you want to ever see Ben Spain alive, again." He smiled disarmingly, but his eyes were hard glass. "No trouble." His English was smooth. Too smooth, and cold. That was it! He sounded like that monster in Catalina! Harumi noted, as she pushed out a breath, feeling her excitement sag. Again she eyed the well-built man. "My car is over there, miss. Come with me now, or I'll kill you where you stand." This time his smile was irresistible.

Forty-nine

The Falcon 4000 turned its stubby nose well sharply to the left and rolled slowly to an isolated area of Ottawa International Airport, as Gregori Ovsyannikov paced the cabin nervously, his tender stump now pressing painfully into his artificial leg. Finally, the pilot shut down his engines and out of the darkness a double-wheeled fuel truck arrived, as the ground crew began refueling the jet. Once the high-speed nozzles were inserted in the wing tanks, with a dull clank, the Russian relaxed as he sat next to Spain.

"Where is she?"

"I'll have her brought out, when we're ready to taxi."

"That's a nice touch, killing us together. You're a real artist, Gregori!" The bitterness boiled over in Spain."

"I won't tell when, Spain. At least it'll be clean and painless."

Spain laughed. "You asshole! That's like saying I want to go to heaven but I don't want to die first! You're a fucking gift from the sewers!"

Ovsyannikov shook his head sadly. "I warned you, damn it! It has all gone too far. You think I want this?" For the first time the Russian grew visibly angry. He stared at Spain with those cold black eyes, then laughed nervously. "I know what you're doing. You want me to kill you right now, but it won't work."

"What the hell twisted you so much, Gregori?"

"The same pressures that reduced you to a parable. The parable of a proud man who drank shaving lotion and begged for money in the slums. Scruggs told me all about how he found you."

"Scruggs," Spain bitterly repeated, a thick tone of betrayal in his throat.

Gregori pushed his head back onto the headrest. "I didn't kill him, Ben. I only said so, because you had it in your mind."

"Who did then? The fucking tooth fairy?"

"I don't know." He shook his head.

The sound of the cabin door opening, forced the Russian painfully to his feet. A moment later, Harumi was holding Spain, her hands on his face.

"You okay, Benny?" She rubbed her hands through his curly hair. "I got it!" she said excitedly. "The hard evidence you said I needed!" She squeezed his hand. "Oh God, Ben, we have so much work to do!"

"Forget it, Harumi. This guy's not punching our ticket for round-trip."

Harumi stared up at Ovsyannikov, the hostility growing in her face and eyes. "So this is the bastard! The Ghost! The pig who killed my friend Kim Dubin!" She started to rise in her seat, lunging for the Russian, before Spain stopped her body with his cuffed hands.

451

"I don't want to fight with the two of you any longer. I'm tired of all this!" He raised his hands into the air and limped off toward the flight deck.

"You know what's so ironic, Benny. We finally uncovered a real piece of history and we won't live to tell about it!" She turned to him, tears rimming her large brown eyes. "What about you? The crazy monk in Wales?"

Spain leaned back and spent the next half hour telling her about Alvin Dvorak. When he had finished, he drew a deep breath.

"You know, Harumi, there's a reason why Ovsyannikov hasn't killed us yet."

She turned in her seat. "What?"

"Gregori has problems. He's not in control. I know him. He says he didn't kill Jack Scruggs."

"Because he says it, doesn't mean it's gospel."

"It is with him. He can't lie. It's not part of his code. That part of him is still intact."

Suddenly, the heavy silence surrounding them was broken by the whine of the turbines as the pilot throttled up his engines. A moment later, they began the long taxi run to wait their turn, in the late night at Ottawa International.

"Where are they taking us, Benny?"

"I don't know." He gripped her hand with his shackled hands. "Maybe Gregori's taking us to visit the Mukhabarat, in Baghdad."

"The who?"

The Iraqi secret police. Awhile back, I heard that Gregori did some work for them."

"Charming fellow."

"I can be." Ovsyannikov peered down at them and

smiled thinly. "To answer your question, our next destination is Dawson, in the Yukon Territory."

"He's going to hide out with the Eskimos," Harumi quipped.

"No, he's taking the Great Northern Pacific circle route to somewhere."

"Very good, Ben. You always were a great navigator."

"He's taking us back to the Soviet Union. Aren't you, Gregori? But this bird needs refueling and his Cuban friends are cozy with the Canadians."

"Close. We're cleared all the way to Fukui in Central Japan, via a final refueling stop at Petropavlovsk in the Soviet Union."

"That's where his gold is, Harumi," Spain explained. " 'The noble metal,' " Alvin Dvorak said. "That last unplayed bargaining chip of World War Two."

"Ben, I won't cuff this woman, if she promises to stay quiet." Ovsyannikov raised his eyebrows. "It's twenty hours to Japan."

"Talk to me, damn it! I'm not a piece of sausage to be bargained over, you bastard!"

Gregori bowed his eyes. "Sorry. No offense intended. It's cultural. So, Miss van Horn, what is your choice?"

"Not much, I'm afraid. I won't do anything," she finally replied softly.

"Ben said you were smart," Ovsyannikov mumbled, as he limped toward the rear of the plane. A moment later, the Falcon lifted into the Canadian night, on a heading for the Northwest Territory, at four hundred fifty knots an hour.

* * *

The deep cobalt sky finally matched the hue of Tsugara Bay, on the Sea of Japan. Since well before sunrise, the three people had huddled for warmth in the small boathouse, on a small pier, at the base of a series of precarious wooden steps that wound up the steep rock cliff to the home above.

Hours before, in the blackness, the launch had secretly dropped them next to a well-kept old yacht in a narrow finger of isolated bay, almost invisible from the open sea.

Spain, his wrists still painfully cuffed, looked down at the old silencer that tipped the barrel of the Russian Makarov pistol. For the past three hours, both he and Harumi had watched Ovsyannikov lose his razor edge, replaced by something dark and taut. Spain knew the look, the tension in his muscles, the dryness in his mouth. He was preparing to take someone. More than once, Harumi had pushed at the Russian only to find the tip of the gun in her nose. The remoteness of his hard eyes, visible even in that doubtful light, made her shiver and back away, as the roar of the distant breakers eating at the rock cliffs outside the inlet, filled the boathouse.

"Just a little longer, Ben." Gregori held up the automatic as the rising sun turned the sky and water a soft pink.

Spain nodded as Harumi rested her head against his shoulder. For a time, they all studied the yacht. In the morning light it was a relic of beauty. An old, hundred-foot blue water classic, with its bright work and highly polished mahogany gleaming from its sharp clipper bows, to its racked stern. The twin sail masts, offset against the tall thin funnel, gave them the feeling of squeezing into a time warp from the turn of the century.

"What the hell is this?" Spain finally moved his face close to the Russian. "You're going to take some people out! Take these things off, for Chrissakes!"

Ovsyannikov shook his head. "Shut up, Spain! One more word and I'll kill this woman where she stands! No fucking drama, damn it! Too much is at stake!"

The sound of voices echoing from somewhere in the cove forced Ovsyannikov to put a hand to his mouth. Slowly, he opened the wooden door a crack, to allow his field of vision to take in the base of the steps. The voices, a strange toxic mixture of Spanish and Japanese, floated down the steps, as a large group of people descended the narrow stairs. Silently, Gregori unlocked Spain's handcuffs, then he nodded. With the stealth of a cat, Ovsyannikov raised the barrel of the gun, taking a sight on where the steps met the wooden pier.

Fifty

Then before them, stood the old hunched *Samurai* ghost, Toshiyuki Mizutari, and his lithe granddaughter, Katsuko, their wooden sandals clunking over the pier. Behind them trailed Senora Hilda Castillo Soria and Sed Cruz, his tall, lean body a lethal counterpoint to his deep-set eyes, which carried a stare of the cold ashes of death.

Spain couldn't see much from behind the Russian, but, instinctively, he knew that the lean man with the savage eyes was carrying a gun and was volatile and dangerous.

With insect stillness, Ovsyannikov watched as the group huddled about the gangway of the yacht. A little more patience now would get him what he wanted. Carefully he measured his options. Could he take these people here? He drew a bead on Sed Cruz, dressed in the dark military fatigues of his leader, Castro. He hated the bastard and killing him would be a pleasure. He was only fifty feet away, but had to be careful that his follow-through would be perfect. Suddenly, Harumi coughed with a sound that floated leisurely across the wharf.

"What was that?" Hilda Soria backed up a step as Sed Cruz moved quickly forward, gun drawn and aimed, his body acting as a shield to protect the Cuban minister. Even in that frozen moment, Soria admired Cruz's quickness and animal instincts.

"Helar!" Cruz shouted, jerking open the boathouse door with one motion. As fast as he was, Sed Cruz wasn't as quick as Gregori Ovsyannikov.

"Hello, you bastard!" As the door swung back and Cruz raised his gun, Gregori smiled at him with those dazzling teeth, then fired off three quick 9mm rounds with a whining thump, into Cruz's chest, slamming the Cuban onto his back. Now Cruz's dark khaki shirt was smeared with black pools of blood. Somehow Cruz forced his gaunt eyes to look down at his chest and stomach, realizing the worst nightmare of his life, anger stamped indelibly on his disbelieving face.

"Does it hurt, Cruz?" Ovsyannikov stood over him blocking his light. "I took your woman, Soria, last week, in Havana." Then he laughed bitterly. "I wanted you to know that before you died." Then Gregori kneeled down, his face very close to the Cuban.

"You tried to take me out last week, close to that seaside restaurant in Havana, didn't you?" he questioned in English. "Don't ever send a boy to do a man's work, you little banana bastard!" Out of the corner of his eye, he watched the shadow movement of the Cuban minister as she drew closer.

Then Ovsyannikov pulled up Cruz by the neck. "Don't leave me yet, Cuban! I killed you for General Lutz! I know you murdered him and his staff, because you were greedy! Just like you double-crossed me, coming here a week early. You were predictable in your greed!" Gregori smiled gently, then casually fired a slug into the Cuban's ear, killing him instantly. Then in a half step he whirled, leveling the weapon at the Cuban woman.

"Don't even think about it, Hilda!" He smiled again, watching the expression of horror and grief spread across the woman's face. "You should have thought this out more carefully," he whispered, his eyes now taking in the old Japanese man and the girl, standing idly, waiting stoically for the drama to play itself out.

"*Dios Mio!* Why did you kill my Sed?" Doubt filled her face and her eyes glistened with pain as she bent down and closed his eyes with her long trembling fingers. Slowly, Ovsyannikov raised the Makarov automatic, brushing it against the minister's head.

"Sleeping with me did not give you license to eliminate me from this project." The Russian held up his free hand as a question mark. "Nor was the gift that General Lutz offered you, a license to kill him! The general and the emperor's messenger," Gregori said flatly, pointing over at Toshiyuki Mizutari, "negotiated an honorable agreement, then you greedy Cuban bastards decided to change the order of things!"

"You can kill me if you want," the minister replied with a cold bravado, "but you will operate without a brain. My task is not to debate the deaths of Sed Cruz and General Lutz, but to see that we operate with efficiency. What matters now is the retrieval of the bullion."

Encouraged by the doubt spreading across the Russian's face, Hilda Soria smiled coolly. "The world is run by the survivors, Gregori. Not the best, but the survivors." She reached out to touch his face, trying to rekindle a shared moment from the week past.

Instantly, the butt of his gun struck her cruelly in the cheek, forcing her to fall. Now sprawled on the pier, the woman thrashed about, holding her face. "Get up, Comrade Princess!" he commanded with the weapon. "As my *amigo* Ben Spain says, 'you're a piece of work!' Now, we are going to take our little cruise. Nothing changes, except you will be locked in your cabin and watched at all times." He rubbed the tip of the gun silencer on the painful blood bruise that was beginning to rise on her face. "Is that agreeable?"

"Yes." She pointed toward Spain and Harumi, who had emerged from the boathouse. "Who are they?"

"The people you kept urging me to kill and the man you tried to kidnap!" Ovsyannikov smiled. "They are also going with us, for the sake of history." He glanced at Harumi and nodded.

Slowly, the ancient rhythm of the cove returned, the imperial yacht tugging impatiently at her mooring lines, as the morning high tide began to withdraw into the Sea of Japan.

Ovsyannikov turned to acknowledge Toshiyuki Mizutari and his granddaughter. He faced the old man and bowed from the waist, then turned to Katsuko and bowed again.

"*Ohayo gozaimasu. Ikaga desu ka?*"

The old Japanese master was truly pleased. "My English is passable, but I am pleased with your gesture." He dipped his eyes out of respect. "In General Lutz's eyes you were a legend. I knew you would come. I asked the Cuban, where the Russian was and she said you were no longer alive. She has no honor. The *O-jo-san* is not worthy."

"Are we prepared to leave now?"

"Yes, my crew is aboard. We are stored and fueled and our boiler is fired and ready to go." He smiled at Ovsyannikov, then turned his eyes to a distraction that seemed far off.

"Gregori, look out!" Spain screamed, but it was too late, as Hilda Soria fired off a single round from the small gold, .25 caliber automatic, striking Ovsyannikov in the small of his back. As he fell, his body turned and in slow motion, he watched Spain dive down over the dead body of Sed Cruz, reach for the gun, lying close to him and fire off two quick rounds at the Cuban woman. Suddenly, it was over, with Hilda Soria floating face up in the inlet, her dead black eyes staring up vacantly at the pink, soft morning haze.

In a moment, both Mizutari and Spain were at Ovsyannikov's side. The bullet had struck the Russian beneath the right kidney. "See, you tried to protect me, Ben! I am still your brother!" He tried to sit up, but fell back, a thin ribbon of crimson trickling from his mouth.

"I'm all torn up inside, Ben," he whispered. "I can feel it. My share—" He grimaced, as a sharp pain rippled through him with a shock.

"Mister Mizutari, we need a doctor, fast!" Spain looked up helplessly at the old man. "Can you call one?"

"No, no!" Ovsyannikov shook his head. "Time," he muttered. "No time, Ben! Toshiyuki will take you to his secret place and show you." His voice was now a death rattle. "He's the only one who knows except for—" He paused again, forcing air painfully into his damaged lungs, filling rapidly with blood.

"Amazing what one little bullet can do. Ben, take care of yourself. They're closing in on us! No more hunting, just heat sensors and electronic lock-ons. There's no place — no place for us to go. We're doomed. The moon is down for us."

Then Gregori's fading eyes found the old, weather-stained face of the Master. "Spain is a soldier with honor. Treat him with the same respect you would offer me. He is my — my brother. Promise me. *Oo nyeh khorosho*. Damn! I'm very cold now. *Pazhaloosta!*" he whispered in Russian.

"I promise you, *Musuko!*"

Ovsyannikov smiled, the crimson ribbon now a dark flow from the corner of his mouth. "Now I have a father and a brother!" He closed his eyes, the searing pain blanching his face, then with a tremendous effort he opened them again.

"Come close, Ben," he barely uttered into Spain's ear. He coughed again, spilling warm, dark foaming blood all over Spain's arm. "Ben." Now the timber was almost gone from his voice. He mouthed something into Spain's ear, then his head dropped to the wooden pier with a sickening thud.

Seven hours later, the *Hatsukaza* slowed, to barely hold station with the Izu current, as the yacht entered the Straits of Korea, on a heading of south by southwest.

Silently, Spain and the mechanic carried the sealed canvas sail bag to the quarterdeck of the old ship as Toshiyuki Mizutari raised a single sheet of rice paper to his face. For a moment he turned to the gathered group, acknowledging his granddaughter, Harumi, and Spain with a slight bow of his bald melon-shaped head. With a

461

tremor in his hand, the old *Samurai* placed a pair of wire reading glasses on his nose, then addressed himself to the paper, in silence. Finally he looked up and stared out at the yellow-green sea.

"We will honor this fallen soldier with a *Haiku* that I have prepared for this occasion." He spoke in thick English. "I hope that it brings honor to Gregori Ovsyannikov, his family, and to the purpose of our voyage.

Then he began to read:

The Quietness;
A tiny leaf falls
into the light spring sea.
A drop of life
completes the cycle.
A lifetime passes
so simply.

Then they gently lifted the weighted canvas form of Gregori Ovsyannikov over the brass railing. A moment later, a muted splash marked the Russian's watery gravestone.

"The Black Ghost is dead," Spain muttered aloud. "I don't know why I feel terrible. He made our lives a living hell."

Harumi pushed out a dark, tired breath. "A piece of you died. He was your twin as a soldier," she said softly. Then she put her arms around him, feeling his warmth as they watched the shapeless canvas bag sink slowly beneath the waves.

Fifty-one

Slowly, the first day at sea passed without incident, as the *Hatsukaze*, built by Mitsubishi Shipyards for Emperor Hirohito, in honor of his birth in 1901, steamed to the northeast, bucking a stiff current. Then the wood and steel yacht slid to the south skirting Chiburi Shima Island, gateway to the Strait of Korea. As dusk gave way to the blackness, the *Hatsukaze* steered her course into the Eastern Channel of the Korea Strait, the muted throbbing of her ancient *Miyabra* engine finding its own meter and harmony with the sea.

The old warrior, Toshiyuki Mizutari, stood attentively at the giant birch wheel, his trained eyes and hands moving in symphony, in the small wheelhouse.

For just an instant, Toshiyuki turned his eyes as the mahogany door opened to the outside, allowing Harumi and Spain to enter. Out of respect to their host, Harumi bowed.

"Konban was. Go-chiso-sama deshita," she offered, turning her eyes from Toshiyuki to Katsuko, leaning over the small navigation table, a small light shining down on a chart.

"We can speak in English, Miss van Horn. My grandfather understands the language well." Katsuko smiled. "My grandfather and I thank you and welcome you aboard. We wish you to share our hospitality." The young woman's natural beauty radiated through, despite the meager light, as Harumi nodded and withdrew from the bridge.

"Mister Spain," Toshiyuki called. "Will you take dinner with us this evening? I wish to talk of the Russian and your relationship." For an instant he turned his eyes to meet Spain, their intensity and focus a surprise.

"There is much irony in all this."

"There certainly is." Spain turned his gaze toward the sharp bows of the old one-hundred-twenty-three-ton ship, through the high, square wood-framed windows. He was amazed. The yacht was immaculate, as if it had never been to sea before. It was a living page out of Victorian England. The only update in the wheelhouse were a simple surface radar system and a fathometer.

"Is there a radio aboard, Mister Mizutari?"

"Yes. But only a small unit. During the Second World War, the ship was filled with radios, but the emperor never used the yacht. He was a marine biologist and felt this vessel was too small and too eloquent to be used for his work on the outskirts of Tokyo Bay." The old man raised his thick gray eyebrows. "Of course, after Nineteen forty-three, with the Allied bombings and their air superiority, even those voyages stopped. After the war ended, I removed most of the communications equipment."

Spain cocked his head. The emperor? Who was the name of that messenger that the monk, Alvin Dvorak, spoke of at Caldey Island? For a long time, Spain stared at the old man in silence, the only sound, the rhythmic clicking of the automatic fathometer, sounding the ocean floor, as the ship moved south. Finally, Spain shook off an uneasy feeling as he stared out at the darkness, happy for the light rolling of the sea beneath his feet.

"This is a most magnificent ship. How old is she?"

"Her keel was laid in Nineteen hundred and one and she was launched in Nineteen hundred and three. In Nineteen thirty-four and again in Nineteen forty, she was refitted. The *Hatsukaze* is one of a kind."

Spain thought about it for a moment. "What is her draft?"

Toshiyuki smiled. "Only seven feet. I can tell, like me, you are an old sailor."

Spain peered at him, then his eyes widened, his voice as soft as his question. "Did you serve during World War Two?"

"Yes, I was a naval gunnery officer, then I was called to serve—"

"Ah, Grandfather, we are coming up on our first mark, the Light at *Hi-no-Misaki*," Katsuko interrupted.

Mizutari glanced off to his portside and watched the automated lighthouse spiraling its powerful white beam out over the dark sea. "What is the new course, Katsuko?"

"The new course is red, two zero five, magnetic."

"Coming left to the new course of two zero five, magnetic," the old man repeated, turning the helm with a watchful eye on the large brass compass and binnacle before him.

"You have trained her well," Spain said softly. "She is a fine navigator."

"Indeed she is. She is also a skilled sailor," Toshiyuki said with pride. "When will we be at our second mark?"

"At the present speed and course, we will reach Tsushima Island by sunrise tomorrow. We must keep a sharp eye out, since we are now in the major shipping lanes!"

"We are close to the Korean coast, Mister Spain. The port of Pusan is close by, where a cargo container vessel exits or enters that major port every fifteen minutes."

But Spain wasn't really listening. He was focused on the story that Alvin Dvorak had told him of the transfer of Amelia Earhart and Fred Noonan to the *Arizona,* the week before Pearl Harbor. Their escort had been a naval officer, Dvorak had said. He would talk to Harumi.

"What else did you do during the war?" Spain held his breath as the words dropped into the silence of the wheelhouse.

"In Nineteen forty-three I was called to serve the emperor and his staff in Tokyo." The old man turned his steady eyes and searched Spain's face. "What about you? What is your background and bond to the Russian?"

"I'm a diver and Gregori Ovsyannikov and I faced each other in combat, in Central America, then we worked as brothers to survive over the next decade. During Vietnam, I was a navy diver and today I'm still a diver." For a moment, Spain hesitated, not certain where to take the thrust of the conversation. Then he made a decision. "As a commercial diver, my current assignment is diving and surveying damage on the battleship *Arizona.*" Then Spain watched the passive expression on the warrior's face begin to tense about his eyes.

For a time, Toshiyuki Mizutari set his jaw, his narrow intense eyes, tending to the helm of the *Hatsukaze.* As the ancient yacht steamed past a series of sharp, black rocks, which jutted up into the growing ocean chop, they entered the Eastern Channel of the Korea Strait, heading south.

"The bottom is very shallow here, Mister Spain. I'm

sure you can appreciate that fact. Many of the shoals and rock pinnacles that break the surface are not on our charts, so I must focus my energies upon the moment."

"My grandfather wishes to continue his discussion with you at dinner tonight," Katsuko interrupted politely. "He does not wish to divert his attentions from the importance of your company." She smiled and bowed slightly and finally Spain understood he was being summarily dismissed.

Spain sat in the corner of their lavish stateroom, decorated in the reds and golds of the Imperial Household, gazing out the large main deck window, at the sea, growing restless and more impatient with movement as the early evening wore on. His eyes then moved to Harumi sleeping on the bed, below a very old traditional Japanese silk screen, depicting an ancient workshop, with skilled craftsmen forging the blade of a long *Samurai* sword. Off in one corner, an *Ashigaru*, foot soldier, stood guard. The stateroom was a definite curiosity. A Japanese room, from the turn of the century, yet decorated with chairs, a bed, and other defined occidental tastes. Obviously, the stateroom was the Western guest quarters. Spain smiled to himself, for at the courtesy the old Japanese *Samurai* and his granddaughter had extended, based solely on the dying words of Gregori Ovsyannikov. Spain looked down at his hands and shivered at the thought that Gregori was dead, yet he felt a great flood of relief. It was the first time in weeks that he didn't feel the angst of some unknown sniper or lawman waiting for them.

"Hey, you okay?" Harumi sat up in bed, staring at him, with a start.

"Guess I was talking out loud," he said sheepishly. He surveyed the large ornate stateroom again. "Some place, huh?" He shook his head in wonder. "From the Nickel sewer of downtown L.A. to the emperor's yacht." He glanced over at Harumi, her taut, naked body outlined against the white silk sheets. "Mind-blowing!"

Harumi yawned and ran her fingers through her hair. "God, I hate this! My hair," she said softly. "My mother's long black hair, bleached and shorn like a—"

"A criminal," Ben laughed.

"That's the first time you've really laughed since all this started." She smiled openly. "That makes me happy, Benny." Pulling her naked form off the bed, she padded to the bathroom, then returned with a large towel wrapped around her.

"Can I ask you something?"

Spain raised his eyes. "That depends."

"What did Ovsyannikov whisper in your ear before he died?"

Spain's face folded into a strange mask, his eyes dropping.

"Ben?" Harumi moved across the stateroom to him.

"I'm not sure, Harumi. I'm just not sure. It was garbled. Maybe it was a final, zany metaphor to all this."

"Why won't you tell me?" she pushed.

"Because it doesn't make any sense. I think Gregori was hurting terribly inside and confused." Spain buried his head in his hands. "God, I can't believe he's dead." He looked up at Harumi, tears suddenly rolling down his cheeks. "I saw that goddamned woman pull out that gun! It was all in slow motion. I was too damned slow and too fucking old!" He turned away staring out at the dark waters of the Korea Strait, listening to the soft rhythm of the

468

beating engine against the sea. "I failed him" he whispered.

Harumi pulled his hands away from his face, clutching him to her breasts. "No, Ben, you didn't fail him. He failed himself. He was truly your brother, wasn't he? I guess I never realized that before. You were both emotional refugees. It must have been just as difficult for him, when he was stalking you."

Spain nodded, the distance still in his eyes. "You just can't imagine what we went through together."

"It's about living. Now," she said tenderly, "he's dead and life is for the living."

"If any of this gold is ever recovered, I have to keep my promise to his family in Moscow." He shook his head, wiping his face. "It's all I can do."

"Benny, Ovsyannikov was you. You both tried to overcome the same emotional wreckage."

"I know that." Then he tried to smile. Then for a moment he stared at her. "At least this death game had some meaning."

"How so? We've paid a terrible price."

"We've got the goods, here. The real, legitimate goods on this Earhart and Pearl Harbor business. No one has ever been able to do that until now! You're going to be the sensation of the book-of-the-month clubs and the talk shows for a long time to come." Then he found the strength to laugh. *"People* magazine will even do a page on you and Mollie. I can see it now. 'Tofu-Eating Eurasian Historian Finds—"

"Shut up, Benny!"

He shook his head. "No. All kidding aside, as I said to that monk on Caldey Island, you have a responsibility to tell the truth. A responsibility to the souls of Earhart,

469

Noonan, and all those people who died at Pearl Harbor."

"You're part of this, too!"

Spain slowly shook his head. "Not this time, kid. Someone has to sit on the curb and clap when the hero's float comes by, during the parade. That's my job." He shrugged. "I really don't mind." He gently held her narrow shoulders. "You've earned every bit of it! This is your show. Your skill and tenacity have been the glue of this ragtag operation. We just have to quietly pull all the evidence together and then you sit at your computer and tell the world a whale of a real tale."

"Speaking of that, where'd you hide Noonan and the emperor's yellow pouch?"

Spain raised an eyebrow. "Remember that snotty little fart at the Mauna Kea? That manager who took us to the computer room?"

"Sure. The one my father strong-armed."

"Well, when he took us in, he showed us the bronze plaque in the garden, honoring the visit of Emperor Hirohito and his wife in Nineteen seventy-six." Spain rubbed his hair. "I buried the stuff, right behind it. I liked the irony of it." He laughed. "Besides, who the hell would ever look there for it!"

"God, Benny." She held him close to her, feeling his strength and firm roundness against her breasts. "Do you think we'll live to have that parade?" Her voice was barely audible.

"I really don't know anymore." He touched her hair gently, then drew a breath that seemed to come from his toes, as they held each other.

Fifty-two

The Grand Salon had been cleared for dinner, floral *tatami* mats now covering the thickly carpeted floor, yet the cabin was still dominated by the glass case holding the ancient and priceless *Dojigiri Samurai* sword, on its *tachi* stand.

Spain knocked back another warm shot of saki, his head growing lighter by the moment, as he and Harumi sat cross-legged across from the old man and his grand-daughter, the *Hatsukaze* sliding farther south toward the Tropic of Cancer. The outside air had grown distinctly lighter and warmer, laced with a special spice fragrance that held some unique restorative power.

Silently, an elderly woman attendant appeared, placing lacquered bowls of steaming *Miso* soup before them. With the swish of silk against her body, the woman was gone and Toshiyuki moved his eyes to Spain.

"I have given this a great deal of thought. This relationship between you, Mister Spain, and the Russian, Ovsyannikov. I witnessed his death, as you did, and I watched the pain live in your eyes as he died in your arms." The old man nodded, pausing, as he carefully collected his thoughts in both Japanese and English. Then his smile vanished. "Wisdom tells me that I should have you both killed, but a relationship born out of fire, is one like the *bonsai*, that continues to grow strong, changing with the seasons and the years. But you must first start with a young tree and build a strong, robust foundation."

"Pardon my interruption, Grandfather, but I believe, through my observations, that these people have the potential to make spaces for the birds to fly through."

Spain moved his puzzled eyes to Harumi.

"*Sumimasen ga.* It is always important to shape a *bonsai* or a relationship in the spring, is it not?" Harumi smiled at her host.

"You know of the *bonsai*, Harumi?" The old man's eyes lightened.

"My dead mother loved to contemplate their beauty. She would tell of the times when she was a child in Japan and she would visit the exhibits with her father. She always remembered the vivid blends of *midori iro, akai, and chairo*." Harumi bowed her eyes. She felt something familiar and powerful in this old man. A comfort and warmth she had not felt since the death of her mother. This man and his granddaughter had become a link with her past. Unlike Spain, she felt no threat from these people. She felt only honor and warmth.

Suddenly, she raised her eyes and addressed Toshiyuki in Japanese. "Our business here is not of gold, but of history, clarity, and truth."

The old man was pleased and honored that she spoke to him in Japanese. "You have not forgotten the ways of your mother's teachings. What history and relative truth do you seek, *ko, kodomo?*"

"The truth of Japan's involvement with Amelia

472

Earhart and her companion Fred Noonan." Harumi held her breath, watching his eyes cloud.

Reluctantly, he bowed his head, a great astonishment growing in his face. "How do you know of this?"

"Spain has recently spoken with a man, a former intelligence agent with the U.S. Government." Harumi paused collecting her thoughts. She would only get one shot at this man, then he would withdraw in traditional silence. She paused for a moment, then bailed out. "This man said you met him during the first few days of December, Nineteen forty-one, where you presented him with vital materials to be passed on to President Roosevelt."

She swallowed, the thick silence in the salon overwhelming as her eyes swept from the surprise in Katsuko's face to the passive stillness of the old man. "This man also said you turned over the American fliers to him on the *Arizona,* at —" Damn, she couldn't recall the island!

"Johnston Island," the old man helped softly. "Yes, I was the young naval officer who was assigned the task of escorting those fliers to a rendezvous with the battleship *Arizona.*" Then his voice dropped away as he weighed the thoughts in his mind.

"Could you tell me about that in some detail?" Harumi probed in Japanese.

Toshiyuki raised a cautionary hand. "It was a half century ago and time has stained my memory. But yes, I was sent by my emperor, as his personal emissary, to the island of Saipan. There I had released into my custody, the two fliers you speak of."

Spain's eyes moved in frustration, from Harumi to Toshiyuki, as he fought to gain some understanding of their conversation.

"This was all done in secret, as the emperor fought against certain elements in his government. That is all he ever told me about the circumstance. It was not my place to ask." His gnarled fingers drew little invisible circles on the table before him. "My honored station was that of messenger, holding an imperial rescript, to do so. I will say that when I forced the fliers release from Garapan Prison, on Saipan, they were very weak from torture and disease. It still brings shame to me, when I think of it."

Then he looked up at Harumi, his voice turning flat and cold. "However, they were spies. They admitted to that crime and should have immediately been put to death, but torture?" He shook his head.

Harumi leaned back. Garapan Prison! The metal bracelet she had found in the pouch! It had been Noonan's prison ID bracelet from Garapan Prison!

"Ah, Mister Mizutari?" Harumi asked. "Do you remember anything of the messages you turned over to the American agent?"

Toshiyuki shook his head. "The emperor personally handed me a sealed yellow pouch, to be delivered to the American President. I will always remember the emperor telling me of the importance of the pouch and how it's contents might prevent the start of war in the Pacific." The old man laughed. "I chaffed at the thought. I was a descendant of a great *Samurai* warrior family. I was a keeper of the faith and the weapons. I had also lived in America as a student, learned the language and liked the people. But I still carried a young man's anger, without wisdom." He grunted. "I had much to learn of death and war, but the wisdom of *arahito-gami*, the god incarnate, was within the soul Emperor Hirohito! That must be restored!" Then he held up his hand again.

"That however, is not your question nor your issue." His eyes turned to Spain. "I have watched the fury grow in this man's eyes, as we talked," he said in English. "I understand this frustration." He bowed his head at Spain, then rubbed the top of his head.

The woman appeared from the shadows, quietly serving raw octopus surrounded on a platter, by fish heads and rice.

Spain swallowed hard into his throat, thinking how he was going to eat the meal without becoming ill. "Mister Mizutari, where are we going?"

Toshiyuki looked up from his plate, slowly placing his chopsticks down as he ate a wet leg, regarding Spain and thinking about the question. "In death, the Russian had ordained the two of you to take his place." The old man nodded as he spoke. "I had great faith in his honor, even in death, and now I will bestow that same honor on the two of you. It is all I have left to give." He smiled benignly.

"But," he cautioned, the steel instantly back in his voice, "you are keepers of the secret now." Then he nodded at the stoic, porcelain face of Katsuko. "Tell them."

Katsuko bowed her eyes. "We are going to the northern Philippine Islands." Then she laughed. "It is my favorite place in the entire world!" Then she glanced at her grandfather and her voice grew serious and masked once again. "It is called Calauit Island, in the Calamian Group. We have visited the island each spring since I can remember. I call it Giraffe Island." Katsuko wiped her mouth with the cotton napkin, her eyes growing dark.

"It is also called the island of the deep cave."

Spain glanced at Harumi and pushed out a breath. "Is that where the lost Philippine treasury is buried?"

The old man nodded crisply. "In Nineteen forty-three

I was assigned by the emperor the task of guarding the island and the cave."

"Were you aware that the gold was moved at one point?"

Toshiyuki nodded at Spain. "Yes, by that time I was a permanent member of the Imperial Household Staff, as a naval attaché."

"Did you know an American agent involved in this?"

"Yes." He looked at Spain in a funny way. "I will never forget him. For some reason, that I was never privy to, he was close to the emperor. He supervised the transfer of the bullion to Calauit Island, from an area in the Paraclae district of the Philippines, southeast of Manila. He knew all about the bullion and where the Americans originally hid it." He closed his eyes, remembering. "General Honjo, head of the Imperial Guard, wanted to execute him, but this man received some invisible protection, masquerading as a German national. His name was Severin."

The old man sipped his saki. "For some reason he was given permission to back channel and promote the myth that Japanese soldiers stole the gold from the Philippine people. That was and still is a lie!" For the first time his voice rose to an angry pitch.

"Grandfather, do not upset yourself." Katsuko reached over and gently touched his bare arm.

"Yes." He removed his wire glasses and cleaned them with the balls of his thumbs, just as the emperor had done a half century before. "Yes, Katsuko. I am in control now. Thank you."

Again he turned his eyes to Spain and Harumi. "It was this bastard of life that floated the story that General Tomoyuki Yamashita, commander of the Japanese forces, which occupied the Philippines, raped the islands of gold bullion and great art treasures." Then the old man stopped himself. "It is true that he dishonored himself and Japan, by brutalizing the people, but this story was manufactured as a lie by this American Severin."

"What?" Harumi was shocked. Then she thought about it in the silence of the dining salon. "What a brilliant thing to do! The great diversion! For half a century the world has been chasing the nonexistent Yamashita Treasury in Manila, taking the heat off of the real gold!" She glanced at the dark expression on Toshiyuki's face, then bowed her head.

"I hope I have not offended you, sir."

"No. This man Severin had every member of the transportation and construction team shot, when the new holding facility was ready for the gold."

"I don't understand?" Spain turned to Harumi.

The old man bowed his head. "Severin used American prisoners of war, captured in the Philippines campaign. Some of the men had even been in his unit on the island of Corregidor, when it surrendered to Japan."

"He ordered American soldiers and sailors, shot?"

"Yes, Mister Spain. He set up execution squads. I was the only staff officer present, as a representative of the emperor, but I was powerless to stop it!"

"How many men were killed by Severin?" Spain whispered.

"Close to two hundred. Then he had lye spread on their bodies and they were buried in massive graves in the jungle."

"Where did this happen?"

"On Calauit Island, of course," the old man said, his voice growing hoarse.

"He killed every witness," Spain muttered. "His own men!"

"I'm alive, Mister Spain." Toshiyuki rubbed his hands together, then folded his arms.

Spain closed his eyes remembering the hate in Wittenberg's and Dvorak's eyes, when they spoke of Severin.

Suddenly, the old man and his granddaughter were on their feet, bowing from the waist. "I am very tired now. Please stay and finish your meal. This conversation has been very painful for me. I am thankful there is a qualified crew aboard. Old men shouldn't be in command, right, Mister Spain?"

"I agree."

As they reached the door, Toshiyuki turned back. "When we arrive at the island I will give you a weapon, Mister Spain. I would feel better if you would agree to that."

The Island

Fifty-three

Five days passed, the *Hatsukaze* steaming on a southerly heading, finally crossing the Tropic of Cancer as they passed the island of Taiwan. During the voyage, Toshiyuki had continued to proudly tell Spain of the crew that helped to run the ship, but after a time he realized that there were only two other people aboard; the woman who served their food and the old crusty mechanic who stood the late and overnight watches on the bridge, while the old warrior slept. Spain was truly amazed at the skill and resource of this elderly crew, as well as Katsuko, who provided all navigation, LORAN and radar fixes.

Spain yawned and leaned back against the highly polished brass rail on the bridge, watching the narrow bows of the *Hatsukaze* slice steadily through a brilliant, emerald-green South China Sea, with Toshiyuki Mizutari at the helm. Even after all these years, the old man was still a fine seaman and Spain admired those skills.

While Toshiyuki kept his eyes to the bow and the course, his ears were always alert to the rhythmic click of the fathometer. Occasionally he would glance over at the stylus as it charted the sea floor to be certain there was always enough water under their keel. A missed coral head could easily rip out her bottom like soft butter.

Harumi sipped from a large cup of green tea as she watched the morning ritual on the bridge of the yacht. For a moment she closed her eyes, inhaling the warm tropical air, reminding her of Hawaii.

"We are leaving the Bashi Channel and entering the Luzon Straits," Katsuko called out excitedly. For as many times as she had made this annual spring voyage, she always grew elated as they approached her beloved Giraffe Island.

Spain moved forward through the easy motion of the sea and stared out the large wood-framed rectangular bridge window.

"Are you searching for something, Mister Spain?"

Spain swallowed, suddenly feeling a deep hollow pang in his stomach. An emptiness as black as night. "I don't know," he mumbled, his eyes sweeping the lush green tropical island of Batan, off to his left, crowded with arcing coconut palms. "What is our latitude now, Katsuko?"

"Just about twenty-two degrees."

Spain grunted and retreated to the navigation table, checking the chart of the South China Sea. For a moment his eyes swept down the Philippine Island chain, south into Indonesia. Then idly, his eye caught the crescent-shaped Vietnamese coastline to the east. Then he blanched, a searing pain rising in his throat as his eyes found the port city of Haiphong. Latitude twenty-two degrees! He closed his eyes as a wave of nausea swept through him, his hands holding his young face-less Chief, who died so many years before. Spain groaned aloud, his shattered psyche held together with a frail patch.

"Benny, what is it?" Harumi was next to him. "You look awful." Then she glanced down at the chart, her eyes taking in Vietnam.

"My body knew I was close, but my mind blocked it." He shrugged helplessly. "So, after all these years, the forces of dark pulled me back. My leaving here alive was a mistake."

"What the hell are you talking about?"

"It's simple. The old message inside is clear. I shouldn't leave here alive!" Then he left the bridge, walking slowly to the foredeck, watching a fleet of *Bangkas,* native Philippine outrigger boats, modernized with outboard engines, powering their way out to their traditional fishing reefs.

Breathing deeply, in the fragrant morning air, Spain's stomach muscles began to relax, the nausea and living nightmare retreating back into his unconscious. For a long time, in the clear inviting waters, he watched colorful schools of large bright red and blue groupers, chasing a group of silver unicorn sturgeon fish. Then he leaned over the railing, guessing that visibility at close to seventy feet. In many places he could see massive rich coral heads of every conceivable color rising up toward the surface.

"It is most refreshing for the spirit."

Startled, Spain turned to find the old man standing next to him.

"Harumi informed me of your trouble. I hope you do not mind my inquiry?" It wasn't a question.

Spain peered up into the bridge window and watched Katsuko expertly piloting the *Hatsukaze.* "Your granddaughter is truly remarkable and poised for her age." Spain smiled politely.

"Indeed. She has the heart and stamina of a *Samurai*

warrior." The old man glanced up at her and nodded. "She has filled many dark voids in my life. I owe her a great deal."

An awkward silence filled the air as they stared out to sea. Finally Toshiyuki spoke. "War is a terrible thing. Often necessary, as an instrument of power, but for the warrior, it can be very difficult, since it is our destiny." Uncharacteristically, he grabbed Spain's arm with a thin, but powerful hand. "That is our lot, our joy, and our burden!"

Spain nodded slowly, thinking about it.

Suddenly, Toshiyuki thrust a battered old pistol into Spain's hand. "Here is the gun, we spoke of."

Spain wrinkled his face, looking down at the automatic that looked like a German luger. "What is it?"

"A very old Nambu. My old service automatic from the war. It is fully loaded. Unfortunately, the eight rounds in the gun clip are all that exist."

"Why do you want me to carry this?"

The old man put a weathered hand on Spain's shoulder. "The growth of this project has taken two long generations, like the growth of a strong *bonsai*." His eyes were a combination of toughness and patience. "I am too old now to offer proper protection. I have too many calluses on my hands."

"Those calluses should make it easier to grip the gun."

Toshiyuki smiled. "There is wisdom in you, but this is a time for a sharp eye and a quiet bow. I don't know what damage the Cubans did to us, or what awaits us on the island." The old man drew a long breath then moved very close to Spain's face.

"Things never go as planned. If something goes wrong, please protect Katsuko. She is young and awaits

484

her opportunity at life. Help her if she needs you."

"Do you have any evidence that your secret has been violated."

"No." Then he pointed to the east, toward the invisible Vietnamese coast. "Like you, with a warrior's instincts, it is not what is seen, but what is felt." He turned and stared at Spain, the cold steel back in his eyes. "I feel there will be trouble on Giraffe Island, and I have never felt that before."

Spain watched the fear grow as a fast, deadly cancer in the old man's eyes, for the first time. "We will know for certain tomorrow morning."

As the sun rose over Pinnacle Rock, on the eastern shore of Calauit Island, the small rubber raft worked its way through the treacherous reef of the shallow Palawan shelf, into a narrow swampy estuary lined with thick mangrove trees.

"What was that!" Spain aimed the old Japanese Nambu pistol at the crunching sound, but Harumi, the old man, and his granddaughter, didn't even turn their heads.

After they beached the boat on a muddy flat, hidden from view under a broad mangrove, the party climbed a shallow bank revealing a lush island of grassy plains, mahogany forests, and stands of wild bamboo growing on worn, rolling hills. Immediately, a fragrance overtook them as they started across a broad savanna, splashed in a vast array of greens and yellows. Even the humidity was less oppressive than at sea.

"My God, what is this place?" Harumi searched the horizon as they hiked toward the distant purple hills. "Benny, it's beautiful! There's a music to this place!"

485

Katsuko put her arm around Harumi as they walked. "This is a wildlife sanctuary!" She shook her head eagerly at Harumi's skepticism.

"I don't understand? I thought this was where the cave holding the treasure was?"

"It is," Toshiyuki interrupted, a large dark shadow passing close to their heads. "Calauit Island also happens to be a—"

"Look out!" Spain shouted, diving and rolling into the tall grass, aiming the gun at the large shadow towering over them.

"No! Don't shoot!" Katsuko was panicked as she lunged at Spain and the gun. A moment later, a huge eighteen-foot African giraffe, camouflaged in rich browns and yellows, lowered her head into the grass and began to lick Spain and Katsuko with a rough, wet tongue. Every so often, she would stop and stare at them through curious cow eyes.

"That is what I love about this place." Katsuko turned to Spain, laughing and petting the massive bony head of the giraffe. "They have no natural enemies," she giggled, pushing the large head toward Spain. "The island is filled with deer, gazelles, topi, and waterbuck. There are even giant python snakes, but they only eat the rodents and ship rats."

"Katsuko, I don't want to stay out in the open!" For the first time, Toshiyuki Mizutari's sharp voice vented his growing anxiety. "I want to move into the forest, quickly!" Then he picked up speed, with the giraffe easily keeping pace to the rear, occasionally leaning over and taking a lick at someone's head.

Another half mile and the low, thickening jungle canopy kept the giraffe from following as they moved silently to the west. Eventually, the mahogany forest began to thin, with shafts of intense blue morning light marking the trail.

As they trekked in single file through the rain forest, the old man dropped back to Spain, who had positioned himself at the rear, his gun drawn.

"Up ahead," Toshiyuki whispered, "a very large python is resting on a low branch of a tree that crosses our path."

Instinctively, Spain raised the old Japanese automatic, but the old man held his wrist. "Do not shoot or be alarmed! The snake's eyes are milky and he is sleeping. Our presence will not bother him. Besides, I do not want any noise!"

"Terrific." Spain rolled his eyes as he carefully watched the black and yellow snake, shimmering in the dim light, its girth as thick as a utility pole, his gut swollen with an undigested meal. As they passed within three feet of the snake, the python's fierce yellow eyes, looking out from a long arrow-shaped head, watched their every movement, wishing his stomach wasn't full.

"His eyes don't look cloudy to me," Spain muttered as he ducked his head. "The damned thing must be twenty feet long! Looks like he swallowed a deer, for Chrissakes!" Spain shivered at the thought. "How did all these animals get here?"

The old man shrugged. "For us it was truly a gift. They appeared thirteen years ago, when Katsuko was a child of five, and she delighted in the distraction. It also created within her, a great love for animals."

"What about other people?" Spain helped the old man cross a small, freshwater creek, as the trail began to move up into the old hills.

"There are a few rangers, who tend to the animals and that is all. The island is open and large enough to vanish in."

"What about the cave? Any problems?"

Toshiyuki shook his head. "It is at the base of a remote hill, covered with a thick stand of giant green bamboo. No one has ever tampered with it. Not since Nineteen forty-three, when the vault was constructed." He glanced at Spain as they traversed a narrow hairpin in the trail. A large green squawking parrot with a brilliant red head swooped low over the group, then disappeared beyond the next hill.

"Mister Spain, I was trained as a gunnery officer and have combat experience with explosives, so I have taken precautions." He smiled vaguely, stopping to wipe the sweat from his forehead. "Double precautions."

"What about the animals?" Spain was intrigued. "This place is in the middle of nowhere. African animals? They had to come from somewhere?"

"They did. From Manila, which is only a hundred eighty miles north, across Mindoro Strait. All I was ever able to find out was that the Marcos took an interest in African animals and imported them. Actually, it was perfect for us."

"Why? Be careful!" Spain stopped the old man from stepping on a large sleeping green lizard, lying across the trail.

"There is perfect balance on this island. The animals have apparently all they need to eat and they don't have any fears of man since none are ever present." Toshiyuki smiled. "Since the deaths of my wife and son, many years ago, the raising of my granddaughter and our annual ritual of visiting this place, has been a tonic."

"Grandfather!" Katsuko was next to the old man, her eyes large and fearful. "Someone has been to the cave!"

Spain shivered as he pushed past them, heading for the head of the trail and his first view of the cave.

Fifty-four

Spain crouched in the brush, his restless eyes silently taking in the scene of a shallow hill with a small obscure entrance, masked by a growth of old bamboo. If one wasn't searching for a cave, it would only appear as a dull shadow on the rocks, with the bamboo filtering out any real definition. Its camouflage was as subtle and natural as the surrounding island landscape.

It was hard to believe that so much history and gold could be hidden in such a remote place. Spain wasn't sure what he had expected to find, but a boulder-strewn, shallow mountain, guarded by green bamboo, wasn't it. How many people had died for this? A light tap on his shoulder brought Spain back to the moment. It was the old man, with a finger pointing at something up ahead, that Spain couldn't see. Finally he caught his eyes, now dazed and troubled. Slowly Spain swung his eyes back to the view ahead, but it was clear.

"What do you see?" the old man whispered, his passive face twisted into a frown.

"Nothing."

Toshiyuki pointed to a place on the worn path. "There.

A simple series of five white stones, in the pattern of a square with a stone in its center, has been kicked aside."

Spain's eyes found the stones, scattered by the kick of someone's foot. "Maybe a large animal did it."

Toshiyuki shook his head. "Large game won't use the trail and never in all the years of coming here, has the stone box been tampered with."

Spain signaled Harumi to come forward. "I'm going to circle around through the tall grass to the cave, and then double back. You take the gun, Harumi." He thrust it into her hands.

"Benny!"

Spain mashed his face. "Damn it! For once, just once in your life, can you do something, based on faith?" His anger bubbled through his low whispering voice. "You know how to use it now, so do it!" Then he disappeared off the trail, heading first into the tall yellow grass that gave way to the giant bamboo. Beyond lay the hill and the cave entrance.

Slowly, he made his way through the high grass, stopping every so often, raising his head for a bearing. The earth was reasonably soft, indicating that there was adequate rainfall in this place that teemed with life. Off in the distance, a flight of parrots, frightened by something, left a large mahogany tree en masse, creating a shrieking cacophony.

Fighting down his fear, Spain began to sense something hostile. A blackness he couldn't touch, or see, but something lurking close by. Kneeling down, his hand found a fist-sized rock. "Jesus," he muttered. "Good going, Spain." Cautiously, he lifted his eyes for a quick view, the morning trade winds beginning to create funny flat patterns in the sea of grass.

Fighting the fear in his belly, Spain moved on toward the cave entrance, his body brushing the grass as he crawled. Something obscure tugged at his consciousness as he finally cleared the grass, facing the stand of bamboo.

For a long time, Spain waited just inside the first stand of bamboo, watching and listening to this strange environment. Only his instincts were on edge, as the peaceful island continued to seduce and haunt him. Something lethal was there, but it was out of reach.

Spain then threaded his way through the last stand of bamboo, the stalks as thick as a man's fist, into a small clearing close to the cave entrance. Squatting, Spain watched and listened to the wind, giving life to his surroundings. He must be insane, he thought, out here without any protection except for a rock. He shook his head and ran for the cave entrance, up a slight incline, about thirty feet away from the bamboo trees.

Spain dove headfirst into the small entrance, sliding into the moist earth. As he looked up, he realized he had landed inside a small natural porch, set back from the real cave entrance. Beyond lay a single rusted steel door, weather-stained hues of browns and reds. It blended perfectly with the hill. Now Spain noted a small black wire running around the perimeter of the large entrance door.

Remembering Toshiyuki's warning about some vague precautions, Spain approached the door, wiping his sweating hands on his now damp pants. Midway down the door, a small steel junction box was bolted to the jamb, connecting the wires.

For a moment, Spain stood back, not quite certain how to proceed. "Let's not blow up now, old sport," he mumbled aloud. "Okay, count three and touch the door."

Then Spain reached out and brushed his fingers against the junction box. Then he moved his hands flush against the door, flakes of rust falling to the ground, as he moved his hands gently toward the massive outside bolt, with the touch of a safe cracker.

Disbelieving, his hands froze on the door. The bolt wasn't locked! "Jesus!" he croaked. Reaching down, he now touched the open bolt, slowly lifting the protective steel guard, when his world seared red; a terrible, blunt pain forcing his eyes to see only a deep abyssal void and then he was falling into that empty, sickening void.

Fifty-five

Slowly his eyes began to focus in a vague, cheap blackness, with a swaying sun the only sign of hope. Now the sun was humming. Jesus, it was alive! He closed his eyes, then opened them again, the swinging sun now a small light bulb, gyrating from the top of a steel cage that was moving!

Suddenly, a horrid Satanic face, with dark, piercing eyes was very close to him, large yellow teeth sneering with the intensity of a wild animal devouring its prey. Then the animal raised its head in the cage and roared with a crazed laugh.

When the hungry eyes dipped and focused again on Spain, they were quieter, but darker. The face—Spain knew that face!

"You're a strong mother fucking bastard! I hit you with a tire iron!"

The voice! God help me with the voice! But Spain's senses were dull, his movements sluggish. He knew he was hurt and that his head was wounded. He couldn't tell about the remainder of his body. He couldn't feel it.

Then the humming in his brain grew faint and the

494

cage door opened. He tried to lift his head, but his neck couldn't support its dead weight.

"Who—" Spain whispered into his aching throat. Then he mouthed the words, not sure this Satan staring at him, could hear or understand. "Who are you? Where is this?"

Then, gruff hands were dragging him over the floor, out of the cage. Spain's head was going to explode. He had never felt such pain. Then he realized he had been in an elevator!

A burst of cold struck him in the face. It was cool, wet, and salty. Satan had thrown a bucket of briny water in his face. Slowly, the thick cotton webbing began to clear away and he was in a dim tunnel of some sort. A mine shaft? That was it! It was warm; not hot, but warm, with a great deal of moisture.

"Feeling better?" The voice was deep and smooth, with just a hint of a distant accent. My God!

Spain stared up at the man, different from the Satan who had scared him to death, in the elevator.

"Erik!" Spain blurted out. Then his head squeezed his mouth shut in pain. Finally the spasm of pain subsided enough to speak. "I don't understand?" Spain was in shock, as Erik van Horn looked down at him. "Erik, what the hell are you doing here!" Spain tried to swallow but couldn't. His worst demons were swimming in his consciousness. Maybe it was a dream. That damned river dream from Haiphong Harbor. His mind was ticking, clearing the watery mine fields. Spain opened his eyes again, but his mind shifted down to a dark, forbidden place that didn't exist. A place where his dreams and nightmares merged. As the blur lifted from Spain's mind it was suddenly filled with a hopeless dread.

Now friendly hands gently lifted Spain's head and a cup of cool sweet water was at his lips. "Drink this, Ben." Van Horn bent over Spain tending to him. "Can you sit up?"

Spain nodded and those old, massive strong hands lifted Spain into a sitting position. "What hit me?" He tried to touch the back of his head, but a lightning bolt shot through him, forcing him to retch. A moment later, van Horn held the cup close to his lips. "I'm sorry, Ben. God, I'm sorry," van Horn whispered, his voice heavy with regret. "Why didn't you listen to me, damn it!"

Spain turned and looked into his sad face. "You knew, didn't you? You sent us around the world the other way, to get rid of us!"

"To save your lives!" Van Horn shook his head, a shock of remorse rippling through his eyes.

Spain watched the deep sadness grow in his eyes. "How is my daughter?

"About fifteen minutes ago, she was fine, just outside the cave."

Van Horn nodded and motioned to someone waiting beyond Spain's vision. *"Ngayon! Ngayon! Pasukan! Pasukan!"* Van Horn pointed up one level toward the cave entrance.

"I told one of our boys in Fillpino, to go up and get the others."

"You're just a bundle of information!" Spain laid his head down heavily on the floor of the cave. "You knew. You were waiting for us!"

Van Horn shook his head vehemently. "No, damn it! Not you! Not my daughter," he said softly. "But I'm well acquainted with Toshiyuki Mizutari, the Black Ghost, General Lutz, and the Cubans; but not you!"

"Why, damn it! You sent us to Russell Witten! You found the code name Pandora's Box!" Spain swallowed with difficulty, then closed his eyes. "You tried to have me killed!" He paused for a moment. "You killed Jack Scruggs, didn't you?"

"It was me, you bastard!" Spain looked up and standing above van Horn was that hideous face. Satan with that death laugh. "I cut a separate deal with Lutz and Ovsyannikov and used van Horn's authority. Van Horn knew but he didn't want to know, if you follow my drift."

"Shut up, Severin!"

Spain's eyes widened in shock. Severin! The American agent who had disappeared during the war. The OSS agent!

"—you hear me, Spain?" Severin was talking to him.

"I know you, but where?" He couldn't put it together. He was too tired, too worn down by the nightmare, in the dimness of the cave.

"I'm Willy Ashmore. The airline agent who took your gun and put you and Harumi aboard a flight to the mainland. I set up the fake killing at the hotel and the police at your door."

Spain shook his head, trying to fit together the pieces. "But, Erik, you, and this butcher! How?"

Van Horn cringed, his voice barely audible. "Ah, I first heard about Brilliant Fire, Manila, when I was serving in occupied Europe. I had an entire network of contacts. You know what has to be done in intelligence work. I knew all the German field commanders in proximity of the Siegfried Line on the German French Border. Then I worked my way into the confidence of the inner circles of the Abwehr and Admiral Wilhelm Canaris. I was one of the few friendly Dutchmen, the Germans could count on, and that is how I worked my way into the top echelon's favor, within a group called the Abteilung II; a special duties section. It was then that I became aware of the German agent who had been planted in Pearl City." A rush of self-anger flooded through van Horn.

"But I never meant to hurt you, or God forbid, my beloved Harumi!"

"The road to hell is paved with good intentions!" Spain sneered. "What about this fucking traitor, standing over your head?"

"Kill the bastard, now, or better yet I'll do it!" Severin hissed, raising his fists.

Slowly, van Horn stood, his frame towering over the shorter former OSS agent. "You lay another fucking glove on Spain or my daughter and I'll feed you to that python on the trail!" Then he grabbed Severin's dirty shirt. "Speak to me, Edward!"

Severin pulled free. "Just keep the prick out of my way!" he shouted as he walked away. "I've waited too damned long!" Then he stopped. "He gets in our way, he's dead!" Severin snapped his fingers, the fire in his voice.

"I think Harumi told you part of it, but that's all she knows."

Spain laughed painfully.

"What's so funny?"

"You, you hypocritical bastard! You made me spill my guts out in your living room, about my sordid past, and you sat there sipping your fucking bourbon, like a gentleman — and all the time you were a predator; a fucking cannibal!" His eyes glistened in the meager light. "You're no better than the rest of us! The stink is all over you! You just let someone else do the killing, then you move in to feed on the hot flesh!"

Van Horn nodded, balancing Spain's anger against his own sadness. After a moment he continued, in a rush, expelling his long pent-up guilt.

"When the war ended, I had nothing! My life was in ruins! My first wife had been killed by the Nazis, when they overran Amsterdam. I was a valued member of the Dutch Underground and later an OSS agent." Van Horn found a stool and sat down heavily next to Spain.

"I did some odd jobs in identifying ex-Nazis, as they tried to run through the underground into Italy and then South America. There was alot of wet work. I killed more than I turned in," he said with a distant satisfaction in his voice.

"Well, that counts for something."

"Not much, Spain. By early Nineteen forty-six, I drifted to Japan, doing some rooting out for the OSS of Japanese army war criminals. That's where I really got to know Russell Witten, old Beads. During the war, we didn't want to know much about each other."

Spain coughed. "Let me finish it for you. In hunting down Japanese war criminals for the upcoming War Crimes Trials, in Tokyo, you found Lieutenant Edward Severin, hiding somewhere in the sewers of the Imperial Palace."

"That's about it. Everyone wanted him and when I found Severin he made me an offer. His life for the Philippine gold. At the time I didn't realize it would take the rest of my life to get it!"

"You did a deal with the devil!" Spain coughed again. "He killed his own men, right on this spot! Vets of the Philippine Campaign! You're as guilty as he is!"

"I know that now." His face flushed.

"But you got caught up in all this, didn't you? What did Alvin Dvorak say, 'noble greed for the noble metal'?"

"You got to Dvorak on that English Island?" Van Horn was shocked. "Well, you were better than I gave you credit for."

"You fool," Spain whispered. "It wasn't me, it was your daughter! Your own loins and genes, Harumi! She was the muscle and push behind all of this!" He shook his head.

"I was shit! A mule for the operation." Spain closed his eyes, the cave whirling around, as sharp waves of nausea swept over him again, then he lay exhausted, trying to catch his breath. Finally he needed to speak.

"So with Severin's help, you watched and waited, knowing that only the old Japanese warrior was left in your way. Obviously you had already agreed to a deal with Ovsyannikov's team."

"It got far more complicated than that, Spain." Van Horn took a long drink from his water canteen. "We knew we had to wait for at least twenty years. Until things really began to cool off, after the war."

"Why? Gold is gold."

"Not so. These bullion bars are the distinctive seventy-five kilogram gold bars, almost pure, except for a bit of silver for strength, known in the trade as World War Two-era bullion. Not that easy to launder or melt down, without giving the store away."

"That's tough!" Spain said sarcastically. "Problems of the rich! How many billions would you have to give away? Five, six or maybe seven, to keep two billion? Christ! The disease of greed!" He studied van Horn's face for a long time. "You make me sick!" Spain waved a weak hand in the air. "Go ahead, finish it."

Van Horn pushed his hands into a steeple under his chin. "I worked out a deal with Severin, when I found him hiding in Tokyo, for an even split and I bought him a new life in Hilo on the Big Island, where you found him. There wasn't a week that went by that we didn't talk about it and plan." Van Horn shook his head. "You wouldn't understand."

"Understand what? The gold belongs to the people of the Philippines. They sure as hell need it today!"

Van Horn dismissed the thought. "In the early Nineteen seventies, Ferdinand Marcos squeezed down on the Philippine people and really began his campaign of terror and greed. He went looking for our gold!"

"Did he find it?"

"Yes, in Nineteen seventy-six. We're not quite sure how, but he did! At least we know he got the door open, but he was beginning to have real political problems at home and in the States, so he decided to do the best possible thing he could. He ignored this island and placed a bunch of wild African animals on it, kicked out the few natives and turned it into an isolated national park! It was declared off limits. It was a brilliant move," van Horn said softly. "His own island vault."

"So for all the Marcos years, you couldn't get near the gold?" Spain raised his head, then leaned back against the cave wall.

"What about the old warrior? He's been coming here for years, ever since the end of the war?"

"We had him watched. He didn't do any harm, he just updated and maintained the vault on a yearly basis."

"He turned the golden egg for you in the warmth of the incubator."

"Something like that. We don't think Marcos ever knew about the old man. He was only here for a week every year and never disturbed anything."

"So why the move now?"

"I found out from Scruggs that General Lutz had joined forces with the old warrior, including your Russian friend. They tried to move past us! Beat us out of our share!" He held up a hand. "But that's not what forced us to move. It was when General Lutz brought Fidel Castro into the picture. They tipped the balance. It was a game of dominoes. When the first one went down the remainder started toppling."

"Then Harumi and I stumbled onto the scene and you didn't know what the hell to do! Just because of a skull and a little yellow pouch."

"Yes," van Horn said softly. "I knew I couldn't stop Harumi."

"So you sent us around the world in the opposite direction and put out a contract on me, careful to preserve your daughter's life."

"Yes, that's about it." Van Horn closed his eyes, not sure what to do.

Spain forced eye contact with van Horn. "The Russian told me before he died, to 'beware of the Flying Dutchman and his greed.' I agonized over those death words and I couldn't figure them out!" Spain rose unsteadily to his feet, holding onto a rusted steel girder for support. "Your reputation preceded you, Erik! Even Alvin 'the monk' Dvorak said you were a rotten bastard!" His voice was filled with hate.

"That's what Gregori said before he died!" Harumi ran to Spain, holding him up. Then she turned to her father. "Oh, Poppa, why?" Tears filled her eyes. "Oh why? Momma would be so ashamed! You were my friend for life!" She rubbed Spain's head. "Oh, Benny, I'm so sorry. Gregori knew, didn't he?" she cried softly. "He tried to spare both of us, especially me from the pain and hurt I feel now!"

Then Harumi turned to her father and slowly approached him.

"Oh, baby!" van Horn cried, reaching for his daughter. "I didn't want this to happen, you know that!"

She searched his old face for a long time. Suddenly his features had grown thicker and more frail. "You could have stopped it, anytime you wanted! We almost died! The police were after us and so were Gregori's goons!" Her rage turned to fear and angst.

"You betrayed my mother." She looked up into his sad helpless eyes.

"Not to worry, friends!" It was Ed Severin, holding an Uzi machine pistol at his hip.

Harumi whirled around. "You gonna kill me, Uncle Willy? I sat on your lap as a child!"

Severin opened his mouth, like a snake ready to taste the wind. "Nothing personal." He turned and herded Toshiyuki Mizutari and Katsuko, around, in front of him. Then he turned the machine pistol on van Horn. "You stay here! I'll take care of this! I'll take them down into the main vault and let them see what they're going to die for!"

Fifty-six

Ed Severin prodded the group down the main tunnel for probably an eighth of a mile, then they turned left into a smaller feeder tunnel. Spain noted that there were at least six feeder tunnels that he could see leading into the main chamber.

"That's it! Move!" He jabbed the gun painfully into Spain's kidneys as he pushed them all along. "Okay, hold it!" Then he reached up and turned on a large series of lights and the view was dazzling. It was the most incredible sight Harumi had ever seen in her life. Below them, in a tunnel that must have stretched for fifty yards, sat brilliant gold bars, stacked on the cave floor. She couldn't even begin to guess how many bars were crowded into just that one tunnel.

"How much is here, Uncle Willy?" Her voice was laced with sarcasm. "Now my uncle's going to kill me!"

"Stop it, Harumi! I didn't want this!" He looked at her, then shook his head. "I'm just taking care of business. I can't let you matter. We did our best to get you out of the way, but as usual you wouldn't listen!"

Spain laughed. "He killed two hundred of his own

men and buried them right outside this cave, what's a few more!"

"Knock it off, big mouth!"

"How much is here, Willy?" Harumi asked flatly.

"About four hundred metric hundred tons alone, in this tunnel. Each seventy-five-kilogram gold bar on the open market is worth about one million bucks American!"

"Why did you lie to me all these years, Uncle Willy?"

"Stop it, Harumi! You're the wild one. The crazy daughter with balls. You have no right to pass judgment on me! Besides, truth and war are not good friends!"

"He's a fucking poet!" Spain quipped.

Severin viciously jammed the nose of the Uzi into his back, dropping Spain to his knees. Then he chambered a round into the machine pistol. "Time to pray, kids!" then he laughed darkly, as Harumi suddenly whirled and fired the old Japanese Nanbu automatic at almost point-blank range into Severin's stomach. By reflex action, she continued to pull the trigger, pumping three more 8mm bullets into Severin as he was jerked backward. Almost in slow motion, his bullet-torn body seemed to hesitate for a moment, then tumbled into the bullion pit, landing with a sickening thud, facedown on a ten-foot-high stack of gold bars.

"Harumi!" The echo came down the passageway as van Horn reached the entrance to the feeder tunnel. Then the elder van Horn entered the room carrying a small pistol, as Toshiyuki Mizutari, reacting with lightning reflexes, grabbed the Nambu pistol from Harumi, locked his arm and fired once, spinning the man to the ground.

"My God!" Harumi shrieked. Before she could reach her father, he held up his pistol and fired once, the bullet slamming into the old Japanese warrior's side.

Slowly at first, then with more authority, Toshiyuki began to crawl toward a small junction box near the entrance to the feeder tunnel. Painfully, with blood staining his light blue silk garment, the old man pushed himself beyond human limits, waving off his granddaughter's attempts to help him.

Five feet, then three feet, then he was at the old junction box. With the light fading from his eyes, Toshiyuki pulled open the small steel door and jerked down a round black lever. Exhausted, his smiling eyes found Katsuko, then he nodded his head.

"Kamawanai de kudasai, Katsuko!"

Tenderly, tears flowing down her lovely stoic face, Katsuko held her grandfather's head as he died in her arms. Then she rose slowly, as if in a dream. "We have to leave now. The entire cave is wired with massive explosives. My grandfather did this many years ago and he was an expert at it! We will be buried alive with the gold in five minutes! Please hurry!" She motioned to Harumi and Spain. "Please, I don't want these deaths not to have witness and meaning!"

Harumi kissed her father's dead lips, then nodded solemnly, rising to her feet. "I knew, Spain. I knew in my heart!" She looked at him with her eyes reflecting that horrifying deep pain of shock and loss. Then the small band of survivors made their way to the lift, for the short trip to the surface, shouting for the few Philippine workers, still in the cave, to get out.

Fifty-seven

Harumi glanced up at the bright night, flashes of her first night dive on the *Arizona* only six weeks before, pushing at her mind, as she watched the background lights of Pearl City throw a misty ambient softness over the Pearl Harbor Memorial. She shivered as a heavy feeling of déjà vu suddenly overcame her; she checked her watch. It was almost three in the morning and the next navy patrol boat would be making its rounds in another fifteen minutes.

From somewhere in the East Loch, a series of small waves from a moving ship rolled under the rubber zodiac, as she glanced up at the glowing light dancing through the side openings that provided that special openness with the marble-walled Shrine Room. Within that hallowed room, the names of all those killed in the *Arizona* were engraved into its soft white marble.

She wasn't even frightened, just sad, as a sharp noise drew her eyes to the dark shadow of the ancient mooring quay of the battleship *Arizona*. In the night light she could barely make out the black stencil sign on the quay:

For a long time she stared at the empty quay as a shiver in her upper torso forced her to cry again. It had been this way for the past month. The anger, the loss of her father, the joy of Spain and their historic discoveries. She wasn't sure how they were going to live. Money would be short and teaching was out of the question. She and Spain had agreed that they would keep her father's home on the Big Island. It would become their sanctuary.

The sound of large air bubbles erupting on the surface twenty feet from her, told her Spain was close to the surface and almost out of the hulk.

"Thank you, God," she said. "Thank you for sending him back to me!"

Suddenly he was on the black surface, moving slowly toward her. Finally, a gloved hand held onto the side of the zodiac, as Spain spat out his regulator and pulled off his face mask. He was smiling. Even in the dark she could tell that much. With effort she moved to him. In a strange way, this final dive by Spain on the *Arizona* was the memorial service for her father and the old Japanese warrior. She nodded as she helped Spain roll himself into the boat.

"Hi." He wiped his nose. "Cold down there!"

"Did you find the pouch holding Earhart's diary?"

"Of course I did." Carefully, he reached over the side of the boat into his large net bag and pulled out the second yellow pouch that she was sure she had seen that night she dived into the ship. Then, gingerly, he held the skull of Amelia Earhart in his hands.

509

"Oh thank God!" She clutched the pouch, then held the skull tightly. "I can almost feel that woman's thoughts, Spain. God, what a powerful moment." Then she glanced down into the water, a thin phosphorescent trail of oil from the *Arizona* forming a beckoning portrait of Gregori Ovsyannikov's face.

Hopelessly she stared at the apparition, then at the small black waves moving his face around the stern of the boat.

"What are you looking at?" Spain held a towel around his head.

"I just saw something. Ah, Gregori's image in the water." Then she shivered.

Tenderly he took her hand. "That's happened to me, too." Then he reached back over the side into his carry bag. "Had a helluva time doing this." His back was to her, as he strained at something heavy.

"Got a surprise for you!"

"What?"

Then he turned around in the boat, struggling to lift a single one-hundred-sixty-five pound bar of gold bullion. "I just found a way to pay the bills. Christ, that's heavy!"

"Where'd that come from! I thought it was all buried!"

"No," he interrupted. "There's just enough here for us, Katsuko, and Gregori's family in Moscow. The gold is just where the monk said it was!"

Harumi shook her head and smiled at him through the darkness of Pearl Harbor.